rse

1964 by Robert A. Heinlein

rved

arrangement with G. P. Putnam's Sons, Inc.

blished by G. P. Putnam's Sons, Inc.

568-9

MEDALLION BOOKS are published by
shing Corporation
Avenue
.Y. 10016

MEDALLION BOOKS ® TM 757,375

United States of America

MEDALLION EDITION,

RINTING

"Bomb warning. *Third bomb warning. This is not a drill. Take shelter at once. Any shelter. You are going to be atom-bombed in the next few minutes. So get the lead out, you stupid fools, and quit listening to this chatter!* TAKE SHELTER!"

For Hugh Farnham this warning was something he had long expected, and for which he had carefully prepared. But not even the wisest man could have taken precautions against the extraordinary world into which Hugh and his little family party were catapulted.

This is a powerful and prophetic novel about what happens after a massive nuclear attack to one American family who survive to face a strange, harrowing, and all-too-possible future . . .

"Robert Heinlein wears imagination as though it were his private suit of clothes. What makes his work so rich is that he combines his lively creative sense with an approach which is at once literate and exciting."
—*New York Times*

ALSO BY ROBERT A. HEINLEIN

I WILL FEAR NO EVIL

STRANGER IN A STRANGE LAND

ORPHANS OF THE SKY

GLORY ROAD

PODKAYNE OF MARS

THE MOON IS A HARSH MISTRESS

STARSHIP TROOPERS

TOMORROW, THE STARS
(ed. by Robert A. Heinlein)

ROBE
HEINL
FARNHAM'S F

A BERKLEY MEDALLIO
published by
BERKLEY PUBLISHING CO

To Alan N

Copyright

All rights

Published

Originally

SBN 425-

BERKLE
Berkley F
200 Mad
New Yor

BERKL

Printed i

BERKL
Thirtee

1

"It's not a hearing aid," Hubert Farnham explained. "It's a radio, tuned to the emergency frequency."

Barbara Wells stopped with a bite halfway to her mouth. "Mr. Farnham! You think they are going to attack?"

Her host shrugged. "The Kremlin doesn't let me in on its secrets."

His son said, "Dad, quit scaring the ladies. Mrs. Wells—"

"Call me 'Barbara.' I'm going to ask the court to let me drop the 'Mrs.' "

"You don't need permission."

"Watch it, Barb," his sister Karen said. "Free advice is expensive."

"Shaddap. Barbara, with all respect to my worthy father, he sees spooks. There is not going to be a war."

"I hope you're right," Barbara Wells said soberly. "Why do you think so?"

"Because the communists are realists. They never risk a war that would hurt them, even if they could win. So they won't risk one they can't win."

"Then I wish," his mother said, "that they would stop having these dreadful crises. Cuba. All that fuss about Berlin—as if anybody cared! And now this. It makes a person nervous. *Joseph!*"

"Yes, ma'am?"

"You fetch me coffee. And brandy. Café royale."

"Yes, ma'am." The houseboy, a young Negro, removed her plate, barely touched.

5

Young Farnham said, "Dad, it's not these phony crises that has Mother upset; it's the panicky way you behave. You must stop it."

"No."

"You must! Mother didn't eat her dinner . . . and all because of that silly button in your ear. You can't—"

"Drop it, Duke."

"Sir?"

"When you moved into your own apartment, we agreed to live as friends. As my friend your opinions are welcome. But that does not make you free to interfere between your mother—my wife—and myself."

His wife said, "Now, Hubert."

"Sorry, Grace."

"You're too harsh on the boy. It does make me nervous."

"Duke is not a boy. And I've done nothing to make you nervous. Sorry."

"I'm sorry, too, Mother. But if Dad regards it as interference, well—" Duke forced a grin. "I'll have to find a wife of my own to annoy. Barbara, will you marry me?"

"No, Duke."

"I told you she was smart, Duke," his sister volunteered.

"Karen, pipe down. Why not, Barbara? I'm young, I'm healthy. Why, someday I might even have clients. In the meantime you can support us."

"No, Duke. I agree with your father."

"Huh?"

"I should say that my father agrees with your father. I don't know that my pops is carrying around a radio tonight but I'm certain that he is listening to one. Duke, every car in our family has a survival kit."

"No fooling!"

"My car out in your father's driveway, the one Karen and I drove down from school has a kit in its trunk that Pops picked before I re-entered college. Pops takes it seriously, so I do."

Duke Farnham opened his mouth, closed it. His father asked, "Barbara, what did your father select?"

6

"Oh, lots of things. Ten gallons of water. Food. A jeep can of gasoline. Medicines. A sleeping bag. A gun—"

"Can you use a gun?"

"Pops made me learn. A shovel. An ax. Clothes. Oh, yes, a radio. But the important thing was 'Where?'—so he kept saying. If I were at school, he would expect me to head for the basement of the gym. But here— Pops would expect me to head up into the mountains."

"You won't need to."

"Sir?"

"Dad means," explained Karen, "that you are welcome in our panic hole."

Barbara showed a questioning look. Her host said, "Our bomb shelter. 'Farnham's Folly' my son calls it. I think you would be safer there than you would be running for the hills—despite the fact that we are only ten miles from a MAMMA Base. If an alarm comes, we'll duck into it. Right, Joseph?"

"Yes, sir! That way I stay on your payroll."

"The hell you do. You're fired the instant the sirens sound—and I start charging you rent."

"Do I pay rent, too?" asked Barbara.

"You wash dishes. Everybody does. Even Duke."

"Count me out," Duke said grimly.

"Eh? Not that many dishes, Son."

"I'm not joking, Dad. Khrushchev said he would bury us—and you're making it come true. I'm not going to crawl into a hole in the ground!"

"As you wish, sir."

"Sonny boy!" His mother put down her cup. "If an attack comes, of course you're going into the shelter!" She blinked back tears. "Promise Mother."

Young Farnham looked stubborn, then sighed. "All right. If an attack comes— If an alarm sounds, I mean; there isn't going to be an attack— I'll go into your panic hole. But, Dad, this is just to soothe Mother's nerves."

"Nevertheless you are welcome."

"Okay. Let's go into the living room and break out the cards—with a firm understanding that we drop the subject. Suits?"

7

"Agreed." His father got up and offered his arm to his wife. "My dear?"

In the living room, Grace Farnham declined to play bridge. "No, dear, I'm too upset. You play with the young people, and— Joseph! Joseph, bring me just a teensy bit more coffee. Royale, I mean. Don't look that way, Hubert; it helps, you know it does."

"Would you like a Miltown, dear?"

"I don't need drugs. I'll just have a drop more coffee."

They cut for partners; Duke shook his head sadly. "Poor Barbara! Stuck with Dad— Did you warn her, Sis?"

"Keep your warnings to yourself," his father advised.

"She's entitled to know, Dad. Barbara, that juvenile delinquent across from you is as optimistic in contract as he is pessimistic in—well, in other matters. Watch out for psychic bids. If he has a Yarborough—"

"Drop dead, Duke. Barbara, what system do you prefer? Italian?"

Her eyes widened. "The only Italian I know is vermouth, Mr. Farnham. I play Goren. Nothing fancy, I just try to go by the book."

" 'By the book,' " Hubert Farnham agreed.

" 'By the book,' " his son echoed. "Which book? Dad likes to ring in the Farmers' Almanac, especially when you're vulnerable, doubled and redoubled. Then he'll point out how, if you had led diamonds—"

"Counselor," his father interrupted, "will you deal those cards? Or shall I stuff them down your throat?"

"I'll go quietly. Put a little blood in it? A cent a point?"

Barbara said hastily, "That's steep for me."

Duke answered, "You gals aren't in it. Just Dad and myself. That's how I pay my office rent."

"Duke means," his father corrected, "that is how he gets deep into debt to his old man. I was beating him out of his allowance when he was still in junior high."

Barbara shut up and played cards. The stakes made her tense, even though it was not her money. Her nervousness was increased by suspicion that her partner was a match player.

8

Her nerves relaxed, though not her care, as it began to appear that Mr. Farnham found her bidding satisfactory. But she welcomed the rest that came from being dummy. She spent these vacations studying Hubert Farnham.

She decided that she liked him, for the way he handled his family and for the way he played bridge—quietly, thoughtfully, exact in bidding, precise and sometimes brilliant in play. She admired the way he squeezed out the last trick, of a contract in which she had forced them too high, by having the boldness to sluff an ace.

She knew that Karen expected her to pair off with Duke this weekend and admitted that it seemed reasonable. Duke was as handsome as Karen was pretty—and a catch . . . rising young lawyer, a year older than herself, with a fresh and disarming wolfishness.

She wondered if he expected to make out with her? Did Karen expect it and was she watching, secretly amused?

Well, it wasn't going to happen!

She did not mind admitting that she was a one-time loser but she resented the assumption that any divorcee was available. Damn it, she hadn't been in bed with *anybody* since that dreadful night when she had packed and left. Why did people think—

Duke was looking at her; she locked eyes with him, blushed, and looked away, looked at his father instead.

Mr. Farnham was fiftyish, she decided. And looked it. Hair thinning and already gray, himself thin, almost gaunt, but with a slight potbelly, tired eyes, lines around them, and deep lines down his cheeks. Not handsome—

With sudden warmth she realized that if Duke Farnham had half the strong masculine charm his father had, a panty girdle wouldn't be much protection. She dismissed it by being quickly angry with Grace Farnham. What excuse did a woman have for being an incipient alcoholic, fretful and fat and self-indulgent, when she had *this* man?

The thought was chased away by the realization that Mrs. Farnham was what Karen might become. Mother and daughter looked alike, save that Karen had not gone to pot. Barbara did not like this thought. She liked Karen better than any other sorority sister she had found when she went back to finish college. Karen was sweet and generous and gay—

But perhaps Grace Farnham had been so, once. Did women *have* to become fretful and useless?

Hubert Farnham looked up from the last trick. "Three spades, game and rubber. Well bid, partner."

She flushed again. "Well played, you mean. I invited too much."

"Not at all. At worst we would have been down one. If you don't bet, you can't win. Karen, has Joseph gone to bed?"

"Studying. He's got a quiz."

"I thought we might invite him to cut in. Barbara, Joseph is the best player in this house—always audacity at the right time. Plus the fact that he is studying to be an accountant and never forgets a card. Karen, can you find us something without disturbing Joseph?"

" 'Spect ah kin, Boss. Vodka and tonic for you?"

"And munching food."

"Come on, Barbara. Let's buttle."

Hubert Farnham watched them go, while thinking it was a shame that so nice a child as Mrs. Wells should have had a sour marriage. A sound game of bridge and a good disposition— Gangly and horsefaced, perhaps— But a nice smile and a mind of her own. If Duke had any gumption—

But Duke didn't have any. He went to where his wife was nodding by the television receiver, and said, "Grace? Grace darling, ready for bed?"—then helped her into her bedroom.

When he came back, he found his son alone. He sat down and said, "Duke, I'm sorry about that difference of opinion at dinner."

"That? Oh, forget it."

"I would rather have your respect than your tolerance. I know that you disapprove of my 'panic hole.' But we have never discussed why I built it."

"What is there to discuss? You think the Soviet Union is going to attack. You think that hole in the ground will save your life. Both ideas are unhealthy. Sick. Especially unhealthy for Mother. You are driving her to drink. I don't like it. I liked it still less to have you remind me—*me*, a lawyer!—that I must not interfere between husband and wife." Duke started to get up. "I'll be going."

"Please, Son! Doesn't the defense get a chance?"

"Uh— All right, all right!" Duke sat down.

"I respect your opinions. I don't share them but many people do. Perhaps most people, since most Americans have made no effort to save themselves. But on the points you made, you are mistaken. I don't expect the USSR to attack—and I doubt if our shelter is enough to save our lives."

"Then why go around with that plug in your ear scaring Mother out of her wits?"

"I've never had an automobile accident. But I carry auto insurance. That shelter is my insurance policy."

"But you just said it wouldn't save your life!"

"No, I said I doubted that it would be enough. It could save our lives if we lived a hundred miles away. But Mountain Springs is a prime target . . . and no citizen can build anything strong enough to stop a direct hit."

"Then why bother?"

"I told you. The best insurance I can afford. Our shelter won't stop a direct hit. But it will stand up to a near miss—and Russians aren't supermen and rockets are temperamental. I've minimized the risk. That's the best I can do."

Duke hesitated. "Dad, I can't be diplomatic."

"Then don't try."

"So I'll be blunt. Do you have to ruin Mother's life, turn her into a lush, just on the chance that a hole in the ground will let you live a few years longer? Will it be worth while to be alive—afterwards—with the country devastated and all your friends dead?"

"Probably not."

"Then *why?*"

"Duke, you aren't married."

"Obviously."

"Son, I must be blunt myself. It has been years since

11

I've had any real interest in staying alive. You are grown and on your own, and your sister is a grown woman, even though she is still in school. As for myself—" He shrugged. "The most satisfying thing left is the fiddling pleasure of a game of bridge. As you are aware, there isn't much companionship left in my marriage."

"I am aware, all right. But it's your fault. You're crowding Mother into a nervous breakdown."

"I wish it were that simple. In the first place— You were at law school when I built the shelter, during that Berlin crisis. Your mother perked up and stayed sober. She would take a martini and let it go at that—instead of four as she did tonight. Duke, Grace *wants* that shelter."

"Well—maybe so. But you aren't soothing her by trotting around with that plug in your ear."

"Perhaps not. But I have no choice."

"What do you mean?"

"Grace is my *wife,* Son. 'To love and to cherish' includes keeping her alive if I can. That shelter may keep her alive. But *only* if she is in it. How much warning today? Fifteen minutes, if we're lucky. But three minutes could be time enough to get her into the shelter. But if I don't hear the alert, I won't have three minutes. So I listen. During any crisis."

"Suppose it happens when you are asleep?"

His father smiled. "If the news is bad, I sleep with this button taped into my ear. When it's really bad—as it is tonight—Grace and I sleep in the shelter. The girls will be urged to sleep there. And you are invited."

"Not likely!"

"I didn't think so."

"Dad, stipulating that an attack is possible—merely stipulating, as the Russians aren't crazy—why build a shelter smack on a target? Why don't you pick a place far from any target, build there—again stipulating that Mother needs one for her nerves, which may be true—and get Mother off the sauce?"

Hubert Farnham sighed. "Son, she won't have it. This is her home."

"Make her!"

12

."Duke, have you ever tried to make a woman do anything she really didn't want to do? Besides that, a weakness for the sauce—hell, growing alcoholism—is not that simple. I must cope with it as best I can. However— Duke, I told you that I did not have much reason to stay alive. But I do have one reason."

"Such as?"

"If those lying, cheating bastards ever throw their murder weapons at the United States, I want to live long enough to go to hell in style—with eight Russian sideboys!"

Farnham twisted in his chair. "I mean it, Duke. America is the best thing in history, *I* think, and if those scoundrels kill our country, I want to kill a few of them. Eight sideboys. Not less. I felt relieved when Grace refused to consider moving."

"Why, dad?"

"Because I don't want that pig-faced peasant with the manners of a pig to run me out of my home! I'm a free man. I intend to stay free. I've made every preparation I can. But I couldn't relish running away. I— Here come the girls!"

Karen came in carrying drinks, followed by Barbara. "Hi! Barb got a look at our kitchen and decided to make crêpes Suzettes. Why are you two looking grim? More bad news?"

"No, but if you will snap the television on, we might get part of the ten o'clock roundup. Barbara, those glorified pancakes smell wonderful. Want a job as a cook?"

"What about Joseph?"

"We'll keep Joseph as housekeeper."

"I accept."

Duke said, "Hey! You refused my offer of honorable matrimony and turn around and agree to live in sin with my old man. How come?"

"I didn't hear 'sin' mentioned."

"Don't you *know?* Barbara . . . Dad is a notorious sex criminal."

"Is this true, Mr. Farnham?"

"Well . . ."

13

"That's why I studied law, Barbara. It was breaking us to bring Jerry Giesler all the way from Los Angeles every time Dad got into a jam."

"Those were the good old days!" Duke's father agreed. "But Barbara, that was years ago. Contract is my weakness now."

"In that case I would expect a higher salary—"

"Hush, children!" Karen said forcefully. She turned up the sound:

"*—agreed in principal to three out of four of the President's major points and has agreed to meet again to discuss the fourth point, the presence of their nuclear submarines in our coastal waters. It may now be safely stated that the crisis, the most acute in post-World-War-Two years, does seem to be tapering off to a mutual accommodation that both countries can live with. We pause to bring you exciting news from General Motors followed by an analysis in depth—*"

Karen turned it down. Duke said, "Just as I said, Dad. You can take that cork out of your ear."

"Later. I'm busy with crêpes Suzettes. Barbara, I'll expect these for breakfast every morning."

"Dad, quit trying to seduce her and cut the cards. I want to win back what I've lost."

"That'll be a long night." Mr. Farnham finished eating, stood up to put his plate aside; the doorbell rang. "I'll answer it."

He went to the door, returned shortly. Karen said, "Who was it, Daddy? I cut for you. You and I are partners. Look pleased."

"I'm delighted. But remember that a count of eleven is not an opening bid. Somebody lost, I guess. Possibly a nut."

"My date. You scared him off."

"Possibly. A baldheaded old coot, very weather-beaten and ragged."

"My date," Karen confirmed. "President of the Dekes. Go get him, Daddy."

"Too late. He took one look at me and fled. Whose bid is it?"

. Barbara continued to try to play like a machine. But it seemed to her that Duke was overbidding; she found herself thereby bidding timidly and had to force herself to overcome it. They went set several times in a long, dreary rubber which they "won" but lost on points.

It was a pleasure to lose the next rubber with Karen as her partner. They shifted and again she was Mr. Farnham's partner. He smiled at her. "This time we clobber them!"

"I'll try."

"Just play as you did. By the book. Duke will supply the mistakes."

"Put your money where your mouth is, Dad. Want a side bet of a hundred dollars on this rubber?"

"A hundred it is."

Barbara thought about seventeen lonely dollars in her purse and got nervous. She was still more nervous when the first hand ended at five clubs, bid and made—by Duke—and realized that he had overbid and would have been down one had she covered his finesse.

Duke said, "Care to double that bet, Governor?"

"Okay. Deal."

Her morale was bolstered by the second hand: her contract at four spades and made possible by voids; she was able to ruff before cleaning out trumps. Her partner's smile was reward enough. But it left her shaky.

Duke said, "Both teams vulnerable, no part score. How's your blood pressure, Daddy-o? Double again?"

"Planning on firing your secretary?"

"Speak up, or accept a white feather."

"Four hundred. You can sell your car."

Mr. Farnham dealt. Barbara picked up her hand and frowned. The count was not bad—two queens, a couple of jacks, an ace, a king—but no biddable suit and the king was unguarded. It was a strength and distribution which she had long tagged as "just good enough to go set on." She hoped that it would be one of those sigh-of-relief hands in which everyone passes.

Her partner picked up his hand and glanced at it. "Three no trump."

Barbara repressed a gasp, Karen did gasp. "Daddy, are you feverish?"

"Bid."

"Pass!"

Barbara said to herself, " 'God oh god, what I do now?' "

Her partner's bid promised twenty-five points—and invited slam. She held thirteen points. Thirty-eight points in the two hands—grand slam.

That's what the book said! Barbara girl, "three no trump" is twenty-five, twenty-six, or twenty-seven points—add thirteen and it reads "Grand Slam."

But was Mr. Farnham playing by the book? Or was he bidding a shut-out to grab the rubber and nail down that preposterous bet?

If she passed, then game and rubber—and four hundred dollars—was certain. But grand slam (if they made it) was, uh, around fifteen dollars at the stakes Duke and his father were playing. Risk four hundred dollars of her partner's money against a chance of fifteen? Ridiculous!

Could she sneak up on it with the Blackwood Convention? No, no!—there hadn't been background bidding.

Was this one of those bids Duke had warned her about? (But her partner had said, "Play by the book.")

"Seven no trump," she said firmly.

Duke whistled. "Thanks, Barbara. We're ganging up on you, Dad. Double."

"Pass."

"Pass," Karen echoed.

Barbara again counted her hand. That singleton king looked awfully naked. But . . . either the home team had thirty-eight points—or it didn't. "Redouble."

Duke grinned. "Thanks, sweetie pie. Your lead, Karen."

Mr. Farnham put down his hand and abruptly left the table. His son said, "Hey! Come back and take your medicine!"

Mr. Farnham snapped on the television, moved on and switched on the radio, changed its setting. "Red alert!" he snapped. "Somebody tell Joseph!" He ran out of the room.

"Come back! You can't duck this with that kind of stunt!"

"Shut up, Duke!" Karen snapped.

The television screen flickered into life: "*—closing down. Tune at once to your emergency station. Good luck, good-bye, and God bless you all!*"

As the screen went blank the radio cut in: "*—not a drill. This is not a drill. Take shelter. Emergency personnel report to their stations. Do not go out on the street. If you have no shelter, stay in the best protected room of your home. This is not a drill. Unidentified ballistic objects have been radar-sighted by our early-warning screens and it must be assumed that they are missiles. Take shelter. Emergency personnel report to their—*"

"He means it," Karen said in an awed voice. "Duke, show Barb where to go. I'll wake Joseph." She ran out of the room.

Duke said, "I don't believe it."

"Duke, how do we get into the shelter?"

"I'll show you." He stood up unhurriedly, picked up the hands, put each in a separate pocket. "Mine and Sis's in my trousers, yours and Dad's in my coat. Come on. Want your suitcase?"

"No!"

17

2

Duke led her through the kitchen to the basement stairs. Mr. Farnham was halfway down, his wife in his arms. She seemed asleep. Duke snapped out of his attitude. "Hold it, Dad! I'll take her."

"Get on down and open the door!"

The door was steel set into the wall of the basement. Seconds were lost because Duke did not know how to handle its latch. At last Mr. Farnham passed his wife over to his son, opened it himself. Beyond, stairs led farther down. They managed it by carrying Mrs. Farnham, hands and feet, a limp doll, and took her through a second door into a room beyond. Its floor was six feet lower than the basement and under, Barbara decided, their back garden. She hung back while Mrs. Farnham was carried inside.

Mr. Farnham reappeared. "Barbara! Get in here! Where's Joseph? Where's Karen?"

Those two came rushing down the basement stairs as he spoke. Karen was flushed and seemed excited and happy. Joseph was looking wild-eyed and was dressed in undershirt and trousers, his feet bare.

He stopped short. "Mr. Farnham! Are they going to hit us?"

"I'm afraid so. Get inside."

The young Negro turned and yelled, *"Doctor Livingstone I presume!"* and dashed back upstairs.

Mr. Farnham said, "Oh, God!" and pressed his fists against his temples. He added in his usual voice, "Get inside, girls. Karen, bolt the door but listen for me. I'll wait

18

as long as I can." He glanced at his watch. "Five minutes."

The girls went in. Barbara whispered, "What happened to Joseph? Flipped?"

"Well, sort of. Dr.-Livingstone-I-Presume is our cat. Loves Joseph, tolerates us." Karen started bolting the inner door, heavy steel, and secured with ten inch-thick bolts.

She stopped. "I'm damned if I'll bolt this all the way while Daddy is outside!"

"Don't bolt it at all."

Karen shook her head. "I'll use a couple, so he can hear me draw them. That cat may be a mile away."

Barbara looked around. It was an L-shaped room; they had entered the end of one arm. Two bunks were on the right-hand wall; Grace Farnham was in the lower and still asleep. The left wall was solid with packed shelves; the passage was hardly wider than the door. The ceiling was low and arched and of corrugated steel. She could see the ends of two more bunks at the bend. Duke was not in sight but he quickly appeared from around the bend, started setting up a card table in the space there. She watched in amazement as he got out the cards he had picked up—how long ago? It seemed an hour. Probably less than five minutes.

Duke saw her, grinned, and placed folding chairs around the table.

There came a clanging at the door. Karen unbolted it; Joseph tumbled in, followed by Mr. Farnham. A lordly red Persian cat jumped out of Joseph's arms, started an inspection. Karen and her father bolted the door. He glanced at his wife, then said, "Joseph! Help me crank."

"Yes, sir!"

Duke came over. "Got her buttoned up, Skipper?"

"All but the sliding door. It has to be cranked."

"Then come take your licking." Duke waved at the table.

His father stared. "Duke, are you seriously proposing to finish a *card game* while we're being attacked?"

"I'm four hundred dollars serious. And another hundred says we aren't being attacked. In a half hour they'll call it off and tomorrow's papers will say the northern lights fouled up the radar. Play the hand? Or default?"

"Mmmm— My partner will play it; I'm busy."

"You stand behind the way she plays it?"

"Of course."

Barbara found herself sitting down at the table with a feeling that she had wandered into a dream. She picked up her partner's hand, studied it. "Lead, Karen."

Karen said, "Oh, hell!" and led the trey of clubs. Duke picked up the dummy, laid it out in suits. "What do you want on it?" he asked.

"Doesn't matter. I'll play both hands face up."

"Better not."

"It's solid." She exposed the cards.

Duke studied them. "I see," he admitted. "Leave the hands; Dad will want to see this." He did some figuring. "Call it twenty-four hundred points. Dad!"

"Yes, Son?"

"I'm writing a check for four hundred and ninety-two dollars—and let that be a lesson to me."

"You don't need to—"

All lights went out, the floor slammed against their feet. Barbara felt frightening pressure on her chest, tried to stand up and was knocked over. All around was a noise of giant subway trains, and the floor heaved like a ship in a cross sea.

"Dad!"

"Yes, Duke! Are you hurt?"

"I don't know. But make that *five* hundred and ninety-two dollars!"

The subterranean rumbling went on. Through this roar Barbara heard Mr. Farnham chuckle. "Forget it!" he called out. "The dollar just depreciated."

Mrs. Farnham started to scream. "Hubert! Hubert, where are you? *Hubert!* Make it *stop!*"

"Coming, dear!" A pencil of light cut the blackness, moved toward the bunks near the door. Barbara raised her head, made out that it was her host, on hands and knees with a flashlight in his teeth. He reached the bunk, succeeded in quieting Grace, her screams ceased. "Karen?"

"Yes, Daddy."

"Are you all right?"

"Yes, just bruised. My chair went over."

"All right. Get the emergency lighting on in this bay. Don't stand up. Crawl. I'll light you from here. Then get the hypo kit and—*ow!* Joseph!"

"Yes, sir."

"You in one piece?"

"I'm okay, Boss."

"Persuade your furry-faced Falstaff to join you. He jumped on me."

"He's just friendly, Mr. Farnham."

"Yes, yes. But I don't want him doing that while I'm giving a hypo. Call him."

"Sure thing. Here, Doc! Doc, Doc, Doc! Fish, Doc!"

Some minutes later the rumbling had died out, the floor was steady, Mrs. Farnham had been knocked out by injected drug, two tiny lights were glowing in the first bay, and Mr. Farnham was inspecting.

Damage was slight. Despite guardrails, cans had popped off shelves; a fifth of rum was broken. But liquor was almost the only thing stored in glass, and liquor had been left in cases, the rest of it had come through. The worst casualty was the shelter's battery-driven radio, torn loose from the wall and smashed.

Mr. Farnham was on his knees, retrieving bits of it. His son looked down. "Don't bother, Dad. Sweep it up and throw it away."

"Some parts can be salvaged."

"What do you know about radios?"

"Nothing," his father admitted. "But I have books."

"A book won't fix that. You should have stocked a spare."

"I have a spare."

"Then for God's sake get it! I want to know what's happened."

His father got up slowly and looked at Duke. "I would like to know, too. I can't hear anything over this radio I'm wearing. Not surprising, it's short range. But the spare is

21

packed in foam and probably wasn't hurt."

"Then get it hooked up."

"Later."

"Later, hell. Where is it?"

Mr. Farnham breathed hard. "I've had all the yap I'm going to take."

"Huh? Sorry. Just tell me where the spare is."

"I shan't. We might lose it, too. I'm going to wait until I'm sure the attack is over."

His son shrugged. "Okay, if you want to be difficult. But all of us want to hear the news. It's a shabby trick if you ask me."

"Nobody asked you. I told you I've had all the yap I'm going to take. If you're itching to know what's happening outside, you can leave. I'll unbolt this door, crank back the armor door, and you can open the upper door yourself."

"Eh? Don't be silly."

"But close it after you. I don't want it open—both for blast and radioactivity."

"That's another thing. Don't you have any way to measure radioactivity? We ought to take steps to—"

"SHUT UP!"

"What? Dad, don't pull the heavy-handed father on me."

"Duke, I ask you to keep quiet and listen. Will you?"

"Well . . . all right. But I don't appreciate being bawled out in the presence of others."

"Then keep your voice down." They were in the first bay near the door. Mrs. Farnham was snoring by them; the others had retreated around the bend, unwilling to witness. "Are you ready to listen?"

"Very well, sir," Duke said stiffly.

"Good. Son, I was not joking. Either leave . . . or do exactly as I tell you. That includes keeping your mouth shut when I tell you to. Which will it be? Absolute obedience, prompt and cheerful? Or will you leave?"

"Aren't you being rather high-handed?"

"I intend to be. This shelter is a lifeboat and I am boat officer. For the safety of all I shall maintain discipline.

Even if it means tossing somebody overboard."

"That's a farfetched simile. Dad, it's a shame you were in the Navy. It gives you romantic ideas."

"*I* think it's a shame, Duke, that *you* never had service. You're not realistic. Well, which is it? Will you take orders? Or leave?"

"You know I'm not going to leave. And you're not serious in talking about it. It's death out there."

"Then you'll take orders?"

"Uh, I'll be cooperative. But this absolute dictatorship—Dad, tonight you made quite a point of the fact that you are a free man. Well, so am I. I'll cooperate. But I won't take unreasonable orders, and as for keeping my mouth shut, I'll try to be diplomatic. But when I think it's necessary, I'll voice my opinion. Free speech. Fair enough?"

His father sighed. "Not nearly good enough, Duke. Stand aside, I want to unbolt the door."

"Don't push a joke too far, Dad."

"I'm not joking. I'm putting you out."

"Dad . . . I hate to say this . . . but I don't think you are man enough. I'm bigger than you are and a lot younger."

"I know. I've no intention of fighting you."

"Then let's drop this silly talk."

"Duke, please! I built this shelter. Not two hours ago you were sneering at it, telling me that it was a 'sick' thing to do. Now you want to use it, since it turned out you were wrong. Can't you admit that?"

"Oh, certainly. You've made your point."

"Yet you are telling me how to run it. Telling me that I should have provided a spare radio. When *you* hadn't provided anything. Can't you be a man, give in, and do as I tell you? When your life depends on my hospitality?"

"Cripes! I told you I would cooperate."

"But you haven't been doing so. You've been making silly remarks, getting in my way, giving me lip, wasting my time when I have urgent things to do. Duke, I don't want your cooperation, on your terms, according to your judgment. While we are in this shelter I want your absolute obedience."

Duke shook his head. "Get it through your head that I'm no longer a child, Dad. My cooperation, yes. But I won't promise the other."

Mr. Farnham shook his head sorrowfully. "Maybe it would be better if you took charge and I obeyed you. But I've given these circumstances thought and you haven't. Son, I anticipated that your mother might be hysterical; I had everything ready to handle it. Don't you think I anticipated this situation?"

"How so? It's pure chance that I'm here at all."

" 'This situation' I said. It could be anybody. Duke, if we had been entertaining friends tonight—or if strangers had popped up, say that old fellow who rang the doorbell—I would have taken them in; I planned on extras. Don't you think, with all the planning I have done, that I would realize that somebody might get out of hand? And plan how to force them into line?"

"How?"

"In a lifeboat, how do you tell the boat officer?"

"Is that a riddle?"

"No. The boat officer is the one with the gun."

"Oh. I suppose you do have guns down here. But you don't have one now, and"— Duke grinned—"Dad, I can't see you shooting me. Can you?"

His father stared, then dropped his eyes. "No. A stranger, maybe. But you're my son." He sighed. "Well, I hope you cooperate."

"I will. I promise you that much."

"Thank you. If you'll excuse me, I have work to do." Mr. Farnham turned away. "Joseph!"

"Yes, sir?"

"It's condition seven."

"Condition *seven*, sir?"

"Yes, and getting worse. Be careful with the instruments and don't waste time."

"Right away, sir!"

"Thank you." He turned to his son. "Duke, if you really want to cooperate, you could pick up the pieces of this radio. It's the same model as the one in reserve. There may be pieces we can use to repair the other one if it becomes necessary. Will you do that?"

"Sure, sure. I *told* you I would cooperate." Duke got on his knees, started to complete the task he had interrupted.

"Thank you." His father turned away, moved toward the junction of the bays.

"Mr. Duke! Get your hands up!"

Duke looked over his shoulder, saw Joseph by the card table, aiming a Thompson submachine gun at him. He jumped to his feet. "What the hell!"

"Stay there!" Joseph said. "I'll shoot."

"Yes," agreed Duke's father, "he doesn't have the compunctions you thought I had. Joseph, if he moves, shoot him."

"Daddy! What's going on?"

Mr. Farnham turned to face his daughter. "Get back!"

"But, Daddy—"

"Shut up. Both of you get into that lower bunk. Karen on the inside. *Move!*"

Karen moved. Barbara looked wide-eyed at the automatic her host now held in his hand and got quickly into the lower bunk of the other bay. "Arms around each other," he said briskly. "Don't either of you let the other one move." He went back to the first bay.

"Duke."

"Yes?"

"Lower your hands slowly and unfasten your trousers. Let them fall but don't step out of them. Then turn slowly and face the door. Unfasten the bolts."

"Dad—"

"Shut up. Joseph, if he does anything but exactly what I told him to, shoot. Try for his legs, but hit him."

Face white, expression dazed, Duke did as he was told: let his trousers fall until he was hobbled, turned and started unbolting the door. His father let him continue until half the bolts were drawn. "Duke. Stop. The next few seconds determine whether you go—or stay. You know the terms."

Duke barely hesitated. "I accept."

"I must elaborate. You will not only obey me, you will obey Joseph."

"Joseph?"

"My second-in-command. I have to have one, Duke; I can't stay awake all the time. I would gladly have had you as deputy—but you would have nothing to do with it. So I trained Joseph. He knows where everything is, how it works, how to repair it. So he's my deputy. Well? Will you obey him just as cheerfully? No back talk?"

Duke said slowly, "I promise."

"Good. But a promise made under duress isn't binding. There is another commitment always given under duress and nevertheless binding, a point which as a lawyer you will appreciate. I want your parole as a prisoner. Will you give me your parole to abide by the conditions until we leave the shelter? A straight quid-pro-quo: your parole in exchange for not being forced outside?"

"You have my parole."

"Thank you. Throw the bolts and fasten your trousers. Joseph, stow the Tommy gun."

"Okay, Boss."

Duke secured the door, secured his pants. As he turned around, his father offered him the automatic, butt first. "What's this for?" Duke asked.

"Suit yourself. If your parole isn't good, I would rather find it out now."

Duke took the gun, removed the clip, worked the slide and caught the cartridge from the chamber, put it back into the clip and reloaded the gun—handed it back. "My parole is good. Here."

"Keep it. You were always a headstrong boy, Duke, but you were never a liar."

"Okay . . . Boss." His son put the pistol in a pocket. "Hot in here."

"And going to get hotter."

"Eh? How much radiation do you think we're getting?"

"I don't mean radiation. Fire storm." He walked into the space where the bays joined, looked at a thermometer, then at his wrist. "Eighty-four and only twenty-three minutes since we were hit. It'll get worse."

"How much worse?"

"How would I know, Duke? I don't know how far away

the hit was, how many megatons, how widespread the fire. I don't even know whether the house is burning overhead, or was blasted away. Normal temperature in here is about fifty degrees. That doesn't look good. But there is nothing to do about it. Yes, there's one thing. Strip down to shorts. I shall."

He went into the other bay. The girls were still in the lower bunk, arms around each other, keeping quiet. Joseph was on the floor with his back to the wall, the cat in his lap. Karen looked round-eyed as her father approached but she said nothing.

"You kids can get up."

"Thanks," said Karen. "Pretty warm for snuggling." Barbara backed out and Karen sat up.

"So it is. Did you hear what just happened?"

"Some sort of argument," Karen said cautiously.

"Yes. And it's the last one. I'm boss and Joseph is my deputy. Understood?"

"Yes, Daddy."

"Mrs. Wells?"

"Me? Why, of course! It's your shelter. I'm grateful to be in it—I'm grateful to be alive! And please call me Barbara, Mr. Farnham."

"Sorry. Hmmm— Call me 'Hugh,' I prefer it to "Hubert.' Duke, everybody—first names from now on. Don't call me 'Dad,' call me 'Hugh.' Joe, knock off the 'mister and the 'miss.' Catch?"

"Okay, Boss, if you say so."

"Make that 'Okay, Hugh.' Now you girls peel down, panties and bra or such, then get Grace peeled to her skin and turn the light out there. It's hot, it's going to get hotter. Joe, strip to your shorts." Mr. Farnham took his jacket off, started unbuttoning his shirt.

Joseph said, "Uh, I'm comfortable."

"I wasn't asking, I was telling you."

"Uh . . . *Boss, I'm not wearing shorts!*"

"He's not," Karen confirmed. "I rushed him."

"So?" Hugh looked at his ex-houseboy and chuckled. "Joe, you're a sissy. I should have made Karen straw boss."

27

"Suits me."

"Get a pair out of stores and you can change in the toilet space. While you're about it, show Duke where it is. Karen, the same for Barbara. Then we'll gather for a powwow."

The powwow started five minutes later. Hugh Farnham was at the table, dealing out bridge hands, assessing them. When they were seated he said, "Anybody for bridge?"

"Daddy, you're joking."

"My name is 'Hugh.' I was not joking, a rubber of bridge might quiet your nerves. Put away that cigarette, Duke."

"Uh . . . sorry."

"You can smoke tomorrow, I think. Tonight I've got pure oxygen cracked pretty wide and we are taking in no air. You saw the bottles in the toilet space?" The space between the bays was filled by pressure bottles, a water tank, a camp toilet, stores, and a small area where a person might manage a stand-up bath. Air intakes and exhausts, capped off, were there, plus a hand-or-power blower, and scavengers for carbon dioxide and water vapor. This space was reached by an archway between the tiers of bunks. ·

"Oxygen in those? I thought it was air."

"Couldn't afford the space penalty. So we can't risk fire, even a cigarette. I opened one inlet for a check. Very hot—heat 'hot' as well as making a Geiger counter chatter. Folks, I don't know how long we'll be on bottled breathing. I figured thirty-six hours for four people, so it's nominally twenty-four hours for six, but that's not the pinch. I'm sweating—and so are you. We can take it to about a hundred and twenty. Above that, we'll have to use oxygen to cool the place. It might end in a fine balance between heat and suffocation. Or worse."

"Daddy—'Hugh,' I mean. Are you breaking it gently that we are going to be baked alive?"

"You won't be, Karen. I won't let you be."

"Well . . . I prefer a bullet."

"Nor will you be shot. I have enough sleeping pills to

let twenty people die painlessly. But we aren't here to die. We've had vast luck; with a little more we'll make it. So don't be morbid."

"How about radioactivity?" asked Duke.

"Can you read an integrating counter?"

"No."

"Take my word for it that we are in no danger yet. Now about sleeping— This side, where Grace is, is the girl's dorm; this other side is ours. Only four bunks but that's okay; one person has to monitor air and heat, and the other one without a bed can keep him awake. However, I'm taking the watch tonight and won't need company; I've taken Dexedrine."

"I'll stand watch."

"I'll stay up with you."

"I'm not sleepy."

"Slow down!" Hugh said. "Joe, you can't stand watch now because you have to relieve me when I'm tuckered out. You and I will alternate until the situation is safe."

Joe shrugged and kept quiet. Duke said, "Then it's my privilege."

"Can't either of you add? Two bunks for women, two for men. What's left over? We'll fold this table and the gal left over can sprawl on the floor here. Joe, break out the blankets and put a couple here and a couple in the tank space for me."

"Right away, Hugh!"

Both girls insisted on standing watch. Hugh shut them off. "Cut for it."

"But—"

"Pipe down, Barbara. Ace low, and low girl sleeps in a bunk, the other here on the floor. Duke, do you want a sleeping pill?"

"That's one habit I don't have."

"Don't be an iron man."

"Well . . . a rain check?"

"Surely. Joe? Seconal?"

"Well, I'm so relieved that I don't have to take that quiz tomorrow . . ."

29

"Glad somebody is happy. All right."

"I was going to add that I'm pretty keyed up. You're sure you won't need me?"

"I'm sure. Karen, get one for Joe. You know where?"

"Yes, and I'm going to get one for me, since I won the cut. I'm no iron man! And a Miltown on top of it."

"Do that. Sorry, Barbara, you can't have one; I might have to wake you and have you keep me awake. You can have Miltown. You'll probably sleep from it."

"I don't need it."

"As you wish. Bed, everybody. It's midnight and two of you are going on watch in eight hours."

In a few minutes all were in bed, with Barbara where the table had been; all lights out save one in the tank space. Hugh squatted on blankets there, playing solitaire—badly.

Again the floor heaved, again came that terrifying rumble. Karen screamed.

Hugh was up at once. This one was not as violent; he was able to stay on his feet. He hurried into the girls' dorm. "Baby! Where are you?" He fumbled, found the light switch.

"Up here, Daddy. Oh, I'm scared! I was just dropping off and it almost threw me out. Help me down."

He did so; she clung to him, sobbing. "There, there," he said, patting her. "You've been a brave girl, don't let it throw you."

"I'm not brave. I've been scared silly all along. I just didn't want it to show."

"Well . . . I'm scared too. So let's not show it, huh? Better have another pill. And a stiff drink."

"All right. Both. I'm not going to sleep in that bunk. It's too hot up there, as well as scary when it shakes."

"All right, I'll pull the mattress down. Where's your panties and bra, baby girl? Better put 'em on."

"Up there. I don't care, I just want people. Oh, I suppose I should. Shock Joseph if I didn't."

"Just a moment. Here are your pants. But where did you hide your brassiere?"

"Maybe it got pushed down behind."

Hugh dragged the mattress down. "I don't find it."

"The hell with it. Joe can look the other way. I want that drink."

"All right. Joe's a gentleman."

Duke and Barbara were sitting on the blanket she had been napping on; they were looking very solemn. Hugh said, "Where's Joe? He wasn't hurt, was he?"

Duke gave a short laugh. "Want to see 'Sleeping Innocence'? That bottom bunk."

Hugh found his second-in-command sprawled on his back, snoring, as deeply unconscious as Grace Farnham. Dr.-Livingstone-I-Presume was curled up on his chest. Hugh came back. "Well, that blast was farther away. I'm glad Joe could sleep."

"It was too damned close to suit me! When are they going to run out of those things?"

"Soon, I hope. Folks, Karen and I have just formed the 'I'm-scared-too' club and are about to celebrate with a drink. Any candidates?"

"I'm a charter member!"

"So am I," agreed Barbara. "God, yes!"

Hugh fetched paper cups, and bottles—Scotch, Seconal, and Miltown. "Water, anyone?"

Duke said, "I don't want anything interfering with the liquor."

"Water, please," Barbara answered. "It's so hot."

"How hot is it, Daddy?"

"Duke, I put the thermometer in the tank room. Go see, will you?"

"Sure. And may I use that rain check?"

"Certainly." Hugh gave Karen another Seconal capsule, another Miltown pill, and told Barbara that she must take a Miltown—then took one himself, having decided that Dexedrine had made him edgy. Duke returned.

"One hundred and four degrees," he announced. "I opened the valve another quarter turn. All right?"

"Have to open it still wider soon. Here are your pills, Duke—a double dose of Seconal and a Miltown."

"Thanks." Duke swallowed them, chased them with whisky. "I'm going to sleep on the floor, too. Coolest place in the house."

"Smart of you. All right, let's settle down. Give the pills a chance."

Hugh sat with Karen after she bedded down, then gently extracted his hand from hers and returned to the tank room. The temperature was up two degrees. He opened the valve on the working tank still wider, listened to it sigh to emptiness, shook his head, got a wrench and shifted the gauge to a full tank. Before he opened it, he attached a hose, led it out into the main room. Then he went back to pretending to play solitaire.

A few minutes later Barbara appeared in the doorway. "I'm not sleepy," she said. "Could you use some company?"

"You've been crying."

"Does it show? I'm sorry."

"Come sit down. Want to play cards?"

"If you want to. All I want is company."

"We'll talk. Would you like another drink?"

"Oh, would I! Can you spare it?"

"I stocked plenty. Barbara, can you think of a better night to have a drink? But both of us will have to see to it that the other one doesn't go to sleep."

"All right. I'll keep you awake."

They shared a cup, Scotch with water from the tank. It poured out as sweat faster than they drank it. Hugh increased the gas flow again and found that the ceiling was unpleasantly hot. "Barbara, the house must have burned over us. There is thirty inches of concrete above us and then two feet of dirt."

"How hot do you suppose it is outside?"

"Couldn't guess. We must have been close to the fireball." He felt the ceiling again. "I beefed this thing up—roof, walls, and floor are all one steel-reinforced box. It was none too much. We may have trouble getting the doors open. All this heat— And probably warped by concussion."

She said quietly, "Are we trapped?"

"No, no. Under these bottles is a hatch to a tunnel. Thirty inch culvert pipe with concrete around it. Leads to the gully back of the garden. We can break out—crowbars and a hydraulic jack—even if the end is crushed in and covered with crater glass. I'm not worried about that; I'm worried about how long we can stay inside . . . and whether it will be safe when we leave."

"How bad is the radioactivity?"

He hesitated. "Barbara, would it mean anything to you? Know anything about radiation?"

"Enough. I'm majoring—I *was* majoring—in botany; I've used isotopes in genetics experiments. I can stand bad news, Hugh, but not knowing—well, that's why I was crying."

"Mmm— The situation is worse than I told Duke." He jerked his thumb over his shoulder. "Integrating counter back of the bottles. Go look."

She went to it, stayed several minutes. When she came back, she sat down without speaking. "Well?" he asked.

"Could I have another drink?"

"Certainly." He mixed it.

She sipped it, then said quietly, "If the slope doesn't change, we'll hit the red line by morning." She frowned. "But that marks a conservative limit. If I remember the figures, we probably won't start vomiting for at least another day."

"Yes. And the curve should level off soon. That's why heat worries me more than radiation." He looked at the thermometer, cracked the valve still wider. "I've been running the water-vapor getter on battery; I don't think we should crank the blower in this heat. I'm not going to worry about Cee-Oh-Two until we start to pant."

"Seems reasonable."

"Let's forget the hazards. Anything you'd like to talk about? Yourself?"

"Little to tell, Hugh. Female, white, twenty-five years old. Back in school, or was, after a bad marriage. A brother in the Air Force—so possibly he's all right. My parents were in Acapulco, so perhaps they are, too. No pets, thank God—and I was so pleased that Joe saved his

cat. No regrets, Hugh, and not afraid . . . not really. Just
. . . sad." She sniffed. "It was a pretty nice world, even if I
did crumb up my marriage."

"Don't cry."

"I'm not crying! Those drops are sweat."

"Yes. Surely."

"They are. It's terribly hot." Suddenly she reached both
hands behind her ribs. "Do you mind? If I take this off?
Like Karen? It's smothering me."

"Go ahead. Child, if you can get comfortable—or less
uncomfortable—do so. I've seen Karen all her life, Grace
even longer. Skin doesn't shock me." He stood up, went
behind the oxygen bottles, and looked at the record of radiation. Having done so, he checked the thermometer and
increased the flow of oxygen.

As he sat down he remarked, "I might as well have
stored air instead of oxygen, then we could smoke. But I
did not expect to use it for cooling." He ignored the fact
that she had accepted his invitation to be comfortable. He
added, "I was worried about heating the place. I tried to
design a stove to use contaminated air safely. Possible.
But difficult."

"I think you did amazingly well. This is the only shelter
I've heard of with stored air. You're a scientist. Aren't
you?"

"Me? Heavens, no. High school only. What little I
know I picked up here and there. Some in the Navy, metal
work and correspondence courses. Then I worked for a
public utility and learned something about construction
and pipelines. Then I became a contractor." He smiled.
"No, Barbara, I'm a 'general specialist.' 'The Elephant
Child's 'satiable curiosity.' Like Dr.-Livingstone-I-Pre-
sume."

"How did a cat get a name like that?"

"Karen. Because he's a great explorer. That cat can get
into anything. Do you like cats?"

"I don't know much about them. But Dr. Livingstone is
a beauty."

"So he is but I like all cats. You don't own a cat, he is a
free citizen. Take dogs; dogs are friendly and fun and
34

loyal. But slaves. Not their fault, they've been bred for it. But slavery makes me queasy, even in animals."

He frowned. "Barbara, I'm not as sad over what has happened as you are. It might be good for us. I don't mean us six; I mean our country."

She looked startled. "How?"

"Well— It's hard to take the long view when you are crouching in a shelter and wondering how long you can hold out. But— Barbara, I've worried for years about our country. It seemes to me that we have been breeding slaves—and I believe in freedom. This war may have turned the tide. This may be the first war in history which kills the stupid rather than the bright and able—where it makes any distinction."

"How do you figure that, Hugh?"

"Well, wars have always been hardest on the best young men. This time the boys in service are as safe or safer than civilians. And of civilians those who used their heads and made preparations stand a far better chance. Not every case, but on the average, and that will improve the breed. When it's over, things will be tough, and that will improve the breed still more. For years the surest way of surviving has been to be utterly worthless and breed a lot of worthless kids. All that will change."

She nodded thoughtfully. "That's standard genetics. But it seems cruel."

"It *is* cruel. But no government yet has been able to repeal natural laws, though they keep trying."

She shivered in spite of the heat. "I suppose you're right. No, I *know* you're right. But I could face it more cheerfully if I thought there was going to be any country left. Killing the poorest third is good genetics . . . but there is nothing good about killing them all."

"Mmm, yes. I hate to think about it. But I did think about it. Barbara, I didn't stockpile oxygen just against radiation and fire storm. I had in mind worse things."

"Worse? How?"

"All the talk about the horrors of World War Three has been about atomic weapons—fallout, hundred-megaton-bombs, neutron bombs. The disarmament talks and the

35

pacifist parades have all been about the Bomb, the Bomb, the Bomb—as if A-weapons were the only thing that could kill. This may not be just an A-weapons war; more likely it is an ABC war—atomic, biological, and chemical." He hooked a thumb at the tanks. "That's why I stocked that bottled breathing. Against nerve gas. Aerosols. Viruses. God knows what. The communists won't smash this country if they can kill us without destroying our wealth. I wouldn't be surprised to learn that bombs had been used only on military targets like the antimissile base here, but that New York and Detroit and such received nerve gas. Or a twenty-four hour plague with eighty percent mortality. The horrid possibilities are endless. The air outside could be loaded with death that a counter won't detect and a filter can't stop." He smiled grimly. "Sorry. You had better go back to bed."

"I'm miserable anyway and don't want to be alone. May I stay?"

"Certainly. I'm happier with you present no matter how gloomy I sound."

"What you've been saying isn't nearly as gloomy as the thoughts I have alone. I wish we knew what was going on outside!" She added, "I wish we had a periscope."

"We do have."

"Huh? *Where?*"

"Did have. Sorry. That pipe over there. I tried to raise it but it won't budge. However— Barbie, I tromped on Duke for demanding that I break out our spare radio before the attack was over. But maybe it's over. What do you think?"

"Me. How would I know?"

"You know as much as I do. That first missile was intended to take out the MAMMA base; they wouldn't bother with us otherwise. If they are spotting from orbiting spaceships, then that second one was another try at the same target. The timing fits, time of flight from Kamchatka is about half an hour and the second hit about forty-five minutes after the first. That one was probably a bull'e-eye—and they know it, because more than an hour has passed and no third missile. That means they are through with us. Logical?"

"Sounds logical to me."

"It's crumby logic, my dear. Not enough data. Perhaps both missiles failed to knock out MAMMA, and MAMMA is now knocking out anything they throw. Perhaps the Russkis have run out of missiles. Perhaps the third round will be delivered by bomber. We don't know. But I'm itching to find out. Twist my arm."

"I would certainly like to hear some news."

"We'll try. If it's good news, we'll wake the others." Hugh Farnham dug into a corner, came out with a box, unpacked a radio. "Doesn't have a scratch. Let's try it without an antenna.

"Nothing but static," he announced shortly. "Not surprised. Although its mate could pull in local stations without an aerial. Now we'll hook to the fixed antenna. Wait here."

He returned shortly. "No soap. Stands to reason that there isn't anything left of the fixed antenna. So we'll try the emergency one."

Hugh took a wrench and removed a cap from an inch pipe that stuck down through the ceiling. He tested the opening with a radiation counter. "A little more count." He got two steel rods, each five feet long; with one he probed the pipe. "Doesn't go up as far as it should. The top of this pipe was buried just belowground. Trouble." He screwed the second rod into the first.

"Now comes the touchy part. Stand back, there may be debris—hot both ways—spilling down."

"It'll get on you."

"On my hands, maybe. I'll scrub afterwards. You can go over me with a Geiger counter." He tapped with a sledge on the bottom of the joined rods. Up they went about eighteen inches. "Something solid. I'll have to bang it."

Many blows later the rod was seated into the pipe. "It felt," he said, as he stopped to scrub his hands, "as if we passed into open air the last foot or so. But it should have stuck out five feet above ground. Rubble, I suppose. What's left of our home. Want to use the counter on me?"

"Hush, you say that as casually as 'What's left of yesterday's milk.' "

He shrugged. "Barbie girl, I was broke when I joined the Navy, I've been flat busted since; I will not waste tears over a roof and some plumbing. Getting any count?"

"You're clean."

"Check the floor under the pipe."

There were hot spots on the floor; Hugh wiped them with damp Kleenex, disposed of it in a metal waste can. She checked his hands afterwards, and the spots on the floor.

"Well, that used up a gallon of water; this radio had better work." He clipped the antenna lead to the rod, switched it on.

Ten minutes later they admitted that they were getting nothing. Noise—static all over the dial—but no signal. He sighed. "I'm not surprised. I don't know what ionization does to radio waves, but that must be a sorcerer's brew of hot isotopes over our heads. I had hoped we could get Salt Lake City."

"Not Denver?"

"No. Denver had an ICBM base. I'll leave the gain up; maybe we'll hear something."

"Don't you want to save the battery?"

"Not really. Let's sit down and recite limericks." He looked at the integrating counter, whistled softly, then checked the thermometer. "I'll give our sleeping beauties a little more relief from the heat. How well are you standing it, Barbie?"

"Truthfully, I had forgotten it. The sweat pours off and that's that."

"Me, too."

"Well, don't use more oxygen on my account. How many bottles are left?"

"Not many."

"How many?"

"Less than half. Don't fret. I'll bet you five hundred thousand dollars—fifty cents in the new currency—that

38

you can't recite a limerick I don't know."

"Clean or dirty?"

"Are there clean ones?"

"Okay. 'A playful young fellow named Scott—' "

The limerick session was a flop. Hugh accused her of having a clean mind. She answered, "Not really, Hugh. But my mind isn't working."

"I'm not at my sharpest. Another drink?"

"Yes. With water, please, I sweat so; I'm dry. Hugh?"

"Yes, Barbie?"

"We're going to die. Aren't we?"

"Yes."

"I thought so. Before morning?"

"Oh, no! I feel sure we can live till noon. If we want to."

"I see. Hugh, would you mind if I moved over by you? Would you put your arm around me? Or is it too hot?"

"Any time I'm too hot to put my arm around a girl I'll know I'm dead and in hell."

"Thanks."

"Room enough?"

"Plenty."

"You're a little girl."

"I weigh a hundred and thirty-two pounds and I'm five feet eight and that's not little."

"You're a little girl. Put the cup aside. Tilt your face up."

"Mmmm— Again. Please, again."

"A greedy little girl."

"Yes. Very greedy. Thank you, Hugh."

"Such pretty ones."

"They're my best feature. My face isn't much. But Karen's are prettier."

"A matter of opinion. Your opinion."

"Well— I won't argue. Scrunch over a little, dear. Dear Hugh—"

"All right?"

"Room enough. Wonderfully all right. And kiss me, too. Please?"

"Barbara, Barbara!"

"Hugh darling! I love you. Oh!"

"I love you, Barbara."

"Yes. Yes! Oh, please! *Now!*"

"Right now!"

"You all right, Barbie?"

"I've never been more all right. I've never been happier in my life."

"I wish that were true."

"It *is* true. Hugh darling, I'm utterly happy now and not at all afraid. I feel wonderful. Not even too warm."

"I'm dripping sweat on you."

"I don't mind. There are two drops on your chin and one on the end of your nose. And I'm so sweaty my hair is soaked. Doesn't matter. Hugh dearest, this is what I wanted. You. I don't mind dying—now."

"I do!"

"I'm sorry."

"No, no! Barbie hon, I didn't mind dying, before. Now suddenly life is worth living."

"Oh. I think it's the same feeling."

"Probably. But we aren't going to die, if I can swing it. Want to move now?"

"If you want to. If you'll put your arm around me after we do."

"Try to stop me. But first I'm going to make us a long, tall drink. I'm thirsty again. And breathless."

"Me, too. Your heart is pounding."

"It has every excuse. Barbie girl, do you realize that I am more than twice your age? Old enough to be your father."

"Yes, Daddy."

"Why, you little squirt! Talk that way and I'll drink this all myself."

"Yes, Hugh. Hugh my beloved. But we are the same age . . . because we are going to die at the same time."

"Don't talk about dying. I'm going to find some way to outwit it."

"If anybody can, you will. Hugh, I'm not feeling morbid. I've looked it in the face and I'm no longer afraid—not afraid to die, not afraid to live. But— Hugh, I'd like one favor."

"Name it."

"When you give the pills to the others—the overdose—I don't want them."

"Uh . . . it might be needful."

"I didn't mean that I wouldn't; I will when you tell me to. But not when the others do. Not until you do."

"Mmm, Barbie, I don't plan on taking them."

"Then please don't make me take them."

"Well— I'll think about it. Now shut up. Kiss me."

"Yes, dear."

"Such long legs you have, Barbie. Strong, too."

"And such big feet."

"Quit fishing for compliments. I like your feet. You would look unfinished without them."

"Be inconvenient, too. Hugh, do you know what I would like to do?"

"Again?"

"No, no. Well, yes. But right now."

"Sleep? Go ahead, dear. I won't fall asleep."

"No, not sleep. I'm not ever going to sleep again. Never. I can't spare one minute we've got left. I was thinking that I would like to play contract again—as your partner."

"Well— We might be able to rouse Joe. Not the others; three grains of Seconal is pretty convincing. We could play three-handed."

"No, no. I don't want any company but you. But I so enjoyed playing, as your partner."

"You're a good partner, honey. The best. When you say 'by the book,' you mean it."

"Not 'the best.' I'm not in your class. But I wish that we had—oh, years and years!—so that I could get to be. And I wish the attack had held off ten minutes, so that you could have played that grand slam."

"Didn't need to. When you answered my bid I knew it was a lay-down." He squeezed her shoulders. "Three grand slams in one night."

"Three?"

41

"Didn't you consider that H-bomb a grand slam?"

"Oh. And then there was the second bomb, later."

"I was not counting the second bomb, it was too far away. If you don't know what I counted, I refuse to draw a diagram."

"*Oh!* In that case, there could easily be a fourth grand slam. I can't make another forcing bid; my bra is gone and—"

"Was that a forcing bid?"

"Of course it was. But you can make the next forcing bid. I'll spot it."

"Slow down! Three grand slams is maximum. A small slam, maybe—if I take another Dexedrine. But four grand slams? Impossible. You know how old I am."

"We'll see. I think we'll get a fourth."

At that moment the biggest slam of all hit them.

3

The light went out, Grace Farnham screamed, Dr. Liv-ingstone-I-Presume wailed, Barbara was knocked silly and came to heaped over a steel bottle and disoriented by blackness and no floors or walls.

She groped around, found a leg, found Hugh attached to it. He was limp. She felt for his heartbeat, could not find it.

She shouted: "Hello! *Hello!* Anybody!"

Duke answered, "Barbara?"

"Yes, yes!"

"Are you all right?"

"I'm all right. Hugh is hurt. I think he's dead."

"Take it easy. When I find my trousers, I'll light a match—if I can get off my shoulders. I'm standing on them."

"Hubert! *Hubert!*"

"Yes, Mother! Wait." Grace continued to scream; Duke alternated reassurances and cursing the darkness. Barbara felt around, slipped on loose oxygen bottles, hurt her shin, and found a flat surface. She could not tell what it was; it was canted steeply.

Duke called out, "Got 'em!" A match flared up, torchbright in oxygen-rich air.

Joe's voice said, "Better put that out. Fire hazard." A flashlight beam cut the gloom.

Barbara called out, "Joe! Help me with Hugh!"

"Got to see about lights."

"He may be dying."

"Can't do a thing without light." Barbara shut up, tried

again to find heartbeat—found it and clutched Hugh's head, sobbing.

Lights came on in the men's bay; enough trickled in so that Barbara could make out her surroundings. The floor sloped about thirty degrees; she, Hugh, steel bottles, water tank, and other gear were jumbled in the lower corner. The tank had sprung a leak and was flooding the toilet space. She saw that, had the tilt been the other way, she and Hugh would have been buried under steel and water.

Minutes later Duke and Joe joined her, letting themselves down through the door. Joe carried a camp lamp. Duke said to Joe, "How are we going to move him?"

"We don't. It might be his spine."

"Still have to move him."

"We don't move him," Joe said firmly. "Barbara, have you moved him?"

"I took his head in my lap."

"Well, don't move him anymore." Joe looked his patient over, touching him gently. "I can't see any gross injuries," he decided. "Barbara, if you can stay put, we'll wait until he comes to. Then I can check his eyes for concussion, see if he can wiggle his toes, things like that."

"I'll hold still. Anybody else hurt?"

"Not to speak of," Duke assured her. "Joe thinks he's cracked some ribs and I wrenched a shoulder. Mother just got rolled into the corner of her bunk. Sis is soothing her. Sis is okay—a lump on her head where a can konked her. Are *you* all right?"

"Just bruises. Hugh and I were playing double solitaire and trying to keep cool when it hit." She wondered how long the lie would stand up. Duke had no more on than she did and didn't seem troubled by it; Joe was dressed in underwear shorts. She added, "The cat? Is he all right?"

"Dr.-Livingstone-I-Presume," Joe answered seriously, "escaped injury. But he is vexed that his sandbox was dumped over. He's cleaning himself and criticizing."

"I'm glad he wasn't hurt."

"Notice anything about this blast?"

"What, Joe? It was the hardest of the three. Much the hardest."

"Yes. But no rumbling. Just one great, big, grand slam, then . . . nothing."

"What does that indicate?"

"I don't know. Barbara, can you stay here and not move? I want to get more lights on, check the damage, and see what to do about it."

"I won't move." Hugh seemed to be breathing easily. In the silence she could hear his heart beat. She decided that she didn't have anything to be unhappy about.

Karen joined her, carrying a flashlight and moving carefully on the slant. "How's Daddy?"

"No change."

"Knocked cold, I guess. So was I. You okay?" She played the flashlight over Barbara.

"Not hurt."

"Well! I'm glad you're in uniform, too. I can't find my pants. Joe ignores it so carefully, it's painful. Is that boy square!"

"I don't know where my clothes are."

"Joe has the only pants among us. What happened to you? Were you asleep?"

"No. I was here. We were talking."

"Hmm— Further deponent sayeth not. I'll keep your grisly secret. Mother won't know; I gave her another hypo."

"Aren't you jumping at conclusions?"

"My favorite exercise. I hope my nasty suspicions are correct. I wish *I* had had something better to do than sleep last night. Since it's probably our last night." She leaned over and kissed Barbara. "I like you."

"Thanks, Karen. Me, too. You."

"Let's hold a funeral and preach about what nice guys we are. You made my daddy happy when you had the guts to bid that slam. If you made him happier still, I'm in favor of it." She straightened up. " 'Bye. I'll go sort groceries. If Daddy wakes up, yell." She left.

"Barbara?"

"Yes, Hugh? Yes!"

"Keep your voice down. I heard what my daughter said."

45

"You did?"

"Yes. She's a gentleman. Barbara? I love you. I may not have another chance to say so."

"I love you."

"Darling."

"Shall I call the others?"

"Shortly. Are you comfortable?"

"Oh, very!"

"Then let me rest a bit. I feel woozy."

"As long as you like. Uh, can you wiggle your toes? Do you hurt anyplace?"

"I hurt lots of places, but not too much. Let me see— Yes, I can move everything. All right, call Joe."

"No hurry."

"Better call him. Work to do."

Shortly Mr. Farnham was back in charge. Joe required him to move himself—a mass of bruises but no break, sprain, nor concussion. It seemed to Barbara that Hugh had landed on the bottles and that she had landed on him. She did not discuss her theory.

Hugh's first act was to bind Joe's ribs with elastic bandage. Joe gasped as it tightened but seemed more comfortable with it. The lump on Karen's head was inspected; Hugh decided that there was nothing he could do for it.

"Will somebody fetch the thermometer?" he asked. "Duke?"

"It's busted."

"It's a bimetal job. Shockproof."

"I looked for it," Duke explained, "while you were doctoring. Seems cooler to me. While it may be shockproof, it couldn't stand being mashed between two tanks."

"Oh. Well, it's no big loss."

"Dad? Wouldn't this be a good time to try the spare radio? Just a suggestion."

"I suppose so, but—I hate to tell you, Duke, but you'll probably find it smashed, too. We tried it earlier. No results." He glanced at his wrist. "An hour and half ago. At two A.M. Has anyone else the time?"

Duke's watch agreed.

"We seem to be in fair shape," Hugh decided, "except

for water. There are some plastic jugs of water but we need to salvage the tank water; we may have to drink it. With Halazone tablets. Joe, we need utensils of any sort, and everybody bail. Keep it as clean as you can." He added, "When Joe can spare you, Karen, scrounge some breakfast. We've got to eat, even if this is Armageddon."

"And Armageddon sick of it," Karen offered.

Her father winced. "Baby girl, you will write on the blackboard one thousand times: 'I will not make bad puns before breakfast.' "

"I thought it was pretty good, Hugh."

"Don't encourage her, Barbara. All right, get with it."

Karen returned shortly, carrying Dr. Livingstone. "I wasn't much help," she announced, "because somebody has to hang onto this damn cat. He wants to help."

"Kablerrrrt!"

"You did so! I'm going to entice him with sardines and get breakfast. What do you want, Daddy Hugh Boss? Crêpes Suzettes?"

"Yes."

"What you'll get is Spam and crackers."

"All right. How's the bailing going?"

"Daddy, I won't drink that water even with Halazone." She made a face. "You know where it wound up."

"We may have to drink it."

"Well . . . if you cut it with whisky—"

"Mmm— Every case of liquor is leaking. The two I've opened each has one fifth, unbroken."

"Daddy, you've ruined breakfast."

"The question is, do I ration it evenly? Or save it all for Grace?"

"Oh." Karen's features screwed up in painful decision. "She can have my share. But the others shouldn't be deprived just because Gracie has a yen."

"Karen, at this stage it's not a yen. In a way, for her it's medicine."

"Yeah, sure. And diamond bracelets and sable coats are medicine for me."

"Baby, there's no point in blaming her. It may be my fault. Duke thinks so. When you are my age, you will

47

learn to take people as they are."

"Hush mah mouf. Maybe I'm harsh—but I get tired of bringing friends home and having Mom pass out about dinner time. Or try to kiss my boyfriends in the kitchen."

"She does that?"

"Haven't you seen? No, you probably haven't. Sorry."

"I'm sorry, too. But only on your account. It's a peccadillo, at most. As I was saying, when you get to be my age—"

"Daddy, I don't expect to get to be your age—and we both know it. If we've got even two fifths of liquor, it's probably enough. Why don't you just serve it to whoever needs it?"

The lines in his face got deeper. "Karen, I haven't given up. It's distinctly cooler. We may get out of this yet."

"Well— I guess that's the proper attitude. Speaking of medicine, didn't you squirrel away some Antabuse when we built this monster?"

"Karen, Antabuse doesn't stop the craving; it simply makes the patient deathly ill if he drinks. If your estimate of our chances is correct, can you see any reason why I should force Grace to spend her last hours miserably? I'm not her judge, I'm her husband."

Karen sighed. "Daddy, you have an annoying habit of being right. All right, she can have mine."

"I was merely asking your opinion. You've helped. I've decided."

"Decided how?"

"None of your business, half pint. Get breakfast."

"I'm going to put kerosene in yours. Give me a kiss, Daddy."

He did. "Now pipe down and get to work."

Five of them gathered for breakfast, sitting on the floor as chairs would not stand up. Mrs. Farnham was still lethargic from heavy sedation. The others shared canned meat, crackers, cold Nescafé, canned peaches, and warm comradeship. They were dressed, the men in shorts, Karen in shorts and halter, and Barbara in a muumuu belonging to Karen. Her underwear had been salvaged but was soaked and the air was too moist to dry it.

Hugh announced, "Time for a conference. Suggestions are welcome." He looked at his son.

"One item, Dad—Hugh," Duke answered. "The backhouse took a beating. I patched it and rigged a platform out of boards that had secured the air bottles. Just one thing—" He turned to his sister. "You setter types be careful. It's shaky."

"*You* be careful. You were the one hard to housebreak. Ask Daddy."

"Stow it, Karen. Good job, Duke. But with six of us I think we should rig a second one. Can we manage that, Joe?"

"Yes, we could. But . . ."

"But what?"

"Do you know how much oxy is left?"

"I do. We must shift to blower and filter soon. And there is not a working radiation counter left. So we won't know what we'll be letting in. However we've got to breathe."

"But did you look at the blower?"

"It looked all right."

"It's not. I don't think I can repair it."

Mr. Farnham sighed. "I've had a spare on order for six months. Well, I'll look at it, too. And you, Duke; maybe one of us can fix it."

"Okay."

"Let's assume we can't repair it. Then we use the oxygen as sparingly as possible. After that we can get along, for a while, on the air inside. But there will come a time when we have to open the door."

Nobody said anything. "Smile, somebody!" Hugh went on. "We aren't licked. We'll rig dust filters out of sheets in the door—better than nothing. We still have one radio—the one you mistook for a hearing aid, Barbara. I wrapped it and put it away; it wasn't hurt. I'll go outside and put up an antenna and we can listen to it down here; it could save us. We'll rig a flagpole, from the sides of a bunk perhaps, and fly a flag. A hunting shirt. No, the American flag; I've got one. If we don't make it, we'll go down with our colors flying!"

Karen started clapping. "Don't scoff, Karen."

"I'm not scoffing, Daddy! I'm crying. *'The rockets' red glare—the bombs bursting in air—gave proof through the night—that our flag was still—' "* Her voice broke and she buried her face in her hands.

Barbara put an arm around her. Hugh Farnham went on as if nothing had happened. "But we won't go down. Soon they will search this area for survivors. They'll see our flag and take us out—helicopter, probably.

"So our business is to be alive when they come." He stopped to think. "No unnecessary work, no exercise. Sleeping pills for everybody and try to sleep twelve hours a day and lie down all the time; it will make the air last as long as possible. The only work is to repair that blower and we'll knock that off if we can't fix it. Let's see— Water must be rationed. Duke, you are water marshal. See how much pure water there is; work out a schedule to stretch it. There is a one-ounce glass with the medicines; use it to dispense water. That's all, I guess: repair the blower, minimum exercise, maximum sleep, rationed water. Oh, yes! Sweat is wasteful. It's still hot and, Barbara, you've sweat right through that sack. Take it off."

"May I leave the room?"

"Certainly." She left, walking carefully on the steep floor, went into the tank room, and returned wearing her soaked underwater. "That's better," he approved. "Now—"

"Hubert! *Hubert!* Where are you? I'm thirsty."

"Duke, give her one ounce. Charge it to her."

"Yes, sir."

"Don't forget that the cat has to have water."

"The dirty water, maybe?"

"Hmm. We won't die through playing fair with our guest. Let's keep our pride."

"He's been drinking the dirty water."

"Well— You boss it. Suggestions, anyone? Joe, do the plans suit you?"

"Well— No, sir."

"So?"

"No exercise, least oxygen used, makes sense. But when

50

it comes time to open the door, where are we?"

"We take our chances."

"I mean, *can* we? Short on air, panting, thirsty, maybe sick— I'd like to be certain that anyone, Karen say, with a broken arm, can get that door open."

"I see."

"I'd like to try all three doors. I'd like to leave the armor door open. A girl can't handle that crank. I volunteer to try the upper door."

"Sorry, it's my privilege. I go along with the rest. That's why I asked for suggestions. I'm tired, Joe; my mind is fuzzy."

"And if the doors are blocked? Probably rubble against the upper door—"

"We have the jack."

"Well, if we can't use the doors, we should make sure of the escape tunnel. Duke's shoulder isn't so good. My ribs are sore but I can work—today. Tomorrow Duke and I will be stiff and twice as sore. There are those steel bottles cluttering the hatch and plunder stored in the hole. Takes work. Boss, I say we've got to be sure of our escape—while we're still in pretty good shape."

"I hate to order heavy work. But you've convinced me." Hugh stood up, suppressing a groan. "Let's get busy."

"I've got one more suggestion."

"So?"

"You ought to sack in. You haven't been to bed at all and you got banged up pretty hard."

"I'm okay. Duke has a bad shoulder, you've got cracked ribs. And there's heavy work to be done."

"I plan to use block and tackle to skid those bottles aside. Barbara can help. She's husky, for a girl."

"Certainly I can," agreed Barbara. "I'm bigger than Joe is. Excuse me, Joe."

"No argument. Boss. Hugh. I don't like to emphasize it but *I* thought of this. You admit you're tired. Not surprising, you've been on the go twenty-four hours. Do you mind my saying that I would feel more confident you could get us through if you would rest?"

"He's right, Hugh."

"Barbara, you haven't had any sleep."

"I don't have to make decisions. But I'll lie down and Joe can call me when he needs me. Okay, Joe?"

"Fine, Barbara."

Hugh grinned. "Ganging up on me. All right, I'll take a nap."

A few minutes later he was in the bottom bunk in the men's dormitory, his feet braced against the footboard. He closed his eyes and was asleep before he could get his worries organized.

Duke and Joe found that five of the bolts of the inner door were stuck. "We'll let them be," Joe decided. "We can always drift them back with a sledgehammer. Let's crank back the armor door."

The armor door, beyond the bolted door, was intended to withstand as much blast as the walls. It was cranked into place, or out, by a rack and gear driven by a long crank.

Joe could not budge it. Duke, heavier by forty pounds, put his weight on it—no results. Then they leaned on it together.

"Frozen."

"Yeah."

"Joe, you mentioned a sledgehammer."

The young Negro frowned. "Duke, I would rather your father tried that. We could break the crank. Or a tooth on the rack."

"The trouble is, we're trying to crank a ton or so of door uphill, when it was meant to move on the level."

"Yes. But this door always has been pesky."

"What do we do?"

"We get at the escape tunnel."

A block and tackle was fastened to a hook in the ceiling; the giant bottles were hauled out of the jumble and stacked, with Barbara and Karen heaving on the line and the men guiding them and then bracing them so that the stack could not roll. When the middle of the floor was clear they were able to get at the manhole cover to the tunnel. It was the massive, heavy-traffic sort and the hook in the ceiling was for lifting it.

It came up, creaking. It swung suddenly because of the 30° out-of-plumb of everything, taking a nick out of Duke's shin and an oath out of Duke.

The hole was packed with provisions. The girls dug them out, Karen, being smaller, going down inside as they got deeper and Barbara stacking the stuff.

Karen stuck her head up. "Hey! Water Boss! There's canned water here."

"Well, goody for me!"

Joe said, "I had forgotten that. This hatch hasn't been opened since the shelter was stocked."

"Joe, shall I knock out the braces?"

"I'll get 'em. You clear out the supplies. Duke, this isn't armored the way the door is. Those braces hold a piece of boiler plate against the opening, with the supplies behind it and the manhole cover holding it all down. Inside the tunnel, at ten-foot intervals, are walls of sandbags, and the mouth has dirt over it. Your father said the idea was to cofferdam a blast. Let it in, slow it down, a piece at a time."

"We'll find those sandbags jammed against that boiler plate."

"If so, we'll dig 'em out."

"Why didn't he use real armor?"

"He thought this was safer. You saw what happened to the doors. I would hate to have to pry loose a steel barrier in that tunnel."

"I see. Joe, I'm sorry I ever called this place a 'hole in the ground.' "

"Well, it isn't. It's a machine—a survival machine."

"I'm through," Karen announced. "Some gentleman help me up. Or you, Duke."

"I'll put the lid on with you under it." Duke helped his sister to climb out.

Joe climbed down, flinching at the strain on his ribs. Dr. Livingstone had been superintending. Now he followed his friend into the hole, using Joe's shoulders as a landing.

"Duke, if you'll hand me that sledge—stay out of the

53

way, Doc. Get your tail down."

"Want me to take him?' asked Karen.

"No, he likes to be in on things. Somebody hold the light." The braces were removed and piled on the floor above.

"Duke, I need the tackle now. I don't want to hoist the plate. Just take its weight so I can swing it back. It's heavy."

"Here it comes."

"That's good. *Doc!* Darn you, Doc! Get out from under my feet! Just a steady strain, Duke. Somebody hand me the flashlight. I'll swing her back and have a look."

"And get a face full of isotopes."

"Have to chance it. A touch more— That's got her, she's swinging free."

Then Joe didn't say anything. At last Duke said, "What do you see?"

"I'm not sure. Let me swing it back, and hand me one brace."

"Right over your head. Joe, what do you see?"

The Negro was swinging the plate back when suddenly he grunted. "Doc! Doc, come back here! That little scamp! Between my legs and into the tunnel. *Doc!*"

"He can't get far."

"Well— Karen, will you go wake your father?"

"Damn it, Joe! *What do you see?*"

"Duke, I don't know. That's why I need Hugh."

"I'm coming down."

"There isn't room. I'm coming up, so Hugh can go down."

Hugh arrived as Joe scrambled out. "Joe, what do you have?"

"Hugh, I would rather you looked yourself."

"Well— I should have built a ladder for this. Give me a hand." Hugh went down, removed the brace, swung back the plate.

He stared even longer than Joe had, then called up. "Duke! Let's heave this plate out."

"What is it, Dad?"

"Get the plate out, then you can come down." It was

hoisted out; father and son exchanged places. Duke stared down the tunnel. "That's enough, Duke. Here's a hand."

Duke rejoined them; his father said, "What do you think?"

"I don't believe it."

"Daddy," Karen said tensely, "somebody is going to talk, or I'm going to wrap this sledgehammer around somebody's skull."

"Yes, baby. Uh, there's room for you girls to go down together."

Barbara was handed down by Duke and Hugh, she helped Karen down over her. Both girls scrunched down and looked.

Karen said softly, "I'll be goldarned!" She started crawling into the tunnel.

Hugh called out, "Baby! Come back!" Karen did not answer. He added, "Barbara, tell me what you see."

"I see," Barbara said slowly, "a beautiful wooded hillside, green trees, bushes, and a lovely sunny day."

"That's what we saw."

"But it's impossible."

"Yes."

"Karen is outside. The tunnel isn't more than eight feet long. She's holding Dr. Livingstone. She says, 'Come on out!' "

"Tell her to get away from the mouth. It's probably radioactive."

"Karen! Get away from the tunnel! Hugh, what time is it?"

"Just past seven."

"Well, it's more like noon outside. I think."

"I've quit thinking."

"Hugh, I want to go out."

"Uh— Oh, hell! Don't tarry at the mouth. And be careful."

"I will." She started to crawl.

4

Hugh turned to his deputy. "Joe, I'm going out. Get me a forty-five and a belt. I shouldn't have let those girls go out unarmed." He eased himself down the hole. "You two guard the place."

His son said, "Against what? There's nothing to guard in here."

His father hesitated. "I don't know. Just a spooky feeling. All right, come along. But arm yourself. Joe!"

"Coming!"

"Joe, arm Duke and yourself. Then wait until we get outside. If we don't come back right away, use your judgment. This situation I hadn't anticipated. It just *can't be*."

"But it is."

"So it is, Duke." Hugh buckled on the pistol, dropped to his knees. Framed in the tunnel's mouth was still the vision of lush greenness where there should have been blasted countryside and crater glass. He started to crawl.

He stood up and moved away from the mouth, then looked around.

"Daddy! Isn't this *lovely!*"

Karen was below him on a slope that ran down to a stream. Across it the land rose and was covered with trees. On this side was a semi-clearing. The sky was blue, sunlight warm and bright, and there was no sign of war's devastation, nor any sign of man—not a building, a road, a path, no contrails in the sky. It was wilderness, and there was nothing that he recognized.

"Daddy, I'm going down to the creek."

"Come here! Where's Barbara?"

"Up here, Hugh." He turned and saw her up the slope, above the shelter. "I'm trying to figure out what happened. What do you think?"

The shelter sat cocked on the slope, a huge square monolith. Dirt clung to it save where the tunnel had cracked off and a jagged place where the stairwell had been. The armor door was exposed just above him.

"I don't think," he admitted.

Duke emerged, dragging a rifle. He stood up, looked around, and said nothing.

Barbara and Karen joined them. Dr.-Livingstone-I-Presume came bounding up to tag Hugh on the ankle and dash away. Obviously the Persian gave the place full approval; it was just right for cats.

Duke said, "I give up. Tell me."

Hugh did not answer. Karen said, "Daddy, why can't I go down to the creek? I'm going to take a bath. I stink."

"It won't hurt you to stink. I'm confused. I don't want to be confused still more by worrying about your drowning—"

"It's shallow."

"—or eaten by a bear, or falling in quicksand. You girls go inside, arm yourselves, and then come out if you want to. But stick close and keep your eyes peeled. Tell Joe to come out."

"Yes, sir." The girls went.

"What do you think, Duke?"

"Well . . . I reserve my opinion."

"If you have one, it's more than I have. Duke, I'm stonkered. I planned for all sorts of things. This wasn't on the list. If you have opinions, for God's sake spill them."

"Well— This looks like mountain country in Central America. Of course that's impossible."

"No point in worrying about whether it's possible. Suppose it was Central America. What would you watch for?"

"Let me see. Might be cougars. Snakes certainly. Tarantulas and scorpions. Malaria mosquitoes. You mentioned bears."

"I meant bears as a symbol. We're going to have to watch everything, every minute, until we know what we're up against."

Joe came out, carrying a rifle. He kept quiet and looked around. Duke said. "We won't starve. Off to the left down by the stream."

Hugh looked. A dappled fawn, hardly waist high, was staring at them, apparently unafraid. Duke said, "Shall I drop it?" He raised his rifle.

"No. Unless you are dead set on fresh meat."

"All right. Pretty thing, isn't it?"

"Very. But it's no North American deer I ever saw. Duke? Where are we? And how did we get here?"

Duke gave a lopsided grin. "Dad, you appointed yourself Fuehrer. I'm not supposed to think."

"Oh, rats!"

"Anyhow, I don't know. Maybe the Russkis developed a hallucination bomb."

"But would we all see the same thing?"

"No opinion. But if I had shot that deer, I'll bet we could have eaten it."

"I think so, too. Joe? Ideas, opinions, suggestions?"

Joe scratched his head. "Mighty pretty country. But I'm a city boy."

"One thing you can do, Hugh."

"What, Duke?"

"Your little radio. Try it."

"Good idea." Hugh crawled inside, caught Karen about to climb down, sent her back for it. While he waited, he wondered what he had that was suitable for a ladder? Chinning themselves in a six-foot manhole was tedious.

The radio picked up static but nothing else. Hugh switched it off. "We'll try it tonight. I've gotten Mexico with it at night, even Canada." He frowned. "Something ought to be on the air. Unless they smeared us completely."

"Dad, you aren't thinking straight."

"How, Duke?"

"This area did not get smeared."

"That's why I can't understand a radio silence."

"Yet Mountain Springs really caught it. Ergo, we aren't in Mountain Springs."

"Who said we were?" Karen answered. "There's nothing like this in Mountain Springs. Nor the whole state."

Hugh frowned. "I guess that's obvious." He looked at the shelter—gross, huge, massive. "But where are we?"

"Don't you read comic books, Daddy? We're on another planet."

"Don't joke, baby girl. I'm worried."

"I wasn't joking. There is nothing like this within a thousand miles of home—yet here we are. Might as well be another planet. The one we had was getting used up."

"Hugh," Joe said, "it sounds silly. But I agree with Karen."

"Why, Joe?"

"Well, we're *someplace*. What happens when an H bomb explodes dead on you?"

"You're vaporized."

"I don't *feel* vaporized. And I can't see that big hunk of concrete sailing a thousand miles or so, and crashing down with nothing to show for it but cracked ribs and a hurt shoulder. But Karen's idea—" He shrugged. "Call it the fourth dimension. That last big one nudged us through the fourth dimension."

"Just what I said, Daddy. We're on a strange planet! Let's explore!"

"Slow down, honey. As for another planet— Well, there isn't any rule saying we have to know where we are when we don't. The problem is to cope."

Barbara said, "Karen, I don't see how this can be anything but Earth."

"Why? Spoilsport."

"Well—" Barbara chucked a pebble at a tree. "That's a eucalyptus, and an acacia beyond it. Not at all like Mountain Springs but a normal grouping of tropical and subtropical flora. Unless your 'new planet' evolved plants just like Earth, this has to be Earth."

"Spoilsport," Karen repeated. "Why shouldn't plants evolve the same way on another planet?'

"Well, that would be as remarkable as finding the same—"

"Hubert! *Hubert!* Where are you? I can't *find* you!" Grace Farnham's voice echoed out the tunnel.

Hugh ducked into the tunnel. "Coming!"

They ate lunch under a tree a little distance from the shelter. Hugh decided that the tunnel had been buried so deeply that the chance of its mouth being more radioactive than the interior was negligible. As for the roof, he was not certain. So he placed a dosimeter (the only sort of radiation instrument that had come through the pummeling) on top of the shelter to compare it later with one inside. He was relieved to see that the dosimeters agreed that they had suffered less than lethal dosage—although large—and that they checked each other.

The only other precaution he took was for them to keep guns by them—all but his wife. Grace Farnham "couldn't stand guns," and resented having to eat with guns in sight.

But she ate with good appetite. Duke had built a fire and they were blessed with hot coffee, hot canned beef, hot peas, hot canned sweet potatoes, and canned fruit salad—and cigarettes with no worry about air or fire.

"That was lovely," Grace admitted. "Hubert dear? Do you know what it would take to make it just perfect? You don't approve of drinking in the middle of the day but these are special circumstances and my nerves are still a teensy bit on edge—so, Joseph, if you will just run back inside and fetch a bottle of that Spanish brandy—"

"Grace."

"What, dear? —then all of us could celebrate our miraculous escape. You were saying?'

"I'm not sure there is any."

"What? Why, we stored two cases of it!"

"Most of the liquor was broken. That brings up something else. Duke, you are out of a job as water boss. I'd like you to take over as bartender. There are at least two unbroken fifths. Whatever you find, split it six ways and make it share and share alike, whether it's several bottles each, or just a part of a bottle."

Mrs. Farnham looked blank, Duke looked uneasy. Karen said hastily, "Daddy, you know what I said."

"Oh, yes. Duke, your sister is on the wagon. So hold her share as a medicinal reserve. Unless she changes her mind."

"I don't want the job," said Duke.

"We have to divide up the chores, Duke. Oh yes, do the same with cigarettes. When they are gone, they're gone, whereas I have hopes that we can distill liquor later." He turned to his wife. "Why not have a Miltown, dear?"

"Drugs! Hubert Farnham, are you telling me that I *can't* have a drink?"

"Not at all. At least two fifths came through. Your share would be about a half pint. If you want a drink, go ahead."

"Well! Joseph, run inside and fetch me a bottle of brandy."

"No!" her husband countermanded. "If you want it, Grace, fetch it yourself."

"Oh, shucks, Hugh, I don't mind."

"I do. Grace, Joe's ribs are cracked. It hurts him to climb. You can manage the climb with those boxes as steps—and you're the only one who wasn't hurt."

"That's not true!"

"Not a scratch. Everybody else was bruised or worse. Now about jobs— I want you to take over as cook. Karen will be your assistant. Okay, Karen?"

"Certainly, Daddy."

"It will keep you both busy. We'll build a grill and Dutch oven, but it will be cook over a campfire and wash dishes in the creek for a while."

"So? And will you please tell me, Mr. Farnham, what Joseph is going to do in the meantime? To earn his wages?"

"Will *you* please tell *me* how we'll pay wages? Dear,

dear—can't you see that things have changed?"

"Don't be preposterous! Joseph will get every cent coming to him and he knows it—just as soon as this mess is straightened out. After all, we've saved his life. And we've always been good to him, he won't mind waiting. Will you, Joseph?"

"Grace! Quiet down and listen. Joe is no longer our servant. He is our partner in adversity. We'll never pay him wages again. Quit acting like a child and face the facts. We're broke. We're never going to have any money again. Our house is gone. My business is gone. The Mountain Exchange Bank is gone. We're wiped out . . . save for what we stored in the shelter. But we are lucky. We're alive and by some miracle have a chance of scratching a living out of the ground. Lucky. Do you understand?"

"I understand you are using it as an excuse to bully me!"

"You've merely been assigned a job to fit your talents."

"Kitchen drudge! I was your kitchen slave for twenty-five years! That's long enough. I won't do it! Do you understand me?"

"You are wrong on both points. You've had a maid most of our married life . . . and Karen washed dishes from the time she could see over the sink. Granted, we had lean years. Now we're going to have more lean years—and you're going to help. Grace, you are a fine cook when you want to be. You will cook . . . or you won't eat."

"Oh!" She burst into tears and fled into the shelter.

Her behind was disappearing when Duke got up to follow. His father stopped him. "Duke!"

"Yes."

"One word and you can join your mother. I'm going exploring, I want you to go with me."

Duke hesitated. "All right."

"We'll start shortly. I think your job should be 'hunter.' You're a better shot than I am and Joe has never hunted. What do you think?"

"Uh— All right."

"Good. Well, go soothe her down and, Duke, see if you can make her see the facts."

"Maybe. But I agree with Mother. You were bullying her."

"As may be. Go ahead."

Duke turned abruptly and left. Karen said quietly, "I think so too, Daddy. You were bullying."

"I intended to. I judged it called for bullying. Karen, if I hadn't tromped on it, she would do no work . . . and would order Joe around, treat him as a hired cook."

"Shucks, Hugh, I don't mind cooking. It was a pleasure to rustle lunch."

"She's a better cook than you are, Joe, and she's going to cook. Don't let me catch you fetching and carrying for her."

The younger man grinned. "You won't catch me."

"Better not. Or I'll skin you and nail it to the barn. Barbara, what do you know about farming?"

"Very little."

"You're a botanist."

"No, I simply might have been one, someday."

"Which makes you eight times as much of a farmer as the rest of us. I can barely tell a rose from a dandelion; Duke knows even less and Karen thinks you dig potatoes out of gravy. You heard Joe say he was a city boy. But we have seeds and a small supply of fertilizers. Also garden tools and books about farming. Look over what we've got and find a spot for a garden. Joe and I will do the spading and such. But you will have to boss."

"All right. Any flower seeds?"

"How did you know?"

"I just hoped."

"Annuals and perennials both. Don't look for a spot this afternoon; I don't want you girls away from the shelter until we know the hazards. Joe, today we should accomplish two things, a ladder and two privies. Barbara, how are you as a carpenter?"

"Just middlin'. I can drive a nail."

"Don't let Joe do what you can do; those ribs have to

63

heal. But we need a ladder. Karen, my little flower, you have the privilege of digging privies."

"Gosh. Thanks!"

"Just straddle ditches, one as the powder room, the other for us coarser types. Joe and I will build proper Chic Sales jobs later. Then we'll tackle a log cabin. Or a stone-wall job."

"I was wondering if you planned to do any work, Daddy."

"Brainpower, darling. Management. Supervision. Can't you see me sweating?" He yawned. "Well, a pleasant afternoon, all. I'll stroll down to the club, have a Turkish bath, then enjoy a long, tall planter's punch."

"Daddy, go soak your head. Privies, indeed!"

"The Kappas would be proud of you, dear."

Hugh and his son left a half hour later. "Joe," Hugh cautioned, "we plan to be back before dark but if we get caught, we'll keep a fire going all night and come back tomorrow. If you do have to search for us, don't go alone; take one of the girls. No, take Karen; Barbara has no shoes, just some spikeheeled sandals. Damn. Moccasins we'll have to make. Got it?"

"Sure."

"We'll head for that hill—that one. I want to get high enough to get the lay of the land—and maybe spot signs of civilization." They set out—rifles, canteens, hand ax, machete, matches, iron rations, compasses, binoculars, mountain boots, coveralls. Coveralls and boots fitted Duke as well as Hugh; Duke found that his father had stocked clothes for him.

They took turns, with the man following blazing trail and counting paces, the leader keeping lookout, compass direction, and record.

The high hill Hugh had picked was across the stream. They explored its bank and found a place to wade. Everywhere they flushed game. The miniature deer were abundant and apparently had never been hunted. By man, at least— Duke saw a mountain lion and twice they saw bears.

It seemed to be about three o'clock local time as they approached the summit. The climb was steep, cluttered with undergrowth, and neither man was in training. When they reached the flattish summit Hugh wanted to throw himself on the ground.

Instead he looked around. To the east the ground dropped off. He stared out over miles of prairie.

He could see no sign of human life.

He adjusted his binoculars and started searching. He saw moving figures, decided that they were antelope—or cattle; he made mental note that these herds must be watched. Later, later—

"Hugh?"

He lowered his binoculars. "Yes, Duke?"

"See that peak? It's fourteen thousand one hundred and ten feet high."

"I won't argue."

"That's Mount James. Dad, we're *home!*"

"What do you mean?"

"Look southwest. Those three gendarmes on that profile. The middle one is where I broke my leg when I was thirteen. That pointed mountain between there and Mount James—Hunter's Horn. Can't you *see?* The skyline is as distinctive as a fingerprint. This is Mountain Springs!"

Hugh stared. This skyline he knew. His bedroom window had been planned to let him see it at dawn; many sunsets he had watched it from his roof.

"Yes."

"Yes," Duke agreed. "Damned if I know how. But as I figure it"—he stomped the ground—"we're on the high reservoir. Where it ought to be. And—" His brow wrinkled. "As near as I can tell, our shelter is smack on our lot. Dad, we didn't go anywhere!"

Hugh took out the notebook in which were recorded paces and compasses courses, did some arithmetic. "Yes. Within the limits of error."

"Well? How do you figure it?"

Hugh looked at the skyline. "I don't. Duke, how much daylight do we have?"

65

"Well . . . three hours. The sun will be behind the mountains in two."

"It took two hours to get here; we should make it back in less. Do you have any cigarettes?"

"Yes.

"May I have one? Charged against me of course. I would like to rest about one cigarette, then start back." He looked around. "It's open up here. I don't think a bear would approach us." He placed his rifle and belt on the ground, settled down.

Duke offered a cigarette to his father, took one himself. "Dad, you're a cold fish. Nothing excites you."

"So? I'm so excitable that I had to learn never to give into it."

"Doesn't seem that way to other people." They smoked in silence, Duke seated, Hugh sprawled out. He was close to exhaustion and wished that he did not have to hike back.

Presently Duke added, "Besides that, you enjoy bullying."

His father answered, "I suppose so, if you class what I do as bullying. No one ever does anything but what he wants to do—'enjoys'—within the possibilities open to him. If I change a tire, it's because I enjoy it more than being stranded."

"Don't get fancy. You enjoy bullying Mother. You enjoyed spanking me as a kid . . . until Mother put her foot down and made you stop."

His father said, "We had better start back." He reached for his belt and rifle.

"Just a second. I want to show you something. Never mind your gear, this won't take a moment."

Hugh stood up. "What is it?"

"Just this. Your Captain Bligh act is finished." He clouted his father. "That's for bullying Mother!" He clouted him from the other side and harder, knocking his father off his feet. "And that's for having that nigger pull a gun on me!"

Hugh Farnham lay where he had fallen. "Not 'nigger,' Duke. Negro."

"He's a Negro as long as he behaves himself. Pulling a gun on me makes him a goddam nigger. You can get up. I won't hit you again."

Hugh Farnham got to his feet. "Let's start back."

"Is that all you've got to say? Go ahead. Hit me. I won't hit back."

"No."

"I didn't break my parole. I waited until we left the shelter."

"Conceded. Shall I lead? Better, perhaps."

"Do you think I'm afraid you might shoot me in the back? Look, Dad, I *had* to do it!"

"Did you?"

"Hell, yes. For my own self-respect."

"Very well." Hugh buckled on his belt, picked up his gun, and headed for the last blaze.

They hiked in silence. At last Duke said, "Dad?"

"Yes, Duke?"

"I'm sorry."

"Forget it."

They went on, found where they had forded the stream, crossed it. Hugh hurried, as it was growing darker. Duke closed up again. "Just one thing, Dad. Why didn't you assign Barbara as cook? She's the freeloader. Why pick on Mother?"

Hugh took his time in answering. "Barbara is no more a freeloader than you are, Duke, and cooking is the only thing Grace knows. Or were you suggesting that she loaf while the rest of us work?"

"No. Oh, we all have to pitch in—granted. But no more bullying, no more bawling Mother out in public. Understand me?"

"Duke."

"Yeah?"

"I've been studying karate three afternoons a week the past year."

"So?"

"Don't try it again. Shooting me in the back is safer."

"I hear you."

"Until you decide to shoot me, it would be well to accept my leadership. Or do you wish to assume the responsibility?"

"Are you offering it?"

"I am not in a position to. Perhaps the group would accept you. Your mother would. Possibly your sister would prefer you. Concerning Barbara and Joe, I offer no opinion."

"How about *you*, Dad?"

"I won't answer that; I owe you nothing. But until you decide to make a bid for leadership, I expect the same willing discipline you showed under parole."

" 'Willing discipline' indeed!"

"In the long run there is no other sort. I can't quell a mutiny every few hours—and I've had two from you plus an utter lack of discipline from your mother. No leader can function on those terms. So I will assume your willing discipline. That includes no interference should I decide again to use what you call 'bullying.' "

"Now see here, I told you I would not stand for—"

"Quiet! Unless you make up your mind to that, your safest choice is to shoot me in the back. Don't come at me with bare hands or risk giving me a chance to shoot first. At the next sign of trouble, Duke, I will kill you. If possible. One of us will surely be killed."

They trudged along in silence, Mr. Farnham never looking back. At last Duke said, "Dad, for Christ's sake, why can't you run things democratically? I don't want to boss things, I simply want you to be fair about it."

"Mmm, you don't want to boss. You want to be a backseat driver—with a veto over the driver."

"Nuts! I simply want things run democratically."

"You do? Shall we vote on whether Grace is to work like the rest of us? Whether she shall hog the liquor? Shall we use Robert's Rules of Order? Should she withdraw while we debate it? Or should she stay and defend herself against charges of indolence and drunkenness? Do you wish to submit your mother to such ignominy?"

"Don't be silly!"

"I am trying to find out what you mean by 'democratically.' If you mean putting every decision to a vote, I am willing—if you will bind yourself to abide by every majority decision. You're welcome to run for chairman. I'm sick of the responsibility and I know that Joe does not like being my deputy."

"That's another thing. Why should Joe have any voice in these matters?"

"I thought you wanted to do it 'democratically'?"

"Yes, but he is—"

"What, Duke? A 'nigger'? Or a servant?"

"You've got a nasty way of putting things."

"You've got nasty ideas. We'll try formal democracy—rules of order, debate, secret ballot, everything —any time you want to try such foolishness. Especially any time you want to move a vote of no confidence and take over the leadership . . . and I'm so bitter as to hope that you succeed. In the meantime we *do* have democracy."

"How do you figure?"

"I'm serving by consent of the majority—four to two, I think. But that doesn't suit me; I want it to be unanimous, I can't put up indefinitely with wrangling from the minority. You and your mother, I mean. I want it to be five to one before we get back, with your assurance that you will not interfere in my efforts to persuade, or cajole, or *bully*, your mother into accepting her share of the load—until you care to risk a vote of no confidence."

"You're asking me to agree to *that?*"

"No. I'm *telling* you. Willing discipline on your part . . . or at the next clash one of us will be killed. I won't give you the slightest warning. That's why your safest course is to shoot me in the back."

"Quit talking nonsense! You know I won't shoot you in the back."

"So? *I* will shoot *you* in the back or anywhere at the next hint of trouble. Duke, I can see only one alternative. If you find it impossible to give willing disciplined consent, if you don't think you can displace me, if you can't bring yourself to kill me, if you don't care to risk a clash in which one of us will be killed, then there is still a peaceful solution."

"What is it?"

"Any time you wish, you can leave. I'll give you a rifle, ammunition, salt, matches, a knife, whatever you find needful. You don't deserve them but I won't turn you out with nothing."

Duke gave a bitter laugh. "Sending me out to play Robinson Crusoe . . . and leaving all the women with you!"

"Oh, no! Any who wish are free to go. With a fair share of anything and some to boot. All three women if you can sell the idea."

"I'll think about it."

"Do. And do a little politicking and size up your chances of winning a vote against me 'democratically'—while being extraordinarily careful not to cross wills with me and thereby bring on a showdown sooner than you wish. I warn you, I'm feeling very short-tempered; you loosened one of my teeth."

"I didn't mean to."

"That wasn't the way it felt. There's the shelter; you can start that 'willing discipline' by pretending that we've had a lovely afternoon."

"Look, Dad, if you won't mention—"

"Shut up. I'm sick of you."

As they neared the shelter Karen saw them and yoo-hooed; Joe and Barbara came crawling out the tunnel. Karen waved her shovel. "Come see what I've done!"

She had dug privies on each side of the shelter. Saplings formed frameworks which had been screened by tacking cardboard from liquor cases. Seats had been built of lumber remnants from the tank room. "Well?" demanded Karen. "Aren't they *gorgeous?*"

"Yes," agreed Hugh. "Much more lavish than I had expected." He refrained from saying that they had cost most of the lumber.

"I didn't do it all. Barbara did the carpentry. You should hear her swear when she hits her thumb."

"You hurt your thumb, Barbara?"

"It'll get well. Come try the ladder."

"Sure thing." He started inside; Joe stopped him.

"Hugh, while we've still got light, how about seeing something?"

"All right. What?"

"The shelter. You've been talking about building a cabin. Suppose we do: what do we have? A mud floor and a roof that leaks, no glass for windows and no doors. Seems to me the shelter is better."

"Well, perhaps," agreed Hugh. "I had thought we could use it while pioneering, if we had to."

"I don't think it's too radioactive, Hugh. That dosimeter should have gone sky-high if the roof is really 'hot.' It hasn't."

"That's good news. But, Joe, look at it. A slant of thirty degrees is uncomfortable. We need a house with a level floor."

"That's what I mean. Hugh, that hydraulic jack—it's rated at thirty tons. How much does the shelter weigh?"

"Oh. Let me think how many yards of mix we used and how much steel." Hugh pondered it, got out his notebook. "Call it two hundred fifty tons."

"Well, it was an idea."

"Maybe it's a good idea." Hugh prowled around the shelter, a block twenty feet square and twelve high, sizing up angles, estimating yardages.

"It can be done," Hugh decided. "We dig under on the uphill side, to the center line, cutting out enough to let that side settle down level. Damn, I wish we had power tools."

"How long will it take?"

"Two men could do it in a week if they didn't run into boulders. With no dynamite a boulder can be a problem."

"Too much of a problem?"

"Always some way to cope. Let's pray we don't run into solid rock. As we get it dug out, we brace it with logs. At the end we snag the logs out with block and tackle. Then we put the jack under the downhill side and tilt it into place, shore it up and fill with what we've removed. Lots of sweat."

"I'll start bright and early tomorrow."

"You will like hell. Not until your ribs have healed. I

will start tomorrow, with two husky girls. Plus Duke, if his shoulder isn't sore, after he shoots us a deer; we've got to conserve canned goods. Reminds me—what was done with the dirty cans?"

"Buried 'em."

"Dig them up and wash them. A tin can is more valuable than gold; we'll use them for all sorts of things. Let's go in. I've still to admire the ladder."

The ladder was two trimmed saplings with treads cut from boards and notched and nailed. Hugh reflected again that lumber had been used too lavishly; treads should have been fashioned from limbs. Damn it, there were so *many* things that could no longer be ordered by picking up a telephone. Those rolls of Scottissue, one at each privy— They shouldn't be left outdoors; what if it rained? All too soon it would be either a handful of leaves, or do without.

So many, many things they had always taken for granted! Kotex— How long would their supply last. And what did primitive women use? Something, no doubt, but *what?*

He must warn them that anything manufactured, a scrap of paper, a dirty rag, a pin, all must be hoarded. Caution them, hound them, nag them endlessly.

"That's a beautiful ladder, Barbara!"

She looked very pleased. "Joe did the hard parts."

"I did not," Joe denied. "I just gave advice and touched up the chisel."

"Well, whoever did it, it's lovely. Now we'll see if it will take my weight."

"Oh, it will!" Barbara said proudly.

The shelter had all lights burning. Have to caution them about batteries, too. Must tell the girls to look up how to make candles. "Where's Grace, Karen?"

"Mother isn't well. She's lying down."

"So? You had better start dinner." Hugh went into the women's bay, saw what sort of not-well his wife suffered. She was sleeping heavily, mouth open, snoring, and was fully dressed. He reached down, peeled back an eyelid; she did not stir. "Duke."

"Yes?"

"Come here. Everybody else outside."

Duke joined him. Hugh said, "After lunch, did you give Grace a drink?"

"Huh? You didn't say not to."

"I wasn't criticizing. How much?"

"Just a highball. An ounce and a half of Scotch, with water."

"Does that look like one highball? Try to rouse her."

Duke tried, then straightened up. "Dad, I know you think I'm a fool. But I gave her just one drink. Damn it, I'm more opposed to her drinking than you are!"

"Take it easy, Duke. I assume that she got at the bottle after you left."

"Well, maybe." Duke frowned. "As soon as I found an unbroken bottle I gave Mother that drink. Then I took inventory. I think I found it all, unless you have some hidden away—"

"No, the cases were together. Six cases."

"Right. I found thirteen unbroken bottles, twelve fifths and a quart of bourbon. I remember thinking that was two fifths each and the quart I would keep in reserve. I had opened one bottle of King's Ransom. I made a pencil mark on it. We'll know if she found it."

"You hid the liquor?"

"I stashed it in the upper bunk on the other side; I figured it would be hard for her to climb up there— I'm not a complete fool, Dad. She couldn't see me, she was in her bunk. But maybe she guessed."

"Let's check."

Thirteen bottles were between springs and mattress; twelve were unopened, the thirteenth was nearly full. Duke held it up. "See? Right to the line. But there was another bottle we had a snort from, after that second bombing. What happened to it?"

"Barbara and I had some after you went to sleep, Duke. There was some left. I never saw it again. It was in the tank room."

"Oh! I did, while we were bailing. Busted. I give up—where *did* she get it?"

"She didn't, Duke."

"What do you mean?"

"It wasn't liquor." Hugh went to the medicines drawer, got a bottle with a broken seal. "Count these Seconal capsules. You had two last night."

"Yeah."

"Karen had one at bedtime, one later; Joe had one. Neither Barbara nor I had any, nor Grace. Five."

"Hold it, I'm counting."

His father began to count as Duke pushed them aside.

"Ninety-one," Duke announced.

"Check." Hugh put the capsules back. "So she took four."

"What do we do, Dad? Stomach pump? Emetic?"

"Nothing."

"Why, you heartless— She tried to kill herself!"

"Slow down, Duke. She did nothing of the sort. Four capsules, six grains, simply produces stupor in a healthy person—and she's healthy as a horse; she had a physical a month ago. No, she snitched those pills to get drunk on." Hugh scowled. "An alcohol drunk is bad enough. But people kill themselves without meaning to with sleeping pills."

"Dad, what do you mean, 'she took them to get drunk on'?"

"You don't use them?"

"I never had one in my life until those two last night."

"Do you remember how you felt just before you went to sleep? Warm and happy and woozy?"

"No. I just lay down and konked out. Next thing I knew I was against the wall on my shoulders."

"You haven't developed tolerance for them. Grace knows what they can do. Drunk, a very happy drunk. I've never known her to take more than one but she's never been chopped off from liquor before. When a person eats sleeping pills because he can't get liquor, he's in a bad way."

"Dad, you should have kept liquor away from her long ago!"

"How, Duke? Tell her she couldn't have a drink? Take

74

them away from her at parties? Quarrel with her in public? Fight with her in front of Joe? Not let her have cash, close out her bank account, see that she had no credit? Would that have stopped her from pawning furs?"

"Mother would never have done *that.*"

"It's typical behavior in such cases. Duke, it is impossible to keep liquor away from any adult who is determined to have it. The United States Government wasn't that powerful. I'll go further. It is impossible for anyone to be responsible for another person's behavior. I spoke of myself as 'responsible' for this group, that was verbal shorthand. The most I can do—or you, or any leader—is to encourage each one to be responsible for himself."

Hugh chewed his thumb and looked anguished. "Perhaps my mistake was in letting her loaf. But she considered me stingy because I let her have only a houseboy and a cleaning woman. Duke, do you see *anything* I could have done short of beating her?"

"Uh . . . that's beside the point. What do we do now?"

"So it is, counselor. Well, we keep these pills away from her."

"And I'm damned well going to chop off the liquor completely!"

"Oh, I wouldn't."

"You wouldn't, eh? Did I hear correctly when you said I was liquor boss?"

"The decision is up to you. I simply said that *I* wouldn't. I think it's a mistake."

"Well, I don't. Dad, I won't go into the matter of whether you could, or should, have stopped Mother from getting the way she is. But *I* intend to stop it."

"Very well, Duke. Mmm, she's going to be cut off anyhow in a matter of days. It might be easier to taper her off. If you decide to, I'll contribute a bottle from my share. Hell, you can have both of mine. I like a snort as well as the next man. But Grace needs it."

"That won't be necessary," his son said crisply. "I'm not going to let her have any. Get it over with, she'll be well that much sooner."

"Your decision. May I offer a suggestion?"

"What?"

"In the morning, be up before she is. Move the liquor out and bury it, someplace known only to you. Then have open one bottle at a time and dispense it by the ounce. Tell the others to drink where she can't see it. You had better ditch the open bottle outdoors, too."

"Sounds reasonable."

"But that makes it all the more urgent to keep sleeping pills away from her."

"Bury them?"

"No. We need them inside, and it's not just sleeping pills. Demerol. Hypodermic needles. Several drugs, some poisonous and some addictive and all irreplaceable. If she can't find Seconal—five bottles of a hundred each, it's bulky—there's no telling what she might get into. We'll use the vault."

"Eh?"

"A little safe let into concrete back of that cupboard. Nothing in it but birth certificates and such, and some reserve ammo, and two thousand silver dollars. Toss the money in with the hardware, we'll use it as metal. The combo is 'July 4th, 1776'—'74-17-76.' Better change it, Grace may know it."

"At once!"

"No rush, she won't wake up. 'Reserve ammo—' Duke, you were liquor and cigarette boss and now you are drugs boss. I'm going whole hog, you are rationing officer. Responsible for everything that can't be replaced: liquor, tobacco, ammunition, nails, toilet tissue, matches, dry cells, Kleenex, needles—"

"Good God! Got any more dirty jobs?"

"Lots of them. Duke, I'm trying to make it each according to his talents. Joe is too diffident—and he missed obvious economies today. Karen doesn't think ahead. Barbara feels like a freeloader even though she's not, she wouldn't crack down. I would, but I'm swamped. You are a natural for it; you don't hesitate to assert yourself. And you have foresight when you take the trouble to use it."

76

"Thank you too much. All right."

"The hardest thing to drill into them will be saving every scrap of metal and paper and cloth and lumber, things Americans have wasted for years. Fishhooks. Groceries aren't as important; we'll replace them, you by hunting, Barbara by gardening. Nevertheless, better note what can't be replaced. Salt. You must ration salt especially."

"Salt?"

"Unless you run across a salt lick in hunting. Salt— Damn it, we're going to have to tan leather. All I used to do with a hide was rub it with salt and give it to the taxidermist. Is salt necessary?"

"I don't know."

"I'll look it up. Damnation, we're going to find that I failed to stock endless things we'll be miserable without."

"Dad," Duke admitted, "I think you've done mighty well."

"So? That's pleasant to hear. We'll manage to—"

"*Daddy!*"

"Yes?" Hugh went to the tank room. Karen's head stuck up out of the manhole.

"Daddy, can we *please* come in? It's dark and scary and something *big* chased Doc in. Joe won't let us until you say."

"Sorry, Baby. Everybody come in. And we'll put the lid on."

"Yes, sir. But Daddy, you ought to look outside. Stars. The Milky Way like a neon sign! And the Big Dipper—so maybe this isn't another planet? Or would we still see the Big Dipper?"

"I'm not certain." He recalled that the discovery that they were still in James County, Mountain Springs area, had not been shared. But Duke must tell it; it was his deduction. "Duke, want to take a look before we close up?"

"Thanks, I've seen a star."

"As you wish." Hugh went outside, waited while his eyes adjusted, saw that Karen was right: Never before had

77

he seen the heavens on a clear mountain night with no
other light, nor trace of smog, to dim its glory.

"Beautiful!"

Karen slipped her hand into his. "Yes," she agreed.
"But I could use some streetlights. There are *things* out
there. And we heard coyotes."

"There are bears and Duke saw a mountain lion. Joe,
better keep the cat in at night, and try to keep him close in
the daytime."

"He won't go far, he's timid. And something just taught
him a lesson."

"And me, too!" announced Karen. "Bears! Come, Barbie, let's go in. Daddy, if the Moon comes up, this must be
Earth—and I'll never trust a comic book again."

"Go ask your brother."

Duke's discovery was the main subject at dinner.
Karen's disappointment was offset by her interest in how
they had mislaid Mountain Springs. "Duke, are you *sure*
you saw what you thought you saw?"

"No possible mistake," Hugh answered for him. "If it
weren't for the trees, you could have spotted it. We had to
climb Reservoir Hill to get a clear view."

"You were gone all that time just to Reservoir Hill?
Why, that's only five minutes away!"

"Duke, explain to your sister about automobiles."

"I think the bomb did it," Barbara said suddenly.

"Why, certainly, Barb. The question is *how?*"

"I mean the enormous H-bomb the Russians claimed to
have in orbit. The one they called the 'Cosmic Bomb.' I
think it hit us."

"Go on, Barbara."

"Well, the first bomb was awful and the second one was
bad; they almost burned us up. But the third one just hit
us *whammy!* and then no noise, no heat, no rumbling, and
the radioactivity got less instead of worse. Here's my notion: You've heard of parallel worlds? A million worlds
side by side, almost alike but not quite? Worlds where
Elizabeth married Essex and Mark Anthony hated
redheads? And Ben Franklin got electrocuted with his
kite? Well, this is one."

"First automobiles and now Benjamin Franklin. I'll go watch Ben Casey."

"Like this, Karen. The Cosmic Bomb hits us, dead on—and kicks us into the next world. One exactly like the one we were in, except that it never had men in it."

"I'm not sure I like a world with no men. I'd rather have a strange planet, with warlords riding thoats. Or is it zitidars?"

"What do you think of my theory, Hugh?"

"I'm keeping an open mind. I'll go this far: We should not count on finding other human beings."

"I go for your theory, Barbara," Duke offered. "It accounts for the facts. Squeezed out like a melon seed. *Pht!*"

"And we landed here."

Duke shrugged. "Let it be known as the Barbara Wells Theory of Cosmic Transportation and stand adopted. Here we are; we're stuck with it—and I'm going to bed. Who sleeps where, Hugh?"

"Just a second. Folks, meet the Rationing Officer. Take a bow, Duke." Hugh explained the austerity program. "Duke will work it out but that's the idea. For example, I noticed a bent nail on the ground in the powder room. That calls for being spread-eagled and flogged. For a serious offense, such as wasting a match, it's keelhauling. Second offense—hang him at the yardarm!"

"Gee! Do we get to watch?"

"Shut up, Karen. No punishments, just the miserable knowledge that you have deprived the rest of something necessary to life, health, or comfort. So don't give Duke any back talk. I want to make another assignment. Baby, you know shorthand."

"That's putting it strongly. Mr. Gregg wouldn't think so."

"Hugh, I take shorthand. What do you want?"

"Okay, Barbara, you are historian. Today is Day One. Or start with the calendar we are used to, but we may adjust it; those were winter stars. Every night jot down the events and put it in longhand later. Your title is Keeper of the Flame. As soon as possible, you really will be Keeper of the Flame; we will have to light a fire, then bank it

79

every night. Sorry to have held you up, Duke."

"I'll sleep in the tank room, Hugh. You take a bunk."

"Wait a minute. Buddy, would you stay up ten minutes longer? Daddy, could Barbara and I use the tank room for a spit bath? May we have that much water? A girl who digs privies *needs* a bath."

"Sure, Sis," Duke agreed.

"Water is no problem," Hugh told her. "But you can bathe in the stream in the morning. Just one thing: Whenever anyone is bathing, someone should stand guard. I wasn't fooling about bears."

Karen shivered. "I didn't think you were. But that reminds me, Daddy— Do we dash out to the powder room? Or hold it all night? I'm not sure I can. But I'll try—rather than play tag with bears!"

"I thought the toilet was still set up?"

"Well . . . I thought, with brand-new outside plumbing—"

"Of course not."

"I feel better. Okay, buddy boy, give Barb and me a crack at the john and you can go to bed."

"No bath?"

"If we bathe, we can bathe in the girls' dorm after the rest of you go to bed. Thereby sparing your blushes."

"I don't blush."

"You should."

"Hold it," interrupted Hugh. "We need a 'No Blushing' rule. Here we are crowded worse than a Moscow apartment. Do you know the Japanese saying about nakedness?"

"I know they bathe in company," said Karen, "and I would be happy to join them. Hot water! Oh, boy!"

"They say, 'Nakedness is often seen but never looked at.' I'm not urging you to parade around in skin. But we should quit being jumpy. If you come in to change clothes and find that there is no privacy—why, just change. Or take bathing in the stream. The person available to guard might not be the sex of the person who wants the bath. So ignore it." He looked at Joseph. "I mean you. I suspect you're a sissy about it."

Joe looked stubborn. "That's the way I was brought up, Hugh."

"So? I wasn't brought up this way either, but I'm trying to make the best of it. After a sweaty day's work it might be that Barbara is the one available to stand bear watch for you."

"I'll take my chances. I didn't see any bears."

"Joe, I don't want any nonsense. You're my deputy."

"I didn't ask to be."

"Nor will you be, if you don't change your tune. You'll bathe when you need it and you'll accept guard service from anybody."

Joe looked stubborn. "No, thank you."

Hugh Farnham sighed. "I didn't expect damfoolishness from you, Joe. Duke, will you back me? 'Condition seven,' I mean."

"*Dee*lighted!" Duke grabbed the rifle he had carried earlier, started to load it. Joe's chin dropped but he did not move.

"Hold it, Duke. Guns won't be necessary. That's all, Joe. Just the clothes you were wearing last night. Not clothes we stored for you, I paid for those. Nothing else, not even matches. You can change in the tank room; it was your modesty you insisted on saving. But your life is your problem. Get moving."

Joseph said slowly, "Mr. Farnham, do you really mean that?"

"Were those real bullets in that gun you aimed at Duke? You helped me clamp down on him; you heard me clamp down on my wife. Can I pull on them anything that rough—and let *you* get away with it? Good God, I'd get it from the girls next. Then the group would fall apart and die. I'd rather it was just you. You have two minutes to say good-bye to Dr. Livingstone. But leave the cat here; I don't want it eaten."

Dr. Livingstone was in the Negro's lap. Joe got slowly to his feet, still holding it. He seemed dazed.

Hugh added, "Unless you prefer to stay."

"I can?"

"On the same terms as the rest."

Two tears rolled down Joe's cheeks. He looked down at the cat and stroked it, then answered in a low voice. "I would like to stay. I agree."

"Good. Confirm it by apologizing to Barbara."

Barbara looked startled. She appeared to be about to speak, then to think better of it.

"Uh . . . Barbara. I'm sorry."

"It's all right, Joe."

"I'd be . . . happy and proud to have you guard me. While I take a bath, I mean. If you will."

"Any time, Joe. Glad to."

"Thank you."

"And now," said Hugh, "who's for bridge? Karen?"

"Why not?"

"Duke?"

"Bed for me. Anybody wants the pot, step over me."

"Sleep on the floor by the bunks, Duke, and avoid the traffic. No, take the upper bunk."

"You take it."

"I'll be last to bed, I want to look up a subject. Joe? Contract?"

"I don't believe, sir, that I wish to play cards."

"Putting me in my place, eh?"

"I didn't say that, sir."

"You didn't have to. Joe, I was offering an olive branch. One rubber, only. We've had a hard day."

"Thank you. I'd rather not."

"Damn it, Joe, we can't afford to be sulky. Last night Duke had a much rougher time. He was about to be shoved out into a radioactive hell—not just to frolic with some fun-loving bears. Did he sulk?"

Joe dropped his eyes, scratched Dr. Livingstone's skull—suddenly looked up and grinned. "One rubber. And I'm going to beat you hollow!"

"In a pig's eye. Barbie? Make a fourth?"

"Delighted!"

The cut paired Joe with Karen and gave him the deal. He riffled the cards. "Now to stack a Mississippi Heart Hand!"

"Watch him, Barbie."

"Want a side bet, Daddy?"

"What have you to offer?"

"Well— My fair young body?"

"Flabby."

"Why, you utterly utter! I'm not flabby, I'm just deliciously padded. Well, how about my life, my fortune, and my sacred honor?"

"Against what?"

"A diamond bracelet?"

Barbara was surprised to see how badly Hugh played, miscounting and even revoking. She realized that he was groggy with fatigue—why, the poor darling! Somebody was going to have to clamp down on him, too. Or he would kill himself trying to carry the whole load.

Forty minutes later Hugh wrote an I.O.U. for one diamond bracelet, then they got ready for bed. Hugh was pleased to see that Joe undressed completely and got into the lower bunk, as he had been told to. Duke stretched out on the floor, bare. The room was hot; the mass cooled slowly and air no longer circulated with the manhole cover in place, despite the vents in the tank room. Hugh made a note that he must devise a bearproof—and cat-proof—grille in place of the cover. Later, later—

He took the camp lamp into the tank room.

Someone had put the books back on shelves but some were open to dry; he fluffed these, hoped for the best.

The last books in the world—

So it seemed.

He felt sudden grief that abstract knowledge of deaths of millions had not given him. Somehow, the burning of millions of books felt more brutally obscene than the killing of people. All men must die, it was their single common heritage. But a book need never die and should not be killed; books were the immortal part of man. Book burners— To rape a defenseless friendly book.

Books had always been his best friends. In a hundred public libraries they had taught him. From a thousand newsstands they had warmed his loneliness. He suddenly

83

felt that if he had not been able to save some books, it would hardly be worth while to live.

Most of his collection was functional: *The Encyclopaedia Britannica*—Grace had thought the space should be used for a television receiver "because they might be hard to buy afterwards." He had grudged its bulkiness, too, but it was the most compact assemblage of knowledge on the market. "Che" Guevera's *War of the Guerillas*—thank God he wasn't going to need that! Nor those next to it: "Yank" Leivy's manual on resistance fighting, Griffith's Translation of Mao Tse-tung's *On Guerilla Warfare*, Tom Wintringham's *New Ways of War*, the new TR on special operations—forget 'em! Ain't a-gonna study war no more!

The Boy Scout Handbook, Eshbach's *Mechanical Engineering*, *The Radio Repairman's Guide*, Outdoor Life's *Hunting and Fishing*, *Edible Fungi and How to Know them*, *Home Life in the Colonial Days*, *Your Log Cabin*, *Chimneys and Fireplaces*, *The Hobo's Cook Book*, *Medicine Without a Doctor*, *Five Acres and Independence*, *Russian Self-Taught* and English-Russian and Russian-English dictionaries, *The Complete Herbalist*, the survival manuals of the Navy Bureau of Weapons, The Air Force's *Survival Techniques*, *The Practical Carpenter*—all sound books, of the brown and useful sort.

The Oxford Book of English Verse, *A Treasury of American Poetry*, *Hoyle's Book of Games*, Burton's *Anatomy of Melancholy*, a different Burton's *Thousand Nights and a Night*, the good old *Odyssey* with the Wyeth illustrations, Kipling's *Collected Verse*, and his *Just So Stories*, a one-volume Shakespeare, the Book of Common Prayer, The Bible, *Mathematical Recreations and Essays*, *Thus Spake Zarathustra*, T. S. Eliot's *The Old Possum's Book of Practical Cats*, Robert Frost's *Verse*, *Men Against the Sea*—

He wished that he had found time to stock the list of fiction he had started. He wished that he had fetched down his works of Mark Twain regardless of space. He wished—

Too late, too late. This was it. All that was left of a mighty civilization. *"The cloud-capped towers—"*

He jerked awake and found that he had fallen asleep standing up. Why had he come in here? Something important. Oh, yes! Tanning leather— Leather! Barbara was barefooted, Barbara must have moccasins. Better try the *Britannica*. Or that *Colonial Days* volume.

No, thank God, you didn't have to use salt! Find some oak trees. Better yet, have Barbara find them; it would make her feel useful. Find something that only Joe could do, too; make the poor little bastard feel appreciated. Loved. Remember to—

He stumbled back into the main room, looked at the upper bunk and knew that he couldn't make it. He lay down on the blanket they had played cards on and fell instantly asleep.

5

Grace did not get up for breakfast. The girls quietly fed them, then stayed in to clean up. Duke went hunting, carrying a forty-five and a hunting bow. It was his choice; arrows could be recoverd or replaced, bullets were gone forever. Duke tried a few flights and decided that his shoulder was okay.

He checked watches and set out, with an understanding that a smoky fire would be built to home on if he was not back by three.

Hugh told the girls to take outdoors any book not bone-dry, then broke out pick and shovel and started leveling their house. Joe tried to join him; Hugh vetoed it.

"Look Joe, there are a thousand things to do. Do them. But no heavy work."

"Such as what, Hugh?"

"Uh, correct the inventories. Give Duke a hand by starring everything that can't be replaced. In the course of that you'll think of things; write them down. Look up how to make soap and candles. Check both dosimeters. Strap on a gun and keep your eyes open—and see that those girls don't go outside without guns. Hell, figure out a way to get plumbing and running water, with no pipe and no lead and no water closets and no portland cement."

"How in the world could you do that?"

"Somebody did it the first time. And tell this bushy-tailed sidewalk superintendent that I need no help."

"Okay. Come here, Doc! Come, come, come!"

"And Joe. Speaking of bathrooms, you might offer to stand guard for the girls while they bathe. You don't have to look."

"All right, I'll offer. But I'll tell them you suggested it. I don't want them to think—"

"Look, Joe. They are a couple of clean, wholesome, evil-minded American girls. Say what you please, they will still believe you are sneaking a peek. It's part of their credo that they are so fatally irresistible that a man just has to. So don't be too convincing; you'll hurt their feelings."

"I get it. I guess." Joe went away, Hugh started digging, while reflecting that he had never missed a chance, given opportunity without loss of face—but that incorrigible Sunday school lad probably would not sneak a peek at Lady Godiva. A good lad—no imagination but utterly dependable. Shame to have been so rough on him last night—

Very quickly Hugh knew what his worst oversight had been: no wheelbarrow.

He had dug only a little before reaching this new appreciation. Digging by muscle power was bad but carrying it away in buckets was an affront to good sense.

So he carried and thought about how to build a wheel—with no metal, no heating tools, no machine shop, no foundry, no—

Now wait! He had steel bottles. There was strap iron in the bunks and soft iron in the periscope housing. Charcoal he could make and a bellows was simply an animal skin and some branches. Whittle a nozzle. Any damfool who couldn't own a wheel with all that at his disposal deserved to lift and carry.

He had ten thousand trees, didn't he? Finland didn't have a damn thing but trees. Yet Finland was the finest little country in the world.

"Doc, get out from under my feet!" If Finland was still there— Wherever the world was—

Maybe the girls would like a Finnish bath. Down where they could plunge in afterwards and squeal and feel good. Poor kids, they would never see a beauty parlor; maybe a

87

sauna would be a "moral equivalent." Grace might like it. Sweat off that blubber, get her slender again. What a beauty she had been!

Barbara showed up, with a shovel. "Where did you get that? And what do you think you're going to do?'

"It's the one Duke was using. I'm going to dig."

"In bare feet? You're cra— Hey, you're wearing shoes!"

"Joe's. The jeans are his, too. The shirt is Karen's. Where shall I dig?"

"Just beyond me, here. Any boulder over five hundred pounds, ask for help. Where's Karen?"

"Bathing. I decided to stink worse and bathe later."

"When you like. Don't try to stick on this job all day. You can't."

"I like working with you, Hugh. Almost as much as—" She let it hang.

"As playing bridge?"

"As playing bridge as your partner. Yes, you could mention that. Too."

"Barbie girl."

He found that just digging was fun. Gave the mind a rest and the muscles a workout. Happy making. Hadn't tried it for much too long.

Barbara had been digging an hour when Mrs. Farnham came around a corner. Barbara said, "Good morning," added a shovelful to a bucket, picked both up half filled, and disappeared around the other corner.

Grace Farnham said, "Well! I wondered where you were hiding. I was left quite alone. Do you realize that?" She was in the clothes she had slept in. Her features looked puffy.

"You were allowed to sleep, dear."

"It isn't pleasant to wake up in a strange place alone. I'm not accustomed to it."

"Grace, you weren't being slighted. You were being pampered."

"Is that what you call it? Then we'll say no more about it, do you mind?"

"Not at all."

"Really?" She seemed to brace herself, then said bleakly, "Perhaps you can stop long enough to tell me where you have hidden my liquor. *My liquor.* My share. I wouldn't think of touching yours—after the way you've treated me! In front of the servants and strangers, may I add?"

"Grace, you must see Duke."

"What do you mean?"

"Duke is in charge of liquor. I don't know where he put it."

"You're lying!"

"Grace, I haven't lied to you in twenty-seven years."

"Oh! You brutal, brutal man!"

"Perhaps. But I'm not lying and the next time you say I am, it will go hard with you."

"Where's Duke? He won't let you talk to me that way! He told me so, he promised me!"

"Duke has gone hunting. He hopes to be back by three."

She stared, then rushed back around the corner. Barbara reappeared, picked up her shovel. They went on working.

Hugh said, "I'm sorry you were exposed to that."

"To what?"

"Unless you were at least a hundred yards away, you know what."

"Hugh, it's none of my business."

"Under these conditions, anything is everybody's business. You have formed a bad opinion of Grace."

"Hugh, I would not dream of being critical of your wife."

"You have opinions. But I want you to have one in depth. Visualize her as she was, oh, twenty-five years ago. Think of Karen."

"She would have looked like Karen."

"Yes. But Karen has never had responsibility. Grace had and took it well. I was an enlisted man; I wasn't commissioned until after Pearl Harbor. Her people were what is known as 'good family.' Not anxious to have their daughter marry a penniless enlisted man."

"I suppose not."

"Nevertheless, she did. Barbara, have you any notion what it was to be the wife of a junior enlisted man in those days? With no money? Grace's parents wanted her to come home—but would not send her a cent as long as she stuck with me. She stuck."

"Good for Grace."

"Yes. She had no preparation for living in one room and sharing a bath down the hall, nor for waiting in Navy outpatients clinics. For making a dollar go twice as far as it should. For staying alone while I was at sea. Young and pretty and in Norfolk, she could have found excitement. She found a job instead—in a laundry, sorting dirty clothes. And whenever I was home she was bright and cheerful and uncomplaining.

"Alexander was born the next year—"

" 'Alexander'?"

"Duke. Named for his maternal grandpappy; I didn't get a vote. Her parents were anxious to make up once they had a grandson; they were even willing to accept me. Grace stayed cool and never accepted a cent—back to work with our landlady minding the baby in weeks.

"Those years were the roughest. I went up fast and money wasn't such a problem. The War came and I was bucked from chief to j.g. and ended as a lieutenant commander in Seabees. In 1946 I had to choose between going back to chief or becoming a civilian. With Grace's backing, I got out. So I was on the beach with no job, a wife, a son in grammar school, a three-year-old daughter, living in a trailer, prices high and going higher. We had some war bonds.

"That was the second rough period. I took a stab at contracting, lost our savings, went to work for a water company. We didn't starve, but scraped icebox and dishrag soup were on the menu. Barbara, she stood it like a trouper—a hardworking den mother, a pillar of the PTA, and always cheerful.

"I was a construction boss before long and presently I tried contracting again. This time it clicked. I built a house

90

on spec and a shoestring, sold it before it was finished and built two more at once. We've never been broke since."

Hugh Farnham looked puzzled. "That was when she started to slip. When she started having help. When we kept liquor in the house. We didn't quarrel—we never did save over the fact that I tried to raise Duke fairly strictly and Grace couldn't bear to have the boy touched.

"But that was when it started, when I started making money. She isn't built to stand prosperity. Grace has always stood up to adversity magnificently. This is the first time she hasn't. I still think she will."

"Of course she will, Hugh."

"I hope so."

"I'm glad to know more about her, Hugh. I'll try to be considerate."

"Damn it, I'm not asking that. I just want you to know that fat and foolish and self-centered isn't all there is to Grace. Nor was her slipping entirely her fault. I'm not easy to live with, Barbara."

"So?"

"So! When we were able to slow down, I didn't. I let business keep me away evenings. When a woman is left alone, it's easy to slip out for another beer when the commercial comes on and to nibble all evening along with the beer. If I was home, I was more likely to read than to visit, anyhow. And I didn't just let business keep me away; I joined the local duplicate club. She joined but she dropped out. She plays a good social game—but I like to fight for every point. No criticism of her, there's no virtue in playing as if it were life or death. Grace's way is better— Had I been willing to take it easy, too . . . well, she wouldn't be the way she is."

"Nonsense!"

"Pardon me?"

"Hugh Farnham, what a person is can never be somebody else's fault, *I* think. I am what I am because Barbie herself did it. And so did Grace. And so did you." She added in a low voice, "I love you. And that's not your fault, nor is anything we did your fault. I won't listen to

91

you beating your breast and sobbing *'Mea culpa!'* You don't take credit for Grace's virtues. Why take blame for her faults?"

He blinked and smiled. "Seven no trump."

"That's better."

"I love you. Consider yourself kissed."

"Kiss back. Grand slam. But watch it," she said out of the corner of her mouth. "Here come the cops."

It was Karen, clean, shining, hair brushed, fresh lipstick, and smiling. "What an inspiring sight!" she said. "Would you poor slaves like a crust of bread and a pannikin of water?"

"Shortly," her father agreed. "In the meantime don't carry these buckets too heavily loaded."

Karen backed away. "I wasn't volunteering!"

"That's all right. We aren't formal."

"But Daddy, I'm clean!"

"Has the creek gone dry?"

"Daddy! I've got lunch ready. Out front. You're too filthy to come into my lovely clean house."

"Yes, baby. Come along, Barbara." He picked up the buckets.

Mrs. Farnham did not appear for lunch. Karen stated that Mother had decided to eat inside. Hugh let it go at that; there would be enough hell when Duke got back.

Joe said, "Hugh? About that notion of plumbing—"

"Got it figured out?"

"Maybe I see a way to have running water."

"If we get running water, I guarantee to provide plumbing fixtures."

"Really, Daddy? I know what I want. In colored tile. Lavender, I think. And with a dressing table built around—"

"Shut up, infant. Yes, Joe?"

"Well, you know those Roman aqueducts. This stream runs uphill that way. I mean it's higher up that way, so someplace it's higher than the shelter. As I understand it, Roman aqueducts weren't pipe, they were open."

"I see." Farnham considered it. There was a waterfall a

hundred yards upstream. Perhaps above it was high enough. "But that would mean a lot of masonry, whether dry-stone, or mud mortar. And each arch requires a frame while it's being built."

"Couldn't we just split logs and hollow them out? And support them on other logs?"

"We could." Hugh thought about it. "There's an easier way, and one that would kill two birds. Barbara, what sort of country is this?"

"I beg your pardon?"

"You said that this area is at least semitropical. Can you tell what season it is? And what the rest of the year is likely to bring? What I'm driving at is this: Are you going to need irrigation?"

"Good heavens, Hugh, I can't answer that!"

"You can try."

"Well—" She looked around. "I doubt if it ever freezes here. If we had water, we might have crops all year. This is not a tropical rain forest, or the undergrowth would be much more dense. It looks like a place with a rainy season and a dry season."

"Our creek doesn't go dry; it has lots of fish. Where were you thinking of having your garden?"

"How about this stretch downstream to the south? Several trees should come out, though, and a lot of bushes."

"Trees and bushes are no problem. Mmm— Joe, let's take a walk. I'll carry a rifle, you strap on your forty-five. Girls, don't dig so much that it topples down on you. We would miss you."

"Daddy, I was thinking of taking a nap."

"Good. Think about it while you're digging."

Hugh and Joe worked their way upstream. "What are you figuring on, Hugh?"

"A contour-line ditch. We need to lead water to an air vent on the roof. If we can do that, we've got it made. A sanitary toilet. Running water for cooking and washing. And for gardening, coming in high enough to channel it wherever Barbara wants it. But the luxury that will mean most to our women folk is a bath and kitchen. We'll clear

93

the tank room and install both."

"Hugh, I see how you might get water with a ditch. But what about fixtures? You can't just let water splash down through the roof."

"I don't know yet, but we'll build them. Not a flush toilet, it's too complex. But a constant-flow toilet, a sort that used to be common aboard warships. It's a trough with seats. Water runs in one end, out the other. We'll lead it down the manhole, out the tunnel, and away from the house. Have you seen any clay?"

"There is a clay bank at the stream below the house. Karen complained about how sticky it was. She went upstream to bathe, a sandy spot."

"I'll look at it. If we can bake clay, we can make all sorts of things. A toilet. A sink. Dishes. Tile pipe. Build a kiln out of unbaked clay, use the kiln to bake anything. But clay just makes it easier. Water is the real gold; all civilizations were built on water. Joe, we are about high enough."

"Maybe a little higher? It would be embarrassing to dig a ditch a couple of hundred yards long—"

"Longer."

"—or longer, and find that it's too low and no way to get it up to the roof."

"Oh, we'll survey it first."

"*Survey* it? Hugh, maybe you didn't notice but we don't even have a spirit level. That big smash broke its glasses. And there isn't even a tripod, much less a transit and all those things."

"The Egyptians invented surveying with less, Joe. Losing the spirit level doesn't matter. We'll build an unspirit level."

"Are you making fun of me, Hugh?"

"Not at all. Mechanics were building level and square centuries before you could buy instruments. We'll build a plumb-bob level. That's an upside-down T, and a string with a weight to mark the vertical. You can build it about six feet long and six high to give us a long sighting arm—minimize the errors. Have to take apart one of the bunks for boards. It's light, fussy work you can do while

94

your ribs heal. While the girls do the heavy, unfussy excavating."

"You draw it, I'll build it."

"When we get the building leveled we'll mount it on the roof and sight upstream. Have to cut a tree or two but we won't have any trouble running a base line. Intercepts we run with a smaller level. Duck soup, Joe."

"No sweat, huh?"

"Mostly sweat. But twenty feet a day of shallow ditch and we'll have irrigation water when the dry season hits. The bathroom can wait—the gals will be cheered just by the fact that there will be one, someday. Joe, it would suit me if our base line cuts the stream about here. See anything?"

"What should I see?"

"We fell those two trees and they dam the creek. Then chuck in branches, mud, and some brush and still more mud and rocks and the stream backs up in a pond." Hugh added, "Have to devise a gate, and that I do not see, with what we have to work with. Every problem leads straight to another. Damn."

"Hugh, you're counting your chickens before the cows come home."

"I suppose so. Well, let's go see how much the girls have dug while we loafed."

The girls had dug little; Duke had returned with a miniature four-point buck. Barbara and Karen had it strung up against a tree and were trying to butcher it. Karen seemed to have as much blood on her as there was on the ground.

They stopped as the men approached. Barbara wiped her forehead, leaving a red trail. "I hadn't realized they were so complicated inside."

"Or so messy!" sighed Karen.

"With that size it's easier on the ground."

"Now he tells us. Show us, Daddy. We'll watch."

"Me? I'm a gentleman sportsman; the guide did the dirty work. But—Joe, can you lay hands on that little hatchet?"

"Sure. It's sharp; I touched it up yesterday."

Hugh split the breastbone and pelvic girdle and spread the carcass, then peeled out viscera and lungs and spilled them, while silently congratulating the girls on not having pierced the intestines. "All yours, girls. Barbara, if you can get that hide off, you might be wearing it soon. Have you noticed any oaks?"

"There are scrub forms. And sumach, too. You're thinking of tannin?"

"Yes."

"I know how to extract it."

"Then you know more about tanning than I do. I'll bow out. There are books."

"I know, I was looking it up. Doc! Don't sniff at that, boy."

"He won't eat it," Joe assured her, "unless it's good for him. Cats are fussy."

While butchering was going on, Duke and his mother crawled out and joined them. Mrs. Farnham seemed cheerful but did not greet anyone; she simply looked at Duke's kill. "Oh, the poor little thing! Duke dear, how did you have the heart to kill it?"

"It sassed me and I got mad."

"It's a pretty piece of venison, Duke," Hugh said. "Good eating."

His wife glanced at him. "Perhaps you'll eat it; I couldn't bear to."

Karen said, "Have you turned vegetarian, Mother?"

"It's not the same thing. I'm going in, I don't want that on me. Karen, don't you dare come inside until you've washed; I won't have you tracking blood in after I've slaved away getting the place spotless." She headed toward the shelter. "Come inside, Duke."

"In a moment, Mother."

Karen gave the carcass an unnecessarily vicious cut.

"Where did you nail it?" Hugh asked.

"Other side of the ridge. I should have been back sooner."

"Why?"

"Missed an easy shot and splintered an arrow on a

boulder. Buck fever. It has been years since I used a 'bow season' license."

"One lost arrow, one carcass, is good hunting. You saved the arrowhead?"

"Of course. Do I look foolish?"

Karen answered, "No, but I do. Buddy, *I* cleaned house. If Mother did any cleaning, it was a mess she made herself."

"I realized that."

"And I'll bet when she smells these steaks, she won't want Spam!"

"Forget it."

Hugh moved away, signaling Duke to follow.

"I'm glad to see Grace looking cheerful. You must have soothed her."

Duke looked sheepish. "Well— As you pointed out, it's rough, chopping it off completely." He added, "But I rationed her. I gave her one drink and told her she could have one more before dinner."

"That's doing quite well."

"I had better go inside. The bottle is there."

"Perhaps you had."

"Oh, it's all right. I put her on her honor. You don't know how to handle her, Dad."

"That's true. I don't."

From the Journal of Barbara Wells:

I am hobbled by a twisted ankle, so I am lying down and adding to this. I've taken notes every night—but in shorthand. I haven't transcribed very much.

The longhand version goes in the fly leaves of the *Britannica*. There are ten blank pages in each volume, twenty-four volumes, and I'll squeeze a thousand words to a page—240,000 words—enough to record our doings until we reclaim the art of making paper—especially as the longhand version will be censored.

Because I can't let my hair down to anyone—and sometimes a gal needs to! This shorthand record is a diary which no one can read but me, as Karen is as poor at Gregg as she claimed.

Or perhaps Joe knows Gregg. Isn't it required in business colleges? But Joe is a gentleman and would not read this without invitation. I am fond of Joseph; his goodness is not a sham. I am sure he is keeping his lips buttoned on many unhappy thoughts; his position is as anomalous as mine and more difficult.

Grace has quit ordering him around—save that she orders all of us. Hugh gives orders, but for the welfare of all. Nor does he give many; we are settled in a routine. I'm the farmer, and plan my own work; Duke keeps meat on the table and gives me a hand when he doesn't hunt; Hugh hasn't told either of us what to do for a long time, and

Karen has a free hand with the house. Hugh has about two centuries of mechanical work planned out and Joe helps him.

But Grace's orders are for her own comfort. We usually carry them out; it's easier. She gets her own way and more than her share, simply by being difficult.

She got the lion's share of liquor. Liquor doesn't matter to me; I rarely "need" a drink. But I enjoy a glow in company and had to remind myself that it was not my liquor, it was Farnham liquor.

Grace finished her share in three days. Duke's was next to go. And so on. At last all was gone save one quart of bourbon earmarked "medicinal." Grace spotted where Duke had it and dug it up. When Duke came home, she was passed out and the bottle was dead.

The next three days were horrors. She screamed. She wept. She threatened suicide. Hugh and Duke teamed up and one of them was always with her. Hugh acquired a black eye, Duke got scratches down his handsome face. I understand they put a lot of B_1 into her and force-fed her.

On the fourth day she stayed in her bunk; the next day she got up and seemed almost normal.

But during lunch she asserted, as something "everybody knows," that the Russians had attacked because Hugh insisted on building a shelter.

She didn't seem angry—more forgiving. She went on to the happy thought that the war would soon be over and we could all go home.

Nobody argued. What good? Her delusion seems harmless. She has assumed her job, at last, as chief cook—but if she is a better cook than Karen I have yet to see it. Mostly she talks about dishes she could prepare if only she had this, or that. Karen works as hard as ever and sometimes gets so mad that she comes out to cry on me and then hoes furiously.

Duke tells Karen that she must be patient.

I should not criticize Duke; he is probably going to be my husband. I mean, who else is there? I could stand Duke but I'm not sure I could stand Grace as a mother-in-law.

Duke is handsome and is considerate of both me and his sister. He did quarrel with his father at first (foolishly it seemed to me) but they get along perfectly now.

In this vicinity he is quite a catch.

Myself? I'm not soured on marriage even though I struck out once. Hugh assumes that the human race will go on. I'm willing.

(Polygamy? Of course I would! Even with Grace as senior wife. But I haven't been asked. Nor, I feel sure, would Grace permit it. Hugh and I don't discuss such things, we avoid touching the other, we avoid being alone together, and I do not make cow's eyes at him. Finished.)

The trouble is, while I like Duke, no spark jumps. So I am putting it off and avoiding circumstances where he might pat me on the fanny. It would be a hell of a note if I married him and there came a night when I was so irritated at his mother and so vexed with him for indulging her that I would tell him coldly that he is not half the man his father is.

No, that must not happen. Duke does not deserve it.

Joe? My admiration for him is unqualified—and he doesn't have a mother problem.

Joe is the first Negro I've had a chance to know well—and I think most well of him. He plays better contract than I do; I suppose he's smarter than I am. He is fastidious and never comes indoors without bathing. Oh, get downwind after he has spent a day digging and he's pretty whiff. But so is Duke, and Hugh is worse. I don't believe this story about a distinctive "nigger musk."

Have you ever been in a dirty powder room? Women stink worse than men.

The trouble with Joe is the same as with Duke: No spark jumps. Since he is so shy that he is most unlikely to court me— Well, it won't happen.

But I am fond of him—as a younger brother. He is never too busy to be accommodating. He is usually bear guard for Karen and me when we bathe and it's a comfort to know that Joe is alert— Duke has killed five bears and Joe killed one while he was actually guarding us. It took three shots and dropped dead almost in Joe's lap. He stood his ground.

We adjourned without worrying about modesty, which upset Joe more than bears do.

Or wolves, or coyotes, or mountain lions, or a cat which Duke says is a mutated leopard and especially dangerous because it attacks by dropping out of a tree. We don't bathe under trees and don't venture out of our clearing without an armed man. It is as dangerous as crossing Wilshire against the lights.

There are snakes, too. At least one sort is poisonous.

Joe and Hugh were starting one morning on the house-leveling and Joe jumped down into the excavation. Dr.-Livingstone-I-Presume jumped down with him—and here was this snake.

Doc spotted it and hissed; Joe saw it just as it struck, getting him in the calf. Joe killed it with his shovel and dropped to the ground, grabbing at his leg.

Hugh had the wound slashed and was sucking it in split seconds. He had a tourniquet on quickly and permanganate crystals on the wound soon after as I heard the hooraw and came a-runnin'. He followed that with rattlesnake anti-venom.

Moving Joe was a problem; he collapsed in the tunnel. Hugh crawled over him and pulled, I pushed, and it took three of us—Karen, too—to lift him up the ladder. We undressed him and put him to bed.

Around midnight, when his respiration was low and his pulse uncertain, Hugh moved the remaining bottle of oxygen into the room, put over Joe's head a plastic sack in which shirts had been stored and gave him oxygen.

By morning he was better.

In three days he was up and well. Duke says it was a pit viper, perhaps a bushmaster, and that a rattlesnake is a pit viper, too, so rattlesnake anti-venom probably saved Joe's life.

I am not trusting *any* snakes.

It took three weeks to excavate under the house. Boulders! This area is a wide, flat, saucer-shaped valley, with boulders most anywhere. Whenever we hit a big one, we dug around it and the men would worry it out with crowbar and block and tackle.

Mostly the men could get boulders out. But Karen found one that seemed to go down to China. Hugh looked it over and said, "Fine. Now dig a hole just north of it and deeper."

Karen just looked at him.

So we dug. And hit another big boulder. "Good," said Hugh. "Dig another hole north of that one."

We hit a third oversize boulder. But in three days the last one had been tumbled into a hole next to it, the middle one had been worried into a hole where the last one had been, and the one that started the trouble was buried where the middle one had been.

As fast as any spot had been cut deeply enough Hugh propped it up with pieces of log; he was worried lest the shelter shift and crush someone. So when we finished the shelter had a forest of posts under it.

Hugh then set two very heavy posts under the uphill corners and started removing the inner ones, using block and tackle. Sometimes they had to be dug under. Hugh was nervous during this and did all the rigging and digging himself.

At last the uphill half was supported on these two big chunks.

They would not budge.

There was so much weight on those timbers that they sneered at our efforts. I said, "What do we do now, Hugh?"

"Try the next-to-last resort."

"What's the last resort?"

"Burn them. But it would take roaring fires and we would have to clear grass and bushes and trees for quite a distance. Karen, you know where the ammonia is. And the iodine. I want both."

I had wondered why Hugh had stocked so much ammonia. But he had, in used plastic Chlorox bottles; the stuff had ridden through the shocks. I hadn't known that iodine was stocked in quantity, too; I don't handle the drugs.

Soon he had sort of a chemistry lab. "What are you making, Hugh?" I asked.

"Ersatz 'dynamite.' And I don't need company," he said. "The stuff is so touchy it explodes at a harsh look."

"Sorry," I said, backing away.

He looked up and smiled. "It's safe until it dries. I had it in mind in case I ever found myself in an underground. Occupying troops take a sour view of natives having explosives, but there is nothing suspicious about ammonia or iodine. The stuff is safe until you put it together and does not require a primer. But I never expected to use it for construction; it's too treacherous."

"Hugh, I just remembered I don't care whether a floor is level or not."

"If it makes you nervous, take a walk."

Making it was simple; he combined tincture of iodine and ordinary household ammonia; a precipitate settled out. This he filtered through Kleenex. The result was a paste.

Joe drilled holes into those stubborn posts; Hugh wrapped this mess in two batches in paper, and packed a bundle into each hole, tamping with his finger. "Now we wait for it to dry."

Everything that he used he flushed down with water, then took a bath with his clothes on, removed them in the water and left them, weighted down with rocks. That was all that day.

Our armament includes two lovely ladies' guns, .22 magnum rimfires with telescopic sights. Hugh had Duke and Joe sight them in. The sighting-in was done with sandbag rest—heaped-up dirt, that is. Hugh had them expend five bullets each, so I knew he was serious. "One bullet, one bear" is his motto.

When the explosive was dry, everything breakable was removed from the shelter. We women were chased far back, Karen was charged with hanging on to Dr. Livingstone, and I was armed with Duke's bear rifle, just in case.

Duke and Joe were on their bellies a measured hundred

feet from the posts. Hugh stood between them. "Ready for count?"

"Ready, Hugh."—"Ready, Dad."

"Deep breath. Let part of it out. Hold it, steady on target, take up the slack. Five . . . four . . . three . . . two . . . one . . . *fire!*"

A sound like a giant slammed door and the middle of each post disintegrated. The shelter stuck out like a shelf, then tilted ponderously down, touched, and was level.

Karen and I cheered; Grace started to clap; Dr. Livingstone jumped down to investigate. Hugh turned his head and grinned.

And the shelter tilted back the other way as the ridge crumbled; it started to slide. It pivoted on the tunnel protuberance, picked up speed and tobogganed down the slope. I thought it was going to end up in the creek.

But the slope leveled off; it ground to a stop, with the tunnel choked with dirt and the whole thing farther out of plumb than before!

Hugh picked up the shovel he had used to heap up shooting supports, walked down to the shelter, began to dig.

I ran down, tears bursting from my eyes. Joe was there first. Hugh looked up and said, "Joe, dig out the tunnel. I want to know if anything is damaged and the girls will want to get lunch."

"Boss—" Joe choked out. "Boss! Oh, gosh!"

Hugh said, in a tone you use to a child, "Why are you upset, Joe? This has saved us work."

I thought he had flipped. Joe said, *"Huh?"*

"Certainly," Hugh assured him. "See how much lower the roof is? Every foot it dropped saves at least a hundred feet of aqueduct. And leveling will be simple here; the ground is loam and boulders are few. A week, with everybody pitching in. Then we bring water to the house and garden two weeks early."

He was correct. The shelter was level in a week, and this time he triggered the end posts with crosspieces; blasting was not needed. Best of all, the armor door cranked back without a murmur and we had air and sunlight inside— It had been stuffy and candles made it pretty rank. Joe and Hugh started the ditch the same day. In anticipation of the glorious day, Karen sketched on the walls of the tank room lifesize pictures of a washstand, a bathtub, a pot.

Truthfully, we are comfortable. Two mattress covers Karen filled with dried grass; sleeping on the floor is no worse than the bunks. We sit in chairs and play our evening rubber at the table. It is amazing what a difference level floors make and how much better it is to have a door than to climb down a ladder and crawl out a hole.

We had to cook over a campfire a while as our grill and Dutch oven were smashed. Karen and I have thrown together a make-do because, as soon as water is led to the house, Hugh intends to start on ceramics, not only for a toilet and a sink but also for a stove vented out through the periscope hole. Luxury!

My corn is coming up beautifully. I wonder what I can use to grind corn? The thought of hot corn bread buttered with deer grease makes me drool.

December 25th—Merry Christmas!

We think it is. Hugh says we are not more than a day off.

Shortly after we got here Hugh picked a small tree with a flat boulder due north of it and sawed it off so that it placed a sharp shadow on the boulder at noon. As "Keeper of the Flame" it has been my duty to sit by that boulder from before apparent noon and note the shortest shadow—follow it down, mark the shortest position and date it.

That shadow had been growing longer and the days shorter. A week ago it began to be hard to see any change and I told Hugh. So we watched together and three days ago was the turning point . . . so that day became December 22nd and we are celebrating Christmas instead of the Fourth of July. But we got our flag up, as Hugh had planned, to the top of the tallest tree in our clearing, with its branches lopped to make it a pole. As Keeper of the Flame I am charged with raising and lowering it but this was a special occasion; we drew lots and Joe won. We lined up and sang "The Star-Spangled Banner" while he hauled it to the peak—and everyone was crying so hard he could hardly sing.

Then we pledged allegiance. Maybe it is sentimental nonsense by ragged castaways but *I* don't think so. We are still one nation, under God, free and indivisible, with liberty and justice for all.

Hugh held divine services and read the Christmas story from the Gospel According to Luke and called on Karen to pray, then we sang carols. Grace has a strong, sure lead; Joe is a bell-like tenor, and Karen, myself, Hugh, and Duke are soprano, contralto, baritone, and bass. I think we sound good. In any case we enjoyed it, even though Grace got taken by the weeps during "White Christmas" and it was contagious.

We would have had services anyhow as today would be Sunday by the old calendar; Hugh holds them every Sunday. Everybody attends, even Duke who is an avowed atheist. Hugh reads a Psalm or some other chapter; we sing hymns; he prays or invites someone to pray, and ends it with "Bless This House—" We are back to the days when the Old Man is priest.

But Hugh never used the Apostles' Creed and his prayers are so nonsectarian that he does not even end them "In Jesus' Name, Amen."

On a rare occasion when he and I spoke in private —waiting out a noon sight last week—I asked him where he stood on matters of faith? (It is important to me to know where my man stands even though he is not my man and can't be.)

"You could call me an Existentialist."

"You are not a Christian?"

"I didn't say that. I can't express it in the negative because it's affirmative. I shan't define it; it would only add to the confusion. You are wondering why I hold church since I refuse to assert a creed?"

"Well . . . yes."

"It's my duty. Services should be available to those who need them. If there is no good and no God, this ritual is harmless. If God is, it is appropriate—and still harmless. We are bleeding no peasants, offering no bloody sacrifices, raising no vanities to the skies in the name of religion. Or so I see it, Barbara."

That had better hold me; it's all I'll get out of him. In my past life religion was a nice, warm, comfy thing I did on Sundays; I can't say it agonized me. But Hugh's Godless offering to God has become important.

Sundays are important other ways. Hugh discourages work other than barbering and primping or hobby work, and encourages games, or any fun thing. Chess, bridge, Scrabble, modeling in clay, group sings, such like— Or just yakking. Games are important; they mark that we are not just animals trying to stay alive but humans enjoying life and savoring it. That nightly rubber of bridge we never skip. It proclaims that our lives are not just hoeing and digging ditches and butchering.

We keep up our bodies, too. I've become pretty good at cutting hair. Duke grew a beard at first but Hugh shaved every day and presently Duke did, too. I don't know what they will do when blades are no more. I've noticed Joe honing a Gem blade on an oil stone.

It's still Christmas and I'll cut back in when the rubber in progress is finished. Dinner was lavish: Grace and Karen spent two days on it—brook trout savory aux herbes, steamed freshwater prawns, steaks and broiled mushrooms, smoked tongue, bouillon Ursine, crackers (quite a treat), radishes, lettuce, green onions, baby beets à la Grace, and best of all, a pan of fudge, as condensed milk, chocolate, and sugar are irreplaceable. Nescafé and cigarettes, two cups and two cigarettes each.

Presents for everybody— All I saved besides clothes I had on was my purse. I was wearing nylons, took them off soon and haven't worn stockings since; I gave them to Karen. I had a lipstick; Grace got that. I had been plaiting a belt; Joe got that. In my purse was a fancy hanky; I washed it, ironed it by pressing it against smooth concrete—Duke got that.

It was this morning before I figured out anything for Hugh. For years I've carried in my purse a little memo book. It has my maiden name in gold and still has half of a filler. Hugh can use it—but it was my name on it that decided me.

I must run; Grace and I are due to attempt to clobber Hugh and Joe.

I've never had a happier Christmas.

Karen and Barbara were washing themselves, the day's dishes, and the week's laundry. Above them, Joe kept watch. Bushes and then trees had been cut away around the stretch they used for bathing; a predator could not approach without Joe having a clear shot at it. His eyes swung constantly, checking approaches. He wasted no seconds on the Elysian tableau he guarded.

Karen said, "Barbie, this sheet won't stand another laundering. It's rags."

"We need rags."

"But what will we use for sheets? It's this soap." Karen scooped a handful from a bowl on the bank. It was soft and gray and harsh and looked like oatmeal mush. "The stuff eats holes."

"I'm not fretted about sheets but I dread the day when we are down to our last towel."

"Which will belong to Mother," Karen stated. "Our rationing officer will have some excellent reason."

"Nasty, nasty. Karen, Duke has done a wonderful job."

"I wasn't bitching. Duke can't help it. It's his friend Eddie."

"Eddie?"

"Edipus Rex, dear."

Barbara turned away and began rinsing a pair of ragged blue jeans.

Karen said, "You dig me?"

"We all have faults."

"Sure, everybody but me. Even Daddy has a shortcoming. His neck pains him."

Barbara looked up. "Is Hugh having trouble with his neck? Perhaps it would help if we massaged it."

Karen giggled. "Your weakness, sister mine, is that you wouldn't know a joke if it bit you. Daddy is stiff-necked and nothing will cure it. He doesn't have weaknesses and that's his weakness. Don't frown. I love Daddy. I admire him. But I'm glad I'm not like him. I'll take this load up to the thorn bushes. Damn it, why didn't Daddy stock clothespins? Those thorns are as bad as the soap."

"Clothespins we can do without. Hugh did an incredible job. Everything from an eight-day clock—"

"Which got busted, right off."

"—to tools and seeds and books and I don't know what. Karen! Don't climb out naked!"

Karen stopped, one foot on the bank. "Nonsense. Old Stone Face won't look. Humiliating, that's what it is. I think I'll yoo-hoo at him."

"You'll do no such thing. Joe is being a gentleman under trying circumstances. Don't make it harder. Let that load wait and we'll take it all up at once."

"Okay, okay. I can't help wondering if he's human."

"He is. I can vouch for it."

"Hmm— Barbie, don't tell me Saint Joseph made a pass at you?"

"Heavens, no! But he blushes if I squeeze past him in the house."

"How can you tell?"

"Sort of purple. Karen, Joe is sweet. I wish you had heard him explain about Doc."

"Explain what?"

"Well, Doc is beginning to accept me. I was holding Doc yesterday and noticed something and said, 'Joe, Doc is getting terribly fat. Or was he always?'

"That was a time when he blushed. But he answered with sweet seriousness, 'Barbara, Dr. Livingstone isn't as much of a boy cat as he thinks he is. Old Doc is more a girl-type cat. That isn't fat. Uh, you see— Doc is going to have babies.' He blurted it out. Seemed to think it would upset me. Didn't of course, but I was astonished."

"Barbara, you mean you didn't *know* that Dr.-Livingstone-I-Presume is a female?"

"How would I know? Everybody calls him 'he' and he—she—has a male name."

"A doctor can be female. Can't you tell a tomcat?"

"I never thought about it. Doc is pretty fuzzy."

"Mmm, yes, with a Persian one might not be certain at first glance. But a tomcat's badges of authority are prominent."

"Had I noticed, I would have assumed that he had been altered."

Karen looked shocked. "Don't let Daddy hear that! He never allows a cat to be spayed or cut. Daddy thinks cats are citizens. However, you've surprised me. Kittens, huh?"

"So Joe says."

"And I didn't notice." Karen looked puzzled. "Come to think of it, I haven't picked him up lately. Just petted him and tried to keep him out of things. Lately it hasn't been safe to open a drawer; he's into it. Looking for a place to have kittens of course. I should have twigged."

"Karen, why do you keep saying 'he' and 'him'?"

" 'Why?' Joe told you. Doc *thinks* he is a boy cat—and who am I to argue? He's always thought so, he was the feistiest kitten we ever had. Hmm— Kittens. Barbie, the first time Doc came into heat we arranged for Doc to meet a gentleman cat of exalted ancestry. But it wasn't Doc's métier and he beat the hell out of the tomcat. So we quit trying. Mmm— Calendar girl, how long have we been here?"

"Sixty-two days. I've looked it up; it's sixty days with a normal range to seventy."

"So it's any time now. I'll bet you two back rubs that we are up all night tonight. Cats never have kittens at a convenient hour." Karen abruptly changed the subject. "Barbie, what do you miss most? Cigarettes?"

"I've quit thinking of them. Eggs, I guess. Eggs for breakfast."

"Daddy did plan for that. Fertilized eggs and a little incubator. But he hadn't built it and anyhow, eggs would

111

have busted. Yes, I miss eggs. But I wish cows laid eggs and Daddy had figured out how to bring cow eggs along. Ice cream! Cold milk!"

"Butter," agreed Barbara. "Banana splits with whipped cream. Chocolate malts."

"Stop it! Barbie, I'm starving in front of your eyes."

Barbara pinched her. "You aren't fading way. Fact is, you've put on weight."

"Perhaps." Karen shut up and began on the dishes. Presently she said in a low voice, "Barbie, Doc won't hand this household half the surprise I'm going to."

"How, hon?"

"I'm pregnant."

"Huh?"

"You heard me. Pregnant. Knocked up, if you insist on the technical term!"

"Are you sure, dear?"

"Of course I'm sure! I had a test, the froggie winked at me. Hell, I'm four months gone." Karen threw herself into the arms of the older girl. "And I'm *scared!"*

Barbara hugged her. "There, there, dear. It's going to be all right."

"The hell it is," Karen blubbered. "Mother's going to raise hell . . . and there aren't any hospitals . . . nor doctors. Oh, why didn't Duke study medicine? Barbie, I'm going to die. I know I am."

"Karen, that's silly. More babies have been born without doctors and hospitals than ever were wheeled into a delivery room. You're not scared of dying, you're scared of telling your parents."

"Well, that, too." Karen wiped at her eyes and sniffed. "Uh— Barbie, don't be mad . . . but that's why I invited you down that weekend."

"So?"

"I figured Mother wouldn't raise quite so much hell if you were present. Most girls in our chapter are either squares or sluts, and silly heads besides. But you are neither and I knew you would stand up for me."

"Thank you, dear."

"Thank me, hell! I was using you."

"It's the finest compliment another woman ever paid me." Barbara wiped a tear from Karen's face and tweaked her cheek. "I'm glad I'm here. So you haven't told your parents?"

"Well, I was *going* to. But the attack hit . . . and then Mother went to pieces . . . and Daddy has been loaded down with worries and there's never been the right time."

"Karen, you aren't scared to tell your father, just your mother."

"Well . . . Mother mostly. But Daddy, too. Besides being shocked and hurt—he'll think it was silly of me to get caught."

"While he's certain to be surprised, I doubt the other." Barbara hesitated. "Karen, you needn't take this alone. I can share it."

"That's what I had hoped. That's why I asked you to come home with me. I told you."

"I mean really share it. I'm pregnant, too."

"What?"

"Yes. We can tell them together."

"Good Lord, Barbara! How did it happen?"

Barbara shrugged. "Careless. How did it happen to you?"

Karen suddenly grinned. "How? A bee sprinkled pollen on me; how else? 'Who' you mean."

" 'Who' I don't care about. Your business. Well, dear? Shall we go tell them? I'll do the talking."

"Wait a minute. You hadn't planned to tell anybody? Or had you?"

"Why, no," Barbara answered truthfully. "I was going to wait until it showed."

Karen looked at Barbara's waistline. "It doesn't show. Are you sure?"

"I've skipped two periods, I'm pregnant. Or I'm ill, which would be worse. Let's gather up the laundry and tell them."

"Uh, since you don't look it—and I do; I've been careful not to undress around Mother—since you don't, let's hold that back and use it as a whammy if things get sickly."

"If you like, Karen, why not tell Hugh first? Then let him tell your mother."

Karen looked relieved. "You think that's all right?"

"Hugh would rather hear it with your mother not around. Now go find him and tell him. I'll hang the clothes."

"All right, I will!"

"And quit worrying. We'll have our babies and won't have any trouble and we'll raise them together and it'll be fun. We'll be happy."

Karen's eyes lit up. "And you'll have a girl and I'll have a boy and we'll marry them and be grandmothers together!"

"That sounds more like Karen." Barbara kissed her. "Run tell Hugh."

Karen found Hugh bricking up the kiln; she told him that she would like a private talk.

"All right," he agreed. "Let me tell Joe to get this fired up. I should inspect the ditch. Come along and talk?"

He gave her a shovel, carried a rifle. "Now what's on your mind, baby girl?"

"Let's get farther away." They walked a meandering distance. Hugh stopped, exchanged rifle for shovel, and built up a stretch of wall.

"Daddy? Perhaps you've noticed a shortage of men?"

"No. Three men and three women. The usual division."

"Perhaps I should say 'eligible bachelors.'"

"Then say it."

"All right, I've said it. I need advice. Which is worse? Incest? Or miscengenation? Or should I be an old maid?"

He placed another shovelful, tamped it. "I would not urge you to be an old maid."

"That settles that, I feel the same way. How do you size up those other fates?"

"Incest," he answered, "is a bad idea, usually."

"Which leaves just one thing."

"Wait. I said, 'Usually.'" He stared at the shovel. "This is not a problem I ever expected—but we are facing many new problems. Brother-and-sister marriages are not un-

114

common in history. They are not necessarily bad." He frowned. "But there is Barbara. You might have to accept a polygamous household."

"Hold it, Daddy. 'Incest' isn't just brothers."

He stared at her. "You've managed to startle me, Karen."

"Shocked you, you mean."

"No. 'Startled.' Were you seriously suggesting what you implied?"

"Daddy," she said soberly, "it's one subject I can't joke about. If I had to choose between you and Duke—as a husband, I mean—I'd take you and no two ways about it."

Hugh mopped his forehead. "Karen, such a statement can be honored only by taking it seriously—"

"I'm serious!"

"And I so take it. Do I understand that you have eliminated Joseph? Or have you considered him?"

"Certainly I have."

"Well?"

"How could I avoid it, Daddy? Joe is nice. But he's just a boy, even though he's older than I am. If I said, 'Boo!' he would jump out of his skin. No."

"Does his skin have something to do with your choice?"

"Daddy, you tempt me to spit in your face. I'm not Mother!"

"I wanted to be sure. Karen, you know that color does not matter to me. I want to know other things about a man. Is his word good? Does he meet his obligations? Does he do honest work? Is he brave? Will he stand up and be counted? Joe is very much a man by all standards that interest me. I think you are being hasty."

He sighed. "If we were in Mountain Springs, I would not urge you to marry any Negro. The pressures are too great; such a marriage is almost a tragedy. But those barbaric factors do not obtain here. I urge that you give Joe serious thought."

"Daddy, don't you think I *have*? I may marry Joe. But I wanted you to know that if I had my choice, out of you three I would pick *you*."

"Thank you."

"Thank me, hell! I'm a woman and you are the man I would most like to. And a fat lot of good it will do me—and you know why. Mother."

"I know." He suddenly looked weary. "We do not what we wish, but what we can. Karen, I am dreadfully sorry that you do not have a longer list to choose from."

"Daddy, if I've learned anything from you, it is that it's a waste of tears to cry over anything that can't be helped. That's Mother, not me. And Duke, though not as bad. I'm just like you on this point— You count your points and play accordingly. You don't moan about how the cards aren't fair. Dig me, Daddy?"

"Yes."

"I didn't come here to ask you to marry me. Nor even to seduce you though I might as well say, having said so much, that you can have me if you want me. I think you've known that for years. I didn't come here to say *that,* either. I simply had to get things out of the way before I told you something else. Something where I've counted the points and I'm going set and that's that. Can't be helped."

"What? Perhaps I can help."

"Hardly. I'm pregnant, Daddy."

He dropped the shovel, took her in both arms. "Oh, wonderful!"

Presently she said, "Daddy . . . I can't shoot a bear with you hugging me."

He put her down, grabbed the rifle. *"Where?"*

"Nowhere. But you're always warning us."

"Oh. All right, I'll take over guard duty. Who's the father, Karen? Duke? or Joe?"

"Neither. Earlier, at school."

"Oh. Still better!"

"How? Damn it, Daddy, this isn't going the way it's supposed to. A girl comes home ruined, her father is supposed to raise hell. All you say is, 'Just dandy!' You've got me confused."

"Sorry. Under other circumstances, I might feel that you had been careless—"

116

"Oh, I was! I took a chance, like the nigguh mammy who said, 'Oh, hunnuhds of times ain't nuffin happen at all.' You know."

"I'm afraid I do. Under these circumstances I am delighted. I had assumed that you were inexperienced. To learn that, instead, you have gone ahead and given us a child and one whose father is from outside our group— Don't you *see*, dear? You have almost doubled the chances of this colony surviving."

"I have?"

"Figure it out, you're not stupid. Your child's father— Good stock?"

"Would I have been doing what I most certainly did if I hadn't thought pretty well of him, Daddy?"

"Sorry, dear. It was a stupid question." He smiled. "I don't feel like working. Let's spread the good news."

"All right. But, Daddy— *What do we tell Mother?*"

"The truth, and I'll do the telling. Don't worry, baby girl. You have that baby and I will take care of all else."

"Yes, sir. Daddy, I feel real good now."

"That's fine."

"I feel so good that I almost forgot something. Did you know that Dr.-Livingstone-I-Presume is going to have babies, too?"

"Yes."

"Why didn't you tell me?"

"You had the same chance to notice that I did."

"Well, yes. But it's pretty frowsy, your noticing that Doc is pregnant—and not noticing that I am."

"I thought you had simply been overeating again."

"You did, huh? Daddy, sometimes I like you better than other times. But this time I guess I'm going to have to like you anyhow."

Hugh decided to eat dinner before stirring up Grace.

The decision was justified. From her rantings, it appeared that Karen was an ungrateful daughter, a disgrace, a shameless little tramp, and that Hugh was an unnatural father, a failure, and somehow to blame for his daughter's pregnancy.

Hugh let her rant until she paused for breath. "Grace. Be quiet."

"What? Hubert Farnham, don't you dare tell me to shut up! How can you sit there, when your own daughter has flagrantly dis—"

"Shut up or I will shut you up."

Duke said, "Pipe down, Mother."

"You, too? Oh, that I should ever see the day when—"

"Mother, keep still for a while. Let's hear from Dad."

Grace simmered, then said, "Joseph! Leave the room."

"Joe, sit down," Hugh ordered.

"Yes, Joe," agreed Karen. "Please stay."

"Well! If neither of you has the common decency to—"

"Grace, I am nearer to striking you than I have ever been in all these years. Will you keep quiet and listen?"

She looked at her son; Duke was carefully looking elsewhere. "Very well, I will listen. Not that it can possibly do any good."

"I hope that it will because it is supremely important. Grace, there is no point in heckling Karen. Besides being cruel, it's ridiculous. Her pregnancy is the best thing that has happened to us."

"Hubert Farnham, are you out of your mind?"

"Please. You are reacting in terms of conventional morality, which is foolish."

"Oh? So morals are foolish, are they? You hymn-singing hypocrite!"

"Morals are not foolish; morals must be our bedrock, always. But whether it was moral for Karen to breed a baby at another time and place, in a society that is no more, is irrelevant; we will not discuss it. The fact is, she did—and it is a blessing to us. Please analyze it. Six of us, four from one family. Genetically that is too small a breeding stock. Yet somehow we must flourish—or saving our own lives is wasted. But now we have a seventh, not here in person. That's better than we had any reason to hope. I pray that the twins that run in my family will show up in her. It would strengthen the stock."

"How can you talk about your own daughter as if you were breeding a cow!"

"She is my daughter whom I love. But more important—her supreme importance—is that she is a woman and pregnant. I wish that you and Barbara were pregnant, too—by outsiders. We need variety for the next generation."

"I will not sit here and be insulted!"

"I simply said 'wish.' In Karen we do have this miracle; we must cherish it. Grace, Karen must be treated with every consideration during her pregnancy. You must take care of her."

"Are you insinuating that I wouldn't? You are the one who cares nothing about her welfare. Your own daughter."

"It doesn't matter that she is my daughter. It would apply if it were Barbara, or you, or another woman. No more heavy work for Karen. That laundry she did today—you'll do that; you've loafed long enough. You'll pamper her. But most urgent, there will be no more scoldings, no harsh words, no recriminations. You will be sweet and kind and gentle with her. Don't fail in this, Grace. Or I will punish you."

"You wouldn't dare!"

"I hope I won't be forced to." Hugh faced his son. "Duke. Do I have your backing? Speak up."

"What do you mean by 'punishment,' Dad?"

"Whatever we are forced to use. Words. Social sanctions. Physical punishment if we must. Even expulsion from our group if no other choice remained."

Duke drummed on the table. "That's putting it brutally, Dad."

"Yes. I want you to think about the extremes."

Duke glanced at his sister. "I'll back you. Mother, you've got to behave."

She started to whimper. "My own son has turned against me. Oh, I wish I had never been born!"

"Barbara?"

"My opinion? I agree with you, Hugh. Karen needs kindness. She mustn't be scolded."

"You keep out of this!"

Barbara looked at Grace without expression. "I'm sorry

119

but Hugh asked me. Karen asked me to be in it, too. I think you have behaved abominably, Grace. A baby isn't a calamity."

"That's easy for you to say!"

"Perhaps. But you've been nagging Karen steadily— and really, you mustn't."

Karen said suddenly, "Tell them, Barbara. About yourself."

"You want me to?"

"You'd better. Or now she'll start on you."

"Very well." Barbara bit her lip. "I said that a baby is not a calamity. I'm pregnant, too—and I'm very happy about it."

The silence told Barbara that her purpose of taking the heat off Karen had been achieved. As for herself, she was tranquil for the first time since she had begun to suspect that she was pregnant. She had not shed a tear—oh, no!—but she found that a tension she had not been conscious of was gone.

"Why, you tramp! No wonder my daughter went wrong, exposed to influences like—"

"Stop it, Grace!"

"Yes, Mother," agreed Duke. "Better keep quiet."

"I was just going to say—"

"You're not going to say anything, Mother. I mean it."

Mrs. Farnham subsided. Hugh went on: "Barbara, I hope you are not fibbing. Trying to protect Karen."

Barbara looked at him and could read no expression. "I am not fibbing, Hugh. I am between two and three months pregnant."

"Well, the rejoicing is now doubled. We will have to relieve you of heavy work, too. Duke, can you take on some farming?"

"Certainly."

"Joe can do some, too. Mmm— I must push ahead with the kitchen and bathroom. You'll both need such comforts long before either baby is born. Joe, that bearproof extra room can't be put off now; nursery space will be essential and we men will have to move out. I think—"

"Hugh—"

"Yes, Barbara?"

"Don't worry tonight. I can garden, I'm not as far along as Karen and I've had no morning sickness. I'll let you know when I need help."

He looked thoughtful, "No."

"Oh, heaven! I *like* gardening. Pioneer mothers always worked when pregnant. They stopped when the pains came."

"And it killed them, too. Barbara, we can't spare either of you. We'll treat you as the precious jewels you are." He looked around. "Right?"

"Right, Dad."

"Sure thing, Hugh!"

Mrs. Farnham stood up. "Really, this conversation is making me ill."

"Good night, Grace. No farming for you, Barbara."

"But I like my farm. I'll quit in time."

"You can supervise. Don't let me catch you using a spading fork. Nor weeding. You might shake something loose. You're a gentleman farmer now."

"Does it say in your books how much work a pregnant woman may do?"

"I'll read up on it. But we'll err on the conservative side. Some doctors keep patients in bed for months to avoid losing a baby."

"Daddy, you don't expect us to stay in bed!"

"Probably not, Karen. But we will be very careful." He added, "Barbara is right; it can't all be settled tonight. Bridge, anyone? Or has there been too much excitement?"

"Hell, no!" Karen answered. "I can use pampering but bridge is one thing that *can't* cause a miscarriage. I think."

"No," agreed her father. "But the way you bid might cause heart failure in someone else."

"Pooh. Who wants to bid like a computer? Live dangerously, I always say."

"You do, dear."

They got no further than dealing. Dr. Livingstone, who had been sleeping in the "bathroom," at that moment came into the main room, walking stiff-legged and almost dragging hindquarters. "Joseph," the cat announced, "I am going to have these babies *right now!*"

The cat's anguished wailing, its hobbled gait, made its meaning clear as words. Joe was out of his chair at once. "Doc! What's the matter, Doc?"

He started to pick the cat up. That was not what Dr. Livingstone needed; it wailed louder and struggled. Hugh said, "Joe. Let it be."

"But old Doc *hurts.*"

"So let's take care of the matter. Duke, we'll use electric lights and the camp lamp. Snuff the candles. Karen, blankets on the table and a clean sheet."

"Right away."

Hugh knelt by the cat. "Easy, Doc. It hurts, doesn't it? Never mind, it won't be long. We're here, we're here." He smoothed the fur along the spine, then gently felt the abdomen. "Contraction. Hurry up, Karen."

"Ready, Daddy!"

"Lift with me, Joe."

They placed the cat on the table. Joe said, "What do we do now?"

"Give you a Miltown."

"But Doc *hurts.*"

"Surely she does. We can't do anything about it. She's having a bad time. It's her first litter and she's frightened, and she's older than she should be, for a first. Not good."

"But we have to do *something.*"

"You can help by quieting down; you're communicating your fear to her. Joe, if there were anything I could do, I would. But there isn't much we can do but stand by and let her know that she is not alone. Keep her from being frightened. Do you want that tranquilizer?"

"Uh, I guess so."

"Get it, Duke. Don't leave, Joe; Doc trusts you."

"Hubert, if you are going to stay up all night over a cat again, I'll need a sleeping pill. You can't expect a person to sleep with all this fuss."

"A Seconal for your mother, Duke. Can anybody think of anything we can use as a kitten bed?" Hugh Farnham searched his memory. Every box, every scrap of lumber, had been used and re-used and re-re-used in endless make-do building. Build a nest of bricks? Not sooner than daylight and this poor animal needed a safe and comforting spot tonight. Take apart some shelves?

"Daddy, how about the bottom wardrobe drawer?"

"Perfect! Pile everything on a bunk. Pad it. Use my hunting jacket. Duke, rig a frame to support a blanket; she'll want a little cave she'll feel safe in. You know."

"Of course we know," Karen chided. "Quit jittering, Daddy. This isn't our first litter."

"Sorry, baby. We are about to have a kitten. See that, Joe?" Fur rippled from the cat's middle down toward the tail, then did so again.

Karen hurriedly threw everything out of the lowest wardrobe drawer, placed it against the wall and put the hunting jacket in it, rushed back. "Did I miss it?"

"No," Hugh assured her. "But right now!"

Doc stopped panting to give one wail and was delivered of a kitten in two quick convulsions.

"Why, it's wrapped in cellophane," Barbara said wonderingly.

"Didn't you know?" asked Karen. "Daddy, it's *gray!* Doc, *where* have you been? Though maybe I shouldn't bring that up."

Neither Hugh nor Dr. Livingstone answered. The mother cat started vigorously licking her offspring, broke the covering, and tiny ratlike arms and legs waved helplessly. A squeak so thin and high as to be almost inaudible announced its opinion of the world. Doc bit the cord and went on licking, cleaning off blood and mucus and purring loudly at the same time. The baby didn't like it and again vented almost silent protest.

"Boss," demanded Joe, "what's wrong with it? It's so skinny and little."

"It's a fine kitten. It's a pretty baby, Doc. He's a bachelor, he doesn't know." Hugh spoke cooingly and rubbed the cat between her ears. He went on in normal tones, "And the worst case of bar sinister I ever saw—smooth-haired, tiger-striped, and gray."

Doc looked up reprovingly, gave a shudder and delivered the afterbirth, began chewing the bloody mass.

Barbara gulped and rushed to the door, fumbled at a bolt. Karen went after her, opened it and steadied her while she threw up.

"Duke!" Hugh snapped. "Bear guard!"

Duke followed them, stuck his head out. Karen said, "Go 'way! We're safe. Bright moonlight."

"Well . . . leave the door open." He withdrew.

Karen said, "I thought you weren't having morning sickness?"

"I'm not. *Oh!*" Retching again hit her. "It was what Doc did."

"Oh, that. Cats always do that. Let me wipe your mouth, dear."

"It's awful."

"It's normal. Good for them. Hormones, or something; you can ask Hugh. All right now?"

"I think so. *Karen!* We don't have to do *that?* Do we? I won't, I won't!"

"Huh? *Oh!* Never thought of it. Oh, I know we don't—or they would have told us in Smut One."

"Lots of things they don't mention in Smut One," Barbara said darkly. "When I had to take it, it was taught by an old maid. But I *won't*. I'll resign first, not have this baby."

"Comrade," Karen said grimly, "that's something we both should have thought of earlier. Stand aside, it's my turn to heave."

Presently they went inside, pale but steady. Dr. Livingstone had three more kittens and Barbara managed to watch without further rushes for the door. Of the other birthings only the third was notable: a tiny tomcat but large in its tininess. He was a breech presentation, the skull did not pass easily, and Doc in her pain clamped down.

Hugh was busy at once, pulling gently on the little body with his whole hand and sweating like a surgeon. Doc wailed and bit his thumb. He did not let it stop him nor hurry him.

Suddenly the kitten came free; he bent over and blew in its mouth, was rewarded with a thin, indignant squeak. He

124

put the baby down, let Dr. Livingstone clean it. "That was close," he said shakily.

"Old Doc didn't mean to," Joe said softly.

"Of course not. Which of you girls feels like fixing this for me?"

Barbara dressed the wound, while telling herself that she must not, *must not,* bite when her own time came.

The kittens were, in order, smooth-haired gray, fluffy white, midnight black with white jabot and mittens, and calico. After much argument between Karen and Joe, they were named: Happy New Year, Snow Princess Magnificent, Dr. Ebony Midnight, and Patchwork Girl of Oz—Happy, Maggie, Midnight, and Patches.

By midnight mother and children were bedded in the drawer with food, water, and sandbox near, and everyone went to bed. Joe slept on the floor with his head by the kitten nest.

When everyone was quiet, he raised up, used the flash to look in. Dr. Livingstone had one kitten in her arms, three more at suck; she stopped cleaning Maggie and looked inquiringly at him.

"They're *beautiful* kittens, Doc," he told her. "The *best* babies."

She spread her royal whiskers and purred agreement.

8

Hugh leaned on his shovel. "That does it, Joe."

"Let me tidy up around the gate." They were at the upper end of their ditch where the stream had been dammed against the dry season. It had been on them for weeks; the forest was sere, the heat oppressive. They were extremely careful about fire.

But no longer so careful about bears. It was still standard practice to be armed, but Duke had killed so many carnivores, ursine and feline, they seldom saw one.

The water spilling over the dam was only a trickle but there was water for irrigation and for household needs. Without the ditch they would have lost their garden.

It was necessary every day or so to adjust the flow. Hugh had not built a water gate; paucity of tools, scarcity of metal, and a total lack of lumber had baffled him. Instead he had devised an expedient. The point where water was taken from the pond had been faced with brick and a spillway set of half-round tile. To increase the flow this was taken out, the spill cut deeper, bricks adjusted, and tiles replaced. It was clumsy; it worked.

The bottom of the ditch was tiled all the way to house and garden; a minimum of water was lost. Their kiln had worked day and night; most of their capital gain had come out of the clay bank below the house and it was becoming difficult to dig good clay.

This did not worry Hugh; they had almost everything they needed.

Their bathroom was no longer a joke. Water flowed in a two-stall trough toilet partitioned with deerhide; tile drainpipe "leaded" with clay ran down the manhole, out the tunnel, and to a cesspool.

Forming drainpipe Hugh had found very difficult. After many failures he had whittled a male form in three parts—in parts, because it was necessary to shape the clay over it, let it dry enough to take out the form before it cracked from shrinking over the form.

With practice he cut his failures to about 25 percent in forming, 25 percent in firing.

The damaged water tank he had cut painfully, mallet and chisel, lengthwise into tubs, a bathtub indoors and a washtub outdoors. The seams he had calked with shaved hide; the tubs did not leak—much.

A brick fireplace-oven filled one corner of the bath-kitchen. It was not in use; days were long and hot; they cooked outdoors and ate under an awning of empty bears—but it was ready against the next rainy season.

Their house now had two stories. Hugh had concluded that an addition strong enough to stop bears and tight enough to discourage snakes would have to be of stone, and solidly roofed. That he could do—but how about windows and doors? Glass he would make someday if he solved the problems of soda and lime. But not soon. A stout door and tight shutters he could manage, but such a cabin would be stuffy.

So they had built a shed on the roof, a grass shack. With the ladder up, a bear faced a twelve-foot wall. Unsure that a wall would stop all their neighbors, Hugh had arranged trip lines around the edge so that disturbing them would cause an oxygen bottle to fall over. Their alarm was tripped the first week, scaring off the intruder. It had also, Hugh admitted, scared the bejasus out of him.

Anything that could not be hurt by weather had been moved out and the main room was rearranged into a women's dormitory and nursery.

Hugh stared downstream while Joe finished fussing. He could make out the roof of his penthouse. Good enough, he mused. Everything was in fair shape and next year would be better. So much better that they might take time to explore. Even Duke had not been as much as twenty miles away. Nothing but feet for travel and too busy scratching to live—

Next year would be soon enough.

"A man's reach should exceed his grasp, or what's a heaven for?" They had started with neither pot nor window. This year a pot— Next year a window? No hurry— Things were going well. Even Grace seemed contented. He felt certain that she would settle down and be a happy grandmother. Grace liked babies, Grace did well with babies— How well he remembered.

Not long now. Baby Karen was fuzzily vague but her guesses seemed to show that D-day was about two weeks off, and her condition matched her guess, as near as he could tell.

The sooner the better! Hugh had studied everything in his library on pregnancy and childbirth; he had made every preparation he could. His patients seemed to be in perfect health, both had satisfactory pelvic measurements, both seemed unafraid, and they helped each other with friendly nagging, not to gain too much weight. With Barbara to hold Karen's hand, with Karen to hold Barbara's hand, with Grace's motherly experience to bolster them, Hugh could see no trouble ahead.

It would be wonderful to have babies in the house.

With a warm wave of euphoria Hugh Farnham realized that he had never been so happy in his life.

"That's it Hugh. Let's catch those tiles on the way back."

"Okay. Take the rifle, I'll carry the tools."

"I think," Joe said, "we ought to—"

His words chopped off at a gunshot; they froze. It was followed by two more.

They ran.

Barbara was in the door. She held up a gun and waved, went inside. She came out before they reached the house, stepping carefully down off the stoop and moving slowly;

she was very gravid. Her belly bulged huge in shorts made from worn-out jeans that had belonged to Duke; she wore a man's shirt altered to support her breasts. She was bare-footed and no longer carried the gun.

Joe outdistanced Hugh, met her near the house. "Karen?" he demanded.

"Yes. She's started."

Joe hurried inside. Hugh arrived, stood panting. "Well?"

"Her bag of waters burst. Then the pains started. That was when I fired."

"Why didn't you— Never mind. What else?"

"Grace is with her. But she wants you."

"Let me catch my breath." Hugh wiped his face, tried to control his trembling. He took a deep breath, held it, let it out slowly. He went inside, Barbara following.

The bunks near the door had been taken down. A bed stuck out into the doorway but space cleared by removing shelves left passage. One bunk was now a cot in the living corner. The bed was padded with a grass mattress and a bear rug; a calico cat was on it.

Hugh squeezed past, felt another cat brush his ankles. He went into the other bay. The bunks there had been re-built into a bed across the end; Karen was in bed, Grace was seated, fanning her, and Joe stood by with an air of grave concern.

Hugh smiled at his daughter. "Hi, Fatty!" He stopped and kissed her. "How are you? Hurting?"

"Not now. But I'm glad you're here."

"We hurried."

A cat jumped up, landing on Karen. *"Unh!* Damn you, Maggie!"

"Joe," said Hugh, "round up the cats and put them in Coventry." The tunnel mouth had been bricked up, but with air holes, and a cat door which could be filled with a large brick. The cats had a low opinion of this but it had been built after Happy New Year had become missing and presumed dead.

Karen said, "Daddy, I want Maggie with me!"

"Joe, make that all but Maggie. When we get busy, grab Maggie and shut her up, too."

"Can do, Hugh." Joe left, passing Barbara coming in.

Hugh felt Karen's cheeks, took her pulse. He said to his wife, "Is she shaved?"

"There hasn't been time."

"You and Barbara get her shaved and washed. Punkin', when did your bowels move?"

"Just did. I was on the pot when it happened. Just sitting there minding my own business—and all of a sudden I'm Niagara Falls!"

"But your bowels moved?"

"Oh, yes!"

"That's one less thing to worry about." He smiled. "Not that there's anything to worry about, you'll play bridge most of the night. Like kittens, babies show up in the wee, sma' hours."

"All night? I want to have this little bastard and get it over with."

"I want it over with, too, but babies have minds of their own." He added, "You'll be busy a while and so will I. I'm dirty." He started to leave.

"Daddy, wait a minute. Do I have to stay back here? It's hot."

"No. The light is better by the door. Especially if young Tarzan has the decency to arrive during daylight. Barbara, turn that used bear over; it'll be cooler. Put this sheet on it. Or a clean one if there is one."

"The sterilized one?"

"No. Don't unpack the boiled sheet until the riot starts." Hugh patted his patient's hand. "Try not to have a pain until I'm clean."

"Daddy, you should have been a doctor."

"I *am* a doctor. The best doctor in the world."

As he left the house he encountered Duke, soaked from a long run. "I heard three shots. Sis?"

"Yes. No hurry, labor just started. I'm about to take a bath. Want to join me?"

"I want to say hello to Sis first."

130

"Hurry up; they're about to bathe her. And grab Joe; he's incarcerating cats. They'll want us out of the way."

"Shouldn't we be boiling water?"

"Do so, if it will calm you. Duke, my O.B. kit, such as it is, has been ready for a month. There are six jars of boiled water, for this and that. Go kiss your sister and don't let her see that you're worried."

"You're a cold fish, Dad."

"Son, I'm scared silly. I can list thirteen major complications—and I'm not prepared to cope with any of them. Mostly I pat her hand and tell her that everything is dandy—and that's what she needs. I examine her, solemn as a judge, and don't know what to look for. It's just to reassure her . . . and I'll thank you to help out."

Duke said soberly, "I will, sir. I'll kid her along."

"Don't overdo it. Just let her see that you share her confidence in old Doc Farnham."

"I will."

"If Joe gets the jitters, get him out. He's the worst. Grace is doing fine. Hurry up or they won't let you in."

Later, bathed and calmed down, Hugh climbed out of the stream ahead of Joe and Duke, walked back carrying his clothes and letting the air dry him. He paused outside, put on clean shorts. "Knock, knock!"

"Stay out," Grace called. "We're busy."

"Then cover her. I want to scrub."

"Don't be silly, Mother. Come in, Daddy."

He went in, squeezing around Barbara and Grace, and on into the bathroom. He trimmed his nails very closely, scrubbed his hands with ditch water—then again with boiled water, and repeated it. He shook them dry and went into the main room, being careful not to touch anything.

Karen was on the bed at the door, a ragged half sheet over her. Her shoulders were swaddled in a grayish garment that had been the shirt Hugh had worn the night of the attack. Grace and Barbara were seated on the bed, Duke stood outside the door, and Joe sat mournfully on the bunk beyond the bed.

Hugh smiled at her. "How is it going? Any twinges?"

"Nary a twinge, damn it. I want to have him before dinner."

"You will. Because you don't get any dinner."

"Beast. My daddy is a beast."

"Doctor Beast, please, Skedaddle, friends, I want to examine my patient. Everyone but Grace. Barbara, go lie down."

"I'm not tired."

"You may be awake most of the night. Take a nap. I don't want to cope with a seven-month preemie."

He folded back the sheet, looked Karen over, and palpated her swollen belly. "Has he been kicking?"

"Has he! I'm going to sign him up with the Green Bay Packers. I think he's wearing shoes."

"Wouldn't be surprised. Did you have shoes on when you started him?"

"What? Daddy, you are a nasty man. Yes."

"Prenatal influence. Next time take them off." He tried to judge whether the child was in the head-down position, or whether it was—God forbid!—a breech presentation. He was unable to decide. So he smiled at Karen and lied. "Shoes won't bother us, as he is head down, just as he should be. It's going to be an easy birth."

"How can you tell, Daddy?"

"Put your hand where mine is. That's his little pointy head, all set to take the dive. Feel it?"

"I guess so."

"You could see, if you were where I am." He tried to see if she was dilated. There was a little blood and he decided against a tactile examination—he did not know how it should feel and handling the birth canal would increase danger of infection. He knew that a rectal exploration should tell him something but he did not know what—so there was no point in submitting Karen to that indignity.

He looked up, caught his wife's eye and thought of asking her opinion, decided not to. Despite having borne children, Grace knew no more about it than he did; the only result would be to shake Karen's confidence.

132

Instead he got his "stethoscope" (three end papers from his encyclopaedia, rolled into a tube) and listened for fetal heartbeat. He had often heard it lately. But he got only a variety of noises which he lumped in his mind as "gut rumble."

"Ticking like a metronome," he announced, putting the tube down and covering her. "Your baby's in fine shape, baby girl, and so are you. Grace, did you start a log when the first pain showed?"

"Barbara did."

"Will you keep it, please? But first tell Duke to take the ropes off the other bed and rig them here."

"Hubert, are you sure she should pull on ropes? Neither of my doctors had me do anything of the sort."

"It's the latest thing," he reassured her. "All hospitals use them now." Hugh had read somewhere that midwives often had their patients pull on ropes while bearing down. He had looked for this in his books, could not find it. But it struck him as sound mechanics; a woman should be able to bear down better.

Grace looked doubtful but dropped the matter and left the shelter. Hugh started to get up. Karen grabbed his hand. "Don't go 'way, Daddy!"

"Pain?"

"No. Something to tell you. I asked Joe to marry me. Last week. And he accepted."

"I'm glad to hear it, dear. I think you are getting a prize."

"I do, too. Oh, it's Hobson's choice but I do love him, quite a lot. But we won't get married until I'm up and around and strong. I couldn't face the row with Mother, not now."

"I won't tell her."

"Better not tell Duke, either. Barbara knows, she thinks it's swell."

A contraction hit Karen while Duke was adjusting ropes. She yelped, chopped it off and gritted her teeth, reached for the ropes as Duke hastily handed them to her. Hugh put his hand on her belly, felt her womb harden as

133

increasing pain showed in her face. "Bear down, baby," he told her. "And pant; it helps."

She started to pant, it turned into a scream.

Endless seconds later she relaxed, forced a smile and said, "They went that a-way! Sorry about the sound effects, Daddy."

"Yell if you want to. But panting does more good. Now rest while you can. Let's get organized. Joe, you're drafted as cook. I want Barbera to rest and Grace to nurse—so you cook dinner, please. Fix some cold supper, too. Grace, did you log it?"

"Yes."

"Did you time the contraction?"

"I did," Barbara answered. "Forty-five seconds."

Karen looked indignant. "Barb, you are out of your mind! It was over an hour."

"Call it forty-five seconds," Hugh said. "I want the time of each pain and how long it lasts."

Seven minutes later the next one hit. Karen managed to pant, screamed only a little. But she did not feel like joking afterwards; she turned her face away. The contraction had been long and severe. Though shaken by his daughter's agony, Hugh felt encouraged; it seemed certain that labor was going to be short.

It was not. All that hot and weary day the woman brought to bed fought to void herself of her burden—white-faced and shrieking, belly hardening with each attempt, muscles in arms and neck standing out as she strained—then fell back limp as the contraction died away, tired and trembling, not speaking, uninterested in anything but the ordeal.

It got steadily worse. Contractions became only three minutes apart, each one longer and seeming to hurt more. Once Hugh told her not to use the ropes; he could not see that they helped. Quickly she asked for them and seemed not to have heard him. She did seem slightly less uncomfortable braced against them.

At nine that night there was bleeding. Grace became frantic; she had heard many stories of the dangers of hemorrhage. Hugh assured her that it was normal and showed that the baby would arrive soon. He believed it, as it was not massive and did not continue—and it did not seem possible that birth could be far away.

Grace looked angry and got up; Barbara slipped into the chair she vacated. Hugh hoped that Grace would rest—the women had been taking turns.

But Grace returned a few minutes later. "Hubert," she said in a high, brittle voice. "Hubert, I'm going to call a doctor."

"Do that," he agreed, his eyes on Karen.

"You listen to me, Hubert Farnham. You should have called a doctor at once. You're killing her, you hear me? I'm going to call a doctor—and you are not going to stop me."

"Yes, Grace. The telephone is in there." He pointed into the other wing. Grace looked puzzled, then turned suddenly and went away. *Duke!*"

His son hurried in. "Yes, Dad?"

Hugh said forcefully, "Duke, your mother has decided to telephone for a doctor. You go help her. *Do you understand?*"

Duke's eyes widened. "Where are the needles?"

"In the smaller bundle on the table. Don't touch the large bundle; it's sterile."

"Got it. What dosage?"

"Two c.c. Don't let her see the needle, or she'll jerk." Hugh's head jerked; he realized that he was groggy. "Make that three c.c.; I want her to go out like a light and sleep until morning. She can tolerate it."

"Right away." Duke left.

Karen had been lying quiet between contractions, apparently in semi-coma. Now she whispered, "Poor Daddy. Your women give you a lot of grief."

"Rest, dear."

"I— Oh, God, here it comes again!"

Then she was saying between screams: "It *hurts!* Make it stop! Oh, Daddy, I do want a doctor! Please, Daddy! *Get me a doctor!*"

135

"Bear down, darling. Bear down."

It went on and on, far into the night, no respite and getting worse. It stopped being worth while to log contractions; they almost overlapped. Karen no longer could be said to talk; she screamed incoherent demands for relief when she strained, spoke unresponsively or did not answer in the brief periods between contractions.

Around dawn—it seemed to Hugh that the torture had been going on for weeks but his watch showed that Karen had been in labor eighteen hours—Barbara said urgently, "Hugh, she can't take any more."

"I know," he admitted, looking at his daughter. She was at the peak of a pain, face gray and contorted, mouth squared in agony, high sobbing moans coming out between her teeth.

"Well?"

"I suppose she should have had a Caesarean. But I'm no surgeon."

"I wonder."

"I don't. I'm not."

"You know more about it than the first man who ever did one! You know how to keep it sterile. We have sulfa drugs and you can load her up with Demerol." She did not try to keep Karen from hearing; the patient was beyond caring.

"No."

"Hugh, you must. She's dying."

"I know." He sighed. "But it's too late for a Caesarean, even if I knew how. To save Karen with one, I mean. We might save her baby." He blinked and swayed. "Only it would not. *Who's to wet-nurse?* You can't, not yet. And cows we don't have."

He took a deep breath, tried to get a grip on himself. "Only one thing left. Try to get it out Eskimo style."

"What's that?"

"Get her up and let gravity help. Maybe it'll work. Call the boys, we'll need them. I've got to scrub again; I might have to do an episiotomy. Oh, God."

Five minutes and two contractions later they were ready

to try it. When Karen lay back exhausted after the second one, Hugh tried to explain what they were going to do. It was hard to get her attention. At last she nodded slightly and whispered, "I don't care."

Hugh went to the table where his equipment was now opened out, got his one scalpel, took the camp lamp in his other hand. "All right, boys. As soon as she starts, pick her up."

They had only seconds to wait. Hugh saw the contraction start, nodded to Duke. "Now!"

"With me, Joe." They started to lift her, each with an arm under her back, a hand under a thigh.

Karen screamed and fought them off. "No, no! Don't touch me—*I can't stand it!* Daddy, make them stop! *Daddy!*"

They stopped. Duke said, "Dad?"

"Lift her up! *Now!*"

They got her high in a squatting position, thighs pulled open. Barbara got behind Karen, arms around her, and pressed down on the girl's tortured belly. Karen screamed and struggled; they held her fast. Hugh got hurriedly to the floor, shined the light up. "Bear down, Karen, bear down!"

"Ooooooh!"

Suddenly he saw the baby's scalp, gray-blue. He started to lay the knife aside; the head retreated. "Try again, Karen!"

He readjusted the lamp. He wondered whether he was supposed to make the incision in front? Or in back? Or both? He saw the scalp show again and stop; with his hand suddenly rock steady and with no conscious decision he reached up and made one small cut.

He barely had time to drop the knife before he had both hands full of wet, slippery, bloody baby. He knew there was something else he should do now but all he could think of was to get it by both feet in his left hand, lift it and slap its tiny bottom.

It let out a choked wail.

"Get her on the bed, boys—but easy! It's still fastened by the cord."

137

They made it, Hugh on his knees and burdened with a feebly wiggling load. Once they had Karen down, Hugh started to put her baby in her arms—but saw that Karen was not up to it. She seemed to be awake—her eyes were open. But she was in total collapse.

Hugh was close to collapse. He looked dazedly around, handed the baby to Barbara. "Stay close," he told her, unnecessarily.

"Dad?" said Duke. "Aren't you supposed to cut the cord?"

"Not yet." Where was that knife? He found it, rubbed it quickly with iodine—hoped that it was sterile. Placed it by two boiled lengths of cotton string—turned and felt the cord to see if it was pulsing.

"He's beautiful," Joe said softly.

"She," Hugh corrected. "The baby is a girl. Now, Barbara, if you—"

He broke off. Suddenly everything happened too fast. The baby started to choke; Hugh grabbed it, turned it upside down, dug into its mouth, scooped out a plug of mucus, handed the baby back, started again to check the cord—saw that Karen was in trouble.

With a nightmare feeling that he needed to be twins he got one of the strings, tied a square knot around the cord near the baby's belly, trying to control his trembling so as not to tie it too hard—started to tie the second, saw that it was not needed; Karen suddenly delivered the placenta and was hemorrhaging. She moaned.

With one slash Hugh cut the cord, snapped at Barbara, "Get a bellyband on it!"—turned to take care of the mother.

She was flowing like a river; her face was gray and she seemed unconscious. Too late to attempt to take stitches in the cut he had made and the tears that followed; he could see that this flood was from inside, not from the damaged portal. He tried to stop it by packing her inside with their last roll of gauze while shouting to Joe and to Duke to get a bellyband and compress on Karen herself to put pressure on her uterus.

Some agonized time later the belly compress was in

place and the gauze was backed by a dam of sanitary napkins—one irreplaceable, Hugh thought tiredly, they hadn't needed much. He raised his eyes and looked at Karen's face—then in sudden panic tried to find her pulse.

Karen had survived the birth of her daughter by less than seven minutes.

9

Katherine Josephine survived her mother by a day. Hugh baptized her with that name and a drop of water an hour after Karen died; it was clear that the baby might not last long. She had trouble breathing.

Once when the baby choked, Barbara started her up again by mouth-to-mouth suction, getting a mouthful of something she spat out hastily. Little Jodie seemed better then for quite a while.

But Hugh knew that it was only a reprieve; he could see no chance of keeping the baby alive long enough—two months—to let Barbara feed it. Only two cans of Carnation milk were left in their stores.

Nevertheless they worked grimly around the clock.

Grace mixed a formula from memory—evaporated milk, boiled water, a hoarded can of white Karo. They had no food cells, not even a nipple. An orphaned baby was a crisis for which Hugh had not planned. In hindsight it seemed the most glaring of probable emergencies. He tried not to brood over his failure, dedicated himself to keeping Karen's daughter alive.

A plastic-barreled eyedropper was the nearest to a nipple they could find. They used it to pick up the formula, try to match the pressure with the infant's attempts to suck.

It did not work well. Little Jodie continued to have trouble breathing and tended to choke every time they tried to feed her; they spent as much time trying to clear her throat and get her cranked up again as they did in feeding her. She seemed reluctant to suck on the harsh substitute and if they squirted food into her mouth anyway, she always choked. Twice Grace was able to coax her into taking almost an ounce. Both times she threw it up. Barbara and Hugh had even less luck.

Before dawn following her birthday Hugh was awakened by Grace screaming. The child had choked to death.

During the long day in which three of them battled to save the baby, Duke and Joe dug a grave, high up the hill in a sunny spot. They dug deep and stocked a pile of boulders; both held concealed horror that a bear or coyotes might dig up the grave.

Grave dug, boulders waiting, Joe said in a strained voice, "How are we going to build a casket?"

Duke sighed and wiped sweat from his eyes. "Joe, we can't."

"We've *got* to."

"Oh, we could cut trees and split them and adz out some lumber—we've done that when we had to. That kitchen counter. But how long would it take? Joe, this is hot weather—*Karen can't wait!*"

"We've got to tear down something and build out of it. A bed, maybe. Bookcases."

"Taking the wardrobe apart would be easiest."

"Let's start."

"Joe. The only things we could use to build a coffin are in the house. Do you think Hugh will let us go in there *now* and start ripping and tearing and banging? If anyone woke that baby or startled it when they were trying to get it to feed, Dad would kill him. If Barbara or Mother didn't kill him first. No, Joe. No coffin."

They settled for a vault, using all their stock of bricks; these they used to build a box in the bottom of the grave, then cut down their dining canopy to line it, and cut timbers to cover it. Poor as it was, they felt comforted by it.

Next morning the grave received mother and daughter.

Joe and Duke placed them in it, Duke having insisted that his father stay behind and take care of Grace and Barbara. Duke had visualized how awkward it would be, getting the bodies into the grave and arranging them; he

141

would not have had Joe along had not an assistant been necessary. He suggested that his mother not come to the grave at all.

Hugh shook his head. "I thought of that. You try to convince her. I can't budge her."

Nor could Duke. But when he sent Joe down for the others, his sister and her daughter were decently at rest with their winding sheet neatly arranged, and no trace remained of the struggle it had been to place them there, the rebuilding of part of the brick box that had been necessary, or—worst—the moment when the tiny corpse had fallen out of the sheet when they tried to get them both down as one. Karen's face looked peaceful and her daughter was cuddled in her arm as if sleeping.

Duke balanced with a foot on each brick wall, knelt over her. "Good-bye, Sis," he whispered. "I'm sorry." He covered her face and got carefully out of the grave. A little procession was coming up the hill, Hugh assisting his wife, Joe helping Barbara. Beyond the shelter their flag flew at half-mast.

They arranged themselves at the grave, Hugh at the head, his wife on his right, his son on his left, Barbara and Joe at the foot. To Duke's relief no one asked that faces be uncovered nor did his mother seem disturbed at the arrangements.

Hugh took a small black book from his pocket, opened it to a marked page:

" '*I am the Resurrection and the Life* . . .

" '*We brought nothing into this world, and it is certain that we can take nothing out. The Lord gave, and the Lord hath taken—*' "

Grace sobbed and her knees started to fail. Hugh shoved the book into Duke's hands, moved to support his wife. "Take over, Son!"

"Take her back down, Dad!"

Grace said brokenly, "No, no! I must stay."

"Read it, Duke. I've marked the passages."

" '. . . *he heapeth up riches, and cannot tell who shall gather them.*

" "For I am a stranger with thee, and a sojourner, as all my fathers were.

" 'O spare me a little, that I may recover my strength . . .

" 'Man, that is born of woman, hath but a short time to live, and is full of misery . . .

" 'Unto Almighty God we commend the soul of our sister—of our sisters—and we commit their bodies to the ground; earth to earth, ashes to ashes, dust to dust—' "

Duke paused, dropped the tiniest of clods into the grave. He looked back at the book, closed it and said suddenly, "Let us pray."

They took Grace back and put her to bed; Joe and Duke returned to close the grave. Hugh, seeing that his wife appeared to be resting, started to snuff candles in the rear bay. She opened her eyes. "Hubert—"

"Yes, Grace?"

"I told you. I warned you. You wouldn't listen to me."

"About what, Grace?"

"I told you she had to have a doctor! You wouldn't call one. You were too proud. You sacrificed my daughter on the altar of your pride. My baby. You killed her."

"Grace, there are no doctors here. You know that."

"If you were even half a man, you wouldn't make excuses!"

"Grace, please. May I get you something? A Miltown? Or would you like a hypo?"

"No, no!" she said shrilly. "That's how you tricked me when I was going to get a doctor anyway. In spite of you. You'll never again trick me with your drugs. And you'll never touch me again, either. Murderer."

"Yes, Grace." He turned and left.

Barbara was on the stoop, sitting with her head in her hands. Hugh said, "Barbara, the flag must be two-blocked. Do you want me to do it?"

"So soon, Hugh?"

"Yes. We go on."

10

They went on. Duke hunted, Duke and Joe farmed, Hugh worked harder than ever. Grace worked too, and her cooking improved—and her eating; she got fatter. She never mentioned her conviction that her husband had been responsible for the death of their daughter.

She did not speak to him at all. When a problem had to be discussed she spoke to Duke. She quit attending church services.

In the last month of Barbara's pregnancy, Duke sought out his father privately. "Dad, you told me that any time I wanted to leave—or any of us—we could."

Hugh was startled. "Yes."

"A pro-rata share, you said. Ammo, tools, and so forth."

"Better than that; we're a going concern. Duke, you are leaving?"

"Yes—but not just myself. Mother wants to. She's the one who's dead set on it. I've got reasons, but Mother's wishes are the deciding factor."

"Mmm— Let's talk about your reasons. Are you dissatisfied with the way I'm running things? I will gladly step aside. I feel sure that I can get Joe and Barbara to go along, so that you will have unanimous support." He sighed. "I am anxious to turn over the burden."

Duke shook his head. "That's not it, Dad. I don't want to be boss and you've done a good job. Oh, I won't say I liked the high-handed way you started in. But results count and you got results. I'd rather not discuss my reasons except to say that they don't have to do with you—and wouldn't be enough to make me leave if Mother weren't hipped on it. She wants to leave. She's going to leave. I can't let her leave alone."

"Can you tell my why Grace wants to leave?"

Duke hesitated. "Dad, I don't see that it matters; she's made up her mind. I pointed out that I couldn't make things as safe for her—nor as comfortable—as it is here. But she's adamant."

Hugh pondered it. "Duke, if that's how your mother feels, I won't try to persuade her; I've long since lost my influence over her. But I have two ideas. You may find one of them practical."

"I doubt it."

"Hear me. You know we have copper tubing; we used some in the kitchen. We have everything for a still; I stocked the items to build one if a war came along—not just for us but because liquor is money in any primitive society.

"I haven't built it for reasons we both know. But I could and I know how to make liquor." He smiled slightly. "Not book knowledge. While I was in the South Pacific, I bossed a still, with the shut-eye connivance of my C.O. I learned how to turn corn or potatoes or most anything into vodka, or fruit into brandy. Duke, your mother might be happy if she had liquor."

"She would drink herself to death!"

"Duke, Duke! If she is happy doing it, who are we to stop her? What does she have to live for? She loved television, she enjoyed parties, she could spend a happy day at the hairdresser's, followed by a movie, then drinks with one of her friends. That was her life, Duke. Now where is it? Gone, gone! There is just this we can give her to make up for what she has lost. Who are *you* to decide that your mother must not drink herself to death."

"Dad, that's not the situation!"

"So?"

"You know I don't—didn't—approve of Mother's excessive drinking. But I might go along with letting her drink all she wants now. If you build that still, we might be customers. But we would still leave. Because that won't solve Mother's problem."

"Well, Duke, that leaves only my other idea. I'll get out instead. Only—" Hugh frowned. "Duke, tell her that I will leave as soon as Barbara has her baby. I can't walk out on my patient. You can give Grace my assur—"

"Dad, that won't solve a thing!"

"I don't understand."

"Oh, Christ, I might as well spill it. It's Barbara. She's— Well, hell, Mother is nuts on the subject. Can't stand her. Ever since Karen died. She said to me, 'Duke, that woman is *not* going to have her child in my home! Her bastard. I won't have it. You tell your father that he has got to get her out of here.' That's what she said, Dad."

"Good Lord!"

"Yeah. I tried to reason with her. I told her that Barbara couldn't leave. I gave her both barrels, Dad; I said there wasn't a chance that you would ever force Barbara to leave. But as for making her leave now, or even letting her, you would no more do it than you would have driven Karen out. I told her that *I* wouldn't, either, and that Joe and I would fight you to stop it, stipulating that you were crazy enough to try. Which you aren't, of course."

"Thank you."

"That did it. She believes me when I lay it on the line. So *she* decided to leave. I can't stall her any longer. She's leaving. I'm going with her, to take care of her."

His father rubbed his temples. "I guess there is no situation so bad but what it can get worse. Duke, even with you, she hasn't anywhere to go."

"Not quite, Dad."

"Eh?"

"I can swing it, with your help. Do you remember that cave up Collins Canyon, the one they tried to make a tourist attraction? It's still there. Or its twin, I mean. I was hunting up that way that first week. The canyon looked so familiar that I climbed up and looked for the cave. Found it. And Dad, it's habitable and defensible."

"The door? The mouth?"

"No problem. If you can spare that steel plate that blocked off the tunnel."

"Certainly."

"The cave has a vent, higher up. No smoke problem. It has a spring that hasn't failed all this dry weather. Dad, it's as comfortable as the shelter; all it needs is outfitting."

"I capitulate. You can take almost anything now. Beds, of course. Utensils. Your pick of the canned goods. Matches, ammunition, guns. Make a list, I'll help you move."

Duke colored under his tan. "Dad, a few things are up there already."

"So? Did you think I would be pinchpenny?"

"Uh . . . I don't mean the past few days. I moved some things up the first days we were here. You see . . . well, you and I had that row—and then you made me rationing officer. That gave me the idea, and for a week or more I always left here loaded, leaving when no one was watching."

"Stealing."

"I didn't figure it so. I never took as much as one-sixth of anything . . . and just stuff I would have to have in a pinch. Matches. Ammo. That rifle you couldn't find. One blanket. A knife. A little food. Some candles. You see . . . well, look at it from my side. There was always the chance that I would get you sore and either have to fight—one of us killed is the way you put it—or run and not be able to stop for *anything*. I decided not to fight. So I made preparations. But I didn't steal it; you *said* I could have it. Say the word and I'll fetch it all back."

Hugh Farnham peeled a callus, then looked up. "One man's stealing is another man's survival, I suppose. Just one thing—Duke, in that food you took: *Were there any cans of milk?*"

"Not one. Dad, don't you think, if there had been, I would have beaten all records getting up there and back when Karen died?"

"Yes. I'm sorry I asked."

"I was sorry I hadn't snitched a few cans; then they wouldn't have been used up."

"The baby didn't last out the milk we had, Duke. All right, it calls for quick surgery—but don't forget that you can come back, any time. Duke, women sometimes get unreasonable at about your mother's age . . . then get over it and are nice old ladies. Maybe we'll have the family together again. I hope we'll see you occasionally. You're welcome to all the vegetables you can eat, of course."

"I was going to mention that. I can't farm up there. Suppose I still hunt for all of us . . . and when I bring in a load of meat I take away a load of green stuff?"

His father smiled. "We have reinstituted commerce. And we can supply you with pottery and there's no need to do your own tanning. Duke, I suggest you sort out what you want, and tomorrow you and I and Joe will start packing it to your cave. Be lavish. Just one thing—"

"What?"

"The books are mine! Anything you want to look up, you'll have to come here. This is not a circulating library."

"Fair enough."

"I mean it. You can have my razor, you can have my best knife. But snitch one book and I'll skin you alive and bind that book in human skin. There are limits. All right, I'll tell Joe, and get Barbara out of the house and we'll stay away until dark. Good luck, and tell Grace no hard feelings. There are, but tell her that. But I'm not too groused. It takes two to create a heaven . . . but hell can be accomplished by one. I can't say that I've been happy lately and Grace may be smarter than we think."

"That's a polite way of telling us to go to hell, Dad."

"Possibly."

"Whatever you mean, the same to you. It was no accident that I moved away from home as soon as I could."

"*Touché!* Well, get on with it." His father turned and walked away.

Joe made no comment. He simply said that he had better get on with the irrigating. Barbara said nothing until they were alone.

Hugh took a picnic lunch—chunks of corn pone, some strings of jerky, two tomatoes, plus a canteen of water. He fetched a rifle and a blanket. They went up the hill above the grave and picked the shade of a detached tree. Hugh noticed fresh flowers on the grave and wondered if Barbara had been trudging up there. The climb was difficult for her; they had taken it very slowly. Or had Grace been doing it? It seemed still less likely. Then he thought of the obvious: Joe.

Once Barbara had her heavy body comfortable, on her back with knees up, Hugh said, "Well?"

She was silent a long time. "Hugh, I'm dreadfully sorry. It's my fault. Isn't it?"

"*Your* fault? Because a woman sick in her mind fixes on you to hate? You told me once not to blame myself for another person's defect. You should take your own advice."

"That wasn't what I meant, Hugh. I mean: losing your son. Grace could not leave if Duke did not. Did he say anything? About me?"

"Nothing but this ridiculous set that Grace has taken. What should he have said?"

"I wonder if I am free to say? In any case I am going to. Hugh, after Karen died, Duke asked me to marry him. I refused. He was hurt. And surprised. You see— You knew about Karen and Joe?"

"Yes."

"I didn't know whether Karen had told you. When she decided to marry Joe, I made up my mind that I would have to marry Duke. Karen took it for granted and I admitted that I intended to. She may have told Duke. In any case, he expected me to say Yes. I said No. And he was hurt. I'm sorry, Hugh. If you want me to, I'll tell him I've changed my mind."

"Hold on! I think you made a mistake. But I won't have you correcting it to please me. What do you *want* to do? Do you plan to marry Joe, now?"

"Joe? I never planned to marry Joe. Although I would marry him as readily as Duke. Hugh, I want to do what I

149

always want to do. Whatever you want." She turned on her side and faced him. "You know that. If you want me to marry Joe, I will. If you want me to marry Duke, I will. You say it, I'll do it."

"Barbara, Barbara!"

"I mean it, Hugh. Or anything more, or anything less. You're my boss. Not just some, but all. Haven't I done so, all the time we've been together? I play by the book."

"Stop talking nonsense."

"If it's nonsense, it's true nonsense."

"As may be. I want you to marry whom you want to marry."

"That's the one thing I can't do. You are already married."

"Oh."

"Are you surprised? No, I've surprised you only by saying it—when we've kept silent so long. That's how it is and that's how it's always been. Since I can't marry you, I'll marry whom you say. Or never marry."

"Barbara, will you marry me?"

"What did you say?"

"Will you marry me?"

"Yes."

He leaned over and kissed her. She kissed him back, lips open, full surrender.

Presently he straightened up. "Would you like some corn pone?"

"Not yet."

"I thought we might have some to celebrate. It calls for champagne. But corn pone is what we have."

"Oh. Then I'll have a nibble. And a sip of water. Hugh, Hugh my beloved, what are you going to do about Grace?"

"Nothing. She's divorcing me. In fact she divorced me more than a month ago, the day—the day we buried Karen. That she is still here is just housing shortage. It doesn't take a judge to grant a divorce here, any more than it will take a license for me to marry you."

Barbara spread her hands over her swollen belly. "I

have my marriage license, right here!" Her voice was light and happy.

"The child is mine?"

She looked at him. "Look over to the east."

"At what?"

"Do you see Three Wise Men approaching?"

"Oh. Idiot!"

"It is yours, my beloved. A thing a woman can never prove but can be utterly sure of."

He kissed her again. When he stopped she caressed his cheek. "I'd like corn pone now, lots of it. I'm hungry. I feel very full of life and anxious to live."

"Yes! Tomorrow our honeymoon starts."

"Today. It has started. Hugh, I'm going to enter it in our journal. Darling, may I sleep on the roof tonight? I can manage the ladder."

"You want to sleep with me? Lecherous little girl!"

"That wasn't what I meant. I'm not lecherous now, my hormones are all keyed against it. No passion, dear. Just love. I won't be any good for a honeymoon. Oh, I'll happily sleep with you; you could have slept with me all these months. No, dear, I meant that I don't want to sleep in the same room with Grace. I'm afraid of her—afraid for the baby at least. Perhaps that's silly."

"No, it's not. It may not be necessary but it's a precaution we'll take. Barbara, what do you think of Grace?"

"Must I say?"

"Tell me."

"I don't like her. That's apart from being afraid of her; I didn't like her long before I became uneasy about her. I don't like the way she treats me, I don't like the way she treats Joseph, I didn't like the way she treated Karen, I have always resented the way she treats you—and had to pretend not to see it—and I *despise* what she has done to Duke."

"I don't like her, either—not for years. I'm glad she's leaving. Barbara, I would be glad even if you were not here."

"Hugh, I'm relieved to hear that. You know I'm divorced."

151

"Yes."

"When my marriage broke up I swore a solemn oath that I would never break up anyone else's marriage. I've felt guilty ever since the night of the attack."

He shook his head. "Forget it. The marriage was already long dead. All that was left were duties and obligations. Mine, for she didn't feel any. Beloved, had my marriage been a reality, you could have come into my arm that night, and cuddle and comfort would have been all. As it was, we were dying—so we thought—and I was at least as hungry for love as you were. I was parched for love—you gave me yourself."

"Beloved, I will never let you be parched again."

About nine the next morning, they all were outside where chattels for the new household were piled.

Hugh looked over his ex-wife's selections with wry amusement. Grace had taken literally the invitation to "take almost anything"; she had gutted the place—the best blankets, almost all utensils including the teakettle and the one skillet, three of four foam-rubber mattresses, nearly all the remaining canned goods, all the sugar, the lion's share of other irreplaceables, all the plastic dishes.

Hugh made only one objection: salt. When he noted that Grace had grabbed all the salt he insisted on a division. Duke agreed and asked if there was anything else Hugh objected to?

Hugh shook his head. Barbara would not mind making-do. *"Better is a dinner of herbs where love is—"*

Duke had shown restraint, taking one shovel, one ax, a hammer, less than half the nails, and no tool not stocked in duplicate. Instead, Duke remarked that he might want to borrow tools someday. Hugh agreed and offered his services on any two-man job. Duke thanked him. Both men found the situation embarrassing, both covered it by being unusually polite.

A delay in starting was caused by the steel plate for the cave door. Its weight was not too great for a man as husky as Duke, but it was awkward. A pack had to be devised, rugged enough for the trek, comfortable in padding and straps, and so rigged that Duke could fire a rifle.

This resulted in sacrificing the one intact bear hide, the covering of the bed Karen had died in. Hugh minded only the loss of time. It would take six trips by three men to move the plunder Grace had picked; Duke thought that two trips a day would be maximum. If they did not start soon, only one trip could be made that day.

At last they got it on Duke's back with a fur pad protecting his spine. "Feels right," Duke decided. "Let's get packs on you two and get going."

"In a jiffy," Hugh agreed and bent over to pick up his load.

"My God!"

"Trouble, Duke?"

"Look!"

A shape had appeared over the eastern rise. It slanted through the air on a course that would have missed them, but, as it neared the point of closest approach, it stopped dead, turned and headed for them.

It passed majestically overhead. Hugh was unable to guess its size at first; there was nothing to which to relate it—a dark shape proportioned like a domino tile. But as it passed about five hundred feet up, it seemed to him that it was around a hundred feet wide and three times that in length. He could make out no features. It moved swiftly but made no noise.

It swept past, turned, circled—stopped, turned again and came toward them at lower altitude.

Hugh found that he had an arm around Barbara. When the object had appeared, she had been some distance away, putting clothes to soak in the outside tub. Now she was circled by his left arm and he could feel her trembling.

"Hugh, what is it?"

"People."

The thing hovered above their flag. Now they could see people; heads showed above its sides.

A corner detached itself, splitting off sharply. It dove, stopped by the peak of the flagpole. Hugh saw that it was

153

a car about nine feet long and three wide, with one passenger. No details could he see, no clue to motive power; the car enclosed the man's lower body; his trunk projected above.

The man removed the flag, rejoined the main craft. His vehicle blended back in.

The rectangle disintegrated.

It broke into units like that which had filched their flag. Most cars remained in the air; some dozen landed, three in a triangle around the colonists. Duke yelled "Watch it!" and dived for his gun.

He never made it. He leaned forward at an extreme angle, pawed the air with a look of amazement, and was slowly pulled back to vertical.

Barbara gasped in Hugh's ear. "Hugh, what is it?"

"I don't know." He did not need to ask what she meant; he had felt, at the instant his son was stopped, that he seemed to be waist deep in quicksand. "Don't fight it."

"I wasn't going to."

Grace shrilled, "Hubert! Hubert, do some—" Her cries cut off. She seemed to faint but did not fall.

Four cars were about eight feet in the air, lined up abreast, and were cruising over Barbara's farm. Where they passed, everything underneath, cornstalks, tomato plants, beans, squash, lettuce, potato hills, everything including branching ditches was pressed flat into a macadam.

The raw end of the main ditch spilled water over this pavement. One car whipped around, ran a new ditch around the raped area in a wide sweep which allowed the water to circle the destroyed garden and reached the stream at a lower point.

Barbara buried her face against Hugh. He patted her.

That car then went upstream along the old ditch. Soon water ceased to flow.

As the garden was leveled, other cars landed on it. Hugh was unable to figure out what they did, but a large pavilion, glossy black, and ornate in red and gold, grew up in seconds in the clearing.

Duke called out, "Dad! For God's sake, can't you get at your gun?"

Hugh was wearing a forty-five, the weapon he had picked for the hike. His hands were only slightly hampered by whatever held them. But he answered, "I shan't try."

"Are you going to just stand there and let—"

"Yes. Duke, use your head. If we hold still, we may live longer."

Out of the pavilion strode a man. He seemed seven feet tall but some of this was a helmet, plumed and burnished. He wore a flowing skirt of red embroidered in gold and was bare to the waist save that an end of the skirt thrown across one shoulder covered part of his broad chest. He was shod in black boots.

All others were dressed in black coveralls with a red and gold patch at the right shoulder. Hugh felt an impression that this man (there was no slightest doubt that he was master)—that the commander had taken time to change into formal clothes. Hugh felt encouraged. They were prisoners—but if the leader took the trouble to dress up before interviewing them, then they were prisoners of importance and a parley might be fruitful. Or did that follow?

But he was encouraged by the man's face, too. He had an air of good-natured arrogance and his eyes were bright and merry. His forehead was high, his skull massive; he looked intelligent and alert. Hugh could not place his race. His skin was dark brown and shiny. But his mouth was only slightly Negroid; his nose, though broad, was arched, and his black hair was wavy.

He carried a small crop.

He strode up to them, stopped abruptly when he reached Joseph. He gave a curt order to their nearest captor.

Joe stretched and bent his legs. "Thanks."

The man spoke to Joe. Joe answered, "Sorry, I don't understand."

The man spoke again. Joe shrugged helplessly. The man grinned and patted him on the shoulder, turned away,

155

picked up Duke's rifle. He handled it clumsily, making Hugh flinch.

Nevertheless, he seemed to understand guns. He worked the bolt, ejecting one cartridge, then put it to his shoulder, aimed upstream and fired.

The blast was deafening, he had fired past Hugh's ear. He grinned broadly, tossed the rifle to a subordinate, walked up to Hugh and Barbara, reached out to touch Barbara's child-swollen belly.

Hugh knocked his hand away.

With a gesture almost negligent, certainly without anger, the big man brushed Hugh's hand aside with the crop he carried. It was not a blow, it would not have swatted a fly.

Hugh gasped in agony. His hand burned like fire and his arm was numb to the armpit. "Oh, God!"

Barbara said urgently, "Don't, Hugh. He isn't hurting me."

Nor was he. With a manner of impersonal interest such as a veterinarian might take in feeling a pregnant mare or bitch, the big man felt out the shape of the child she carried, then lifted one of her breasts—while Hugh writhed in that special humiliation of a man unable to protect his woman.

The man finished his palpation, grinned at Barbara and patted her head. Hugh tried to ignore the pain in his hand and dug into his memory for a language imperfectly learned. *"Vooi govoriti'yeh po-Russki, Gospodin?"*

The man glanced at him, made no answer.

Barbara said, *"Sprechen Sie deutsch, mein Herr?"*

That got her a smile. Hugh called out, "Duke, try him in Spanish!"

"Okay. *Habla usted Español, Senor?"* No response—

Hugh sighed. "We've shot our wad."

"M'sieur?" Joe said. *"Est-ce que vous parlez la langue française?"*

The man turned. *"Tiens?"*

"Parlez-vous français, monsieur?"

"Mais oui! Vous êtes française?"

156

"*Non, non! Je suis américain. Nous sommes tous américains.*"

"*Vraiment? Impossible!*"

"*C'est vrai, monsieur. Je vous en assure.*" Joe pointed to the empty flagpole. "*Les Etats-Unis de l'Amérique.*"

The conversation became hard to follow as both sides stumbled along in broken French. At last they paused and Joe said, "Hugh, he asked me—ordered me—to come into his tent and talk. I've asked him to let you all loose first. He says No. 'Hell, no!' it amounts to."

"Ask him to let the women loose."

"I'll try." Joe spoke at length with the big man. "He says the *enceinte femme*—that's Barbara—can sit down where she is. The 'fat one'—Grace he means—is to come with us."

"Good work, Joe. Get us a deal."

"I'll try. I don't understand him very well."

The three went into the pavilion. Barbara found that she could sit down, even stretch out. But the invisible web held Hugh as clingingly as ever.

"Dad," Duke said urgently, "this is our chance, while nobody is around who understands English."

"Duke," Hugh answered wearily, "can't you see they hold trumps? It's my guess that we are alive as long as he isn't annoyed—not one minute longer."

"Aren't you even going to try to fight? Where's that crap you used to spout about how you were a free man and planned to stay free?"

Hugh rubbed his hurt hand. "Duke, I won't argue. You start anything and you'll get us killed. That's how I size it up."

"So it was just crap," Duke said scornfully. "Well, I'm not making any promises."

"All right. Drop it."

"I'm not making promises. Just tell me this, Dad. How does it feel to be shoved around? Instead of shoving?"

"I don't like it."

"Neither did I. I've never forgotten it. I hope you get your bellyful."

Barbara said, "Duke, for heaven's sake, stop talking like a fool!"

Duke looked at her. "I'll shut up. Just one thing. Where *did* you get that baby in you?"

Barbara did not answer. Hugh said quietly, "Duke, if we get out of this, I promise you a beating."

"Any time, old man."

They quit talking. Barbara reached out and patted Hugh's ankle. Five men gathered around the pile of household objects, looking them over. A man came up and gave them an order; they dispersed. He looked at the chattels himself, then peered into the shelter and went inside.

Hugh heard a sound of water, saw a brown wave rushing down the stream bed. Barbara raised her head. "What's that?"

"Our dam is gone. It doesn't matter."

After a long time, Joe came out of the pavilion alone. He came up to Hugh and said, "Well, here's the scoop, as nearly as I got it. Not too near, maybe; he speaks a patois and neither of us is fluent. But here it is. We're trespassers, this is private land. He figured we were escaped prisoners—the word is something else, not French, but that's the idea. I've convinced him—I think I have—that we are innocent people here through no fault of our own.

"Anyhow, he's not sore, even though we are technically criminals—trespass, and planting things where farms aren't supposed to be and building a dam and a house and things like that. I think everything is going to be all right—as long as we do as we're told. He finds us interesting—how we got here and so forth."

Joe looked at Barbara. "You remember your theory about parallel universes?"

"I guess I was right. No?"

"No. This part is as confused as can be. But one thing is certain. Barbara, Hugh—Duke—get this! This is our own world, right here."

Duke said, "Joe, that's preposterous."

"You argue with him. He knows what I mean by the

United States, he knows where France is. And so forth. No question about it."

"Well . . ." Duke paused. "As may be. But what about this? *Where's my mother?* What's the idea of leaving her with that savage?"

"She's all right, she's having lunch with him. And enjoying it. Let it run easy, Duke, and we're going to be okay, I think. Soon as they finish lunch we'll be leaving."

Somewhat later Hugh helped Barbara into one of the odd flying machines, then mounted into one himself, behind the pilot. He found the seat comfortable and, in place of a safety belt, a field of that quicksand enclosed his lower body as he sat down. His pilot, a young Negro who looked remarkably like Joe, glanced back, then took off without noise or fuss and joined the re-forming rectangle in the air. Hugh saw that perhaps half the cars had passengers; they were whites, the pilots were invariably colored, ranging from as light brown as a Javanese to as sooty black as a Fiji Islander.

The car Hugh was in was halfway back in the outside starboard file. He looked around for the others and was only mildly surprised to see Grace riding behind the boss, in the front rank, center position. Joe was behind them, rather buried in cats.

Off to his right, two cars had not joined up. One hovered over the pile of household goods, gathered them up in a nonexistent cargo net, moved away. The second car was over the shelter.

The massive block lifted straight up without disturbing the shack on its roof. The small car and its giant burden took position fifty feet off the starboard side. The formation moved forward and gathered speed but Hugh felt no wind of motion. The car flanking them seemed to have no trouble keeping up. Hugh could not see the other loaded car but assumed that it was on the port side.

The last he saw of their home was a scar where the shelter had rested, a larger scar where Barbara's farm had been, and a meandering track that used to mark an irrigation ditch.

He rubbed his sore hand, reflecting that the whole

thing had been a gross abuse of coincidence. It offended him the way thirteen spades in a putatively honest deal would offend him. He pondered a remark Joe had made before they loaded: "We were incredibly lucky to have encountered a scholar. French is a dead language—'*une langue perdue*,' he called it."

Hugh craned his neck, caught Barbara's eye. She smiled.

11

Memtok, Chief Palace Domestic to the Lord Protector of the Noonday Region, was busy and happy—happy because he was busy, although he was not aware that he was happy and was given to complaining about how hard he had to work, because, as he put it, although he commanded eighteen hundred servants there were not three who could be trusted to empty a slop jar without supervision.

He had just completed a pleasant interview chewing out the head chef; he had suggested that the chef himself, old and tough as he was, nevertheless would make a better roast than the meat the chef had sent in to Their Charity the evening before. One of the duties that Memtok assumed personally was always to sample what his lord ate, despite risk of poison and despite the fact that Their Charity's tastes in cuisine were not his own. It was one of the innumerable ways in which Memtok gave attention to details, diligence that had brought him, still in his prime, to his present supreme eminence.

The head chef had grumbled and Memtok had sent him away with a taste of the lesser whip to remind him that cooks were not that hard to find. Then he had turned happily to his paper work.

There were stacks of it, as he had just completed moving the household from the Palace to the Summer Palace—thirty-eight of the Chosen but only four hundred and sixty-three servants; the summer residence was run with a skeleton staff. The twice-yearly move involved a wash of paper work—purchase orders, musters, inventories, vouchers, shipping lists, revisions of duty rosters, dispatches—and he considered advising his patron to have some likely youngster muted and trained as his clerk. But he rejected the idea; Memtok did not trust servants who could read and write and add, it gave them ideas even if they could not talk.

The truth was, Memtok loved his paper work and did not want to share it. His hands flew over the papers, checking figures, signing his symbol, okaying payments. He held his pen in an odd fashion, nested between the first three fingers of his right hand—this because he had no thumbs.

He did not miss them, could barely remember what it had been like to have them. Nor did he need them. He could handle a spoon, a pen, and a whip without them, and he had no need ever to handle anything else.

Far from missing his thumbs, he was proud of their absence; they proved that he had served his lord in both major capacities, at stud when he was younger and now these many years as a tempered domestic. Every male servant over fourteen (with scarce special exceptions) showed one alteration or the other; very few could exhibit both, only a few hundred on the entire Earth. Those few spoke as equals only to each other, they were an élite.

Someone scratched at the door. "Come!" he called out, then growled, "What do *you* want?" The growl was automatic but he really did dislike this servant for the best of reasons; he was not subject to Memtok's discipline. He was of a different caste, huntsmen, wardens, keepers, and beaters, and was subject to the Majordomo of the Preserve. The Majordomo considered himself to be of the same rank as the Chief Domestic, and nominally was. However, he had thumbs.

Memtok's greatest objection to the Summer Palace was that it put him in contact with these servants who had the unpardonable fault of not being under his orders. While it would take only a word to Their Charity to crack down on one of them, he disliked to ask, and while he could touch one of them without real fear of reprimand, the louse would be sure to complain to his boss. Memtok did not

162

believe in friction between executive servants. Bad for morale.

"Message from Boss. Rayed to tell you Their Charity on his way back. Says four savages with escort. Says you better tear up to the roof, take care of them. All."

" 'All'? Damn you, what do you mean 'All'? Why four savages? And in the Name of Uncle when are they arriving?"

"All," the servant insisted. "Message came in twenty minutes ago. I been looking all over for you."

"*Get out!*" The important part of the message was that Their Charity was arriving home instead of staying away overnight. Chef, Receptionist, Musical Director, Housekeeper, Groundskeeper, all heads of departments—he was phoning orders even as he thought. Four savages? Who cared about savages?

But he was on the roof and accepted their custody. He would have been there anyway, with the Lord Protector arriving.

When they arrived, Hugh had no chance to see Barbara. When he was released from the restraint of the "seat belt," he was confronted by a little baldheaded white man with a waspish face, an abrupt manner, and a whip. He was dressed in a white robe which reminded Hugh of a nightshirt, save that it had on the right shoulder the red and gold patch which Hugh had tentatively identified as the insigne of the big man, the boss. The emblem was repeated in rubies and gold on the chest of the little man as a medallion supported by a heavy gold chain.

The man looked him over with obvious distaste, then turned him and Duke over to another white man in a nightshirt. This man wore no medallion but did carry a small whip. Hugh rubbed his hand and resolved not to test whether this whip was as potent as the ornate one carried by the big boss.

Duke tested it. The angry little man gave instructions to his straw boss, and left. The straw boss gave an order; Hugh interpreted the tone and gesture as: "All right, you guys, get going"—and got going.

163

Duke didn't. The straw boss barely touched him on his calf; Duke yelped. He limped the rest of the way—down a ramp, into a very fast lift, then into a windowless, light, white-walled room which whiffed of hospitals.

Duke understood the order to strip without needing to be stimulated; he cursed but complied. Hugh merely complied. He was beginning to understand the system. The whips were used as spurs are used by a good rider, to exact prompt obedience but not to damage.

From there they were herded into a smaller room, where they were hit from all sides by streams of water. The operator was in a gallery above. He shouted at them, then indicated in pantomime that they were to scrub.

They scrubbed. The jets cut off, they were doused in liquid soap. They scrubbed again and were rinsed and were required to scrub still again, all to gestures that left no doubt as to how thorough a bath was expected. The jets got very hot and harsh, changed to cold and still harsher, were replaced by blasts of hot air.

It was too much like an automatic dishwasher, Hugh felt, but they ended up cleaner than they had been in months. An assistant to the bathmaster then plastered strips over their eyebrows, rubbed an emulsion on their scalps, into their scratchy beards, (neither had shaved that day), over their backs and chests and arms and legs, and finally into their pubic hair. Duke got another lesson in obedience before he submitted to this last. When, thereafter, they were subjected willy-nilly to enemas, he gritted his teeth and took it. The water closet was a whirlpool set in the floor. Their finger- and toenails were cut short.

After that they were bathed again. The eyebrow patches washed away. So did their hair. When they came out, they were both bald all over, save for eyebrows.

The bathmaster made them gargle, showing them what he wanted and spitting into the whirlpool. They gargled three times—a pleasant, pungent liquid—and when it was over, Hugh found that his teeth seemed cleaner than they had ever been in his life. He felt utterly clean, lively, glowing with well-being—but humiliated.

They were taken to another room and examined.

Their examiner wore the conventional white nightshirt and a small insigne on a thin gold chain but he needed no diplomas on the wall to show his profession. His bedside manner would never make him rich, Hugh decided; he had the air of military surgeons Hugh had known—not unkind but impersonal.

He seemed surprised by and interested in a removable bridge he found in Hugh's mouth. He examined it, looked in Hugh's mouth at the gaps it had filled, gave it to one of his assistants with instructions. The assistant went away and Hugh wondered if his chewing was going to be permanently hampered.

The physician took an hour or more over each of them, using instruments Hugh did not recognize—weight, height, and blood pressure were the only familiar tests. Things were done to them, too, none of them really unpleasant—no hypodermic needles, no knives. During this, Hugh's bridge was returned and he was allowed to put it back in.

But the tests and/or treatments often seemed to be indignities even though not painful. Once, when Hugh was stretched out on a table from which Duke had just been released, the younger man said, "How do you like it, Dad?"

"Restful."

Duke snorted.

The fact that both men had appendicitis scars seemed to interest the physician as much as the removable bridge. By acting he indicated a bellyache, then jabbed a thumb into McBurney's point. Hugh conveyed agreement—with difficulty, as nodding the head seemed to be a negative.

An assistant came in and handed the physician a contrivance which turned out to be another dental bridge. Hugh was required to open his mouth; the old one was again taken and the new one seated. It felt to Hugh's tongue as if he again had natural teeth there. The physician probed cavities, cleaned them and filled them —without pain but without anesthesia so far as Hugh was aware.

After that Hugh was suddenly "strapped" (an invisible

165

field) to a table, supine, and his legs were elevated. Another table was wheeled up and Hugh realized that he was being prepared for surgery—and with horror he was sure what sort. "Duke! Don't let them grab you! Get that whip!"

Duke hesitated too long. The therapist did not carry a whip; he merely kept one at hand. Duke lunged for it, the physician got it first. Moments later Duke was on his back, still gasping his agony at the punishment he had taken and having his knees elevated and spread. They both went on protesting.

The physician looked at them thoughtfully and the straw boss who had fetched them was called in. Presently the waspish little man with the big medallion strode in, looked the situation over, stormed out.

There was a long wait. The boss therapist filled in the time by having his assistants complete preparations for surgery and there was no longer the slightest doubt in Hugh's mind, or Duke's, as to what they were in for. Duke pointed out that it would have been better if they had fought—and died—earlier in the day, rather than wind up like this. As they would have fought, he reminded his father, if Hugh hadn't turned chicken.

Hugh didn't argue, he agreed. He tried to tell himself that his docility in being captured was on account of the women. It afforded him little comfort. True, he hadn't used his own much in recent years . . . and might never need them again. But, damn it, he was *used* to them. And it would be rough for Duke, young as he was.

After a long time the little man stormed back in, angrier than ever. He snapped an order; Hugh and Duke were released.

That ended it, save that they were rubbed all over with a fragrant cream. They were given a white nightshirt apiece, conducted through long bare passages and Hugh was shoved into a cell. The door was not locked but he could not open it.

In one corner was a tray, with dishes and a spoon. The food was excellent and some of it unidentifiable; Hugh ate with good appetite, scraping the dishes and drinking the thin beer with it. Then he slept on a soft part of the floor, having blanked his mind of worry.

He was prodded awake by a foot.

He was taken to another plain, windowless room, which turned out to be a schoolroom. Two short white men in nightshirts were there. They were equipped with props, the equivalent of a blackboard (it could be cleared instantly by some magic), patience—and a whip, for the lessons were "taught to the tune of a hickory stick." No error went unnoted.

They both could draw and both were imaginative pantomimists; Hugh was taught to speak.

Hugh discovered that his memory was sharpened by the stimuli of pain; he had little tendency to repeat a mistake. At first he was punished only for forgetting vocabulary, but as he learned, he grew to expect flicks of pain for errors in inflection, construction, idiom, and accent.

This Pavlovian treatment continued—if his mental records were correct—for seventeen days; he did nothing else and saw no one but his teachers. They worked in shifts; Hugh worked every possible minute, about sixteen hours a day. He was never allowed quite enough sleep although he never felt sleepy—he didn't dare—during lessons. Once a day he was bathed and given a clean nightshirt, twice a day he was fed, tasty food and plentiful, three times a day he was policed to the toilet. All other minutes were spent learning to speak, with ever-sharp awareness that any bobble would be punished.

But he learned how to duck punishment. A question, quickly put, would sometimes do. "Teacher, this one understands that there are protocol modes for each status rising and falling, but what this one in its ignorance lacks is knowledge of what each status is—being wholly without experience through the inscrutable ways of Uncle the Mighty—and also is sometimes not aware of the status assumed for teaching purposes by my charitable teacher and of the status this humble one is expected to assume in reply. More than that, this one does not know its own status in the great family. May it please its teacher."

The whip was put down and for the next hour he was

lectured. The problem was more involved than Hugh's question showed. The lowest status was stud. No, there was one lower: servant children. But since children were expected to make mistakes, it did not matter. Next higher was slut, then tempered servant—a category with subtle and unlimited gradations of rank so involved that speech of equals was used if the gradient was not clearly evident.

High above all servants were the Chosen, with unlimited and sometimes changing variations of rank, including those ritual circumstances in which a lady takes precedence over a lord. But that was not usually a worry; always use protocol rising mode. However—

"If two of the Chosen speak to you at once, which one do you answer?"

"The junior," Hugh answered.

"Why?"

"Since the Chosen do not make mistakes, this one's ears were at fault. The senior did not actually speak, for his junior would never have interrupted."

"Correct. You are a tempered gardener and you encounter a Chosen of the same rank as your lord uncle. He speaks. 'Boy, what sort of a flower is that?' "

"As Their Charity knows much better than this one can ever know, if this one's eyes are not mistaken, that plant may be a hydrangea."

"Good. But drop your eyes when you say it. Now about your status—" The teacher looked pained. "You haven't any."

"Please, teacher?"

"Uncle! I've tried to find out. Nobody knows but our Lord Uncle and they have not ruled. You're not a child, you're not a stud, you're not a tempered, you don't belong anywhere. You're a savage and you don't fit."

"But what protocol mode must I use?"

"Always the rising. Oh, not to children. Nor to sluts, no need to overdo it."

Except for changes in inflection caused by status, Hugh found the language simple and logical. It had no irregular verbs and its syntax was orderly; it probably had been tidied up at some time. He suspected, from words that he recognized—"simba," "bwana," "wazir," "étage," "trek," "oncle"—that it had roots in several African languages. But that did not matter; this was "Speech" and, according to his teachers, the only language spoken anywhere.

In addition to protocol modes, quite a chunk of vocabulary was double, one word being used down, its synonym although different in root used up. He had to know both—be able to recognize one and to use the other.

The pronunciation gave him trouble at first, but by the end of the week he could lip smack, click, make the fast glottal stop, and hear and say vowel distinctions he had never suspected existed. By the sixteenth day he was chattering freely, beginning to think in it, and the whip was rarely used.

Late next day the Lord Protector sent for him.

12

Although he had been bathed that day, Hugh was rushed through another bath, rubbed down with fragrant cream, and issued a fresh robe, before being whizzed to the lord's private apartments. There he was bounced past a series of receptionists close on Memtok's heels, and into a large and very sumptuous retiring room.

The lord was not there; Joseph and Dr.-Livingstone-I-Presume were. Joe called out, "Hugh! Wonderful!" and added to the Chief Domestic, "You may go."

Memtok hesitated, then backed away and left. Joe ignored him, slipped his arm in Hugh's, and led him to a divan. "Gosh, it's good to see you! Sit down, we'll talk until Ponse gets here. You look well." Doctor Livingstone checked Hugh's ankles, purred and stropped against them.

"I am well. 'Ponse'?" Hugh scratched the cat's ears.

"Don't you know his name? The Lord Protector, I mean. No, I guess you wouldn't. That's one of his names, one he uses *en famille*. Never mind, have they been treating you right?"

"I suppose so."

"They had better. Ponse gave orders for you to be pampered. Look, if you aren't treated okay, you tell me. I can fix it."

Hugh hesitated. "Joe, have you had one of those odd whips used on you?"

"Me?" Joe seemed astonished. "Of course not. Hugh, have they been abusing you? Peel off that Mother Hubbard and let me have a look."

Hugh shook his head. "There are no marks on me. I

haven't been hurt. But I don't like it."

"But if you've been stroked for no reason— Hugh, that's one thing that Ponse does not tolerate. He's a very humane sort of guy. All he wants is discipline. If anybody—anybody at all, even Memtok—has been cruel to you, somebody is going to catch it."

Hugh thought about it. He rather liked his teachers. They had worked hard and patiently and had been sparing of him once it became possible to talk instead of using the whip. "I haven't been hurt. Just reminded."

"I'm glad to hear it. Actually, Hugh, I didn't see how you could be. That quirt Ponse carries—you could kill a man with it at a thousand feet; it takes skill to use it gently. But those toys the upper servants carry, all they do is tingle and that's all they are supposed to do."

Hugh decided not to argue over what constituted a tingle; he had urgent things on his mind. "Joe, how are the others? Have you seen them?"

"Oh, they're all right. You heard about Barbara?"

"I haven't heard a damn thing! What about Barbara?"

"Slow down. Having her babies, I mean."

"She had her baby?"

" 'Babies.' Twin boys, identical. A week ago."

"How is she? *How is she?*"

"Easy, man! She's fine, couldn't be better. Of course. They are way ahead of us in medicine; losing a mother, or a baby, is unheard of." Joe suddenly looked sad. "It's a shame they didn't run across us months back." He brightened. "Barbara told me that she had intended to name it Karen, if it was a girl. When it turned out to be twin boys, she named one—the one five minutes the elder—'Hugh' and the other 'Karl Joseph.' Nice, eh?"

"I'm flattered. Then you've seen her. Joe, I've got to see her. Right away. How do I arrange it?"

Joe looked astonished. "But you *can't,* Hugh. Surely you know that."

"Why can't I?"

"Why, you're not tempered, that's why. Impossible."

"Oh."

"I'm sorry, but that's the way it is." Joseph suddenly

grinned. "I understand that you were almost made eligible by accident. Ponse laughed his head off at how close you came and how you and Duke yelped."

"I don't see the humor of it."

"Oh, Hugh, he simply has a robust sense of humor. He laughed when he told me about it. I didn't laugh and he decided that I have no sense of humor. Different people laugh at different things. Karen used to use a fake Negro dialect that set my teeth on edge, the times I overheard it. But she didn't mean any harm. Karen— Well, they just don't come any better, and you and I know it and I'll shut up about it. Look, if the vet had gone ahead, without orders, it would have cost him his hands; Ponse sent that word to him. Might have suspended the sentence—good surgeons are valuable. But his assumption was only natural, Hugh; both you and Duke are too tall and too big for stud. However, Ponse doesn't tolerate sloppiness."

"All right, all right. I still don't see the harm in my calling on Barbara and seeing her babies. *You* saw her. And you're not tempered."

Joe looked patiently exasperated. "Hugh, it's not the same thing. Surely you know it."

"Why isn't it?"

Joe sighed. "Hugh, I didn't make the rules. But I'm Chosen and you're not, and that's all there is to it. It's not my fault that you're white."

"All right. Forget it."

"Let's be glad that one of us is in a position to get us some favors. Do you realize that all of you would have been executed? If I hadn't been along?"

"The thought has crossed my mind. Lucky you knew French. And that *he* knows French."

Joe shook his head. "French didn't enter into it, it merely saved time. The point was that *I* was there . . . and the rest of you were excused of any responsibility on that account. What had to be settled then was the degree of my criminality, my neck was in a noose." Joe frowned. "I'm still not in the clear. I mean, Ponse is convinced but my case has to be reviewed by the Supreme Lord Proprietor;

it's his preserve—Ponse is just custodian. I could be executed yet."

"Joe, what in the world is there about it to cause you to talk about being *executed?*"

"Plenty! Look, if you four ofays—whites—had been alone, Ponse would have tried you just by looking at you. Two capital crimes and both self-evident. Escapees. Servants who had run away from their lord. Destructive trespass in a personal domain of the Supreme Proprietor. Open-and-shut on both counts and death for each of them. Don't tell me that wasn't the way it was because I know it and it took me long enough to make Ponse see it, using a language neither one of us knows too well. And my neck is still in jeopardy. However—" He brightened. "Ponse tells me that the Supreme Proprietor is years behind in reviewing criminal cases and that it has been more years since he last set foot on this preserve or even cruised over it . . . and that long before my case can come up there won't be a trace of destruction. They are putting the trees back and there's never an accurate count of bears and deer and other game. He tells me not to worry."

"Well, that's good."

"But maybe you think I haven't done some sweating over it! Just letting your shadow fall across the Supreme Lord Proprietor means your neck and sneezing in his presence is even worse—so you can figure for yourself that trespassing on land that is his personally is nothing to take lightly. But I shan't worry as long as Ponse says not to. He's been treating me as a guest, not as a prisoner. But tell me about yourself. I hear you've been studying the language. So have I—a tutor every day I've had time for it."

Hugh answered, "May it meet with their approval, this one's time has, as they know, been devoted to nothing else."

"Whoo! You speak it better than I do."

"I was given incentive," Hugh said, relapsing into English. "Joe, have you seen Duke? Grace?"

"Duke, no. I haven't tried to. Ponse has been away

173

most of the time and took me along; I've been terribly busy. Grace, yes. It's possible that you might see Grace. She's often in these apartments. That's the only way you could see her, of course. Right here. And in the presence of Ponse. Might happen. He's not a stickler for protocol. In private, I mean; he keeps up appearances in public."

"Hmm— Joe, in that case, couldn't you ask him to let me see Barbara and the twins? Here? In his presence?"

Joe looked exasperated. "Hugh, can't you understand that I'm just a guest? I'm here on sufferance. I don't have a single servant of my own, no money, no title. I said you *might* see Grace; I did not say you would. If you did, it would be because he had sent for you and it suited him not to send her out—not for *your* convenience. As for asking him to let you see Barbara, I can't. And that's *that!* I advise you not to, either. You might learn that his quirt doesn't just tingle."

"All I meant was—"

"Watch it! Here he comes."

Joe went to meet his host. Hugh stood with head bowed, eyes downcast, and waited to be noticed. Ponse came striding in, dressed much as Hugh had seen him before save that the helmet was replaced by a red skullcap. He greeted Joe, sat heavily down on a large divan, stuck out his legs. Doctor Livingstone jumped up into the lord's lap; he stroked it. Two female servants appeared from nowhere, pulled off his boots, wiped his feet with a hot towel, dried them, massaged them, placed slippers on them, and vanished.

While this was going on, the Lord Protector spoke to Joe of matters Hugh could not follow other than as words, but he noticed that the noble used the mode of equals to Joe and that Joe talked in the same fashion to him. Hugh decided that Joe must be in as solid as Doctor Livingstone. Well, Joe did have a pleasing personality.

At last the big man glanced at him. "Sit down, boy."

Hugh sat down, on the floor. The lord went on, "Have you learned Language? We're told that you have."

"May it please Their Charity, this one's time has been devoted singly to that purpose, with what inadequate results known to them far better than their servant would dare venture to estimate."

"Not bad. Accent could be crisper. And you missed an infix. How do you like the weather we've been having?"

"Weather is as Uncle the Mighty ordains it. If it pleases His favorite nephew, it cannot fail to make joyful one so humble as this servant."

"Quite good. Accent blurry but understandable. Work on it. Tell your teachers we said it. Now drop that fancy speech, I haven't time to listen to it. Equals speech, always. In private, I mean."

"All right. I—" Hugh broke off; one of the female servants had returned, to kneel in front of her lord with a drink on a tray.

Ponse glanced sharply at Hugh, then looked at the girl. "It? Doesn't count, it's a deaf mute. You were saying?"

"I was about to say that I couldn't have an opinion about weather because I haven't seen any since I got here."

"I suppose not. I gave orders for you to learn Language as quickly as possible and servants are inclined to follow instructions literally. No imagination. All right, you will walk outdoors an hour each day. Tell whoever is in charge of you. Any petition? Are you getting enough to eat? Are you being treated well?"

"The food is good. I'm used to eating three times a day but—"

"You can eat four times a day if you wish. Again, tell the one in charge of you. All right, now to other matters. Hugh— That's your name, isn't it?"

"Yes, Their Charity."

"Can't you hear? I said, 'Use equals mode.' My private name is Ponse. Use it. Hugh, if I had not picked you people up myself, were I not a scholar, and had I not seen with my own eyes the artifacts in that curious structure, your house, I would not have believed it. As it is, I must. I'm not a superstitious man. Uncle works in mysterious ways, but He doesn't use miracles . . . and I would not hesitate to repeat that in any temple on Earth, unorthodox as it sounds. But— How long does it come to, Joe?"

"Two thousand one hundred and three years."

"Call it two thousand. What's the matter, Hugh?"

"Uh, nothing, nothing."

"If you're going to throw up, go outside; I picked these rugs myself. As I was saying, you've given my scientists something to think about—and a good thing, too; they haven't turned out anything more important than a better mousetrap in years. Lazy scoundrels. I've told them to come up with a sensible answer, no miracles. How five people—or six—and a building of some mass could hurdle twenty centuries and never break an egg. Exaggeration. Joe tells me it broke some bones and other things. Speaking of bones, Joe tells me this won't please you—and it didn't please him—but I ordered my scientists to disturb some bones. Strontium sampling, that sort of thing; I suppose you've never heard of it. Clear proof that the cadaver had matured *before* the period of maximum radioactivity—— Look, I warned you about these rugs. Don't do it!"

Hugh gulped. (*"Karen! Karen! Oh, my darling!"*)

"Better now? Perhaps I should have told you that a priest was present, proper propitiations were made—exactly as if it had been one of the Chosen. Special concession, my orders. And when the tests were completed every atom was returned and the grave closed with proper rites."

"That's true, Hugh," Joseph said gravely. "I was there. And I put on fresh flowers. Flowers that will stay fresh, I'm told."

"Certainly they will," Ponse confirmed, "until they wear out from sheer erosion. I don't know why you use flowers but if there are any other rites or sacrifices necessary to atone for what may seem to you a desecration, just name it. I'm a broad-minded man; I'm aware that other times had other customs."

"No. No, best let it be."

"As you wish. It was done from scientific necessity. It seemed more reasonable than amputating one of your fingers. Other tests also kept my scientists from wiggling out of the obvious. Foods preserved by methods so ancient that I doubt if any modern food expert would know how to duplicate same—and yet the foods were edible. At least some servants were required to eat them; no harm resulted. A fascinating radioactivity gradient between upper and inner sides of the roof structure—I gave them a hint on that. Acting on information received from Joe, I ordered them to look for evidence that this event took place at the beginning of the East-West War that destroyed the Northern Hemisphere.

"So they found it. Calculations lead them to believe that the structure must have been near the origin of an atom-kernel explosion. Yet it was unhurt. That produced a theory so wild that I won't tire your ears with it; I've told them to go on working.

"But the best thing is the historical treasure. I am a man of history, Hugh; history, properly interpreted, tells everything. The treasure, of course, are those books that came along. I am not exaggerating when I say that they are my most precious possessions. There are only two other copies of the *Encyclopaedia Britannica* in the world today—and those are not this edition and are in such poor shape that they are curiosities rather than something a scholar can work with; they weren't cared for during the Turmoil Ages."

Ponse leaned back and looked happy. "But *mine* is in mint condition!"

He added, "I'm not discounting the other books. Treasures, all of them. Especially the *Adventures of Odysseus*, which is known only by reputation. I take it that the pictures date from the time of Odysseus too?"

"I'm afraid not. The artist was alive in my time."

"Too bad. They're interesting, nevertheless. Primitive art, stronger than we have now. But I exaggerated when I said that the books were my chiefest possession."

"Yes?"

"*You* are! There! Doesn't that please you?"

Hugh barely hesitated. "Yes. If true." (If it's true that I am your chattel, you arrogant bastard, I prefer being a valuable one!)

"Oh, quite true. If you had been speaking in protocol mode, you wouldn't have been able to phrase a doubt. I never lie, Hugh; remember that. You and— That other one, Joe?"

"Duke."

" 'Duke.' Although Joe speaks highly of your scholarship, not so highly of its. But let me explain. There are other scholars who read Ancient English. None in my household, true; since it is not a root language to any important degree, few study it. Nevertheless, scholars could be borrowed. But *none* such as yourself. You actually *lived* then; you'll be able to translate knowledgeably, without these maddening four and five interpretations of a single passage that disfigure most translations from ancient sources, all because the scholar doesn't really know what the ancient author was talking about. Lack of cultural context, I mean. And no doubt you will be able to supply explanations for things obscure to me and commonplace to you.

"Right? Right! So you see what I want. Start with the *Encyclopaedia Britannica*. Get busy today, translate it. Just scribble it out quickly, sloppy but fast. Someone else will pretty it up for my eyes. Understand? All right, go do it."

Hugh gulped. "But, Ponse, I can't write Language."

"What?"

"I was taught to speak; I haven't been taught to read and write."

Ponse blinked. "Memtok!"

The Chief Palace Domestic arrived with such speed that one might suspect that he was just outside the door. And so he had been—listening in on private conversation by means Memtok was certain were not known to the Lord Protector . . . inasmuch as Memtok was still breathing. Such measures were risky but he found them indispensable to efficient performance of his duties. At worst, it was safer than planting a slut in there who was not quite a deaf mute.

"Memtok, I told you it was to be taught to speak, read, and write Language."

Hugh listened, eyes downcast, while the Chief Domestic tried to protest that the order had never been given (it had not) but nevertheless had been carried out (obviously false), all without contradicting the Lord Protector (impossible to reconcile, inconceivable to attempt).

"Garbage," Ponse remarked. "I don't know why I don't put you up for adoption. You would look good in a coal mine. That pale skin would be improved by some healthy coal dust." He twitched his quirt and Memtok paled still more. "Very well, let it be corrected. It is to spend half of each day in learning to read and write, the other half in translating and in dictating same into a recorder. I should have thought of that; writing takes too long. Nevertheless, I want it to be able to read and write." He turned to Hugh. "Anything you can think of? That you need?"

Hugh started to phrase a request in the involved indirection which presumed nothing, as required by protocol mode, rising.

Ponse chopped him off. "Speak directly, Hugh. Memtok, close your ears. No ceremony needed in Memtok's presence, he is a member of my inner family, my nephew in spirit if not in the eyes of my senior sister. Spit it out."

Memtok relaxed and looked as beautific as his vinegar features permitted. "Well, Ponse, I need room to work. My cell is the size of that divan."

"Describe your needs."

"Well, I'd like a room with natural light, one with windows, say a third the size of this one. Working tables, bookshelves, writing materials, a comfortable chair—yes, and access to a toilet without having to wait; it interferes with my thinking otherwise."

"Don't you have that?"

"No. And I don't think it helps my thinking to be touched with a whip."

"Memtok, have you been whipping it?"

"No, my uncle. I swear."

"You would swear if you were caught with cream on your lip. Who has been?"

Hugh dared to interrupt. "I'm not complaining, Ponse. But those whips make me nervous. And I never know who can give me orders. Anybody, apparently. I haven't been able to find out my status."

"Mmm— Memtok, where do you have it in the Family?"

The head servant barely conceded that he had not been able to solve that problem.

"Let's solve it. We make it a department head. Mmm —Department of Ancient History. Title: Chief Researcher. Senior head of department, just below you. Pass the word around. I'm doing this to make clear how valuable this servant is to me . . . and anyone who slows up its work is likely to wind up in the stew. I suppose it will really be a one-servant department but you fill it out, make it look good, by transferring its teachers, and whoever looks out for its recorder and prepares the stuff for me, a cleaner or two, an assistant to boss them—I don't want to take up its valuable time on routine. A messenger. You know. There must be dozens of idlers around this house, eating their silly heads off, who would look well in the Department of Ancient History. Now have fetched a lesser whip and a lesser badge. Move."

In moments Hugh was wearing a medallion not much smaller than Memtok's. Ponse took the whip and removed something from it. "Hugh, I'm not giving you a charged whip, you don't know how to use it. If one of your loafers need spurring, Memtok will be glad to help. Later, when you know how, we'll see. Now— Are you satisfied?"

Hugh decided that it was not the time to ask to see Barbara. Not with Memtok present. But he was beginning to hope.

He and Memtok were dismissed together. Memtok did not object when Hugh walked abreast of him.

13

Memtok was silent while he led Hugh back down to servants' country; he was figuring out how to handle this startling development to his own advantage.

This savage's status had troubled the Chief Domestic from arrival. He didn't fit—and in Memtok's world everything had to fit. Well, now the savage had an assigned status; Their Charity had spoken and that was that. But the situation was not improved. The new status was so ridiculous as to make the whole belowstairs structure (the whole world, that is) a mockery.

But Memtok was shrewd and practical. The bedrock of his philosophy was: You can't fight City Hall, and his basic strategy in applying it was the pragmatic rule: When you can't beat 'em, you join 'em.

How could this savage's preposterous promotion be made to appear necessary and proper—and a credit to the Chief Domestic?

Uncle! The savage wasn't even tempered. Nor would he be. At least not yet. Later, possibly—it would make everything so much more tidy. Memtok had been amazed when Their Charity had postponed the obvious. Memtok hardly recalled his own tempering; his emotions and drives before that time were a thin memory—of someone else. There was no reason for the savage to have kicked up a fuss about it; tempering marked promotion into real living. Memtok looked forward to another half century of activity, power, gracious living—what stud could claim that?

But there it was. How to make it look good?

A Curiosity!—that's what the savage was. All great

lords possessed Curiosities; there had been times when visiting in his own caste that he had been embarrassed by the fact that his own lord took no interest in Curiosities; there were not even Siamese twins nor a two-headed freak in the whole household. Not even a flipper-armed dwarf. Their Charity was—let's admit it—too simple in his tastes for his high rank; sometimes Memtok was a little ashamed of him. Spending his time on scrolls and such when he should be upholding the pride of the house.

That lord in Hind— What title? Prince something or other silly. Never mind, he had that big cage where studs and sluts lived and mated with great apes, talked the same jabber—it wasn't Language—and you couldn't tell which was which save that some were hairy and some were smooth. *There* was a Curiosity worthy of a great household! That lord's chief domestic had declared by the Uncle that there were live crossbreeds from the experiment, hidden away where the priests couldn't object. It might be true, since it was a fact that despite official denial crossbreeds between servants and Chosen were possible—and did happen, even though designated bedwarmers were always sterile. But these accidents were never allowed to see the light of day.

A Curiosity, that was the angle. An untempered who was nevertheless a servant executive. A Famous Scholar who had not even been able to speak Language when he was almost as old as Memtok. A man out of nowhere. From the stars. Everybody knew that there were men somewhere in the stars.

Probably a miracle . . . and the temples were investigating and any year now this household would be famous for its unique Curiosity. Yes. A word here, a word there, a veiled hint—

"Hugh," Memtok said cordially. "May I call you 'Hugh'?"

"What? Why, certainly!"

"You must call me 'Memtok.' Let's stroll a bit and pick out space for your departmental headquarters. You would like a sunny place, I understand. Perhaps rooms facing the gardens? And do you want your personal quarters opening off your headquarters? Or would you rather have them elsewhere so that you can get away from it all?" The latter, Memtok decided. Roust out the head gardener and the studmaster and give the savage *both* their quarters—that would make everyone understand how important this Curiosity was. . . . and get both of them sore at the savage, too. He'd soon realize who was his friend. Memtok, namely, and nobody else. Besides, the gardener had been getting uppity, implying that his work didn't come under the Chief Domestic. A touching up was what he needed.

Hugh said, "Oh, I don't need anything fancy."

"Come, come! We want you to have every facility. I wish *I* could get away from it all sometimes. But I can't—problems, problems, problems, every minute of the day; some people have to have all their thinking done for them. It will be a treat to have a man of the mind among us. We'll find you cozy quarters, plenty of room for you and your valet. But separate." Valet? Was there a tempered young buck around, well housebroken and biddable, who could be depended on to report everything and keep his mouth shut? Suppose he had his sister's eldest son tempered now, would the lad shape up in time?

And would his sister see the wisdom in it? He had great hopes for **the boy.** Memtok was coldly aware that he would have to go someday—though not for many years—and **he was** determined that his heir should succeed to his **high office.** But it would take planning, and planning could never start too soon. If his sister could be made to see it—

Memtok led Hugh through crowded passsageways; servants scurried out of the way wherever they went—save one who stumbled and got tingled for his awkwardness.

"My!" said Hugh. "This is a big building."

"This? Wait till you see the Palace—though no doubt it is falling to rack and ruin, under my chief deputy. Hugh, we use only a quarter of the staff here. There is no formal entertaining, just garden parties. And only a handful of guests. In the city the Chosen are always coming and going. Many a time I am rooted out of bed in the night to open apartments for some lord and his ladies without a moment's warning. And that is where planning counts. To be able to open the door of a guest-wing flat and know—*know*, mind you, without looking—that beds are freshly perfumed, refreshments waiting, everything spotless, music softly playing."

"That must take real staff work."

"Staff work!" Memtok snorted. "I wish I could agree. What it takes is for me to inspect every room, every night, no matter how tired I am, before I go to bed. Then stay up to see that mistakes are corrected, not depend on their lies. They're all liars, Hugh. Too much 'Happiness.' Their Charity is generous; he never cuts down on the ration."

"I've found the food ample. And good."

"I didn't say food, I said 'Happiness.' I control the food and I don't believe in starving them, not even as punishment. A tingle is better. They understand that. Always remember one thing, Hugh; most servants don't really have minds. They're as thoughtless as the Chosen—not referring to Their Charity of course; I would never criticize my own patron. I mean Chosen in general. You understand." He winked and gave Hugh a dig in the ribs.

"I don't know much about the Chosen," Hugh admitted. "I've hardly laid eyes on them."

"Well . . . you'll see. It takes more than a dark skin to make brains no matter what they teach in temple. Not that I expect you to quote me nor would I admit it if you did. But— Who do you think runs this household?"

"I haven't been here long enough to express opinions."

"Very shrewd. You could go far if you had ambition. Let me put it this way. If Their Charity goes away, the household goes on smoothly as ever. If I am away, or dare to fall sick— Well, I shudder to think of it." He gestured with his whip. "*They* know. You won't find them scurrying that fast to get out of *his* way."

Hugh changed the subject. "I did not understand your remark about a 'ration of Happiness.'"

"Haven't you been receiving yours?"

"I don't know what it is."

"Oho! One bullock gets you three that it has been issued but never got as far as you. Must look into that. As to what it is, I'll show you." Memtok led him up a ramp and out onto a balcony. Below was the servants' main dining hall, crowded with three queues. "This is issue time—studs at a different hour, of course. They can have it as drink, in chewing form, or to smoke. The dosage is the same but some say that smoking it produces the keenest happiness."

Memtok used words not in Hugh's vocabulary; Hugh told him so. Memtok said, "Never mind. It improves the appetite, steadies the nerves, promotes good health, enhances all pleasures—and wrecks ambition. The trick is to be able to take it or leave it alone. I never took it regularly even when I was at stud; I had ambition. I take it now only on feast days or such—in moderation." Memtok smiled. "You'll find out tonight."

"I will?"

"Didn't I tell you? Banquet in your honor, just after evening prayer."

Hugh was hardly listening. He was searching the far queue, trying to spot Barbara.

Memtok sent the Chief Veterinarian and the Household Engineer as an escort of honor for Hugh. Hugh was mildly embarrassed at this attention from the physician and surgeon in view of the helpless posture he had been in the last time he had seen the man. But the veterinarian was most cordial.

Memtok headed the long table with Hugh on his right. Twenty department heads were seated; there was one lower servant standing behind each guest and endless streams coming in and out from kitchen and pantry. The banquet room was beautiful, its furnishings lavish, and the feast was sumptuous and endless; Hugh wondered what a meal of the Chosen must be like if their upper servants ate this way.

He soon found out, in part. Memtok was served twice, once from the tasty dishes everyone shared, again from another menu. These dishes he sampled, using separate plates, but rarely did more than taste. Of the regular menu he ate sparingly and sometimes passed up dishes.

He noticed Hugh's glance. "The Lord Protector's dinner. Try it. At your own risk, of course."

"What risk?"

"Poison, naturally. When a man is over a hundred years old his heir is certain to be impatient. To say nothing of business competitors, political rivals, and subverted friends. Go ahead; the taster tries it half an hour before Their Charity—or I—touches it, and we've lost only one taster this year."

Hugh decided that his nerve was being tested; he tried a spoonful.

"Like it?" asked the Chief Domestic.

"Seems greasy to me."

"Hear that, Gnou? Our new cousin is a man of taste. Greasy. Someday you'll be fried in your own grease, I fear. The truth is, Hugh, that we eat better than the Chosen do . . . although courses are served more elaborately in the Grand Hall, of course. But I am a gourmet who appreciates artistry; Their Charity doesn't care what it is as long as it doesn't squeal when he bites it. If the sauces are too elaborate, the spices too exotic, he'll send it back with a demand for a slice of roast, a hunk of bread, and a pitcher of milk. True, Gnou?"

"You have said it."

"And frustrating."

"Very," admitted the chef.

"So Cousin Gnou's best cooks work for us, and the Chosen struggle along with ones whose chief skill lies in getting a bird's skin back on without ruffling the feathers. Cousin Hugh, if you will excuse me, I must lift up to the Grand Hall and attempt by proper ceremony to make Cousin Gnou's pièce de résistance seem better than it is. Don't believe what they tell you about me while I'm gone—regrettably it's all true." He exposed his teeth in what must have been a smile and left.

No one spoke for a while. Finally someone—Hugh thought it was the transportation master but he had met too many—said, "Chief Researcher, what household were you with before you were adopted, may one ask?"

"One may. House of Farnham, Freeholder Extraordinary."

"So. I am forced to admit that the title of your Chosen is new to me. A new title, perhaps?"

"Very old," Hugh answered. "Extremely ancient and granted directly by Uncle the Mighty, blessed be His Name. The rank is roughly that of king, but senior to it."

"Really?"

Hugh decided to drop that shovel for a wider one. In earlier conversation he had learned that Memtok knew a great deal about many things—but almost nothing about such trivia as history, geography, and matters outside the household. And from his Language lessons he knew that a servant who could read and write was rare, even among executives, unless the skill was necessary to his duties. Memtok had told him proudly that he had petitioned the opportunity while he was still at stud and had labored at it to the amusement of the other studs. "I had my eyes on the future," he had told Hugh. "I could have had five more years, probably ten, at stud—but as soon as I could read, I petitioned to be tempered. So I had the last laugh—for where are they now?"

Hugh decided on the very widest shovel; a big lie was always easier to sell. "The title is unbroken for three thousand years in House Farnham. The line remained intact by direct intervention of the Uncle right through Turmoil and Change. Because of its Divine origin its holder speaks to the Proprietor as an equal, 'thee' and 'thou.' " Hugh drew himself up proudly. "And *I* was factotum-in-chief to Lord Farnham."

"A noble house indeed. But 'factotum-in-chief? We don't use that designation here. A domestic?"

"Yes and no. The chief domestic works under the factotum."

The man almost gasped. "And so," Hugh went on, "do *all* servant executives, domestic or not—business, political, agrarian, everything. The responsibility is wearing."

"So I should imagine!"

"It is. I was growing old and my health was failing—I

187

suffered a temporary paralysis of my lower limbs. Truthfully I never like responsibility, I am a scholar. So I petitioned to be adopted and here I am—scholar to a Chosen of similar scholarly tastes . . . a fitting occupation for my later years."

Hugh realized that he had stretched one item too far; the veterinarian looked up. "This paralysis, I noted no signs of it."

(Damn it, doctors never cared about anything but their specialty!) "It came on me suddenly one morning," Hugh said smoothly, "and I haven't been troubled by it since. But to a man of my years it was a warning."

"And what are your years? Professional interest, of course. One may ask?"

Hugh tried to make the snub as direct as some he had heard Memtok pass out. "One may *not*. I'll let you know when I need your services. But," he added, to soothe the smart, "it would be fair to say that I was born some years earlier than Their Charity."

"Astonishing. From your physical condition—quite good, I thought—I would have judged you to be no more than sixty, at most."

"Blood will tell," Hugh said smugly. "I am not the only one of my bloodline to live a very long time."

He was saved from further evasions by the return of Memtok. Everyone stood up. Hugh didn't notice in time, so he remained seated and brazened it out. If Memtok resented it, he did not let it show. He clapped Hugh on the shoulder as he sat down. "No doubt they've told you how I eat my own young?"

"I was given the impression of a happy family presided over by a beloved uncle."

"Liars, all of them. Well, I'm through for the evening—until some emergency. Their Charity knows that we are welcoming you; he commanded me not to return to the Grand Hall. So now we can relax and be merry." The Chief Domestic tapped his goblet with a spoon. "Cousins and nephews, a toast to our newest cousin. Possibly you heard what I said—the Lord Protector is pleased at our modest effort to make Cousin Hugh feel at home in Their

188

Family. But I am sure that you already guessed that . . . since one cannot miss that Cousin Hugh carries, not a least whip, but a lesser whip exactly like mine!" Memtok smiled archly. "Let us trust that he will never need to use it."

Loud applause greeted the boss's brilliant sally. He went on solemnly, "You will know that not even my chief deputy carries such authority, much less the ordinary department head . . . and from that I am sure you conclude that a hint from Cousin Hugh, Chief Researcher and Aide in Scholarship to Their Charity by direct appointment—a hint from him is an order from me—so don't let me have to make it a direct order.

"And now the toasts! All cousins together and let Happiness flow freely . . . so let the junior among us give the first toast. Who claims it, who claims it?"

The party got rowdy. Hugh noted that Memtok drank sparingly. He remembered the warning and tried to emulate him. It was impossible. The Chief Domestic could drop out of any toast, merely raise his glass, but Hugh as guest of honor felt compelled to drink them all.

Some unknown time later Memtok led him back to his newly acquired, luxurious quarters. Hugh felt drunk but not unsteady—it was just that the floor was so far away. He felt illuminated, possessed of the wisdom of the ages, floating on silvery clouds, and soaked through with angelic happiness. He still had no idea what was in Happiness drinks. Alcohol? Maybe. Betel nut? Mushrooms? Probably. Marijuana? It seemed certain. He must write down the formula while it was fresh in his mind. This was what Grace should have had! He must— But of course, she *did* have it now. How very nice! Poor old Grace— He had never understood her—all she needed was a little Happiness.

Memtok took him into his bedroom. Sleeping across the foot of his lovely new bed was a female creature, blond and cuddly.

Hugh looked down at her from about a hundred-foot elevation and blinked. "Who *she?*"

"Your bedwarmer. Didn't I say?"

"But—"

"It's quite all right. Yes, yes, I know you are technically a stud. But you can't harm her; this is what she is for. No danger. Not even altered. A natural freemartin."

Hugh turned around to discuss it, wheeling slowly because of his great width and high sail area. Memtok was gone. Hugh found that he could just make it to the bed. "Move over, kitten," he muttered, and fell asleep.

He overslept but the kitten was still there; she had his breakfast waiting. He looked at her with unease—not because he had a hangover; he did not. Apparently Happiness did not exact such payments. He felt physically strong, mentally alert, and morally straight—and very hungry. But this teen-ager was an embarrassment.

"What's your name, kitten?"

"May it please them, this one's name is of such little importance that whatever they please to call it will be a boon."

"Cut it, cut it! Use equals speech."

"I don't really have a name, sir. Mostly they just say, 'Hey, you.'"

"All right, I'll call you 'Kitten.' Does that suit you? You look like a kitten."

She dimpled. "Yes, sir. It's ever so much nicer than 'Hey, you.'"

"All right, your name is 'Kitten.' Tell everybody and don't answer to 'Hey, you.' Tell them that is official because the Chief Researcher says so and if anybody doubts it, tell them to check with the Chief Domestic. If they dare."

"Yes, sir. Thank you, sir. Kitten, Kitten, Kitten," she repeated as if memorizing it, then giggled. "Pretty!"

"Good. Is that my breakfast?"

"Yes, sir."

He ate in bed, offering her bits, and discovered that she expected to be fed, or at least allowed to eat. There was enough for four; between them they ate enough for three. Then he learned that she expected to assist him in the bathroom; he put a stop to that.

Later, ready to go to his assigned duties, he said to her, "What do you do now?"

"I go back to sluts' quarters, sir, as soon as you release me. I come back at bedtime—whatever time you say."

He was about to tell her that she was charming and that he almost regretted passing out the night before but that he did not require her services on future— He stopped. An idea had hit him. "Look. Do you know a tall slut named Barbara? Oh, this much taller than you are. She was adopted something over two weeks ago and she had babies, twin boys, about a week ago."

"Oh, yes, sir. The savage."

"That's the one. Do you know where she is?"

"Oh, yes, sir. She's still in lying-in quarters. I like to go in there and look at the babies." She looked wistful. "It must be nice."

"Uh, yes. Can you take a message to her?"

Kitten looked doubtful. "She might not understand. She's a savage, she can't talk very well."

"Mmm— Damn. No, maybe it's a help. Wait a moment." His quarters were equipped with a desk; he went to it, got one of those extraordinary pens—they didn't stain and didn't wear out and appeared to be solid—found a piece of paper. Hastily he wrote a note, asking Barbara about herself and the twins, reporting his odd promotion, telling her that soon, somehow, he would see her—be patient, dear—and assuring her of his undying devotion.

He added a P.S. "The bearer of this note is 'Kitten'—if the bearer is short, blond, busty, and about fourteen. She is my bedwarmer—which means nothing and you've got an evil mind, wench! I'm going to hang onto her because she is a way—the *only* way, it would appear—for me to communicate with you. I'll try to write every day, I'll darn well expect a note from you every day. If you can. And if anybody does *anything* you don't like, tell me and I'll send you his head on a platter. I think. Things are looking up. Plenty of paper and a pen herewith. Love, love, love—H.

"P.P.S.—go easy on 'Happiness.' It's habit-forming."

He gave the girl the note and writing materials. "You

know the Chief Domestic by sight?"

"Oh, yes, sir. I've warmed his bed. Twice."

"Really? I'm amazed."

"Why, sir?"

"Well, I didn't think he would be interested."

"You mean because he's tempered? Oh, but several of the executives like to have a bedwarmer anyhow. I like it better than being sent upstairs; it's less trouble and you get lots more sleep. The Chief Domestic doesn't usually send for a bedwarmer, though—it's just that he checks us and teaches us manners before we are allowed to serve upstairs." She added, "You see, he knows all about it; he used to be a stud, you know." She looked at Hugh with innocent curiosity. "Is it true what they say about you? May one ask?"

"Uh . . . one may not."

"I'm sorry, sir." She looked crushed. "I didn't mean any harm." She glanced fearfully at his whip, dropped her eyes.

"Kitten."

"Yes, sir."

"See this whip?"

"Uh, *yessir!*"

"You will never, never, never feel my whip. That's a promise. Never. We're friends."

Her face lit up and she looked angelically beautiful instead of pretty. "Oh, thank you, sir!"

"Another thing. The only whip you need fear from now on is the Chief Domestic's—so stay out of his way. Anyone else—any 'least whip'—you tell him, or her, that this lesser whip is what he'll get if he touches you. Tell him to check with the Chief Domestic. Understand me?"

"Yes, sir." She looked smugly happy.

Too smug, Hugh decided. "But you stay out of trouble. Don't do anything to deserve a tingle—or I might turn you over to the Chief Domestic for a real tingling, the sort he is famous for. But as long as you work for me, don't allow anyone but him to tingle you. Now git and deliver that. I'll see you tonight, about two hours after evening prayer. Or come earlier if you are sleepy, and go to bed."

Must remember to have a little bed put here for her, he reminded himself.

Kitten touched her forehead and left. Hugh went to his office and spent a happy day learning the alphabet and dictating three articles from the *Britannica*. He found his vocabulary inadequate, so he sent for one of his teachers and used the man as a dictionary. Even so, he found it necessary to explain almost endlessly; concepts had changed.

Kitten went straight to the Chief Domestic's office, made her report, turned over the note and writing materials. Memtok was much annoyed that he held in his hand what might be important evidence—and no way to read it. It did occur to him that that other one—Duke? Juke? Some such—might be able to read these hen scratches. But not likely, of course, and even under tingling there would be no certainty that Juke would translate honestly, and no way to check on him.

Asking Joe never crossed his mind. Nor did asking Their Charity's new bedwarmer. But the impasse had one intriguing aspect. Was it possible that this savage slut actually could *read*? And perhaps even essay to write a reply?

He stuck the note in his copier, gave it back to the girl. "All right, your name is Kitten. And do exactly as he tells you about not letting yourself be tingled—and be sure to gossip about it; I want it known all over. But get this—" He gave Kitten the gentlest of reminders; she jumped. *"This* whip is waiting for you, if you make any mistakes."

"This one hears and obeys!"

Hugh returned from the executives' dining room rather late; he had sat around and gossiped. He found Kitten asleep in his bed and remembered that he had forgotten to ask for another bed for her.

Clutched in her hand was a folded paper. Gently he worked it out without waking her:

Darling!

How utterly wonderful to see your handwriting! I knew from Joe that you were safe, hadn't heard about your promotion, didn't know whether you knew about the twins. First about them— They are thriving, they both look like their papa, both have his angelic disposition. Six pounds each at birth is my guess, but, although they were weighed, weights here mean nothing to me. Me? I'm a prize cow, dearest, no trouble at all—and the care I received (and am receiving) is fantastically good. I started to labor, was given something to drink, never hurt again although I remember all details of having two babies—as if it had happened to somebody else. So trouble free and actually *pleasant* that I'd be willing to do it every day. And would, if the rewards were as nice as little Hugh and Karl Joseph.

As for the rest, boring except for our fine boys, but I'm learning the language as fast as I can. And somebody should tell the Borden Company about me—which is good, as our scamps are greedy eaters. I'm even able to help out the girl in the next bed, who is short on milk. Just call me Elsie.

I'll be patient. I'm not surprised at your new honors; I expect that you'll be bossing the place in a month. I have confidence in my man. My husband. Such a beautiful word—

As for Kitten, I don't believe your Boy Scout assertions, my lecherous darling; your record shows that you take advantage of innocent young girls. And she's awfully cute.

Seriously, dearest, I know how noble you are and I didn't have an evil-minded thought. But I would not blame you if your nobility slipped—especially as I've picked up enough words to be aware of her odd category in this strange place. I mean, Kitten is not vulnerable and can't go set. If you *did* slip, I would not be jealous—not much, anyhow—but I would not want it to become a habit. Not to the exclusion of me, at least; my hormones are rearranging themselves very rapidly. But I *don't* want you to get rid of her when she is our only way of communicating. Be nice to her; she's a nice kid. But you're always nice to everyone.

I will write every day—and I will cry into my pillow and be worried to death any day I don't hear from you.

My love forever and forever,

B

P.S. The smear is little Hugh's right footprint.

Hugh kissed the letter, then got into bed, clutching it. Kitten did not wake.

14

Hugh found learning to read and write Language not difficult. Spelling was phonetic, a sign for every sound. There were no silent letters and never any question about spelling or pronunciation. Accent was on the penultima unless marked; the system was as free from traps as Esperanto. He could sound out any word as soon as he had learned the 47-letter alphabet, and, with thought, he could spell any word he could pronounce.

Writing and printing were alike, cursive, and a printed page looked like one written by a skilled penman. He was not surprised to find that it looked like Arabic and a search in the *Britannica* confirmed that the alphabet must have derived from Arabic of his time. Half a dozen letters had not changed; some were similar although changed. There were many new letters to cover the expansion into a system of one sound, one sign—plus letters for sounds XXth century Arabic had never used. Search in the *Britannica* convinced him that Arabic, French, and Swahili were the main roots of Language, plus Uncle alone knew what else. He could not confirm this; a dictionary with derivations, such as he had been used to for English, apparently did not exist—and his teachers seemed convinced that Language had *always* been just as they knew it. The concept of change baffled them.

It was only of intellectual interest; Hugh knew neither Arabic, French, nor Swahili. He had learned a little Latin and less German in high school, and had struggled to learn Russian in his later years. He was not equipped to study the roots of Language, he was merely curious.

Nor did he dare spend time on it; he wanted to please Their Charity, butter him up so that he might, eventually, petition the boon of seeing Barbara—and that meant a flood of translated articles. Hugh worked very hard.

The second day after his elevation, Hugh asked for Duke, and Memtok sent for him. Duke was rather worn down—there were lines in his face—but he spoke Language. Duke spoke it not as well as his father and apparently had tangled more with his teachers; his mood seemed to oscillate between hopelessness and rebellion, and he limped badly.

Memtok made no objection to transferring Duke to the Department of Ancient History. "Glad to get rid of him. He's too monstrous big for stud, yet he doesn't seem to be good for anything else. Certainly, put him to work. I can't bear to see a servant lying around, eating his head off, doing nothing."

So Hugh took him. Duke looked over Hugh's private apartment and said, "Christ! You certainly managed to come up smelling like a rose. How come?"

Hugh explained the situation. "So I want you to translate legal articles and related subjects—whatever you can do best."

Duke shoved his fists together and looked stubborn. "You can stuff it."

"Duke, don't take that attitude. This is an opportunity."

"For you, maybe. What are you doing about Mother?"

"What can I do? I'm not allowed to see her, neither are you. You know that. But Joe assures me that she is not only comfortable and well treated, but happy."

"So he says. Or so you say he says. I want to see it myself. I damn well insist on it."

"Very well, insist on it. Go see Memtok about it. But I must warn you, I can't protect you from him."

"Rats. I know what that slimy little bastard would say—and what he would do." Duke scowled and rubbed

197

his injured leg. "It's up to you to arrange it. You've got such an unholy drag around here, the least you can do is use it to protect Mother."

"Duke, I don't have that sort of drag. I'm being pampered for the reason a race horse is pampered . . . and I have just as little to say about it as a race horse has. But I can cut you in on pampering if you cooperate—decent quarters, immunity from mistreatment, a pleasant place to work. But I can no more get you into women's quarters, or have Grace sent here, than I can go to the Moon. They have harem rules here, as you know."

"And you are content to sit here and be a trained seal for that ape, and neglect Mother? Count me out!"

"Duke, I won't argue. I'll assign you a room and send you a volume of the *Britannica* each day. Then it's up to you. If you won't work, I'll try to keep Memtok from knowing it. But I think he has spies all over the place."

Hugh let it go at that. At first he got no help out of Duke. But boredom worked where argument failed; Duke could not stand to be shut up in a room with nothing to do. He was not locked up but he did not venture out much because there was always the chance that he might run into Memtok, or some other whip-carrying upper servant, who might want to know what he was doing, and why—servants were expected to look busy even if they weren't, from morning prayer to evening prayer.

Duke began to produce translations and, with them, a complaint that he was short on vocabulary. Hugh was able to have assigned to him a tempered clerk who had worked in Their Charity's legal affairs.

But he rarely saw Duke—it seemed to be the only way they could stay out of arguments. Duke's output speeded up after the first week but fell off in quality—Duke had discovered the sovereign power of "Happiness."

Hugh considered warning Duke about the drug, decided against it. If it kept Duke contented, who was he to deny him this anodyne? The quality of Duke's translations did not worry Hugh; Their Charity had no way to judge— unless Joe rendered an opinion, which seemed unlikely. He

198

himself was not trying too hard to turn out good translations; "not good, but Wednesday" was the principle he used: Give the boss lucid copy in great quantity—and leave out the hard parts.

Besides, Hugh found that a couple of drinks of Happiness at dinner topped off the day. It allowed him to read Barbara's daily letter in a warm glow, write a cheerful answer for Kitten to carry back, then to bed and sound sleep.

But Hugh did not use much of it; he was afraid of the stuff. Alcohol, he reasoned, had the advantage of being a poison. It gave fair warning if one started drinking heavily. But this stuff exacted no such price; it merely turned anxiety, depression, worry, boredom, any unpleasant emotion, into an uncritical happy glow. Hugh wondered if it was principally methyl meprobamate? But he knew little chemistry and that little was two thousand years behind times.

As a member of the executive servants' mess Hugh could have all he wanted. But he noted that Memtok was not the only boss who used the stuff abstemiously; a man did not fight his way up in the servants' hierarchy by dulling himself with drugs—but sometimes a servant did get high up, then skidded to the bottom, unable to stand prosperity in the form of unrationed Happiness. Hugh never learned what became of them.

Hugh could even keep a bottle in his rooms—and that solved the problem of Kitten.

Hugh had decided not to ask for a bed for Kitten; he did not want to rub Memtok's nose in the fact that he was using the child only as a go-between to women's quarters. Instead he required the girl to make up a bed each night on the divan in his living room.

Kitten was very hurt by this. By now she was sure that Hugh could make better use of a bedwarmer and she regarded it as rebuke to her in her honorable capacity as comfort and solace—and it scared her. If her master did not like her, she might lose the best job she had ever had. (She did not dare report to Memtok that Hugh had no use

199

for her as a bedwarmer; she gave reports on every point but that.)

She wept.

She could not have done better; Hugh Farnham had been a sucker for women's tears all his life. He took her on his knee and explained that he liked her very much (true), that it was a sad thing but he was too old to appreciate a female bedmate (a lie), and that he slept badly and was disturbed by having anyone in bed with him (a half-truth)—and that he was satisfied with her and wanted her to go on serving him. "Now wipe your eyes and have a drink of this."

He knew that she used the stuff; she chewed her ration like bubble gum—chewing gum it was in fact; the powder was added to chicle. Most servants preferred gum because they could go dreamily through the day, chewing it while they worked. Kitten passed her empty days chewing it and chewed the played-out cud in Hugh's quarters after she learned he did not mind. So he did not hesitate to give her a drink.

Kitten went happily to bed and right to sleep, no longer worried that her master might get rid of her. That set a precedent. Each evening, half an hour before Hugh wanted the lights out, he would give her a short drink of it.

For a while he kept track of the level in the bottle. Kitten was often in his quarters when he was not, he knew how much she enjoyed it, and there were no locks in his quarters—his rank entitled him to locks but Memtok had carefully not told him.

He quit bothering when he was convinced that Kitten was not snitching it. In fact, Kitten would have been terrified at the thought of stealing from her master. Her ego was barely big enough for a mouse; she was less than nothing and knew it and had never owned anything, not even a name, until Hugh gave her one. Under his kindness she was beginning to be a person, but it was still the faintest flicker, anything could blow it out. She would no more have risked stealing from him than she would have risked killing him.

Hugh, half by intent, encouraged her confidence. She was a trained bath girl; he gave in and let her scrub his back and handle the nozzles for his bath, dress him, and take care of his clothes. She was a masseuse, too; he sometimes found it pleasant to have his head and neck rubbed after a day spent poring over the fine print or following the lines in a scroll reader—and she was pathetically anxious to do anything to make herself necessary.

"Kitten, what do you do in the daytime?"

"Why, nothing mostly. Sluts of my subcaste mostly don't have to work if they have night duty. Since I'm having duty every night I'm allowed to stay in the sleep room until midday. So I do, even if I'm not sleepy, because the slutmaster is likely to put one to work if he catches one just wandering around. Afternoons— Well, mostly I try to stay out of sight. That's best. Safest."

"I see. You can hide out in here if you like. Or can you?"

Her face lit up. "If you give me a pass, I can."

"All right, I will. You can watch television— No, it's not on at that hour. Mmm, you don't know how to read. Or do you?"

"Oh, no, sir! I wouldn't dare petition."

"Hmm—" Hugh knew that permission to learn to read could not be granted even by Memtok; it required Their Charity's permission and was granted only after investigation of the necessity. Furthermore, anything he did that was out of line jeopardized his thin chances of reunion with Barbara.

But— Damn it, a man had to be a man! "There are scrolls in here and a reader. Do you *want* to learn?"

"Uncle protect us!"

"Don't swear. If you *want* to—and can keep your pretty little mouth shut—I'll teach you. Don't look so damned scared! You don't have to decide now. Tell me later. Just don't talk about it. To anyone."

Kitten did not. It scared her not to report it, but she had a reflex for self-preservation and felt without knowing why that to report this would endanger her happy setup.

Kitten became substitute family life for Hugh. She sent him to work cheerful, greeted him with a smile when he came back, talked if he wanted to talk and never spoke unless spoken to. Most evenings she curled up in front of the television—Hugh thought of it as "the television" and it was in fact closed-circuit television under principles not known to him, in color, in three dimensions, and without lines.

It played every evening in the servants' main hall, from evening prayer until lights-out, to a packed house, and there were outlets in the apartments of executive servants. Hugh had watched it several evenings, expecting to gain insight into this strange society he must learn to live in.

He decided that one might as well try to study the United States by watching *Gunsmoke*. It was blatant melodrama, with acting as stylized as Chinese theater, and the favorite plot seemed to be that of the faithful servant who dies gloriously that his lord may live.

But it was only second in importance to Happiness in the morale of life belowstairs. Kitten loved it.

She would watch it, snapping her gum, and suppressing squeals of excitement, while Hugh read—then sigh happily when the program ended, accept her little drink of Happiness with profuse thanks and a touch of her forehead, and go quietly to sleep. Hugh sometimes went on reading.

He read a great deal—every evening (unless Memtok stopped in to visit) and half of every day. He begrudged the time he spent translating for Their Charity but never neglected it; it was the hopeful key to better things. He had found it necessary to study modern culture if he was to translate matters of ancient history intelligibly. The Summer Palace had a fair library; he was given access when he claimed necessity for his work—Memtok arranged it.

But his true purpose was not translation but to try to understand what had happened to *his* world to produce *this* world.

So he usually had a scroll in the reader, in his office, or in his living room. The scroll system of printing he found admirable; it mechanized the oldest form of book into a system far more efficient than bound leaves—drop the double cylinder into the reader, flip it on, and hold still. The letters raced across in front of his eyes several hundred feet at a whack, to the end of the scroll. Then the scroll flipped over and chased back the following line, which was printed upside down to the one just scanned.

The eye wasted no time flipping back and forth at stacked lines. But a slight pressure speeded the gadget up to whatever the brain could accept. As Hugh got used to the phonetics, he acquired speed faster than he had ever managed in English.

But he did not find what he was looking for.

Somewhere in the past the distinctions between fact, fiction, history, and religious writings seemed to have been rubbed out. Even when he got it clear that the East-West War that had bounced him out of his own century was now dated 703 B.C. (Before the Great Change), he still had trouble matching the world he had known with the "history" set forth in these scrolls.

The war itself he didn't find hard to believe. He had experienced only a worm's-eye view of the first hours but what the scrolls related matched the possibilities: a missile-and-bomb holocaust that had escalated in its first minutes into "brilliant first strike" and "massive retaliation" and smeared cities from Peiping to Chicago, Toronto to Smolensk; fire storms that had done ten times the damage the bombs did; nerve gas and other poisons that had picked up where fire left off; plagues that were incubating when the shocked survivors were picking themselves up and beginning to hope—plagues that were going strong when fallout was no longer deadly.

Yes, he could believe that. The bright boys had made it possible, and the dull boys they worked for had not only never managed to make the possibility unlikely but had never really believed it when the bright boys delivered what the dull boys ordered.

Not, he reminded himself, that he had believed in "Better red than dead"—or believed in it now. The aggression had been one-sided as hell—and he did not regret a megaton of the "massive retaliation."

But there it was. The scrolls said that it had killed off the northern world.

But how about the rest of it? It says here that the United States, at the time of the war, held its black population as slaves. Somebody had chopped out a century. On purpose? Or was it honest confusion and almost no records? There had been, he knew, a great book burning for two centuries during the Turmoil, and even after the Change.

Was it lost history, like Crete? Or did the priests like it better this way?

And since when were the Chinese classed as "white" and the Hindus as "black"? Yes, purely on skin color Chinese and Japanese were as light as the average "white" of his time, and Hindus were certainly as dark as most Africans—but it was not the accepted anthropological ordering of his day.

Of course, if all they meant was skin shade—and apparently that was what they did mean—he couldn't argue. The story maintained that the whites, with their evil ways, destroyed each other almost to the last man . . . leaving the innocent, charitable, merciful dark race—beloved by Uncle the Mighty—to inherit the Earth.

The few white survivors, spared by Uncle's mercy, had been succored and cherished as children and now again were waxing numerous under the benevolent guidance of the Chosen. So it read.

Hugh could see that a war which smeared North America, Europe, all of Asia except India, could kill off most whites and almost all Chinese. But what had happened to the white minority in South America, the whites of the Union of South Africa, and the Australians and New Zealanders?

Search as he would, Hugh could not find out. All that seemed certain was that the Chosen were dark whereas servants were palefaces—and usually small. Hugh and his son towered over the other servants. Contrariwise, the few Chosen he had seen were big men.

If present-day whites were descended from Australians, mostly—No, couldn't be, Aussies had not been runts. And those "Expeditions of Mercy"—were they slave raids? Or pogroms? Or, as the scrolls said, rescue missions for survivors?

The book burnings might account for these discrepancies. It wasn't clear to Hugh whether all books had been put to the torch, or possibly technical books had been spared—for it was clear that the Chosen had technology superior to that of his time; it seemed unlikely that they had started from scratch.

Or was it unlikely? All the technology of his own time that had amounted to a damn had been less than five hundred years old, most of it less than a hundred, and the most amazing parts less than a generation. Could the world have gone back to a dark ages, then pulled out of it and more, in two thousand years? Of course it could!

Either way, the Koran had been the only book officially exempt from the torch—and Hugh harbored a suspicion that the Koran had not been spared either. He had owned a translation of the Koran, had read it several times.

He wished now that he had put it into the shelter, for the Koran as he now read it in "Language" did not match his memory. For one thing, he had thought that Mahomet was a redheaded Arab; this "Koran" mentioned his skin color repeatedly, as black. And he was sure that the Koran was free of racism. This "improved" version was rabid with it.

Furthermore, this Koran had a new testament with a martyred Messiah. He had taught and had been hanged for it—religious scrolls were all marked with a gallows. Hugh did not object to a new testament; there had been time for a new revelation and religions had them as naturally as a cat has kittens. What he objected to was some revisionist working over the words of the Prophet, apparently to make them fit this new book. That wasn't fair, that was cheating.

The social organization Hugh found almost as puzzling.

He was beginning to get a picture of a complex culture, stable, even static—high technology, few innovations, smooth, efficient—and decadent. Church and State were one—"One Tongue, One King, One People, One God." The Lord Proprietor was sovereign and supreme pontiff and owned everything under Uncle's grant, and the Lords Protector such as Ponse were his bishops and held only fiefs. Yet there were plenty of private citizens (Chosen, of course—a white was not a person), shopkeepers, landowners, professional men, etc. A setup for an absolute totalitarian communism yet streaked through with what appeared to be private enterprise—Hell, there were even corporations if he understood what he was reading.

The most interesting point to Hugh (aside from the dismal fact that his own status was fixed by law and custom at zero) was the inheritance system. Family was everything, yet marriage was almost nothing—present but not important. Descent was through the female line—but power was exercised by males.

This confused Hugh until it suddenly fell into place. Ponse was Lord Protector because he was eldest son of an eldest daughter—whose oldest brother had been Lord Protector before Ponse. Ponse's heir therefore was his oldest sister's oldest son—title went down through mother and daughter endlessly, with power vested in the oldest brother of each female heir. It did not matter who Ponse's father was and it mattered even less what sons he had; none of them could inherit. Ponse inherited from his mothers' brother; his heir was his sister's son.

Hugh could see that, under this system, marriage would never be important—bastardy might be a concept so abstract as to be unrecognized—but *family* would be more important than ever. Women (of the Chosen) could never be downgraded; they were more important than males even though they ruled through their brothers—and Religion recognized this; the One God, Uncle the Mighty, had an elder sister, the Eternal Mamaloi . . . so sacred that she was not prayed to and her name was never used in cursing. She was just *there,* the Eternal Female Principle that gave all life and being.

Hugh had a feeling that he had read about this sort of descent before, uncle to nephew through the female line, so he searched the *Britannica*. He was surprised to discover that the setup had prevailed at one time or another in every continent and many cultures.

The Great Change had been when Mamaloi had at last succeeded—working indirectly, as always—in uniting all Her children under one roof and placing their Uncle in charge. Then She could rest.

Hugh's comment was: "And God help the human race!"

Hugh kept expecting Their Charity to send for him. But two months passed and he did not, and Hugh was beginning to fret that he would never have a chance to ask to see Barbara—apparently Ponse had no interest in him as long as he kept on grinding out translations. Translating the *Britannica* looked like a job for several lifetimes; he resolved to stir things up, so he sent one day's batch with a letter to Their Charity.

A week later the Lord Protector sent for him. Memtok came for Hugh, dancing with impatience but insisting that Hugh wash his armpits, rub himself with deodorant, and put on a clean robe.

The Lord Protector did not seem to care how Hugh smelled; he let him wait while he did something else. Hugh stood in silence . . . although Grace was present. She was lounging on a divan, playing with cats and chewing gum. She glanced at Hugh, then ignored him, save that her face took on a secret smile that Hugh knew well— He called it "canary that ate the cat."

Dr.-Livingstone-I-Presume greeted Hugh, jumping down, coming over and rubbing against his ankles. Hugh knew that he should ignore it, wait for the lord to recognize his presence—but this cat had been his friend a long time; he could not snub it. He bent down and stroked the cat.

The skies did not split, Their Charity ignored the breach.

Presently the Lord Protector said, "Boy, come here. What's this about making money from your translations?

What in Uncle gave you the notion I needed money?"

Hugh had got the notion from Memtok. The Chief Domestic had growled about how difficult it was to run things, with pennypinching from on high getting worse every year.

"May it please Their Charity, this one's opinions are of no value, it is true, but—"

"Cut the flowery talk, damn you!"

"Ponse, back where—when—I came from there never was a man so rich but what he needed more money. Usually the richer he was, the more he needed."

The lord grinned. " '*Plus ça change, plus c'est la même chose.*' Hugh, you aren't just sniffing Happiness. Things are the same now. Well? What's your idea? Spit it out."

"It seems to me that there are things in your encyclopaedia which might be turned to a profit. Processes and such that have been lost in the last two thousand years—but might be worth money now."

"All right, do it. The stuff you send up is satisfactory, what I've had time to read. But some of it is trivial. 'Smith, John, born and died—a politician who did nothing much and did that little poorly.' Know what I mean?"

"I think so, Ponse."

"All right, skip that garbage and dig me up four or five juicy ideas I can cash in on."

Hugh hesitated. Ponse said, "Well? Did you understand?"

"I think I need help. You see, I don't know anything really, except what goes on belowstairs. I thought Joe might help."

"How?"

"I understand that he has traveled with you, seen things. He is more likely to be able to pick out subjects that merit study. He could pick the articles, I will translate them, and you can judge whether there is anything to exploit. I can synopsize them, so that you needn't waste time wading through details if the subject doesn't merit it."

"Good idea. I'm sure Joe will be happy to help. All right, send up the encyclopaedia. All."

Hugh was dismissed so abruptly that he had no chance

tò mention Barbara. But, he reflected, he could not have risked it with Grace present.

He considered digging out Duke, telling him that his mother was fat and happy—both literally—but decided against it. He wasn't sure how pleased Duke would be with a truthful report. They didn't see eye to eye and that was that.

15

Joe sent down a volume every day for many days, with pages marked; Hugh slaved to keep up and to make useful translations. After two weeks Hugh was again sent for.

He expected a conference over some business idea. What he found was Ponse, Joe, and a Chosen he had never seen. Hugh instantly prepared to speak protocol mode, rising.

The Lord Protector said, "Come here, Hugh. Cut the cards. And don't start any of that tiresome formality, this is family. Private."

Hugh hesitantly approached. The other Chosen, a big dark man with a permanent scowl, didn't seem pleased. He was carrying his quirt and twitched it. But Joe looked up and smiled. "I've been teaching them contract, Hugh, and our fourth had to be away. I've been telling Ponse that you are the best player any where or when. So don't let me down."

"I'll try not to." Hugh recognized one deck of cards, they had once been his. The other deck appeared to be hand-painted and were beautiful. The card table was not from the shelter; fabulous hand craftsmanship had gone into it.

The cut made Hugh partner of the strange Chosen. Hugh tried not to show how nervous it made him, as his partner clearly did not like it. But the Chosen grunted and accepted it.

His partner's contract, at three spades—by a fluke distribution they made four. His partner growled, "Boy, you underbid, you wasted game. Don't let it happen again."

Hugh kept quiet and dealt.

On the next hand Joe and Ponse made five clubs. Hugh's partner was furious—at Hugh. "If you had led diamonds, we would have set them! *And* you washed out our leg. I warned you. Now I'm—"

"Mrika!" Ponse said sharply. "This is contract. Play it as such. And put that tickler down. The servant played correctly."

"It did not! And I'm damned if I care for letting it in the game anyhow. I can smell the rank, sharp stink of a buck servant no matter how much it's scrubbed. I don't think this one is scrubbed at all."

Hugh felt sweat breaking out in his armpits and flinched. But Ponse said evenly, "Very well, we excuse you. You may leave."

"That suits me!" The Chosen stood up. "Just one thing before I do— If you don't quit stalling, Their Mercy will let the North Star Protectorate—"

"Are you planning to put up the money?" Their Charity said sharply.

"Me? It's a Family matter. Not but what I wouldn't jump at the chance! Forty million hectares and most of it in prime timber? Of course I would! But I hardly have one bullock to jingle against another—and you know why."

"Certainly we know. You gamble."

"Oh, come now! A businessman has to take chances. You can't call it gambling when—"

"We do call it gambling. We do not object to gambling but we have a vast distaste for losing. If you must lose, you will do it with your own bullocks."

"But this isn't gambling, it's a sure thing—as well as getting us in solid with Their Mercy. The Family—"

"We decide what is good for the Family. Your turn will come soon enough. In the meantime we are as anxious to please the Lord Proprietor as you are. But not with bullocks the Family doesn't have in the treasury."

"You could borrow it. The interest would only come to—"

"You wanted to leave, Mrika. We note that you have left." Ponse picked up cards and began to shuffle.

211

The younger Chosen snorted and left.

Ponse laid out a solitaire game, started to play. Presently he said to Joe, "Sometimes that young man gets me so annoyed that I would happily change my will."

Joe looked puzzled. "I thought you could not disinherit him?"

"Oh, no!" Their Charity looked shocked. "Not even a peasant can do that. Where would we be if there were no stability here on Earth? I wouldn't dream of it, even if the law permitted it; he's my heir. I was just thinking of the servants."

Joe said, "I don't follow you."

"Why, you know— No, perhaps you don't. I keep forgetting that you didn't grow up among us. My will disposes of things personally mine. Not much—jewelry, scrolls, such. Value probably less than a million. Trivia. Except household servants. Just the household. I'm not talking about servants in mines or on ranches, or in our shipping lines. It's customary to list all household servants in a will—otherwise they escort their uncle." He grinned. "It would be a good joke on Mrika if he found that he was going to have to raise the money to adopt fifteen hundred, two thousand servants—or shut the house and live in a tent. I can just see that. Why, the lad can't take a pee without four servants to shake it. I doubt if he knows how to put on his boots. Hugh, if you tell me to put the black lady on the red lord, I'll tingle you. I'm not in a good mood."

Hugh said hastily, "Did you miss a play? I hadn't noticed."

"Then why were you staring at the cards?" Hugh had indeed been staring at the game, trying to be invisible. He had been made very nervous by witnessing a quarrel between Ponse and his nephew. But he had missed not a word, he found it extremely interesting.

Ponse went on, "Which would you prefer, Hugh? To escort me to Heaven? Or stay here and serve Mrika? Don't answer too quickly. If you stay here, I venture you may be eating your own toes to stay your hunger before I'm gone

212

a year . . . whereas Heaven is a nice place, so the Good Scroll tells."

"It's a hard choice."

"Well, you don't have to make it, nor will you know. A servant should never know, it keeps him on his toes. That scoundrel Memtok keeps praying me for the honor of being in my escort. If I thought he was sincere, I would dismiss him for incompetence." Ponse swept the cards together. "Damn that lad! He's poor company but I had my liver set on a few good, hard rubbers. Joe, we've got to teach more people to play. Being left without a fourth is annoying."

"Certainly," agreed Joe. "Right now?"

"No, no. I want to play, damn it, not watch some beginner's bumbles. I'm growing addicted. Takes a man's worries off his mind."

Hugh was hit by inspiration. "Ponse, if you don't mind having another servant in the game . . ."

Joe brightened up. "Why, of course! He—"

"Barbara," Hugh cut in fast, before Joe could mention Duke.

Joe blinked. Then he smoothly picked it up. "He—Hugh, I mean—was about to mention a servant named Barbara. Good bridge player."

"Well! You've been teaching this game belowstairs, Hugh?" Ponse added, " 'Barbara'? A name I don't recognize. Not one of the upper servants."

"You remember her," Joe said. "She was with us when you picked us up. The tall one."

"Oh, yes. Bigging, it was. Joe, are you telling me that a *slut* can play this game?"

"She's a top player," Joe assured him. "Plays better than I do. Heavens, Ponse, she can play rings around you. Isn't that right, Hugh?"

"Barbara is an excellent player."

"This I must see to believe."

A few minutes later Barbara, freshly bathed and scared, was fetched in. She glanced at Hugh, looked startled silly, opened her mouth, closed it, and stood mute.

213

Ponse came up to her. "So this is the slut who is supposed to be able to play contract. Stop trembling, little one; nobody's going to eat you." In bluff words he convinced her that she was there only to play bridge and that she was expected to relax and be informal—no fancy talk. "Just behave as if you were downstairs, having a good time with other servants. Hear me?"

"Yes, sir."

"Just one thing." He tapped her on her chest. "When you're my partner, I shan't be angry if you make mistakes—after all, you're only a slut and it's surprising that you can play an intellectual game at all. But"—he paused— "when you are playing against me, if you fail to fight for every trick, if I even suspect that you are trying to let me win, I guarantee you'll tingle when you leave. Understand?"

"That's right," agreed Joe. "Their Charity expects it. Just play by the book, and play your best."

" 'By the book,' " Ponse repeated. "I've never seen this book but that's the way Joe says he has taught me to play. So do it. All right, let's cut the cards."

Hugh hardly listened, he was drinking in the sight of Barbara. She looked well and healthy although it was startling to see her slender again—or almost, he corrected; she was still largish in the fanny and certainly in the bust. She had lost most of her tan and was dressed in the shapeless short robe all female servants wore belowstairs, but he was delighted to see that she had not had her hair removed. It was cropped but could grow back.

He noticed that his own appearance seemed to startle her, realized why. He said, smiling, "I comb my hair with a washrag now, Barbie. No matter, I didn't have enough to matter. Now that I'm used to being hairless, I like it."

"You look distinguished, Hugh."

"He's ugly as sin," said Ponse. "But are we chatting? Or playing bridge? Your bid, Barba."

They played for hours. As it progressed, Barbara seemed to relax and enjoy it. She smiled a great deal, usually at Hugh, but also at Joe and even at Their Charity. She played by the book and Ponse never found fault. Hugh decided that their host was a good player, not yet perfect but he remembered what cards had been played and usually bid accurately. Hugh found him a satisfactory partner and an adequate opponent; it was a good game.

But once, with Barbara as Ponse's partner and contract in her hand, Hugh saw when Ponse laid down the dummy that Ponse had overbid in his answer. So he contrived to lose one sure trick, thereby letting Barbara make contract, game, and rubber.

It got him a glance with no expression from Barbara and Joe gave him a look that had a twinkle in it, but Joe kept his mouth shut. Ponse did not notice. He gave a bass roar, reached across and patted Barbara's head. "Wonderful, wonderful! Little one, you really *can* play contract. Why, I doubt if I could have made that myself."

Nor did Ponse complain when, on the next rubber, Barbara and Hugh gave him and Joe a trouncing. Hugh decided that Ponse had the inborn honesty called "sportsmanship"—plus a good head for cards.

One of the little deaf-mutes trotted in, knelt, and served Their Charity a tumbler of something cold, then another to Joe. Ponse took a swig, wiped his mouth and said, "Ah, that hits the spot!"

Joe made a whispered suggestion to him. Ponse looked startled and said, "Oh, certainly. Why not?"

So Hugh and Barbara were served. Hugh was pleased to discover that it was apple juice; he wasn't sure of his ability to play tight bridge had it been Happiness.

During this rubber Hugh noticed that Barbara was squirming a little and seemed to have trouble in concentrating. When the hand ended he said quietly, "Trouble, hon?"

She glanced at Ponse and whispered, "Some. I was about to feed the boys when I was sent for."

"Oh." Hugh turned to his host. "Ponse, Barbara needs to stop."

Ponse looked up from shuffling. "Plumbing call? One of the maids can show it, I suppose. They must go somewhere."

"Not that. Well, maybe that, too. What I meant was, Barbara has twins."

"Well? Sluts usually have twins, they have two breasts."

"That's the point, she's nursing them and she's hours past time. She has to leave."

Ponse looked annoyed, hesitated, then said, "Oh, garbage. Its milk won't cake from so short a delay. Here, cut the cards."

Hugh did not touch them. Ponse said, "Did you hear me?"

Hugh stood up. His heart was pounding and he felt a shudder of fear. "Ponse, Barbara hurts. She needs to nurse her twins right now. I can't force you to let her—but if you think I'll play cards while you don't let her, you're crazy."

For long moments the big man stared, without expression. Then suddenly he grinned. "Hugh, I like you. You did something like this once before, didn't you? The slut is your sister, I suppose."

"No."

"Then you are the one who is crazy. Do you know how close you came to being cold meat?"

"I can guess."

"I doubt it, you don't look worried. But I like spunk, even in a servant. Very well, I'll have its brats fetched. They can suck while we play."

The twins were fetched and Hugh saw at once that they were the handsomest, healthiest, and loveliest babies that had ever been born; he told Barbara so. He did not immediately get a chance to touch them as Ponse took one in each arm, laughed at them, blew in their faces, and jiggled them. "Fine boys!" he roared. "Fine boys, Barba! Holy little terrors, I'll bet. Go on, swing that fist, kid! Sock Uncle in the nose again. What do you call them, Barba? Do they have names?"

"This one is Hugh—"

"Eh? Does Hugh have something to do with them? Or thinks he has, perhaps?"

"He's their father."

"Well, well! Hugh, you may be ugly, but you have other

216

qualities. If Barba knows what she's talking about. What's this one's name?"

"That one is little Joe. Karl Joseph."

Ponse lifted an eyebrow at Joe. "So you have sluts naming brats for you, Joe? I'll have to watch you, you're a sly one. What did you give Barba?"

"Beg pardon?"

"Birthing present, you idiot. Give her that ring you're wearing. So many brats in this house named after me that I have to order trinkets by the basket load; they know it obliges me to make them a present. Hugh is lucky, he has nothing to give. Hey, Hughie has teeth!"

Hugh got to hold them while they settled down for combined bridge and nursing. Barbara took them one at a time and played cards with her free hand. The little maids fussed over the one not nursing and, in due time, took them away. In spite of the handicap Barbara played well, even brilliantly; the long session ended with Ponse top scorer, Barbara close behind, and Joe and Hugh tied for last. Hugh had cheated very little to make it come out that way; the cards had favored Ponse and Barbara when they were partners; they had made two small slams.

Ponse was feeling very jovial about it. "Barba, come here, little one. You tell the slutmaster I said to find a wet nurse for your brats and that I want the vet to dry you up as soon as possible. I want you available as my bridge partner. Or opponent—you give a man a tough fight."

"Yes, sir. May one speak?"

"One may."

"I would rather nurse them myself. They're all I have."

"Well—" He shrugged. "This seems to be my day for balky servants. I'm afraid you are both still savages. A tingling wouldn't do you any harm, slut. All right, but you'll have to play one-handed sometimes; I won't have brats stopping the game." He grinned. "Besides, I'd like to see the little rascals occasionally, especially that one that bites. You may go. All."

Barbara was dismissed so suddenly that Hugh barely had time to exchange smiles with her; he had hoped to walk down with her, steal a private visit. But His Charity did not dismiss him, so he stayed—with a warm glow in his heart; it had been the happiest time in a long time.

Ponse discussed the articles he had been translating, why none of them offered practical business ventures. "But don't fret, Hugh; keep plugging and we'll strike ore yet." He turned the talk to other matters, still kept Hugh there. Hugh found him a knowledgeable conversationalist, interested in everything, as willing to listen as he was to talk. He seemed to Hugh the epitome of the perfect decadent cynical, a dilettante in arts and sciences, neither merciful nor cruel, unimpressed by his own rank, not racist—he treated Hugh as an intellectual equal.

While they were talking, the little maids served dinner to Ponse and to Joe. Nothing was offered to Hugh, nor did he expect it—nor want it, as he could have meals served in his rooms if he was not on time in the executive servants' dining room and he had long since decided, from samplings, that Memtok was right: the upper servants ate better than the master.

But when Ponse had finished, he shoved his dishes toward Hugh. "Eat."

Hugh hesitated a split second; he did not need to be told that he was being honored—for a servant. There was plenty, at least three times as much left as Ponse had eaten. Hugh could not recall that he had ever eaten someone's leavings, and certainly not with a used spoon. He dug in.

As usual, Their Charity's menu did not especially please Hugh—somewhat greasy and he had no great liking for pork. Pork was hardly ever served belowstairs but was often part of the menus Memtok sampled, Hugh had noticed. It surprised him, as the revised Koran still contained the dietary laws and the Chosen did follow some of the original Muslim customs. They practiced circumcision, did not use alcohol other than a thin beer, and observed Ramadan at least nominally and called it that. Mahomet would have been shocked by the revisions to his straightforward monotheistic teachings but he would have recognized some of the details.

But the bread was good, the fruits were superb, and so were the ices and many other things; it wasn't necessary to dine solely on roast. Hugh kept intact his record for enjoying the inevitable.

Ponse was interested in what the climate had been in this region in Hugh's time. "Joe tells me you sometimes had freezing temperatures. Even snow."

"Oh, yes, every winter."

"Fantastic. How cold did it get?"

Hugh had to think. He had not had occasion to learn how these people marked temperatures. "If you consider the range from freezing of water to boiling, it was not unusual for it to get one third of that range lower than freezing."

Ponse looked surprised. "Are you sure? We call that range, freezing to boiling, one hundred. Are you telling me that it sometimes got as much as thirty-three degrees below freezing?"

Hugh noted with interest that the centigrade scale had survived two millennia—but no reason why not; they used the decimal system in arithmetic and in money. He had to do a conversion in his head. "Yes, that's what I mean. Nearly cold enough to freeze mercury, and cold enough for that, up in those mountains." Hugh pointed out a view window.

"Cold enough," Joe agreed, "to freeze your teeth! Only thing that ever made me long for Mississippi."

"Where," asked Ponse, "is Mississippi?"

"It's not," Joe told him. "It's under water now. And good riddance."

This led to discussion of why the climate had changed and Their Charity sent for the last volume of the *Britannica,* containing ancient maps, and for modern maps. They poured over them together. Where the Mississippi Valley had been, the Gulf now reached far north. Florida and Yucatan were missing and Cuba was a few small islands. California had a central sea and most of northern Canada was gone.

Similar shrinkages had taken place elsewhere. The Scandinavian Peninsula was an island, the British Isles were several small islands, part of the Sahara was under water. What had been lowland anywhere were missing—Holland, Belgium, northern Germany could not be found. Nor Denmark—the Baltic was a gulf of the Atlantic.

Hugh looked at it with odd sorrow and had never felt so homesick. He had known it was so, from reading; this was the first map he had seen of it.

"The question," said Ponse, "is whether the melting of ice was triggered by the dust of the East-West War, or was it a natural change that was, at most, speeded up a little by artificial events? Some of my scientists say one thing, some the other."

"What do you think?" asked Hugh.

The lord shrugged. "I'm not foolish enough to hold opinions when I have insufficient data; I'll leave that folly to scientists. I'm simply glad that Uncle saw fit to let me live in an age in which I can go outdoors without freezing my feet. I visited the South Pole once—I have some mines there. Frost on the ground. Dreadful. The place for ice is in drink."

Ponse went to the window and stood looking out at the silhouette of mountains against darkening sky. "However, if it got that cold up there now, we would root them out in a hurry. Eh, Joe?"

"Back they would come with their tails between their legs," Joe agreed.

Hugh looked puzzled. "Ponse means," Joe explained, "the runners hiding up in the mountains. What they thought you were when we were found."

"Runners and a few aborigines," Ponse supplemented. "Savages. Poor creatures who have never been rescued by civilization. It's hard to save them, Hugh. They don't stand around waiting to be picked up the way you did. They're crafty as wolves. The merest shadow in the sky and they freeze and you can't see them—and they are very destructive of game. Of course we could smoke them out any number of ways. But that would kill the game, can't have that. Hugh, you've lived out there; you must have acquired some feel for it. How would you go about rescuing those critters? Without killing game."

Mr. Hugh Farnham hesitated only long enough to

phrase his reply. "Their Charity knows that this one is a servant. This one's ears must be at fault in thinking that it heard its humble self called on to see the problem as it might appear to the Chosen."

"Why, damn your impudence! Come, come, Hugh, I want your opinion."

"You got my opinion, Ponse. I'm a servant. My sympathies are with the runaways. And the savages. I didn't come here willingly. I was dragged."

"Surely you aren't resenting that now? Of course you were captured, even Joe was. But there was language difficulty. Now you've seen the difference. You *know*."

"Yes, I know."

"Then you know how much your condition has improved. Don't you sleep in a better bed now? Aren't you eating better? Uncle! When we picked you up, you were half starved and infested with vermin. You were barely staying alive with the hardest sort of work, I could *see*. I'm not blind, I'm not stupid; there isn't a member of my Family down to the lowest cleaner that works half as hard as you had to, or sleeps in as poor a bed—and in a stinking little sty; I could hardly bear the stench before we fumigated it—and as for the food, if that is the word, any servant in this house would turn up his nose at what you ate. Isn't all that true?"

"Yes."

"Well?"

"I prefer freedom."

" 'Freedom!' " Their Charity snorted. "A concept without a referent, like 'ghosts.' Meaningless. Hugh, you should study semantics. Modern semantics, I mean; I doubt if they really had such a science in your day. We are all free—to walk our appointed paths. Just as a stone is free to fall when you toss it into the air. No one is free in the abstract meaning you give the word. Do you think *I* am free? Free to change places with you, say? Would I if I could? You bet I would! You have no concept of the worries I have, the work I do. Sometimes I lie awake half the night, worrying which way to turn next—you won't find that in servants' hall. They're happy, they have no worries.

But I have to carry my burden as best I can."

Hugh looked stubborn. Ponse came over and put his arm around Hugh's shoulders. "Come, let's talk this over judicially—two civilized beings. I'm not one of those superstitious persons who thinks a servant can't think because his skin is pale. Surely you know that. Haven't I respected your intellect?"

"Well . . . yes."

"That's better. Let me explain some things—Joe has seen them—and you can ask questions, and we'll arrive at a rational understanding. First—Joe, you've seen Chosen here and there who are what our friend Hugh would no doubt describe as 'free.' Tell him."

Joe snorted. "Hugh, you should see—and you would be glad to be privileged to live in Ponse's household. There is just one phrase I can think of to describe them. Po' black trash. Like the white trash there used to be in Mississippi. Poor black trash, not knowing where their next meal is."

"I follow you."

"I think I do, too," agreed Their Charity. "A pungent phrase. I look forward to the day when every man will have servants. It can't come overnight, they'll have to lift themselves up. But a day when all the Chosen will be served—and all servants as well cared for as they are in my own Family. That's my ideal. In the meantime I do the best I can. I look after their welfare from birth until they're called Home by Uncle. They have nothing to fear, utter security—which they wouldn't have out in those mountains as I'm sure you know better than I. They are happy, they are never overworked—which I am—and they have plenty of fun, which is more than I can say! This bridge game today—the first real fun I've had in a month. And they are never punished, only just enough to remind them when they err. Have to do that, you've seen how stupid most of them are. Not that I am inferring that *you* are— No, I tell you honestly that I think you are smart enough to take care of servants yourself, despite your skin. I'm speaking of the ordinary run. Honestly, Hugh, do you think they could take care of themselves as well as I look out for them?"

222

"Probably not." Hugh had heard all this before, only nights ago, and in almost the same words—from Memtok. With the difference that Ponse seemed to be honestly fond of his servants and earnest about their welfare—whereas the Chief Domestic had been openly contemptuous of them, even more strongly so than his veiled contempt for the Chosen. "No, they couldn't most of them."

"Ah! You agree with me."

"No."

Ponse looked pained. "Hugh, how can we have a rational discussion if you say one thing and contradict it in the next breath?"

"I didn't contradict myself. I agreed that you took fine care of the welfare of your servants. But I did not agree that I prefer it to freedom."

"But *why*, Hugh? Give me a reason, not a philosophical abstraction. If you're not happy, I want to know why. So that I can correct it."

"I can give you one reason. I'm not allowed to live with my wife and children."

"Eh?"

"Barbara. And the twins."

"Oh. Is that important? You have a bedwarmer. Memtok told me, and I congratulated him on having used initiative in an odd situation. Not much gets past that sly old fox. You have one and she is sure to be more expert at her specialty than the ordinary run of breeding slut. As for the brats, no reason why you can't see them—just order them fetched to you whenever you like. But who wants to *live* with brats? Or with a wife? I don't live with my wife and children, you can bet on that. I see them on appropriate occasions. But who would want to live with them?"

"I would."

"Well— Uncle! I want you to be happy. It can be arranged."

"*It can?*"

"Certainly. If you hadn't put up such a fuss over being tempered, you could have had them with you all along—though I confess I don't see why. Do you want to see the vet?"

"Uh . . . no."

"Well, there's another choice. I'll have the slut spayed."

"No!"

Ponse sighed. "You're hard to please. Be practical, Hugh; I can't change a scientific breeding system to pamper one servant. Do you know how many servants are in this family? Here and at the Palace? Around eighteen hundred, I believe. Do you know what would happen if I allowed unrestricted breeding? In ten years there would be twice that number. And what would happen next? They would starve! I can't support them in unlimited breeding. Would if I could, but it's wishing for the Moon. Worse, for we can go to the Moon any time it's worth while but nobody can cope with the way servants will breed if left to their own devices. So which is better? To control it? Or let them starve?"

Their Charity sighed. "I wish you were a head shorter, we could work something out. You've been in studs' quarters?"

"I visited it once, with Memtok."

"You noticed the door? You had to stoop; Memtok walked straight in—he used to be a stud. The doors are that height in every studs' barracks in the world—and no servant is chosen if he can't walk in without stooping. And the slut in this case is too tall, too. A wise law, Hugh. I didn't make it; it was handed down a long time ago by Their Mercy of that time. If they are allowed to breed too tall they start needing to be tingled too often and that's not good, for master or servant. No, Hugh. Anything within reason. But don't ask for the impossible." He moved from the divan where he had been sitting tête-a-tête with Hugh and sat down at the card table, picked up a deck. "So we'll say no more about it. Do you know how to play double solitaire?"

"Yes."

"Then come see if you can beat me and let's be cheerful. A man gets upset when his efforts aren't appreciated."

Hugh shut up. He was thinking glumly that Ponse was not a villain. He was exactly like the members of every ruling class in history: honestly convinced of his benevolence and hurt if it was challenged.

They played a game; Hugh lost, his mind was not on it. They started to lay out another. Their Charity remarked, "I must have more cards painted. These are getting worn."

Hugh said, "Couldn't it be done more quickly, using a printer such as we use for scrolls?"

"Eh? Hadn't thought about it." The big man rubbed one of the XXth century cards. "This doesn't seem much like printing. Were they printed?"

"Oh, yes. Thousands at a time. Millions, I should say, figuring the enormous numbers that used to be sold."

"Really? I wouldn't have thought that bridge, with its demand on the intellect, would have attracted many people."

Hugh suddenly put down his cards. "Ponse? You wanted a way to make money."

"Certainly."

"You have it in your hand. Joe! Come here and let's talk about this. How many decks of cards were sold each year in the United States?"

"Gosh, Hugh, I don't know. Millions, maybe."

"So I would say. At a gross profit of about ninety percent. Mmm— Ponse, bridge and solitaire aren't the only games that can be played with these cards. The possibilities are unlimited. There are games simple as solitaire but played by two or three or more players. There are games a dozen people can play at once. There are hard games and easy games, there is even a form of bridge—'duplicate,' it's called—harder than contract. Ponse, every family —little family—kept one or two or even dozens of decks on hand; it was a rare home that didn't own a deck. I could guess how many were sold. Probably a hundred million decks in use in the United States alone. And you've got a virgin market. All it needs is to get people interested."

"Ponse, Hugh is right," Joe said solemnly. "The possibilities are unlimited."

Ponse pursed up his lips. "If we sold them for a bullock a deck, let us say . . . mmm—"

"Too much," Joe objected. "You would kill your market before you got started."

Hugh said, "Joe, what's that formula for setting a price to maximize profits rather than sales?"

"Works only in a monopoly."

"Well? How is that done here? Patents and copyrights and such? I haven't seen anything about it in what I've read."

Joe looked troubled. "Hugh, the Chosen don't use such a system, they don't need to. Everything is pretty well worked out, things don't change much."

Hugh said, "That's bad. Two weeks after we start, the market will be flooded with imitations."

Ponse said, "What are you two jabbering about? Speak Language." Hugh's question had necessarily been in English; Joe had answered in English.

Joe said, "Sorry, Ponse," and explained the ideas behind patent rights, copyright, and monopoly.

Ponse relaxed. "Oh, that's simple. When a man gets an inspiration from Heaven, the Lord Proprietor forbids anyone else to use it without his let. Doesn't happen often, I recall only two cases in my lifetime. But Mighty Uncle has been known to smile."

Hugh was not surprised to learn how scarce invention was. It was a static culture, with most of what they called "science" in the hands of tempered slaves—and if patenting a new idea was that difficult, there would be little incentive to invent. "Would you say that this idea is an inspiration from Heaven?"

Ponse thought about it. "An inspiration is whatever Their Mercy, in Their wisdom, recognizes as an inspiration." Suddenly he grinned. "In my opinion, anything that will stack bullocks in the Family coffers is an inspiration. The problem is to make the Proprietor see it. But there are ways. Keep talking."

Joe said, "Hugh, the protection should extend not only over playing cards but over the games themselves."

"Of course. If they don't buy Their Charity's cards, they must not play his games. Hard to stop, since anybody can fake a deck of cards. But the monopoly should make it illegal."

"And not just cards like these, but any sort of playing cards. You could play bridge with cards just with numbers on them."

"Yes." Hugh pondered. "Joe, there was a Scrabble set in the shelter."

"It's still around. Ponse's scientists saved everything. Hugh, I see what you're driving at, but nobody here could learn Scrabble. You have to know English."

"What's to keep us from inventing Scrabble all over again—in *Language?* Let me set my staff to making a frequency count of the alphabet as it appears in Language and I'll have a set of Scrabble, board and tiles and rules, suited to Language, the following day."

"What in the name of Uncle is Scrabble?"

"It's a game, Ponse. Quite a good one. But the point is that it's a game that we can charge more for than we can for a deck of cards."

"That's not all," said Hugh. He began ticking on his fingers. "Parcheesi, Monopoly, backgammon, Old Maid for kids—call it something else—dominoes, anagrams, poker chips and racks, jigsaw puzzles—have you seen any?"

"No."

"Good for young and old, and all degrees of difficulty. Tinker Toy. Dice—lots of games with dice. Joe, are there casinos here?"

"Of sorts. There are places to gamble and lots of private gambling."

"Roulette wheels?"

"I don't believe so."

"It gets too big to think about. Ponse, you are going to have to sit up nights, counting your money."

"Servants for such chores. I wish I knew what you two are talking about. May one ask?"

"Sorry, sir. Joe and I were talking about ancient games

. . . and not just games but all sorts of recreations that we used to have and have now been lost. At least I think they have been. Joe?"

"The only one I've seen that looks familiar is chess."

"Chess would hold up if anything would. Ponse, the point is that every one of these things has money in it. Surely, you have games now. But these will be novelties. So old they are new again. Ping-Pong . . . bowling alleys! Joe, have you seen—"

"No."

"Billiards. Pocket pool. I'll stop, we've got a backlog. Ponse, the first problem is to get a protection from Their Mercy to cover it all—and I see a theory that makes it an inspiration from on high. It was a miracle."

"What? Garbage. I don't believe in miracles."

"You don't have to believe in it. Look, we were found on the Proprietor's personal land—and *you* found us. Doesn't that look as if Uncle intended for the Proprietor to know about this? And for you as Lord Protector to protect it?"

Ponse grinned. "An argument could be made for such a theory. Might be expensive. But you can't boil water without feeding the fire, as my aunt used to say." He stood up. "Hugh, let's see that Scrabble game. Soon. Joe, we'll find time for you to explain these other things. We excuse you both. All."

Kitten was asleep when Hugh returned but she was clutching a note:

Oh, darling, it was so wonderful to *see* you! ! ! I can't *wait* until Their Charity asks us to play bridge again! Isn't he an old dear? Even if he was thoughtless at one point. He corrected his mistake and that's the mark of a true gentleman.

I'm so excited at seeing you that I can hardly write, and Kitten is waiting to take this to you.

The twins send you kisses, slobbery ones. Love, love, love!

Your own B.

Hugh read Barbara's note with mixed feelings. He shared her joy in their reunion, limited as it had been, and eagerly looked forward to the next time Ponse's pleasure would permit them to be together. As for the rest— Better get her out of here before she acquired a slave mentality! Surely, Ponse was a gentleman within the accepted meaning of the term. He was conscientious about his responsibilities, generous and tolerant with his inferiors. A gentleman.

But he was a revolving son of a bitch, too! And Barbara ought not to be so ready to overlook the fact. Ignore it, yes—one had to. But not forget it.

He must get her free.

But *how?*

He went to bed.

An aching hour later he got up, went into his living room, stood at his window. He could make out against black sky the blacker blackness of the Rocky Mountains.

Somewhere out there, were free men.

He could break this window, go toward the mountains, be lost in them before daylight—find free companions. He need not even break the window—just slip past a nodding watchman, or use the authority symbolized by his whip to go out despite the watch. No real effort was made to keep house servants locked up. A watch was set more to keep intruders out. Most house servants would no more run away than a dog would.

Dogs— One of the studmaster's duties was keeper of the hounds.

If necessary, he could kill a dog with his hands. *But how do you run when burdened with two small babies?*

He went to a cupboard, poured himself a stiff drink of Happiness, gulped it down, and went back to bed.

16

For the next many days Hugh was busy redesigning the game of Scrabble, translating *Hoyle's Complete Book of Games,* dictating rules and descriptions of games and recreations not in Hoyle (such as Ping-Pong, golf, water skiing), attending conferences with Ponse and Joe—playing bridge.

The last was by far the best. With Joe's help he taught several Chosen the game, but most sessions were play, with Joe, Ponse, and always Barbara. Ponse had the enthusiasm of a convert; when he was in residence he played bridge every minute he could spare, and always wanted the same four, the best players available.

It seemed to Hugh that Their Charity was honestly fond of Barbara, as fond as he was of the cat he called "Doklivstnipsoom"—never "Doc." Ponse extended to cats the courtesy due equals, and Doc, or any cat, was free to jump into his lap even when he was bidding a hand. He extended the same courtesy and affection to Barbara as he knew her better, always called her "Barba," or "Child," and never again referred to her as "it." Barbara called him "Ponse," or "Uncle," and clearly felt happy in his company.

Sometimes Ponse left Barbara and Hugh alone, once for twenty minutes. These were jewels beyond price; they did not risk losing such a privilege by doing more than hold hands.

If it was time to nurse the boys, Barbara said so and

Ponse always ordered them fetched. Once he ordered them fetched when it wasn't necessary, said that he had not seen them for a week and wanted to see how much they had grown. So the game waited while their "Uncle" Ponse got down on the rug and made foolish noises at them.

Then he had them taken away, five minutes of babies was enough. But he said to Barbara, "Child, they're growing like sugar cane. I hope I live to see them grow up."

"You'll live a long time, Uncle."

"Maybe. I've outlived a dozen food tasters, but that salts no fish. Those brats of ours will make magnificent matched footmen. I can see them now, serving in the banquet hall of the Palace—the Residence, I mean, not this cottage. Whose deal is it?"

Hugh saw Grace a few times, but never for more than seconds. If he showed up when she was there, she left at once, displeasure large on her face. If Barbara arrived before Hugh did, Grace was always out of sight. It was clear that she was an habituée of the lord's informal apartments; it was equally clear that she resented Barbara as much as ever, with bile left over for Hugh. But she never said anything and it seemed likely that she had learned not to cross wills with Their Charity.

It was now official that Grace was bedwarmer to Their Charity. Hugh learned this from Kitten. The sluts knew when the lord was in residence (Hugh often did not) by whether Grace was downstairs or up. She was assigned no other duties and was immune to all whips, even Memtok's. She was also, the times Hugh glimpsed her, lavishly dressed and bejeweled.

She was also very fat, so fat that Hugh felt relieved that he no longer had even a nominal obligation to share a bed with her. True, all bedwarmers were fat by Hugh's standards. Even Kitten was plump enough that had she been a XXth century American girl, she would have been at least pretending to diet—Kitten fretted that she was unable to put on weight—and did Hugh like her anyhow?

Kitten was so young that her plumpness was somewhat pleasing, as with a baby. But Hugh found Grace's fatness another matter—somewhere in that jiggling mass was buried the beautiful girl he had married. He tried not to think about it and could not see why Ponse would like it—if he did. But in truth, Hugh admitted, he did not know that Grace was anything more than nominally Ponse's bedwarmer. After all, Ponse was alleged to be more than a century old. Would Ponse have any more use for one than Memtok had? Hugh did not know—nor care. Ponse looked to be perhaps sixty-five and still strong and virile. But Hugh held a private opinion that Grace's role was odalisque, not houri.

While the question did not matter to him it did to Duke. Hugh's first son came storming into Hugh's office one day and demanded a private interview; Hugh led him to his apartment. He had not seen Duke for a month. Translations had been coming in from him; there had been no need to see him.

Hugh tried to make the meeting pleasant. "Sit down, Duke. May I offer you a drink of Happiness?"

"No, thanks! What's this I hear about Mother?"

"What do you hear, Duke?" (Oh, Lord! Here we go—)

"You know damned well what I mean!"

"I'm afraid I don't."

Hugh made him spell it out. Duke had his facts correct and, to Hugh's surprise, had learned them just that day. Since more than four hundred servants had known all along that one of the slut savages—the other one, not the tall skinny one—lived upstairs with Their Charity more than she lived in sluts' quarters, it seemed incredible that Duke had taken so long to find out. However, Duke had little to do with the other servants and was not popular—a "troublemaker," Memtok had called him.

Hugh neither confirmed nor denied Duke's story.

"Well?" Duke demanded. "What are you going to do about it?"

"About what, Duke? Are you suggesting that I put a stop to servants' hall gossip?"

"I don't mean that at all! Are you going to sit there like a turd on a rock while your wife is being raped?"

"Probably. You come in here with some story you've

picked up from a second assistant dishwasher and expect me to do something. I would like to know, first, why do you think this gossip is true? Second, what has what you have told me got to do with rape? Third, what would you expect me to do about it? Fourth, what do you think I *can* do about it? Take them in order and be specific. Then we may talk about what I will do."

"Quit twisting things."

"I'm not twisting anything. Duke, you had an expensive education as a lawyer—I know, I picked up the tab. You used to lecture me about 'rules of evidence.' Now use that education. Take those questions in order. Why do you think this gossip is true?"

"Uh . . . I heard it and checked around. Everybody knows it."

"So? Everybody knew the Earth was flat, at one time. But what is the allegation? Be specific."

"Why, I told you. Mother is assigned as that bastard's bedwarmer."

"Who says so?"

"Why, everybody!"

"Did you ask the slutmaster?"

"Do you think I'm crazy?"

"I'll take that as rhetorical. To shorten this, what 'everybody knows,' as you put it, is that Grace is assigned duties upstairs. This could be verified, if true. Possibly in attendance on Their Charity, possibly waiting on the ladies of the household, or perhaps other duties. Do you want an appointment with the slutmaster, so that you can ask him what duties your mother has? I do not know her duties."

"Uh, you ask him."

"I shan't. I feel sure that Grace would regard it as snooping. Let's assume that *you* have asked him and that he has told you, as you now suspect only from gossip, that her assignment is as bedwarmer. To Their Charity. On this assumption, made solely for the sake of argument since you haven't proved it—on this assumption, where does rape come in?"

Duke looked astonished. "I would not have believed it,

even of you. Do you mean to sit there and say baldly that you think Mother would do such a thing *voluntarily?*"

"I long ago gave up trying to guess what your mother would do. But *I* haven't said she is doing anything. *You* have. I don't know that her assignment is bedwarmer other than through gossip you have repeated without proof. If true, I still would not know if she had ever carried out the assignment by actually getting into his bed, voluntarily or otherwise—I've never seen his bed nor even heard gossip on this point . . . just your evil thoughts. But if those thoughts are correct, I still would have no opinion as to whether or not anything other than sleep had taken place. I have shared beds with females and done nothing but sleep; it can happen. But even stipulating sexual activity—your assumption, not mine—I doubt that Their Charity has ever raped *any* female in his life. I doubt it especially now."

"Crap. There never was a nigger bastard who wouldn't rape a white woman if he had the chance."

"Duke! That's poisonous, insane nonsense. You almost persuade me that you *are* crazy."

"I—"

"*Shut up!* You know that Joseph, to give one example, had endless opportunity to rape any of three white women for nine long months. You also know that his behavior was above reproach."

"Well . . . he didn't have a chance to."

"I told you to shut up this poison. He had endless chance. While you were hunting, any day. He was alone with each of them, many times. Drop it! Slandering Joseph, I mean, even by innuendo. I'm ashamed of you."

"And I'm ashamed of you. Fat cat for a nigger king."

"Very well, the shame is mutual. Speaking of fat cats, I don't really need you. If you want to quit being a fat cat, you can wash dishes or whatever they assign you to."

"Doesn't matter to me."

"Let me know when you wish to be relieved. It will lose you your private cubicle but such luxury is a fat cat privilege. Never mind. I see only one way to get at the facts, if any, underlying these foul suspicions in your mind. Ask the Lord Protector."

"Go right ahead! First sensible thing you've said."

"Oh, not me, Duke. I don't suspect him of rape. But you can ask him. See the Chief Domestic. He'll see any Palace servant who wants to see him. At the servant's risk, but I doubt if he'll tingle anyone in my department without good cause; I do have some fat cat privileges. Tell him you want an audience with the Lord Protector. I think that is all it will take, although you may have to wait a week or two. If Memtok turns you down, tell me. I fancy I can get him to arrange it. Then, when you see the Lord Protector, simply ask him, point-blank."

"And be lied to. If I ever get that close to that black ape, I'm going to kill him!"

Mr. Farnham sighed. "Duke, I don't see how one man can be so wrong-headed so many different ways. If you are granted an audience, Memtok will be at your side. With his whip. The Lord Protector will be about fifty feet away. And the whip *he* carries doesn't just tingle; it's a deadly weapon. The old man has lived a long time, he's not easy to kill."

"I can try!"

"So you can. If a grasshopper tries to fight a lawn-mower, one may admire his courage but not his judgment. But you are equally silly in thinking that Their Charity would lie about it. If he has done what you think he has—raped your mother, forced her to submit—he would feel not the slightest shame, not in any way reluctant to answer you honestly. Duke, he would no more bother to lie to you than it would occur to him to step aside if you were in his way. However—would you believe your mother?"

"Of course I would."

"Then tell him also that you would like to see her. I am almost certain that he would grant the request. For a few minutes and in his presence. The harem rules he can break if he chooses. If you have the guts to tell him that you want to hear *her* confirm whatever he tells you, I think he would be astonished. But I think he would then laugh and grant the petition. If you want to see your mother, assure yourself personally of her welfare and safety, that's all I can suggest. You can't see her otherwise. It's so irregular that your only chance is to spring it on him, face to face."

Duke looked baffled. "Look, why the devil don't *you* ask him? You see him almost every day, so I hear."

"*Me?* Yes. I see him fairly often. But ask him about rape? Is that what you mean?"

"Yes, if you choose to put it that way."

" 'Rape' is what *you* claim to be worried about. But *I* don't suspect him of rape. I won't be a front for your evil suspicions. If it is to be done, you must have the guts to do it yourself." Hugh stood up. "We've wasted enough time. Either get back to work, or go see Memtok."

"I'm not through."

"Oh, yes, you are. That was an order, not a suggestion."

"If you think I'm scared of that whip—"

"Heavens, Duke, I wouldn't tingle you myself. If you force me to it, I'll ask Memtok to chastise you. He's reputed to be expert. Now get out. You've wasted half my morning."

Duke left. Hugh stayed, trying to compose himself. A row with Duke always left him shaking; it had been so when the lad was only twelve. But something else troubled him, too. He had used every sophistry he could think of to divert Duke from a hopeless course. That did not worry him, nor did he share Duke's basic worry. Whatever had happened to Grace, he felt sure that rape was not a factor.

But he was sourly aware of something that Duke, in his delusions, apparently did not realize—the oldest Law of the Conquered, that their women eventually submit—willingly.

Whether his ex-wife had or had not was a matter almost academic. He suspected that she had never been offered opportunity. Either way, she was obviously contented with her lot—smug about it. That troubled him little; he had tried to do his duty by her, she had long since withdrawn herself from him. But he did not want Barbara ever to feel the deadening load of hopelessness that could—and

236

had, all through history—turned chaste women into willing concubines. Much as he loved her, he had no illusions that Barbara was either angel or saint; the Sabine women had stood no chance and neither would she. "Death before dishonor!" was a slogan that did not wear well. In time, it changed to happy cooperation.

He got out his bottle of Happiness, looked at it—put it back. He would never solve his problems that way.

Hugh made no effort to learn if Duke had gone to see Memtok. He got back to work at his endless task of buttering up Their Charity in every way available, whether by good bridge, moneymaking ideas, or simply translating. He no longer had any hope that the boss would eventually permit him to move Barbara and the twins into his apartment; old Ponse had seemed adamant on that. But favor at court could be useful, even indispensable, no matter what happened—and in the meantime it let him see Barbara occasionally.

He never gave up his purpose of escape. As the summer wore on he realized that the chances were slim of escaping—all four of them escaping, twins in arms—that year. Soon the household would move to the city, and so far as he knew the only possible time to escape was when they were near mountains. No matter. A year, two years, even longer, perhaps wait until the boys could walk. Hard enough even then, but nearly impossible with babies in arms. He must tell Barbara, with whispered urgency, the next time they were left alone even for a minute, what he had in mind—urge her to keep her chin up, and wait.

He didn't dare write it to her. Ponse could get it translated—other scholars somewhere understood English, even though Joe would never give him away. Would Grace? He hoped not, but couldn't guess. Probably Ponse knew all about those notes, had them translated every day, chuckled over them, and did not care.

Perhaps he could work out a code—something as simple as first word, first line, then second line, second word, and so on. Might risk it.

He had figured out one thing in their favor, an advantage that might overcome their lack of sophistication in this society. Runaways rarely succeeded simply because of their appearance. A white skin might be disguised—but servants averaged many inches shorter and many pounds lighter than the Chosen.

Both Barbara and Hugh were tall; they were big enough to pass in that respect for Chosen. Features? The Chosen were not uniform in feature; Hindu influence mixed with Negroid and with other things. His baldness was a problem, he would have to steal a wig. Or make one. But with stolen clothes, squirreled food, weapons of some sort (his two hands!) and *makeup*—they might be able to pass for "poor black trash" and take to the road.

If it wasn't too far. If the hounds did not get them. If they did not make some ridiculous bumble through ignorance. But servants, marked by their complexion, were not allowed to go one step outside the household, farm, ranch, or whatever was their lawful cage—without a pass from their patron.

Perhaps he could learn what a pass looked like, forge one. No, Barbara and he could *not* travel as servants on a forged pass for the very reason that made it dimly possible for them to disguise as Chosen: Their size was distinctive, they would be picked up on sight.

The more Hugh thought about it the more it seemed that he would have to wait at least until next summer.

If they were among the servants picked for the Summer Palace next year— If they *both* were— If *all four* were— He had not thought of that. Christ! Their little family might never be all under this one roof again! Perhaps they would have to run for it now, in the short time left before the move—run and take a chance on hounds, on bears, on those nasty little leopards . . . with two nursing babies to protect. God! Was ever a man faced with poorer chances for saving his family?

Yes. He himself—when he built that shelter.

Prepare every way he could . . . and pray for a miracle. He started saving food from meals served in his rooms, such sorts as would keep a while. He kept his eyes open to steal a knife—or anything that could be made into a knife. He kept what he was doing from Kitten's eyes.

Much sooner than he had hoped he got a chance to acquire makeup. A feast day always meant an orgy of Happiness in servants' hall; one came that featured amateur theatricals. Hugh was urged to clown the part of Lord Protector in a comic skit. He did not hesitate to do so, Memtok himself had pointed out that his size made him perfect for the part. Hugh roared through it, brandishing a quirt three times as big as Their Charity ever carried.

He was a dramatic success. He saw Ponse watching from the balcony from which Hugh had first seen Happiness issued, watching and laughing. So Hugh ad-libbed, calling out, "Hey, less noise in the balcony! Memtok! Tingle that critter!"

Their Charity laughed harder than ever, the servants were almost hysterical and, at bridge the following day, Ponse patted him and told him that he was the best Lord of Nonsense the pageant had ever had.

Result: one stolen package of pigment which needed only to be mixed with the plentiful deodorant cream to make him the exact shade of the Lord Protector; one wig which covered his baldness with black wavy hair. It was not the wig he had worn in the skit; he had turned that one back to the chief housekeeper, picking a time under Memtok's eyes and urging Memtok to try it on. No, it was a wig he had tried on out of several saved from year to year—and which had fitted him just as well. He tried it on, dropped it, kicked it into a corner, recovered it in private—and kept it under his robe for several days until it seemed certain that it hadn't been missed. It wound up under a file case in his outer office one night when he chose to work later than his clerks.

He was still looking for something he could grind into a knife.

He did not see Duke during the three weeks following their row. Sometimes Duke's translations came in, sometimes he skipped a day or two; Hugh let him get away with it. But when Hugh could not recall having seen any scrolls come through of the sort Duke was concerned with for a full week, Hugh decided to check up.

Hugh walked to the cubicle that was Duke's privilege

for being a "researcher in history." He scratched on the door—no answer.

He scratched again, decided that Duke was sleeping, or not in; he slid the door up and looked in.

Duke was not asleep but he was out of this world. He was sprawled naked on his bunk in the most all-out Happiness jag Hugh had ever seen. Duke looked up when the door opened, giggled foolishly, made a gesture, and said, "Hiyah, y'ole bas'ard! How's tricks?"

Hugh stepped closer for a better look at what he thought he saw, and felt sick at his stomach. "Son, son!"

"Still crepe-hanging, Hughie? Old hooey Hugh, the fake fart!"

Gulping, Hugh started to back out, and backed almost into the Chief Veterinarian. The surgeon smiled and said, "Visiting my patient? He hardly needs it." He moved past Hugh with a muttered apology, leaned over Duke, peeled an eyelid back, examined him in other ways, said to him jovially, "You're doing fine, cousin. Let's give you another little treatment, then I'll send you in another big meal. How does that sound?"

"Jus' fine, Doc. Jus' dandy! You're m' frien'. Bes' frien' never had!"

The vet set a dial on a little instrument, pressed it against Duke's thigh, waited a moment, and came out. He smiled at Hugh. "Practically recovered. He'll dream a few hours now, wake up hungry, and not know any time has passed. Then we'll feed him and give him another dose. A fine patient, he's rallied beautifully. Doesn't know what's happened—and by the time we're ready to taper him off, he won't be interested."

Who ordered this?

The surgeon looked surprised. "The Chief Domestic, of course. Why?"

"Why wasn't I told?"

"I don't know, better ask him. I got it as a routine order, we carried it out in the routine fashion. Sleeping powder in his evening meal, I mean, then surgery that night. Followed by post-surgical care and usual massive dosage to keep him tranquil. It tends to make some of them a little nervous at first, we vary it to suit the patient. But, as you can see, this patient has taken it as easily as pulling a tooth. By the way, that bridge I installed in your mouth. Satisfactory?"

"What? Yes. Never mind that! I want to know—"

"May it please you, the Chief Domestic is the one to see. Now, if this one may be excused, I'm overdue to hold sick call. I merely stopped by to make sure my patient was happy."

Hugh went to his apartment and threw up. Then he went looking for Memtok.

Memtok received him into his office at once, invited him to sit down. Hugh had begun to value the Chief Domestic as a friend, or as the nearest thing he had to a friend. Memtok had formed a habit of dropping in on Hugh in the evenings occasionally and, despite the boss servant's backgrounds and values, Hugh found him shrewd and stimulating and well informed within his limits. Memtok seemed to have the loneliness that a ship's captain must endure; he seemed pleased to relax and enjoy friendship.

Since the other upper servants were correctly polite with the Chief Researcher rather than warm, Hugh, lonesome himself, had enjoyed Memtok's unbending and had thought of him as his friend. Until this—

Hugh told Memtok bluntly, without protocol, what was on his mind. "Why did you do this?"

Memtok looked surprised. "Such a question! Such a very improper question. Because the Lord Protector ordered it."

"He *did?*"

"My dear cousin! Tempering is always by the lord's order. Oh, I recommend, to be sure. But orders for alterations must come from above. However, if it is any business of yours, in this case I made no recommendation. I was given the order, I had it carried out. All."

"Certainly it was my business! He works for me."

"Oh! But he had already been transferred before this was done. Else I would have made a point of telling you. Propriety, cousin, propriety in all things. I hold subordinates strictly accountable. So I never undercut them. Can't run a taut household if one does. Fair is fair."

"*I* wasn't told he was transferred. Don't you count that as undercutting?"

"Oh, but you were." The Chief Domestic glanced at the rack of pigeonholes backing his desk, searched briefly, pulled out a slip. "There it is."

Hugh looked at it. DUTY ASSIGNMENT, CHANGE IN—ONE SERVANT, MALE (*savage, rescued & adopted*), *known as Duke, description*—Hugh skipped on down.—*relieved of all duties in the Department of Ancient History and assigned to the personal service of Their Charity, effective immediately.* BILLETING & MESSING ASSIGNMENTS: *Unchanged until further*—

"I never saw this!"

"It's my file copy. You got the original." Memtok pointed at the lower left corner. "Your deputy clerk's sign. It always pleases me when my executives can read and write, it makes things so much more orderly. With an ignoramus like the Chief Groundskeeper, one can tell him until one's throat is raw and later the stupid lout will claim that wasn't the way he heard it—yet a tingling improves his memory only for that day. Disheartening. One can't be forever tingling an upper servant, it doesn't work." Memtok sighed. "I'd recommend a change, if his assistant wasn't even stupider."

"Memtok, I never saw this."

"As may be. It was delivered, your deputy receipted for it. Look around your office. One bullock gets you three you'll find it. Perhaps you'd like me to tingle your deputy? Glad to."

"No, no." Memtok was almost certainly right, the order was probably on his own desk, unread. Hugh's department had grown to two or three dozen people; there seemed to be more every day. Most of them seemed to be button sorters, all of them wanted to take up his time. Hugh had long since told the earnest, fairly literate clerk who was his deputy that he was not to be bothered—otherwise Hugh would have accomplished no translating after the first week; Parkinson's Law had taken over. The clerk had obeyed and routine matters stacked up. Every week or so Hugh would go through the stack rapidly, shove it back at his deputy for file or burning or whatever they did with useless papers.

Probably the order transferring Duke was in the current accumulation. If he had seen it in time— Too late, too late! He put his elbows on his knees and covered his face. Too late! Oh, my son!

Memtok touched his shoulder almost gently. "Cousin, take hold of yourself. Your prerogatives were not abridged. You see that, do you not?"

"Yes. Yes, I see it," Hugh mumbled through his hands.

"Then why are you overwrought?"

"He was—he *is*—my son."

"He is? Then why are you behaving as if he were your nephew?" Memtok used the specific form, meaning "your eldest sister's oldest son" and he was honestly puzzled by the savage's odd reaction. He could understand a mother being interested in her son—her oldest son, at least. But a father? Uncle! Memtok had sons, he was certain, throughout the household—"One-Shot Memtok" the former slutmaster used to call him. But he didn't know who they were and could not imagine wanting to know. Or caring.

"Because—" Hugh started. "Oh, forget it. You did your duty. Conceded."

"Well— You still seem upset. I'll send for a bottle of Happiness. I'll join you, this once."

"No. No, thank you."

"Oh, come, come! You need it. A tonic is excellent, it is excess that one must avoid."

"Thanks, Memtok, but I don't want it. Right now I must be sharp. I want to see Their Charity. Right away if possible. Will you arrange it for me?"

"I can't do that."

"Damn it, I know that you *can*. And I know he will see me if you ask him."

"Cousin, I didn't say that I would not; I said 'I *can't.*' Their Charity is not in residence."

"Oh." Then he asked to have word sent to Joe. But the
243

Chief Domestic told him that the young Chosen had left with the Lord Protector. He promised to let Hugh know when either of them returned— Yes, at once, cousin.

Hugh skipped dinner, went to his rooms and brooded. He could not avoid tormenting himself with the thought that it was, in part at least, his own fault—no, no, not for failing to read every useless paper that came into his office the instant it arrived; no, *that* was sheer bad luck. Even if he checked his "junk mail" each morning, it probably would have been too late; the two orders had probably gone out at the same time.

What did anguish his soul was fear that he had pushed the first domino in that quarrel with Duke. He could have lied to the boy, told him that his mother was, to Hugh's certain knowledge, a maid-in-waiting or some such, to the Lord Protector's sister, safe inside the royal harem and never seen by a man. Pampered, living the life of Riley, and happy in it—and that other tale was just gossip servants talk to fill their idle minds.

Duke would have believed it because Duke would have wanted to believe it.

As it was— Perhaps Duke had gone to see Their Charity. Perhaps Memtok had arranged it, or perhaps Duke had simply tried to bull his way in and the row had reached Ponse's ears. It was more than possible, he saw now, that his advice to Duke to see the head man might well have resulted in a scene that would have caused Ponse to order the tempering as casually as he would order his air coach. All too likely—

He tried to tell himself that no one is *ever* responsible for another person's actions. He believed it, he tried to live by it. But he found that cold wisdom no comfort.

At last he quit brooding, got writing materials, and got to work on a letter to Barbara. He had had not even a moment's chance to tell her his plans for them to escape, no chance to work up a code. But she must be ready at no notice; he must tell her, somehow.

Barbara knew German, he had a smattering from one high school year of it. He knew enough Russian to stumble through a simple conversation, Barbara had picked up a few words from him during their time in the wilderness—a game that they could share without giving Grace cause for jealousy.

He wrote a draft, then painfully translated the letter into a mishmash of German, Russian, colloquial English, beatnik jive, literary allusions, pig Latin, and special idioms. In the end he had a message that he was sure Barbara could puzzle out, but he was certain that no student of ancient languages could translate it into Language, even in the unlikely event that the scholar knew English, German, and Russian.

He was not afraid that it might be translated by anyone else. If Grace saw it, she would pronounce it gibberish; she knew no Russian, no German. Duke was off in a drug-ridden dream world. Joe might guess at the meaning—but he trusted Joe not to give him away. Nevertheless, he tried to conceal the meaning even from Joe, hashing the syntax and using deliberate misspellings.

The draft read:

My darling,

I have been planning our escape for some time. I do not know how I will manage it but I want you to be ready, day or night, to grab the twins and simply follow me. Steal food if you can, steal some stout shoes, steal a knife. We'll head for the mountains. I had intended to wait until next summer, let the boys grow some first. But something has happened to change my mind: Duke has been tempered. I don't know why and I'm too heartbroken to talk about it. But it could happen to me next. Worse than that— You remember Ponse's saying that he wanted to see our twins as matched footmen? Darling, studs do not serve in the Banquet Hall. Nor is there any other fate in store for them; they are both going to be tall. It must not happen!

And we can't wait. The capital city of the Protectorate is somewhere near where St. Louis used to be; we *can't* run all the way to the Rocky Mountains carrying our two boys—and we have no way of knowing (and no reason to expect) that all four of us will be sent to the Summer Palace next year.

Be brave. Don't touch any Happiness drug in any form from here on; our chance is likely to be a split-second one, with no warning.

I love you,
Hugh

Kitten came in; he told her to watch the show, not bother him. The child obeyed.

The final draft read:

Luba,

Ya bin smoking komplott seit Hector was weaned. The Count of Monte Cristo bit, dig? Kinder too klein machs nix—ya hawchoo! Goldilocks' troubles machs nix—as the fellow said, it's the only game in town. Good Girl Scouts always follow the Boy Scout motto. Speise, schuhen, messer—what Fagin taught Oliver, nicht? Da! Schnell is die herz von duh apparat; Berlin is too far from the Big Rock Candy and Eliza would never make the final curtain.

Ein ander jahr, nyet. It takes two to tango and four to play bridge, all in ein kammer, or the trek is dreck. A house divided is for the vogelen, like doom. Mehr, ya haben schrecken. Mein Kronprinz now rules only the Duchy of Abelard. Page Christine Jorgenson, he answers—I kid you not. Spilt milk butters no parsnips after the barn is burned so weep no more, my lady—but falsetto is not the pitch for detski whose horoscope reads Gemini. Borjemoi! Old King Coal is a Merry Old Soul but he'll get no zwilling kellneren from thee. Better a bonny bairn beards bären y begegn Karen—is ratification unaminous? Idgay eemay?

Verb. Sap.: I don't drink, smoke, nor chew, nor run around with twists who do. Cloud nine is endsville for this bit. Write soon, even if it's only five dollars utbay swing the jive; the dump is bugged and the Gay Pay Oo is eager.

Forever—H.

Kitten was long asleep before Hugh finished composing this jargon. He tore the draft into bits and dropped it down the whirlpool, went to bed. After a long time haunted by Duke's giggling, foolish, happy, drug-blurred face he got up and broke his own injunction to Barbara, dosed his sorrows and his fears with bottled Happiness.

17

Barbara's answer read:

Darling,
  When you bid three no-trump, my answer is seven no-trump, without hesitation. Then it's a grand slam—or we go set and don't cry. Any time you can get four together we'll be ready to play.
                                        Love always—B.

Nothing else happened that day. Nor the next—or the next. Hugh doggedly dictated translations, his mind not on his work. He was very careful what he ate or drank, since he now knew the surgeon's humane way of sneaking up on a victim; he ate only from dishes Memtok had eaten from, tried to be crafty by never accepting a fruit or a roll that was closest to him when a servant offered him such, avoided drinking anything at the table—he drank only water which he himself had taken from the tap. He continued to have breakfast in his room, but he started passing up many foods in favor of unpeeled fruits and boiled eggs in the shell.

He knew that these precautions were futile—no Borgia would have found them difficult to outwit—and in any case, if orders came to temper him, they need only grab him after subduing him with a whip if it proved difficult to drug him. But he might have time to protest, to demand that he be taken before the Lord Protector.

As for whips— He resumed karate practice, alone in his rooms. A karate blow delivered fast enough would cause even a whip wielder to lose interest. There was no real hope behind any of it; he simply intended not to go peacefully. Duke had been right; it would have been better to have fought and died.

He made no attempt to see Duke.

He continued to hide food from his breakfast tray—sugar, salt, hard bread. He assumed that such food must be undrugged even though he ate none of it at the time, because it did not affect Kitten.

He had been going barefoot most of the time but wearing felt slippers for his daily exercise walks in the servants' garden. Now he complained to Memtok that the gravel hurt his feet through these silly slippers—didn't the household afford anything better?

He was given heavy leather sandals, wore them thereafter in the garden.

He cultivated the household's chief engineer, telling him that, in his youth, he had been in charge of construction for his former lord. The engineer was flattered, being not only one of the junior executive servants but also in the habit of hearing mostly complaints rather than friendly interest. Hugh sat with him after dinner and managed to appear knowledgeable largely by listening.

Hugh was invited to look around the plant, and spent a tiring morning crawling over pipes and looking at plans—the engineer could not write but could read a little and understood drawings. It would have been an interesting day in itself if Hugh had been free from worries; Hugh's background made engineering interesting to him. But he concentrated on trying to memorize every drawing he saw, match it in his mind with the passageways and rooms he was taken through. He had a deadly serious purpose: Despite having lived most of a summer in this big building, he knew only small pieces of it inside and only a walled garden outside. He needed to know all of it; he needed to know every possible exit from servants' quarters, what lay behind the guarded door to sluts' quarters, and most particularly, where in that area Barbara and the twins lived.

He got as far as the meander door that led into the distaff side. The engineer hesitated when the guard suddenly became alert. He said, "Cousin Hugh, I'm sure it's all right for you to go in here, with me—but maybe we had better go up to the Chief Domestic's office and have him write you out a pass."

"Whatever you say, cousin."

"Well, there really isn't anything of interest in here. Just the usual appointments of a barracks—water, lights, air service, plumbing, baths, such things. All the interesting stuff, power plant, incinerator, air control, and so forth, is elsewhere. And you know how the boss is—likely to fret over any variation from routine. If it's all the same to you, I'll make my inspection in there later."

"However you want to arrange things," Hugh answered with a suggestion of affronted dignity.

"Well . . . everybody knows you're not one of those disgusting young studs." The engineer looked embarrassed. "Tell you what— You tell me flatly that you want to see everything . . . in my department that is—and I'll trot up to Memtok and tell him you said so. He knows—Uncle! we all know—that you enjoy the favor of Their Charity. You understand me? I don't mean to presume. Memtok will write out a pass and I'll be in the clear and so will the guard and the head guard. You wait here and be comfortable. I'll hurry."

"Don't bother. There's nothing in there I want to see," Hugh lied. "You've seen one bath, you've seen 'em all, I always say."

The engineer smiled in relief. "That's a good one, I'll remember that. 'You've seen one bath, you've seen 'em all!' Ha Ha! Well, we've still got the carpentry shop and the metal shop."

Hugh went on with him, arm in arm and jovial, while fuming inside. So close! Yet letting Memtok suspect that he had any interest in sluts' quarters was the last thing he wanted.

But the morning was well spent. Not only did Hugh acquire a burglar's insight as to weak points of the building (that delivery door to the unloading dock; if it was merely locked at night, it should be possible to break out) but also he picked up two prizes.

The first was a piece of spring steel about eight inches long. Hugh palmed it from some scrap in the metal shop; it wound up taped to his arm, after an unneeded plumbing call, for he had gone prepared to steal.

The second was even more of a prize: a printed drawing of the lowest level, with engineering installations shown boldly—but with every door and passage marked—including sluts' quarters.

Hugh had admired it. "Uncle, but that's a beautiful drawing! Your own work?"

The engineer shyly admitted that it was. Based on architect's plans, you understand—but changes keep having to be added.

"Beautiful!" Hugh repeated. "It's a shame there isn't more than one copy."

"Oh, plenty of copies, they wear out. Would you like one?"

"I would treasure it. Especially if the artist would inscribe it." When the man hesitated, Hugh moved in fast and said, "May I suggest a wording? Here, I'll write it out and you copy it."

Hugh walked away with the print, inscribed: *To my dear Cousin Hugh, a fellow craftsman who appreciates beautiful work.*

That night he showed it to Kitten. The child was awestruck. She had no concept of maps and was fascinated by the idea that it was possible to put down, just on a piece of paper, the long passages and twisty turns of her world. Hugh showed her how one went from his quarters to the ramp leading up to the executive servants' dining room, where the servants' main hall was, how the passage outside led, by two turns, to the garden. She confirmed the routes slowly, frowning in unaccustomed mental effort.

"You must live somewhere over here, Kitten. That is sluts' quarters."

"It is?"

"Yes. See if you can find where you live. I won't show you, you know how. I'll just sit back."

"Oh. Uncle help me! Let me see. First, I have to come down this ramp—" She paused to think while Hugh kept his face impassive. She had confirmed what he had almost stopped suspecting; the child was a planted spy. "Then . . . this is the door?"

"That's right."

"Then I walk straight ahead past the slutmaster's office, clear to the end, and I turn, and . . . I must live right *there!*" She clapped her hands and giggled.

"Your billet is across from your mess hall?"

"Yes."

"Then you got it right, first time! That's wonderful! Now let's see what else you can figure out."

For the next quarter hour she took him on a tour of sluts' quarters—junior and senior common rooms, messes, virgins' dormitory, bedwarmers' sleep room, nursery, lying-in, children's hall, service stalls, baths, playground door, garden door, offices, senior matron's apartment, everything—and Hugh learned that Barbara was no longer billeted in lying-in. Kitten volunteered it.

"Barbra—you know, the savage slut you write to—she used to be there, and now she right *there.*"

"How can you tell? Those rooms all look alike."

"*I* can tell. It's the second one of the four-mother rooms on this side, when you walk away from the baths."

Hugh noted with deep interest that a maintenance tunnel ran under the baths, with an access manhole in the passage Barbara's room was on—and with even deeper interest that this seemed to connect with another that ran clear across the building. Could it be that here was a wide-open unguarded route between all three main areas of servants' land? Surely not, as the lines seemed to show that any stud with initiative need only crawl a hundred yards to let himself into sluts' quarters.

Yet it might be true—for how would any stud know where those tunnels led?

And why would a stud risk it if he guessed? With the ra-

252

tio of intact males to breeding sluts about that of bulls to cows on a cattle ranch. And could thumbless hands handle the fastenings?

For that matter, could those trap doors be opened from below?

"You're a fast learner, Kitten. Now try a part you don't know as well. Figure out, on the drawing, how to get from our rooms here to my offices. And if you solve that one, here's a harder one. What turns you would take and what ramp you would use if I told you to take a message to the Chief Domestic?"

She solved the first one after puzzling, the second she traced without hesitation.

At lunch next day, with Memtok at his elbow, Hugh called down the table to the engineer. "Pipes, old cousin! That beautiful drawing you gave me yesterday— Do you suppose one of your woodworkers could frame it for me? I'd like to hang it over my desk where people can admire it."

The engineer flushed and grinned widely. "Certainly, Cousin Hugh! How about a nice piece of mahogany?"

"Perfect." Hugh turned to his left. "Cousin Memtok, our cousin is wasted on pipes and plumbing; he's an artist. As soon as I have it hung, you must stop by and see what I mean."

"Glad to, cousin. When I find time. If I find time."

More than a week passed with no word about Their Charity, nor about Joe—a week of no bridge, and no Barbara. At last, one day at lunch, Memtok said, "By the way, I had been meaning to tell you, the young Chosen Joseph has returned. Do you still want to see him?"

"Certainly. Is Their Charity also in residence?"

"No. Their Gracious sister believes that he may not return until after we go home. Ah, you must see that, cousin. Not a cottage like this. Great doings night and day—and this humble servant will be lucky to get three meals in peace all winter. Run, run, run, worry, worry, worry, problems popping right and left," he said with unctuous satisfaction. "Be glad you're a scholar."

Word came a couple of hours later that Joe expected Hugh. He knew his way, having been to Joe's guest rooms to help teach bridge to Chosen, so he went up alone.

Joe greeted him enthusiastically. "Come in, Hugh! Find a seat. No protocol, nobody here but us chickens. Wait till you hear what I've done. Boy, have I been busy! One shop ready to go as a pilot plant before Their Charity finished the wangling for the protection, all on the Q.T. But so organized that we were in production the day protection was granted. Not bad terms, either. Their Mercy takes half, Their Charity hangs onto half and floats the financing, and out of Their Charity's half I'm cut in for ten percent and manage the company. Of course as we branch out and into other lines—the whole thing is called 'Inspired Games' and the charter is written to cover almost any fun you can have out of bed—as we branch out, I'll need help and that's a problem; I'm scared old Ponse is going to want to put some of his dull-witted relatives in. Hope not, there's no place for nepotism when you're trying to hold down costs. Probably best to train servants for it—cheaper in the long run, with the right sort. How about you, Hugh? Do you think you could swing the management of a factory? It's a big job; I've got a hundred and seven people working already."

"I don't see why not. I've employed three times that many and never missed a payroll—and I once bossed two thousand skilled trades in the Seabees. But, Joe, I came up here with something on my mind."

"Uh, all right, spill it. Then I want to show you the plans."

"Joe, you know about Duke?"

"What about Duke?"

"Tempered. Didn't you know?"

"Oh. Yes, I knew. Happened just about as I left. He's not hurt, is he? Complications?"

" 'Hurt?' Joe, he was *tempered*. You act as if he had merely had a tooth pulled. You knew? Did you try to stop it?"

"No."

"In the name of God, *why not?*"

"Let me finish, can't you? I don't recall that *you* tried to stop it, either."

"I never had the chance. I never knew."

"Neither did I. That's what I've been trying to tell you, but you keep jumping down my throat. I learned about it after it happened."

"Oh. Sorry. I thought you meant you just stood by and let it happen."

"Well, I didn't. Don't know what I could have done if I had known. Maybe asked Ponse to call you in first, I suppose. Wouldn't have done any good, so I guess we were both better off not having to fret about it. Maybe all for the best. Now about our plans— If you'll look at this schematic layout, you'll see—"

"Joe!"

"Huh?"

"Can't you see that I'm in no shape to talk about playing-card factories? Duke is my *son.*"

Joe folded up his plans. "I'm sorry, Hugh. Let's talk, if it will make you feel better. Get it off your chest—I suppose you do feel bad about it. Looking at it from one angle."

Joe listened, Hugh talked. Presently Joe shook his head. "Hugh, I can set your mind at rest on one point. Duke never did see the Lord Protector. So your advice to Duke—good advice, I think—could not have had anything to do with his being tempered."

"I hope you're right. I'd feel like cutting my throat if I knew it was my fault."

"It's not, so quit fretting."

"I'll try. Joe, whatever possessed Ponse to do it? He knew how we felt about it, from that time it almost happened through a misunderstanding. So why would he? I thought he was my friend."

Joe looked embarrassed. "You really want to know?"

"I've got to know."

"Well . . . you're bound to find out. Grace did it."

"*What?* Joe, you must be mistaken. Sure, Grace has her

255

faults. But she wouldn't have *that* done—to her own son."

"Well, no, not exactly. I doubt if she knew what it was until after it was done. But just the same, she set it off. She's been wheedling Ponse almost from the day we got here that she wanted her Dukie with her. She was lonesome. 'Ponsie, I'm lonesome. Ponsie, you're being mean to Gracie. Ponsie, I'm going to tickle you until you say Yes. Ponsie, why won't you?'—all in that baby whine she uses. Hugh, I guess you didn't see much of it—"

"None of it."

"I would have wrung her neck. Ponse just ignored her, except when she tickled him. Then he would laugh and they would roll on the floor and he would tell her to shut up, and make her sit quiet for a while. Treated her just like one of the cats. Honest, I don't think he ever—I mean, it doesn't seem likely, from what I saw, that he was interested in her as a—"

"And I'm not interested. Didn't anybody tell Grace what it would entail, for her to have her son with her?"

"Hugh, I don't think so. It would never occur to Ponse that explanation was required . . . and certainly I never discussed it with her. She doesn't like me, I take up too much of her Ponsie's time." Joe wrinkled his nose. "So I doubt if she knew. Of course she should have figured it out; anybody else would have. But, excuse me, since she's your wife, but I'm not sure she's bright enough."

"And hopped up on Happiness, too—every time I caught sight of her. No, she's not bright. But she's not my wife, either. Barbara is my wife."

"Well . . . legally speaking, a servant can't have a wife."

"I wasn't speaking legally, I was speaking the truth. But even though Grace is no longer my wife, I'm somewhat comforted to know that she probably didn't know what it would cost Duke."

Joe looked thoughtful. "Hugh, I don't think she did . . . but I don't think she really cares, either . . . and I'm not sure that you can properly say that it cost Duke anything."

"You might explain. Perhaps I'm dense."

"Well, if Grace minds that Duke has been tempered,

she doesn't show it. She's pleased as punch. And he doesn't seem to mind."

"You've seen them? Since?"

"Oh, yes. I had breakfast with Their Charity yesterday morning. They were there."

"I thought Ponse was away?"

"He was back and now he's gone out to the West Coast. Business. We're really tearing into it. He was here only a couple of days. But he had this birthday present for Grace. Duke, I mean. Yes, I know it wasn't her birthday, and anyhow birthdays aren't anything nowadays; it's nameday that counts. But she told Ponse she was about to have a birthday and kept wheedling him—and you know Ponse, indulgent with animals and kids. So he set it up as a surprise for her. The minute he was back, he made a present of Duke to her. Shucks, they've even got a room off Ponse's private quarters; neither of them sleeps below-stairs, they live up here."

"Okay, I don't care where they sleep. You were telling me how Grace felt about it. And Duke."

"Oh, yes. Can't say just when she found out what had been done to Duke, all I can say is that she is so happy about it all that she was even cordial with me—telling me what a dear Ponsie was to arrange it and doesn't Dukie look just *grand?* In his new clothes? Stuff like that. She's got him dressed in the fancy livery the servants wear up here, not a robe like that you're wearing. She's even put jewelry on him. Ponse doesn't mind. He's an outright gift, a servant's servant. I don't think he does a lick of work, he's just her pet. And she loves it that way."

"But how about Duke?"

"That's what I've been telling you, Hugh; Duke hasn't lost by it. He's snug as a bug in a rug and he knows it. He was almost patronizing to me. You might have thought that I was the one wearing livery. With Grace in solid with the big boss and with her wound around his finger, Duke thinks he's got it made. Well, he *has,* Hugh. And I didn't mind his manner; I could see he was hopped on this tranquilizer you servants use."

257

"You call it 'got it made' when a man is grabbed and drugged and tempered and then kept drugged so that he doesn't *care?* Joe, I'm shocked."

"Certainly I call it that! Hugh, put your prejudices aside and look at it rationally. Duke is happy. If you don't believe it, let me take you in there and you talk to him. Talk to both of them. See for yourself."

"No, I don't think I could stomach it. I'll concede that Duke is happy. I'm well aware that if you feed a man enough of that Happiness drug, he'll be happy as a lark even if you cut off his arms and legs and then start on his head. But you can be that sort of 'happy' on morphine. Or heroin. Or opium. That doesn't make it a good thing. It's a tragedy."

"Oh, don't be melodramatic, Hugh. These things are all relative. Duke was certain to be tempered eventually. It's not lawful for a servant as big as he is to be kept for stud, I'm sure you know that. So what difference does it make whether it's done last week, or next year, or when Ponse dies? The only difference is that he is happy in a life of luxury, instead of hard manual labor in a mine, or a rice swamp, or such. He doesn't know anything useful, he could never hope to rise very high. High for a servant, I mean."

"Joe, do you know what you sound like? Like some white-supremacy apologist telling how well off the darkies used to be, a-sittin' outside their cabins, a-strummin' their banjoes, and singin' spirituals."

Joe blinked. "I could resent that."

Hugh Farnham was angry and feeling reckless. "Go ahead and resent it! I can't stop you. You're a Chosen, I'm a servant. Can I fetch your white sheet for you, Massah? What time does the Klan meet?"

"Shut up!"

Hugh Farnham shut up. Joe went on quietly. "I won't bandy words with you. I suppose it does look that way to you. If so, do you expect me to weep? The shoe is on the other foot, that's all—and high time. I used to be a servant, now I'm a respected businessman—with a good chance of becoming a nephew by marriage of some noble family. Do you think I would swap back, even if I could? For *Duke*? Not for anybody, I'm no hypocrite. I was a servant, now you are one. What are you beefing about?"

"Joe, you were a decently treated employee. You were not a slave."

The younger man's eyes suddenly became opaque and his features took on an ebony hardness Hugh had never seen in him before. "Hugh," he said softly, "have you ever made a bus trip through Alabama? As a 'nigger'?"

"No."

"Then shut up. You don't know what you are talking about." He went on, "The subject is closed and now we'll talk business. I want you to see what I've done and am planning to do. This games notion is the best idea I ever had."

Hugh did not argue whose idea it had been; he listened while the young man went on with eager enthusiasm. At last Joe put down his pen and sat back. "What do you think of it? Any suggestions? You made some useful suggestions when I proposed it to Ponse—keep on being useful and there will be a good place in it for you."

Hugh hesitated. It seemed to him that Joe's plans were too ambitious for a market that was only a potential and a demand that had yet to be created. But all he said was, "It might be worth while to package with each deck, no extra charge, a rule book."

"Oh, no, we'll sell those separately. Make money on them."

"I didn't mean a complete Hoyle. Just a pamphlet with some of the simpler games. Cribbage. A couple of solitaire games. One or two others. Do that and the customers start enjoying them at once. It should lead to more sales."

"Hmm— I'll think about it." Joe folded up his papers, set them aside. "Hugh, you got so shirty a while ago that I didn't tell you one thing I have in mind."

"Yes?"

"Ponse is a grand old man, but he isn't going to live forever. I plan to have my own affairs separate from his by then so that I'll be financially independent. Trade around interests somehow, untangle it. I don't need to tell you that I'm not anxious to have Mrika as my boss—and I didn't tell you, so don't repeat it. But I'll manage it, I'm looking out for number one." He grinned. "And when Mrika is Lord Protector I won't be here. I'll have a household of my own, a modest one—and I'll need servants. Guess whom I plan to adopt when I staff it."

"I couldn't."

"Not you—although you may very well be a business servant to me, if it turns out you really can manage a job. No, I had in mind adopting Grace and Duke."

"Huh?"

"Surprised? Mrika won't want them, that's certain. He despises Grace because of her influence over his uncle, and it's a sure thing he's not going to like Duke any better. Neither of them is trained and it shouldn't be expensive to adopt them if I don't appear too eager. But they would be useful to me. For one thing, since they speak English, I'd be able to talk to them in a language nobody else knows, and that could be an advantage, especially when other servants are around. But best of all— Well, the food here is good but sometimes I get a longing for some plain old American cooking, and Grace is a good cook when she wants to be. So I'll make her a cook. Duke can't cook but he can learn to wait on table and answer the door and such. Houseboy, in other words. How about that?"

Hugh said slowly, "Joe, you don't want them because Grace can cook."

Joe grinned unashamedly. "No, not entirely. I think Duke would look real good as my houseboy. And Grace as my cook. Tit for Tat. Oh, I'll treat them decently, Hugh, don't you worry. They work hard and behave themselves and they won't get tingled. However, I don't doubt but what it will take a few tingles before they get the idea." He twitched his quirt. "And I won't say I won't enjoy teaching them. I owe them a little. Three years, Hugh. Three years of Grace's endless demands, never satisfied with anything—and three years of being treated with patronizing contempt by Duke whenever he was around."

260

Hugh said nothing. Joe said, "Well? What do you think of my plan?"

"I thought better of you, Joe. I thought you were a gentleman. It seems I was wrong."

"So?" Joe barely twitched his quirt. "Boy, we excuse you. All."

18

Hugh came away from Joe's rooms feeling utterly discouraged. He knew that he had been foolish—no, criminally careless!—in letting Joe get his goat. He needed Joe. Until he had Barbara and the twins safely hidden in the mountains, he needed every possible source of favor. Joe, Memtok, Ponse, anyone he could find—and probably Joe most of all. Joe was a Chosen, Joe could go anywhere, tell him things he didn't know, give him things he could not steal. He had even considered, as a last resort, asking Joe to help them to escape.

Not now! Idiot! Utter fool! To risk Barbara and the boys just because you can't hold your bloody temper.

It seemed to him that things were as bad as they could get—and part of it his own folly.

He did not stand around moping; he looked up Memtok. It had become more urgent than ever to set up some way to communicate with Barbara secretly—and that meant that he had to talk to her—and that meant at least one bridge game in the Lord Protector's lounge and a snatch of talk even if he had to talk English in front of Ponse. He had to force matters.

Hugh found the Chief Domestic leaving his office. "Cousin Memtok, could you spare me a word?"

Memtok's habitual frown barely relaxed. "Certainly, cousin. But walk along with me, will you? Trouble, trouble, trouble—you would think that a department head could run his department without someone to wipe his nose, wouldn't you? You'd be wrong. The freezer flunky complains to the leading butcher and he complains to the chef, and it's a maintenance matter, and you would think that Gnou would take it up directly with engineering and between them they would settle it. Oh, no! They both come to me with their troubles. You know something about construction, don't you?"

"Yes," Hugh admitted, "but I'm not up-to-date in the subject. It has been some years." (About two thousand, my friend! But we won't speak of that.)

"Construction is construction. Come along, give me the benefit of your advice."

(And find out that I'm faking. Chum, I'll double-talk you to death.) "Certainly. If this humble one's opinion is worth anything."

"Damned chill room. It's been a headache every summer. I'm glad we'll be back in the Palace soon."

"Has the date been set? May one ask?"

"One may. A week from tomorrow. So it's time to think about packing up your department and being ready to move."

Hugh tried to keep his face calm and his voice steady. "So soon?"

"Why are *you* looking worried? A few files, some office equipment. Have you any idea how many thousands of items *I* have on inventory? And how much gets stolen, or lost, or damaged simply because you can't trust any of these fools? Uncle!"

"It must be terribly wearing," agreed Hugh. "But that brings to mind something. I petitioned you to let me know when Their Charity was next in residence. I learned from the young Chosen, Joseph, that Their Charity returned a day or two ago and is now gone again."

"Are you criticizing?"

"Uncle forbid! I was just asking."

"It is true that Their Charity was physically present for a short time. But he was not officially in residence. Not in the best of health, it seemed to me—Uncle protect him."

"Uncle protect him well!" Hugh answered sincerely. "Under the circumstances naturally you did not ask him to grant me an audience. But could I ask of you the small favor, next time—"

"We'll talk later. Let's see what these two helpless ones

263

have to offer." Head Chef Gnou and the Chief Engineer met them at the entrance to Gnou's domain, they went on through the kitchen, through the butcher shop, and into the cold room. But they lingered in the butcher shop, Memtok impatient, while parka-like garments were fetched, the Chief Domestic having refused the ones offered on the legitimate grounds that they were soiled.

The butcher shop was crowded with live helpers and dead carcasses—birds, beeves, fish, anything. Hugh reflected that thirty-eight Chosen and four hundred and fifty servants ate a lot of meat. He found the place mildly depressing even though he himself had cleaned and cut and trimmed many an animal.

But only his habitual tight control in the presence of Memtok and his "cousins" in service kept him from showing shock at something he saw on the floor, trimmed from a carcass almost cut up on one block.

It was a dainty, plump, very feminine hand.

Hugh felt dizzy, there was a roaring in his ears. He blinked. It was still there. A hand much like Kitten's—

He breathed carefully, controlled the retching within him, kept his back turned until he had command over himself. There had suddenly flooded over him the truth behind certain incongruities, certain idioms, some pointless jokes.

Gnou was making nervous conversation while his boss waited. He moved to the chopping block, unintentionally kicking the dainty little hand underneath into a pile of scraps and said, "Here's one you won't have to bother to taste, Chief Domestic. Unless the old one returns unexpectedly."

"I always bother to taste," Memtok said coldly. "Their Charity expects his table to be perfect whether he is in residence or not."

"Oh, yes, surely," Gnou agreed. "That's what I always tell my cooks. But— Well, this very roast illustrates one of my problems. Too fat. You'll feel that it's greasy—and so it will be. But that's what comes of using sluts. Now, in my opinion, you can't find a nicer piece of meat, marbled but firm, than a buck tempered not older than six, then hung at twice that age."

"No one asked your opinion," Memtok answered. "Their Charity's opinion is the only one that counts. They think that sluts are more tender."

"Oh, I agree, I agree! No offense intended."

"And none taken. In fact I agree with your opinion. I was simply making clear that your opinion—and mine in this matter—is irrelevant. I see they've fetched them. Did they stop to make them?"

The party put on heavy garments, went on inside. The engineer had said nothing up to then, effacing himself other than a nod and a grin to Hugh. Now he explained the problem, a cranky one of refrigeration. Hugh tried to keep his eyes on it, rather than on the contents of the meat storage room.

Most of the meat was beef and fowl. But one long row of hooks down the center held what he knew he would find—human carcasses, gutted and cleaned and frozen, hanging head down, save that the heads were missing. Young sluts and bucks, he could see, but whether the bucks were tempered or not was no longer evident. He gulped and thanked his unlucky stars that that pathetic little hand had given him warning, at least saved him from fainting.

"Well, Cousin Hugh, what do you think?"

"Why, I agree with Pipes."

"That the problem can't be solved?"

"No, no." Hugh had not listened. "His reasoning is correct and he implied the answer. As he says, the problem can't be solved—now. The thing to do is not to try to patch it up, *now*. Wait a week. Tear it out. Put in new equipment."

Memtok looked sour. "Expensive."

"But cheaper in the long run. Good engineering isn't accomplished by grudging a few bullocks. Isn't that right, Pipes?"

The engineer nodded vigorously. "Just what I always say, Cousin Hugh! You're absolutely right."

Memtok still frowned. "Well— Prepare an estimate. Show it to Cousin Hugh before you bring it to me."

"Yes, sir!"

Memtok paused on the way out and patted the loin of a stripling buck carcass. "That's what I would call a nice piece of meat. Eh, Hugh?"

"Beautiful," Hugh agreed with a straight face. "Your nephew, perhaps? Or just a son?"

There was frozen silence. Nobody moved except that Memtok seemed to grow taller. He raised his whip of authority most slightly, no more than tightening his thumbless grip.

Then he grimaced and gave a dry chuckle. "Cousin Hugh, your well-known wit will be the death of me yet. That's a good one. Gnou, remind me to tell that this evening."

The Chief agreed and chuckled, the engineer roared. Memtok gave his cold little laugh again. "I'm afraid I can't claim the honor, Hugh. All of these critters are ranch bred, not one of them is a cousin of ours. Yes, I know how it is in some households, but Their Charity considers it unspeakably vulgar to serve a house servant, even in cases of accidental death— And besides, it makes the servants restless."

"Commendable."

"Yes. It is gratifying to serve one who is a stickler for propriety. Enough, enough, time is wasting. Walk back with me, Hugh."

Once they were clear of the rest Memtok said, "You were saying?"

"Excuse me?"

"Come, come, you're absentminded today. Something about Their Charity not being in residence."

"Oh, yes. Memtok, could you, as a special favor to me, let me know the minute Their Charity returns? Whether officially in residence or not? Not petition anything for me. Just let me know." Damn it, with time pouring away like life through a severed artery his only course might be a belly-scraping apology to Joe, then get Joe to intercede.

"No," said Memtok. "No, I don't think I can."

"I beg your pardon? Has this one offended you?"

"You mean that witticism? Heaven, no! Some might find it vulgar and one bullock gets you three that if you had told it in sluts' quarters some of them would have fainted. But if there is one thing I pride myself on, Hugh, it's my sense of humor—and any day I can't see a joke simply because I am the butt of it, I'll petition to turn in my whip. No, it was simply my turn to have a little joke at your expense. I said, 'I don't think I can.' That is a statement of two meanings—a double-meaning joke, follow me? I don't think I can tell you when Their Charity returns because he has sent word to me that he is not returning. So you'll see him next at the Palace . . . and I promise I'll let you know when he's in residence." The Chief Domestic dug him in the ribs. "I wish you had seen your own face. My joke wasn't nearly as sharp as yours. But your jaw dropped. Very comical."

Hugh excused himself, went to his rooms, took an extra bath, a most thorough one, then simply thought until dinnertime. He braced himself for the ordeal of dinner with a carefully measured dose of Happiness—not enough to affect him later, strong enough to carry him through dinner, now that he knew why "pork" appeared so often on the menu of the Chosen. He suspected that the pork served to servants was really pork. But he intended to eat no more bacon nevertheless. Nor ham, nor pork chops, nor sausage. In fact he might turn vegetarian—at least until they were free in the mountains and it was eat game or starve.

But with a shot of Happiness inside him he was able to smile when Memtok tasted the roast for upstairs and to say, "Greasy?"

"Worse than usual. Taste it."

"No, thanks. I knew it would be. I would cook up better than that—though no doubt I would be terribly stringy. And tough. Though perhaps Cousin Gnou could tenderize me."

Memtok laughed until he choked. "Oh, Hugh, don't ever be that funny while I'm swallowing! You'll kill me yet."

"This one hopes not." Hugh toyed with the beef on his plate, pushed it aside and ate a few nuts.

He was very busy that evening, writing long after Kitten was asleep. It had become utterly necessary to reach Barbara secretly, yet his only means was the insecure route through Kitten. The problem was to write to Barbara in a code that only she could read, and which she would see as a code without having been warned and without the code being explained to her—and yet one which was safe from others. But the double-talk mixture he had last sent her would not do; he was now going to have to give her detailed instructions, ones where it really mattered if she missed a word or failed to guess a concealed meaning.

His last draft was:

Darling,

If you were here, I would love a literary gabfest, a good one. You know what I mean, I am sure. Let's consider Edgar Allan Poe, for example. Can you recall how I claimed that Poe was the best writer both to read and to reread of all the mystery writers before or since, and that this was true because he never could be milked dry on one reading? The answer or answers in The Gold Bug, or certainly that little gem The Murders in the Rue Morgue, or take The Case of the Purloined Letter, or any of them; same rule will apply to them all, when you consider the very subtle way he always had of slanting his meaning so that one reaches a full period in his sentences only after much thought. Poe is grand fun and well worth study. Let's have our old literary talks by letter. How about Mark Twain next? Tired—must go to bed!

Love—

Since Hugh had never discussed Edgar Allan Poe with Barbara at any time, he was certain that she would study the note for a hidden message. The only question was whether or not she would find it. He wanted her to read it as:

"If

you

can

read

this

answer

the

same

way

period"

Having done his best he put it aside, first disposing of all trial work, then prepared to do something else much more risky. At that point he would have given his chances of immortal bliss, plus 10 percent, for a flashlight, then settled for a candle. His rooms were lighted, brilliantly or softly as he wished, by glowing translucent spheres set in the upper corners. Hugh did not know what they were save that they were not any sort of light he had ever known. They gave off no heat, seemed not to require wiring, and were controlled by little cranks.

A similar light, the size of a golf ball, was mounted on his scroll reader. It was controlled by twisting it; he had decided tentatively that twisting these spheres polarized them in some way.

He tried to dismount the scroll reader light.

He finally got it loose by breaking the upper frame. It was now a featureless, brilliantly shining ball and nothing he could do would dim it—which was almost as embarrassing as no light at all.

He found that he could conceal it in an armpit under

his robe. There was still a glow but not much.

He made sure that Kitten was asleep, turned out all lights, raised his corridor door, looked out. The passageway was lighted by a standing light at an intersection fifty yards away. Regrettably he had to go that way. He had expected no lights at this hour.

He felt his "knife" taped to his left arm—not much of a knife, but patient whetting with a rock picked up from a garden path had put an edge on it, and tape had made a firm grip. It needed hours more work and he could work on it only after Kitten was asleep or in time stolen from working hours. But it felt good to have it there and it was the only knife, chisel, screwdriver, or burglar's jimmy that he had.

The manhole to the engineering service tunnels lay in the passage to the right after he had to pass the lighted intersection. Any manhole would do but that one was on the route to the veterinary's quarters; if caught outside his rooms but otherwise without cream on his lip, he planned to plead a sudden stomachache.

The manhole cover swung back easily on a hinge, it was fastened by a clasp that needed only turning to free it. The floor of the tunnel, glimpsed with his shiny sphere, lay four feet below the corridor floor. He started to let himself down and ran into his first trouble.

These manholes and tunnels had been intended for men a foot shorter and fifty pounds lighter than Hugh Farnham, and proportionately smaller in shoulders, hips, hands-and-knees height, and so forth.

But he could make it. He had to.

He wondered how he would make it, crawling and carrying at least one baby. But that he had to do, too. So he would.

He almost trapped himself. Barely in time he found that the underside of the steel door was smooth, no handle, and that it latched automatically by a spring catch.

That settled why no one worried that the studs might gain unplanned access to sluts. But it also settled something else. Hugh had considered snatching this very chance, if he found things quiet at the other end: Wake

Barbara, bring all four of them back via the tunnel—then outside and away, by any of a dozen weak points, away and off to the mountains on foot, reach them before light, find some stream and ford it endwise to throw off hounds. Go, go, *go!* With almost no food, with nothing but a makeshift knife, with no equipment, a "nightshirt" for clothing, and no hope of anything better. Go! And save his family, or die with them. But die *free!*

Perhaps someday his twin sons, wiser in the new ways than himself and toughened by a life fighting nature, could lead an uprising against this foul thing. But all he planned to do, all he could hope for, was get them free, keep them free, alive and free and ungelded, until they were grown and strong.

Or die.

Such was still his plan. He wasted not a moment sorrowing over that spring catch. It merely meant that he *must* communicate with Barbara, set a time with her, because she would have to open the hatch at the far end. Tonight he could only reconnoiter.

He found that tape from his knife handle would hold the spring catch back. He tested it from above; the lid could now be swung back without turning the clasp.

But his wild instincts warned him. The tape might not hold until he was back. He might be trapped inside.

He spent a sweating half hour working on that spring catch, using knife and fingers and holding the light ball in his teeth.

At last he managed to get at and break the spring. He removed the catch entirely. The manhole, closed, now looked normal, but it could be opened from underneath with just a push.

Only then did he let himself down inside and close it over him.

He started out on knees and elbows with the light in his mouth, and stopped almost at once. The damned skirt of his robe kept him from crawling! He tried bunching it around his waist. It slid down.

He inched back to the manhole shaft, took the pesky garment off entirely, left it under the manhole, crawled

271

away without it, naked save for the knife strapped to his arm and the light in his teeth. He then made fair progress, although never able to get fully on hands and knees. His elbows had to be bent, his thighs he could not bring erect, and there were places where valves and fittings of the pipes he crawled past forced him almost to his belly.

Nor could he tell how far he was going. However, there were joints in the tunnel about every thirty feet; he counted them and tried to match them in his mind with the engineering drawing.

Pass under two manholes . . . sharp left turn into another tunnel at next manhole . . . crawl about a hundred and fifty feet and under one manhole—

Something more than an hour later he was under a manhole which had to be the one closest to Barbara.

If he had not lost himself in the bowels of the palace— If he had correctly remembered that complex drawing— If the drawing was up to date— (Had two thousand years made any difference in the lag between engineering changes and revisions of prints to match?) If Kitten knew what she was talking about in locating Barbara's billet by a method so novel to her— If it was still Barbara's billet—

He crouched in the awkward space and tried to press his ear against the shaft's cover.

He heard a baby cry.

About ten minutes later he heard hushed female voices. They approached, passed over him, and someone stopped on the lid.

Hugh unkinked himself, prepared to return. The space was so tight that the obvious way was to back up the way he had come, so he found himself trying to crawl backward through the tunnel.

That worked so poorly that he came back to the shaft and, with contortions and loss of skin, got turned around.

What seemed hours later he was convinced that he was lost. He began to wonder which was the more likely: Would he starve or die of thirst? Or would some repairman get the shock of his life by finding him?

But he kept on crawling.

His hands found his robe before his eyes saw it. Five minutes later he was in it; seven minutes later (he stopped to listen) he was up and out and had the lid closed. He forced himself not to run back to his rooms.

Kitten was awake.

He wasn't aware of it until she followed him into the bath. Then she was saying with wide-eyed horror, "Oh, dear! Your poor knees! And your elbows, too."

"I stumbled and fell down."

She didn't argue it, she simply insisted on bathing him and salving and taping the raw places. When she started to pick up his dirty robe, he told her sharply to go to bed. He did not mind her touching his robe but his knife had been on top of it and only by maneuvering had he managed to keep himself between her and it long enough to flip a fold of cloth over the weapon.

Kitten went silently to bed. Hugh hid the knife in its usual place (much too high for Kitten), then went into his living room and found the child crying. He petted her, soothed her, said he had not meant to sound harsh, and fed her a bonus dose of Happiness—sat with her while she drank it, watched her go happily to sleep.

Then he did not even try to get along without it himself. Kitten had gone to sleep with one hand outside her cover. It looked to Hugh exactly like a forlorn little hand he had seen twelve hours earlier on the floor of a butcher shop.

He was exhausted and the drink let him go to sleep. But not to rest. He found himself at a dinner party, black tie and dressy. But he did not like the menu. Hungarians goulash . . . French fries . . . Chinese noodles . . . po' boy sandwich . . . breast of peasant . . . baked Alaskans—but it was all pork. His host insisted that he taste every dish. "Come, come!" he chided with a wintry smile. "How do you know you don't like it? One bullock gets you three you'll learn to love it."

Hugh moaned and could not wake up.

Kitten did not chatter at breakfast, which suited him. Two hours of nightmare-ridden sleep was not enough, yet it was necessary to go to his office and pretend to work.

Mostly he stared at the print framed over his desk while his scroll reader clicked unnoticed. After lunch he sneaked away and tried to nap. But the engineer scratched at his door and apologetically asked him to look over his estimates on refitting the meat cooler. Hugh poured his guest a dolop of Happiness, then pretended to study figures that meant nothing to him. After a decent time he complimented the man, then scrawled a note to Memtok, recommending that the contract be let.

Barbara's note that night applauded the idea of a literary discussion club by mail and discussed Mark Twain. Hugh was interested only in how it read diagonally:

"Did

    I

        read

            it

                correctly

                darling

                    question

                    mark"

19

"Darling

we

must

escape

next

six

days

or

sooner

be

ready

night

after

letter

275

has

    phrase

        Freedom

            is

                a

                    lonely

                      thing—"

For the next three days Hugh's letters to Barbara were long and chatty and discussed everything from Mark Twain's use of colloquial idiom to the influence of progressive education on the relaxation of grammar. Her answers were lengthy, equally "literary," and reported that she would be ready to open the hatch, confirmed that she understood, that she had a little stock of food, had no knife, no shoes—but that her feet were very calloused—and that her only worry was that the twins might cry or that her roommates might wake up, especially as two of them were still giving night feedings to their babies. But for Hugh not to worry, she would manage.

Hugh drew a fresh bottle of Happiness, taped it near the top of the shaft closest to her billet, instructed her to tell her roommates that she had stolen it, then use it to get them so hopped up on the drug that they would either sleep or be so slaphappy that if they did wake, they would do nothing but giggle—and, if possible, get enough of the drug into the twins that the infants would pass out and not cry no matter how they were handled.

Making an extra trip through the tunnels to plant the bottle was a risk Hugh hated to take. But he made it pay. He not only timed himself by the clock in his rooms and learned beyond any possibility of mistake the rat maze he must follow but also he carried a practice load, a package of scrolls taped together to form a mass bigger and heavier, he felt sure, than one of his infant sons would be. This he tied to his chest with a sling made of stolen cloth; it had been a dust cover for the scroll printer in his offices. He made two such slings, one for Barbara, and tore and tied them so they could be shifted to the back later to permit the babies to be carried papoose style.

He found that it was difficult but not impossible to carry a baby in this fashion through the tunnels, and he spotted the places where it was necessary to inch forward with extreme care not to place any pressure on his dummy "precious burden" and still not let the ties on his back catch on engineering fittings above him.

But it could be done and he got back to his rooms without waking Kitten—he had increased her evening bonus of Happiness. He replaced the scrolls, hid his knife and spherical lamp, washed his knees and elbows and anointed them, then sat down and wrote a long P.S. to the letter he had written earlier to tell Barbara how to find the bottle. This postscript added some afterthoughts about the philosophy of Hemingway and remarked that it seemed odd that a writer would in one story say that "freedom is a lonely thing" and in another story state that—and so on.

That night he gave Kitten her usual amplified nightcap, then said, "Not much left in this bottle. Finish it off and I'll get a fresh one tomorrow."

"Oh, I'd get terribly silly. You wouldn't like me."

"Go ahead, drink it. Have a good time, live it up. What else is life for?"

Half an hour later Kitten was more than willing to be helped to bed. Hugh stayed with her until she was snoring heavily. He covered her hands, stood looking down at her, suddenly knelt and kissed her good-bye.

A few minutes later he was down the first manhole.

He took off his robe, piled on it a bundle of what he had collected for survival—food, sandals, wig, two pots of deodorant cream into which he had blended brown pigment. He did not expect to use disguise and had little faith in it, but if they were overtaken by daylight before they were in the mountains, he intended to darken all four of them, tear their robes into something resembling the breechclout and wrap-around which he had learned were the working clothes of free peasant farmers among the Chosen—"poor black trash" as Joe called them—and try to brazen it out, keeping away from people if possible, until it was dark again.

He tied one baby sling to him with the other inside it and started. He hurried, as time was everything. Even if Barbara managed to pass out her roommates promptly, even if he had no trouble breaking out at his preferred exit, even if the crawl back through the tunnels could be made in less than an hour—doubtful, with the kids—they could not be outdoors earlier than midnight, which allowed them five hours of darkness to reach wild country. Could he hope for three miles an hour? It seemed unlikely, Barbara barefooted and both carrying kids, the country unknown and dark—and those mountains seen from his window seemed to be at least fifteen miles away. It would be a narrow squeak even if everything broke his way.

He made fast time to sluts' quarters, punishing his knees and elbows.

The bottle was missing, he could feel the tacky places where he had fastened it. He settled himself as comfortably as possible and concentrated on quieting his pounding heart, slowing his breathing, and relaxing. He tried to make his mind blank.

He dozed off. But he was instantly alert when the lid over him was raised.

Barbara made no sound. She handed him one of their sons, he stuffed the limp little body as far down the tunnel as he could reach. She handed him the other, he placed it beside the first, then added a pitiful little bundle she had.

But he did not kiss her until they were down inside—only seconds after he had wakened—and the lid had clicked into place over them.

She clung to him, sobbing; he whispered to her fiercely not to make a sound, then added last-minute instructions into her ear. She quieted instantly; they got busy.

It was agonizingly difficult to get ready for the crawl in a space too small for one and nearly impossible for them both. They did it because they had to. First he helped her get out of the shorter garment sluts wore, then he had her lie down with her legs back in the other reach of the tunnel while he tied a baby sling to her, then a baby was stuffed into each sling and knots tightened to keep each child slung as high in its little hammock as possible. Hugh then knotted the skirt of her garment together, stuffed her hoarded food into the sack thus formed, tied the sleeves around his left leg, and let it drag behind. He had planned to tie it around his waist, but the sleeves were too short.

That done (it seemed to take hours), he had Barbara back up into the far reach of the tunnel, then managed painfully to turn himself and get headed the right way without banging little Hughie's skull. Or was it Karl Joseph? He had forgotten to ask. Either one, the baby's warm body against his, its lightly sensed breathing, gave him fresh courage. By God, they would make it! Whatever got in his way would die.

He set out, with the light in his teeth, moving very fast wherever clearance let him do so. He did not slow down for Barbara and had warned her that he would not unless she called out.

She did not, ever. Once her baggage worked loose from his leg. They stopped and he had her tie it to his ankle; that was their only rest. They made good time but it seemed forever before he reached the little pile of plunder he had cached when he set out.

They unslung the babies and caught their breaths.

He helped Barbara back into her shift, rearranged her sling to carry one baby papoose fashion, and made up their luggage into one bundle. All that he held out was his knife taped to his arm, his robe, and the light. He showed her how to hold the light in her mouth, then spread her lips and let the tiniest trickle leak out between her teeth. She tried it.

"You look ghastly," he whispered. 'Like a jack-o'-lantern. Now listen carefully. I'm going up. You be ready to hand me my robe instantly. I may reconnoiter."

"I could help you get it on, right here."

"No. If I'm caught coming out, there will be a fight and it would slow me down. I won't want it, probably, until we reach a storeroom that is our next stop. If it's all clear above, I'll want you to hand out everything fast, including the baby not on your back. But you will have to carry him as well as the bundle and my robe; I've got to have my hands free. Darling, I don't want to kill anybody but if anyone gets in our way, I will. You understand that, don't you?"

She nodded. "So I carry everything. Can do, my husband."

"You follow me, fast. It's about two city blocks to that storeroom and we probably won't see anyone. I jiggered its lock this afternoon, stuffed a wad of Kitten's chewing gum into it. Once inside we'll rearrange things and see if you can wear my sandals."

"My feet are all right. Feel."

"Maybe we'll take turns wearing them. Then I have to break a lock on a delivery door but I spotted some steel bars a week ago which ought still to be there. Anyhow, I'll break out. Then away we go, fast. It should be breakfast before we are missed, sometime after that before they are sure we are gone, still longer before a chase is organized. We'll make it."

"Sure we will.

"Just one thing— If I reach for my robe and then close the lid on you, you stay here. Don't make a sound, don't try to peek out."

"I won't."

"I might be gone an hour. I might fake a bellyache and have to see the vet, then come back when I can."

"All right."

"Barbara, it might be twenty-four hours, if anything goes wrong. Can you stay here and keep the twins quiet that long? If you must?"

"Whatever it takes, Hugh."

He kissed her. "Now put the light back in your mouth and close your lips. I'm going to sneak a peek."

He raised the lid an inch, lowered it. "In luck," he whispered. "Even the standing light is out. Here I go. Be ready to hand things up. Joey first. And don't show a light."

He pushed the lid up and flat down without a sound, raised himself, got his feet to the corridor floor, stood up.

A light hit him. "That's far enough," a dry voice said, "Don't move."

He kicked the whip hand so fast that the whip flew aside as he closed. Then *this*—and *that!*—and sure enough! The man's neck was broken, just as the book said it would be.

Instantly he knelt down. "Everything out! Fast!"

Barbara shoved baby and baggage up to him, was out fast as he took her hand. "Some light," he whispered. "His went out and I've got to dispose of him."

She gave him light.

Memtok—

Hugh quelled his surprise, stuffed the body down the hole, closed the lid. Barbara was ready, baby on back, baby in left arm, bundle in right. "We go on! Stay close on my heels!" He set out for the intersection, holding his course in the dark by fingertips on the wall.

He never saw the whip that got him. All he knew was the pain.

20

For a long time Mr. Hugh Farnham was aware of nothing but pain. When it eased off, he found that he was in a confinement cell like the one in which he had lived his first days under the Protectorate.

He was there three days. He thought it was three days, as he was fed six times. He always knew when they were about to feed him—and to empty his slop jar, for he was not taken outside for any purpose. He would find himslf restrained by invisible spider web, then someone would come inside, leave food, replace the slop jar, and go. It was impossible to get the servant who did this to answer him.

After what may have been three days he found himself unexpectedly caught up by that prisoning field (he had just been fed) and his old colleague and "cousin" the Chief Veterinary came in. Hugh had more than a suspicion as to why; his feeling amounted to a conviction, so he pleaded, demanded to be taken to the Lord Protector, and finally shouted.

The surgeon ignored it. He did something to Hugh's thigh, then left.

To Hugh's limited relief he did not become unconscious, but he found, when the tanglefoot field let up that he could not move anyhow and felt lethargic. Shortly two servants came in, picked him up, placed him in a box like a coffin.

Hugh found that he was being shipped somewhere. His shipping case was given casual but not rough handling; once he felt a lift surge and then surge to a stop; his box was placed in something; and some minutes, hours, or days later it was moved again; and presently he was dumped into another confinement room. He knew it was a different one; the walls were light green instead of white. By the time they fed him he had recovered and was again "tangled" while food was placed inside.

This went on for one hundred and twenty-two meals. Hugh kept track by biting a chunk out of his fingernails and scratching the inside of his left arm. This took him less than five minutes each day; he spent the rest of his time worrying and sometimes sleeping. Sleeping was worse than worrying because he always reenacted his escape attempt in his sleep and it always ended in disaster—although not necessarily at the same point. He did not always kill his friend the Chief Domestic and at least twice they got all the way to the mountains before they were caught. But, long or short, it ended the same way and he would wake up sobbing and calling for Barbara.

He worried most about Barbara—and the twins, although the boys were not as real to him. He had never heard of a slut being severely punished for anything. However, he had never heard of a slut being involved in an attempted escape and a killing, either; he just did not know. But he did know that the Lord Protector preferred slut meat for his table.

He tried to tell himself that old Ponse would do nothing to a slut while she was still nursing babies—and that would be a long time yet; among servants, according to Kitten, mothers nursed babies for at least two years.

He worried about Kitten, too. Would the child be punished for something she had had nothing to do with? A completely innocent bystander? Again he did not know. There was "justice" here; it was a major branch of religious writings. But it resembled so little the concept "justice" of his own culture that he had found the stuff almost unreadable.

He spent most of his time on what he thought of as "constructive" worry, i.e., what he should have done rather than what he had done.

He saw now that his plans had been laughably inadequate. He should never have let himself be panicked into moving too soon. It would have been far better to have built up his connection with Joe, never disagreed with him, tickled his vanity, gone to work for him and, in time, prevailed on him to adopt Barbara and the kids. Joe was an accommodating person and old Ponse was so open-handed that he might simply have made Joe a present of these three useless servants instead of demanding cash. The boys would have been in no danger for years (and perhaps never in danger if Joe owned them), and, in time, Hugh could have expected to become a trusted business servant, with a broad pass allowing him to go anywhere on his master's business—and Hugh would have acquired sophisticated knowledge of how this world worked that a house servant could never acquire.

Once he had learned exactly how it ticked, he could have planned an escape that would work.

Any society man has ever devised, he reminded himself, could be bridged—and a servant who handles money can find ways to steal some. Probably there was an "underground railroad" that ran to the mountains. Yes, he had been far too hasty.

He considered, too, the wider aspects—a slave uprising. He visualized those tunnels being used not for escape but as a secret meeting place—classes in reading and writing, taught in whispers; oaths as mighty as a Mau Mau initiation binding the conspirators as blood brothers with each Chosen having marked against his name a series of dedicated assassins, servants patiently grinding scraps of metal into knives.

This "constructive" dream he enjoyed most—and believed in least. Would these docile sheep *ever* rebel? It seemed unlikely. He had been classed with them by accident of complexion but they were not truly of his breed. Centuries of selective breeding had made them as little like himself as a lap dog is like a timber wolf.

And yet, and yet, *how did he know?* He knew only the tempered males, and the few studs he had seen had all been dulled by a liberal ration of Happiness—to say nothing of what it might do to a man's fighting spirit to lose his thumbs at an early age and be driven around with whips-that-were-more-than-whips.

This matter of racial differences—or the nonsense notion of "racial equality"—had never been examined scientifically; there was too much emotion on both sides. Nobody *wanted* honest data.

Hugh recalled an area of Pernambuco he had seen while in the Navy, a place where rich plantation owners, dignified, polished, educated in France, were black, while their servants and field hands—giggling, shuffling, shiftless knuckleheads "obviously" incapable of better things—were mostly white men. He had stopped telling this anecdote in the States; it was never really believed and it was almost always resented—even by whites who made a big thing of how anxious they were to "help the American Negro improve himself." Hugh had formed the opinion that almost all of those bleeding hearts wanted the Negro's lot improved until it was *almost* as high as their own— and no longer on their consciences—but the idea that the tables could ever be turned was one they rejected emotionally.

Hugh knew that the tables could indeed be turned. He had seen it once, now he was experiencing it.

But Hugh knew that the situation was still more confused. Many Roman citizens had been "black as the ace of spades" and many slaves of Romans had been as blond as Hitler wanted to be—so any "white man" of European ancestry was certain to have a dash of Negro blood. Sometimes more than a dash. That southern Senator, what was his name?—the one who had built his career on "white supremacy." Hugh had come across two sardonic facts: This old boy had died from cancer and had had many transfusions—and his blood type was such that the chances were two hundred to one that its owner had not just a touch of the tarbrush but practically the whole tar barrel. A navy surgeon had gleefully pointed this out to Hugh and had proved both points in medical literature.

Nevertheless, this confused matter of races would *never* be straightened out—because almost nobody wanted the truth.

Take this matter of singing— It had seemed to Hugh that Negroes of his time averaged better singers than had whites; most people seemed to think so. Yet the very persons, white or black, who insisted most loudly that "all races were equal" always seemed happy to agree that Negroes were superior, on the average, in this one way. It reminded Hugh of Orwell's *Animal Farm,* in which "All Animals Are Equal But Some Are More Equal Than Others."

Well, he knew who wasn't equal here—despite his statistically certain drop of black blood. Hugh Farnham, namely. He found that he agreed with Joe; When things were unequal, it was much nicer to be on top!

On the sixty-first day in this new place, if it was the sixty-first, they came for him, bathed him, cut his nails, rubbed him with deodorant cream, and paraded him before the Lord Protector.

Hugh learned that he still could be humiliated by not being given even a nightshirt as clothing, but he conceded that it was a reasonable precaution in handling a prisoner who killed with his bare hands. His escort was two young Chosen, in uniforms which Hugh assumed to be military, and the whips they carried were definitely not "lesser whips."

The route they followed was very long; it was clearly a huge building. The room where he was delivered was very like in spirit to the informal lounge where Hugh had once played bridge. The big view window looked out over a wide tropical river.

Hugh hardly glanced at it; the Lord Protector was there. And so were Barbara and the twins!

The babies were crawling on the floor. But Barbara was breast deep in that invisible quicksand, a trap that claimed Hugh as soon as he was halted. She smiled at him but did not speak. He looked her over carefully. She seemed unhurt and healthy, but was thin and had deep circles under her eyes.

He started to speak; she gestured warningly with eyes and head. Hugh then looked at the Lord Protector—and noticed only then that Joe was lounging near him and that Grace and Duke were playing some card game over in a corner, both of them chewing gum and ostentatiously not seeing that Hugh was there. He looked back at Their Charity.

Hugh decided that Ponse had been ill. Despite the fact that Hugh felt comfortably warm in skin, Ponse was wearing a full robe with a shawl over his lap and he looked, for once, almost his reputed age.

But when he spoke, his voice was still resonant. "You may go, Captain. We excuse you."

The escort withdrew. Their Charity looked Hugh over soberly. At last he said, "Well, boy, you certainly made a mess of things, didn't you?" He looked down and played with something in his lap, caught it and pulled it back to the middle of the shawl. Hugh saw that it was a white mouse. He felt sudden sympathy for the mouse. It didn't seem to like where it was, but if it did manage to escape, the cats would get it. Maggie was watching with deep interest.

Hugh did not anwer, the remark seemed rhetorical. But it had startled him very much. Ponse covered the mouse with his hand, looked up. "Well? Say something!"

"You speak English!"

"Don't look so silly. I'm a scholar, Hugh. Do you think I would let myself be surrounded by people who speak a language I don't understand? I speak it, and I read it, silly as the spelling is. I've been tutored daily by skilled scholars—plus conversation practice with a living dictionary." He jerked his head toward Grace. "Couldn't you guess that I would want to *read* those books of mine? Not be dependent on your hit-or-miss translations? I've read the *Just So Stories* twice—charming!—and I've started on the *Odyssey*."

He shifted back to Language. "But we are not here to discuss literature." Their Charity barely gestured. Four slut servants came running in with a table, placed it in front of the big man, placed things on it. Hugh recognized them—a home-made knife, a wig, two pots for deodorant cream, a bundle, an empty Happiness bottle, a little white

287

sphere now dull, a pair of sandals, two robes, one long, one short, mussed and dirty, and a surprisingly high stack of paper, creased and much written on.

Ponse put the white mouse on the table, stirred the display, said broodingly, "I'm no fool, Hugh. I've owned servants all my life. I had you figured out before you had yourself figured out. Doesn't do to let a man like you mingle with loyal servants, he corrupts them. Gives them ideas they are better off without. I had planned to let you escape as soon as I was through with you, you could have afforded to wait."

"Do you expect me to believe that?"

"Doesn't matter whether you do or don't. I could not afford to keep you very long—one bad apple rots the rest, as my uncle was fond of saying. Nor could I put you up for adoption and let some unwitting buyer pay good money for a servant who would then corrupt others elsewhere in my realm. No, you had to escape."

"Even if that is so, I would never have escaped without Barbara and my boys."

"I said I am not a fool. Kindly remember it. Of course you would not. I was going to use Barba—and these darling brats—to force you to escape. At my selected time. Now you've ruined it. I must make an example of you. For the benefit of the other servants." He frowned and picked up the crude knife. "Poor balance. Hugh, did you really expect to make it with this pitiful tackle? Not even shoes for that child by you. If only you had waited, you would have been given opportunity to steal what you needed."

"Ponse, you are playing with me the way you've been playing with that mouse. You weren't planning to let us escape. Not really escape at least. I would have wound up on your table."

"Please!" The old man made a grimace of distaste. "Hugh, I'm not well, someone has again been trying to poison me—my nephew, I suppose—and this time almost succeeded. So don't talk nasty, it upsets my stomach." He looked Hugh up and down. "Tough. Inedible. An old stud savage is merely garbage. Much too gamy. Besides that, a gentleman doesn't eat members of his own family, no matter what. So let's not talk in bad taste. There's no cause for you to bristle so. I'm not angry with you, just very, very provoked." He glanced at the twins, said, "Hughie, stop pulling Maggie's tail." His voice was neither loud nor sharp; the baby stopped at once. "Admittedly those two would make tasty appetizers were they not of my household. But even had they not been, I would have planned better things for them; they are so cute and so much alike. Did plan better things at first. Until it became clear that they were necessary to forcing you to run."

Ponse sighed. "You still do not believe a word I'm saying. Hugh, you don't understand the system. Well, servants never do. Did you ever grow apples?"

"No."

"A good eating apple, firm and sweetly tart, is never a product of nature; it is the result of long development from something small and sour and hard and hardly fit for animal fodder. Then it has to be scientifically propagated and protected. On the other hand, too highly developed plants—or animals—can go bad, lose their firmness, their flavor, get mushy and soft and worthless. It's a two-horned problem. We have it constantly with servants. You must weed out the troublemakers, not let them breed. On the other hand these very troublemakers, the worst of them, are invaluable breeding stock that must not be lost. So we do both. The run-of-the-crop bad ones we temper and keep. The very worst ones—such as you—we encourage to run. If you live—and some of you do—we can rescue you, or your strong get, at a later time and add you in, judiciously, to a breeding line that has become so soft and docile and stupid that it is no longer worth its keep. Our poor friend Memtok was a result of such pepping up of the breed. One quarter savage he was—he never knew it of course—and a good stud that added strength to a line. But far too dangerous and ambitious to be kept too long at stud; he had to be made to see the advantages of being tempered. Most of my upper servants have a recent strain of savage in them; some of them are Memtok's sons. My engineer, for example. No, Hugh, you would not have wound up on anybody's table. Nor tempered. I would like to have kept you as a pet, you're diverting—and a fair bridge hand in the bargain. But I could not let you stay in contact with loyal servants, even as insulated as you were by your fancy title. Presently you would have been put in touch with the underground."

Hugh opened his mouth and closed it.

"Surprised, eh? But there is always an underground wherever there is a ruling class and a serving class. Which is to say, always. If there were not one, it would be necessary to invent one. However, since there is one, we keep track of it, subsidize it—and use it. In the upper servants' mess its contact is the veterinary—trusted by everyone and quite shamelessly free of sentiment; I don't like him. If you had confided in him, you would have been guided, advised, and helped. I would have used you to cover about a hundred sluts, then sent you on your way. Don't look startled, even Their Mercy uses studs who have to stoop a bit to get through the studs' door when a freshening of the line is indicated—and there was always the danger that you might get yourself, and those dear boys, killed, and thereby have wasted a fine potential."

Their Charity picked up the pile of Kitten-delivered mail. "These things— All my Chief Domestic was expected to do was to thwart you from doing something silly; he never knew the veterinary's second function. Why, I even had to crack down on Memtok a bit to turn his copies of these over to me—when anyone could have guessed that a stud like you would find a way to get in touch with his slut. I deduced that it would happen that time that you stood up to me about her, our first bridge game. Remember? Perhaps you don't. But I sent for Memtok, and sure enough, you had already started. Although he was reluctant to admit it, since he had not reported it."

Hugh was hardly listening. He was turning over in his mind the glaring fact that he was hearing things told only to dead men. None of the four was going to leave this room alive. No, perhaps the twins would. Yes, Ponse wanted the breeding line. But he—and Barbara—would never have a chance to talk.

But Ponse was saying, "You still have a chance to correct your mistakes. And you made lots of them. One note you wrote my scholars assured me was gibberish, not English at all. So I knew it was a secret message whether we could read it or not. Thereafter all your notes were subjected to careful analysis. So of course we found the key—rather naïve to be considered a code, rather clever considering the handicaps. And useful to me. But confound it, Hugh, it cost me! Memtok was naïve about savages, he did not realize that they fight when cornered."

Ponse scowled. "Damn you, Hugh, your recklessness cost me a valuable property. I wouldn't have taken ten thousand bullocks for Memtok's adoption—no, not twenty. And now your life is forfeit. The charge of attempting to run we could overlook, a tingling in front of the other servants would cover that. Destroying your master's property we could cover up if it had been done secretly. Did you know that that bedwarmer I lent you knew most of what you were up to? Saw much of it? Sluts gossip."

"She told you?"

"No, damn it, it didn't tell the half; we had to tingle it out of it. Then it turned out it knew so much that we could not afford to have it talking and the other servants putting one and one together. So it had to go."

"You had her killed." Hugh felt a surge of disgust and said it, knowing that nothing he said could matter now.

"What's it to you? Its life was forfeit, treason to its master. However, I'm not a spiteful man, the little critter has no moral sense and didn't know what it was doing—you must have hypnotized it, Hugh—and I'm a frugal man; I don't waste property. It's adopted so far away that it'll have trouble understanding the accent, much less have its stories believed."

Hugh sighed. "I'm relieved."

"Choice about the slut, eh? Was it that good?"

"She was innocent. I didn't want her hurt."

"As may be. Now, Hugh, you can repair all this costly mess. Pay me back the damage and do yourself a good turn at the same time."

"How?"

"Quite simple. You've cost me my key executive servant, I've no one of his caliber to replace him. So you take his place. No scandal, no fuss, no upset belowstairs—every servant who saw any piece of it is already adopted away. And you can tell any story you like about what happened to Memtok. Or even claim you don't know. Barba, can you refrain from gossip?"

"I certainly can where Hugh's welfare is concerned!"

"That's a good child. I would hate to have you muted, it would hamper our bridge game. Although Hugh will be rather busy for bridge. Hugh, here's the honey that trapped the bear. You take over as Chief Domestic, do the kind of a job I know you can do once you learn the details—and Barba and the twins live with you. What you always wanted. Well, that's the choice. Be my boss servant and have them with you. Or your lives are forfeit. What do you say?"

Hugh Farnham was so dazed that he was gulping trying to accept, when Their Charity added, "Just one thing. I won't be able to let you have them with you right away."

"No?"

"No. I still want to breed a few from you, before you are tempered. Needn't be long, if you are as spry as you look."

Barbara said, "No!"

But Hugh Farnham was making a terrible decision. "Wait, Barbara. Ponse. What about the boys? Will they be tempered, too?"

"Oh." Ponse thought about it. "You drive a hard bargain, Hugh. Suppose we say that they will not be. Let's say that I might use them at stud a bit—but not take their thumbs; it would be a dead giveaway for so private a purpose with studs as tall as they are going to be. Then at fourteen or fifteen I let them escape. Does that suit you?" The old man stopped to cough; a spasm racked him. "Damn it, you're tiring me."

Hugh pondered it. "Ponse, you may not be alive fourteen or fifteen years from now."

"True. But it is very impolite for you to say so."

"Can you bind this bargain for your heir? Mrika?"

Ponse rubbed his hair and grinned. "You're a sharp one, Hugh. What a Chief Domestic you will make! Of course I can't—which is why I want some get from you, without waiting for the boys to mature. But there is always a choice, just as you have a choice now. I can see to it that you are in my heavenly escort. All of you, the boys, too. Or I can have you all kept alive and you can work out a new bargain, if any. *'Le Roi est mort, vive le Roi?'*—which was the ancients' way of saying that when the protector leaves there is always a new protector. Just tell me, I'll do it either way."

Hugh was thinking over the grim choices when Barbara again spoke up. "Their Charity—"

"Yes, child?"

"You had better have my tongue cut out. Right now, before you let me leave this room. Because I will have nothing to do with this wicked scheme. And I will not keep quiet. *No!*"

"Barba, Barba, that's not being a good girl."

"I am not a girl. I am a woman and a wife and a mother! I will never call you 'uncle' again—you are vile! I will not play bridge with you ever again, with or without my tongue. We are helpless . . . but I will give you *nothing*. What is this you offer? You want my husband to agree to this evil thing in exchange for a few scant years of life for me and for our sons—for as long as God lets that evilness you call your body continue to breathe. Then what? You cheat him even then. We die. Or we are left to the mercy of your nephew who is even worse than you are. Oh, I know! The bedwarmers all hate him, they weep when they are called to serve him—and weep even harder when they come back. But I would not let Hugh make this choice, even if you could promise us all a lifetime of luxury. *No!* I won't, I won't! You try to do it, I'll kill my babies! Then myself. Then Hugh will kill himself I know! No matter what you have done to him!" She stopped, spat as far as she could in the old man's direction, then burst into tears.

Their Charity said, "Hughie, I told you to stop teasing that cat. It will scratch you." Slowly he stood up, said,

"Reason with them, Joe," and left the room.

Joe sighed and came over close to them. "Barbara," he said gently, "take hold of yourself. You aren't acting in Hugh's interests even if you think you are. You should advise him to take it. After all, a man Hugh's age doesn't have much to lose by it."

Barbara looked at him as if she had never seen him before in her life. Then she spat again. Joe was close, she got him in the face.

He jumped and raised his hand. Hugh said sharply, "Joe, if you hit her and I ever get loose, I'll break your arm!"

"I wasn't going to hit her," Joe said slowly. "I was just going to wipe my face. I wouldn't hit Barbara, Hugh; I admire her. I just don't think she has good sense." He took a kerchief to the smear of saliva. "I guess there is no use arguing."

"None, Joe. I'm sorry I spit on you."

"That's all right, Barbara. You're upset . . . and you never treated me as a nigger, ever. Well, Hugh?"

"Barbara has decided it. And she always means what she says. I can't say that I'm sorry. Staying alive here just isn't worth it, for any of us. Even if I was not to be tempered."

"I hate to hear you say that, Hugh. All in all, you and I always got along pretty well. Well, if that's your last word, I might as well go tell Their Charity. Is it?"

"Yes."

"Yes, Joe."

"Well— Good-bye, Barbara. Good-bye, Hugh." He left.

The Lord Protector came back in alone, moving with the slow caution of a man old and sick. "So that's what you've decided," he said, sitting down and gathering the shawl around him. He reached out for the mouse, still crouching on the table top; servants came in and cleared off the table. He went on, "Can't say that I'm surprised— I've played bridge with both of you. Well, now we take up the other choice. Your lives are forfeit and I can't let you stay here, other than on those terms. So now we send you back."

"Back where, Ponse?"

"Why, back to your own time, of course. If you make it. Perhaps you will." He stroked the mouse. "This little fellow made it. Two weeks at least. And it didn't hurt him. Though one can only guess what two thousand years would do."

The servants were back and were piling on the table a man's watch, a Canadian dime, a pair of much worn mountain boots, a hunting knife, some badly made moccasins, a pair of Levis, some ragged denim shorts with a very large waistline, a .45 automatic pistol with belt, two ragged and faded shirts, one somewhat altered, a part of a paper of matches, and a small notebook and pencil.

Ponse looked at the collection. "Was there anything else?" He slid the loaded clip from the pistol, held it in his hand. "If not, get dressed."

The invisible field let them loose.

21

"I don't see what there is to be surprised about," Ponse told them. "Hugh, you will remember that I told my scientists that I wanted to know how you got here. No miracles. I told them rather firmly. They understood that I would be most unhappy—and vexed—if the Protectorate's scientists could not solve it when they had so many hints, so much data. So they did. Probably. At least they were able to move this little fellow. He arrived today, which is why I sent for you. Now we will find out if it works backwards in time as well as forwards—and if the big apparatus works as well as the bench model. I understand it is not so much the amount of power—no atom-kernel bombs necessary—as the precise application of power. But we'll soon know."

Hugh asked, "How will you know? *We* will know—if it works. But how will *you* know?"

"Oh, that. My scientists are clever, when they have incentive. One of them will explain it."

The scientists were called in, two Chosen and five servants. There was no introduction; Hugh found himself treated as impersonally as the little white mouse who still tried to meet his death on the floor. Hugh was required to take off his shirt and two servant-scientists taped a small package to Hugh's right shoulder. "What's that?" It seemed surprisingly heavy for its size.

The servants did not answer; the leading Chosen said, "You will be told. Come here. See this."

"This" turned out to be Hugh's former property, a U. S. Geodetic Survey map of James County. "Do you understand this? Or must we explain it?"

"I understand it." Hugh used the equals mode, the Chosen ignored it while continuing to speak in protocol mode, falling.

"Then you know that here is where you arrived."

Hugh agreed, as the man's finger covered the spot where Hugh's home had once stood. The Chosen nodded thoughtfully and added, "Do you understand the meaning of these marks?" He pointed to a tiny x-mark and very small figures beside it.

"Certainly. We call that a 'bench mark.' Exact location and altitude. It's a reference point for all the rest of the map."

"Excellent." The Chosen pointed to a similar mark at the summit of Mount James as shown by the map. "Now, tell us, if you know—but don't lie about it; it will not advantage you—how much error there would be, horizontally and vertically, between these two reference points."

Hugh thought about it, held up his thumb and forefinger about an inch apart. The Chosen blinked. "It would not have been that accurate in those primitive times. We assume that you are lying. Try again. Or admit that you don't know."

"And I suggest that you don't know what you are talking about. It would be at least that accurate." Hugh thought of telling him that he had bossed surveying parties in the Seabees and had done his own surveying when he was getting started as a contractor—and that while he did not know how accurate a geodetic survey was. he did know that enormously more accurate methods had been used in setting those bench marks than were ever used in the ordinary survey.

He decided that explanation would be wasted.

The Chosen looked at him, then glanced at Their Charity. The old man had been listening but his face showed nothing. "Very well. We will assume that the marks are accurate, each to the other. Which is fortunate, as this one is missing"—he pointed to the first one, near where Hugh's home had been—"whereas this one"—he indicated the summit of Mount James—"is still in place, in solid rock. Now search your memory and do not lie again, as it will matter to *you* . . . and it will matter to Their Charity, as a silly lie on your part could waste much effort and Their Charity would be much displeased, we are certain. Where, quite near this reference mark and the same height—certainly no higher!—is—was, I mean, in those primitive times—a flat, level place?"

Hugh thought about it. He knew exactly where that bench mark had been: in the cornerstone of the Southport Savings Bank. It was, or had been a small brass plate let into the stone beside the large dedication plate, about eighteen inches above the sidewalk at the northeast corner of the building. It had been placed there shortly after the Southport shopping center had been built. Hugh had often glanced at it in passing; it had always given him a warm feeling of stability to note a bench mark.

The bank had sided on a parking lot shared by the bank, a Safeway Supermarket, and a couple of other shops. "It is level and flat off this way for a distance of—" (Hugh estimated the width of that ancient parking lot in feet, placed the figure in modern units.) "Or a little farther. That's just an estimate, not wholly accurate."

"But it is flat and level? And no higher than this point?"

"A little lower and sloping away. For drainage."

"Very well. Now place your attention on this configuration." Again it was Hugh's property, a Conoco map of the state. "That object fastened to your back you may think of as a clock. We will not explain it, you could not understand. Suffice to say that radiation decay of a metal inside it measures time. That is why it is heavy; it is cased in lead to protect it. You will take it to *here*." The Chosen pointed to a town on the map; Hugh noted that it was the home of the state university.

At a gesture the Chosen was handed a slip of paper. To Hugh he said, "Can you read this? Or must it be explained?"

"It says 'University State Bank,'" Hugh told him. "I seem to recall that there was an institution of that name in that town. I'm not sure, I don't recall doing business with it."

"There was," the Chosen assured him, "and its ruins were recently uncovered. You will go to it. There was, and still is, a strong room, a vault, in its lowest part. You will place this clock in that vault. Do you understand?"

"I understand."

"By Their Charity's wish, that vault has not yet been opened. After you have gone, it will be opened. The clock will be found and we will read it. Do you understand why this is crucial to the experiment? It will not only tell us that you made the time jump safely but also exactly how long the span was—and from this our instruments will be calibrated." The Chosen looked very fierce. "Do this exactly. Or you will be severely punished."

Ponse caught Hugh's eye at this point. The old man was not laughing but his eyes twinkled. "Do it, Hugh," he said quietly. "That's a good fellow."

Hugh said to the Chosen scientist. "I will do it. I understand."

The Chosen said, "May it please Their Charity, this one is ready to weigh them now, and then leave for the site."

"We've changed our mind," Ponse announced. "We will see this." He added, "Nerve in good shape, Hugh?"

"Quite."

"All of you who made the first jump were given this opportunity, did I tell you? Joe turned it down flatly." The old man glanced over his shoulder. "Grace! Changed your mind, little one?"

Grace looked up, "Ponsie!" she said reproachfully. "You *know* I would never leave you."

"Duke?"

The tempered servant did not even look up. He simply shook his head.

Ponse said to the scientist, "Let's hurry and get them weighed. We intend to sleep at home tonight."

The weighing was done elsewhere in the Palace. Just before the four were placed on the weighing area the Lord Protector held up the cartridge clip he had removed from the pistol Hugh now wore. "Hugh? Will you undertake not to be foolish with this? Or should I have the pellets separated from the explosives?"

"Uh, I'll behave."

"Ah, but how will you behave? If you were impetuous, you might succeed in killing me. But consider what would happen to Barba and our little brats."

(I had thought of that, you old scoundrel. I'll still do what seems best to me.) "Ponse, why don't you let Barbara carry the clip in a pocket? That would keep me from loading and firing very fast even if I did get ideas."

"A good plan. Here, Barba."

The boss scientist seemed unhappy at the total weight of his experimental package. "May it please Their Charity, this one finds that body weights of both adults must have lessened markedly since the time of the figures on which the calculations were made."

"And what do you expect of us?"

"Oh, nothing, nothing, may it please Their Charity. Just a slight delay. The mass must be exact." Hurriedly the Chosen started piling metal discs on the platform.

It gave Hugh an idea. "Ponse, you really expect this to work?"

"If I knew the answer, it would not be necessary to try it. I hope it will work."

"If it does work, we'll need money right away. Especially if I'm to travel half across the state to bury this clock device."

"Reasonable. You used gold, did you not? Or was it silver? I see your idea." The old man gestured. "Stop that weighing."

"We used both, sometimes, but it had to have our own protectorate's stamp. Ponse, there were quite a number of American silver dollars in my house when you took it away from me. Are they available?"

They were available and in the Palace and the old man had no objection to using them to make up the missing weight. The boss scientist was fretted over the delay—he explained to his lord that the adjustments were set for an exact time span as well as exact mass in order to place these specimens at a time *before* East-West War had started, plus a margin for error—but that delay was reducing the margin and might require recalculation and long and painful recalibration. Hugh did not follow the technicalities.

Nor did Ponse. He cut the scientist off abruptly. "Then recalculate if necessary. All."

It took more than an hour to locate the man who could locate the man who knew where these particular items of the savage artifacts were filed, then dig them out and fetch them. Ponse sat brooding and played with his mouse. Barbara nursed the twins, then changed them with the help of slut servants; Hugh petitioned plumbing calls for each of them—granted, under guard—and all this changed all the body weights and everything was started over again.

The silver dollars were still in, or had been replaced in, the $100 rolls in which Hugh had hoarded them. They made quite a stack, and (on the happy assumption that the time jump would work) Hugh was pleased that he had lost while imprisoned the considerable paunch he had regrown during his easy days as "Chief Researcher." However, less than three hundred silver dollars were used in bringing them up to calculated weight—plus a metal slug and some snips of foil.

"If it suits the Lord Protector, this one believes that the specimens should be placed in the container without delay."

"Then do it! Don't waste our time."

The container was floated in. It was a box, metallic, plain, empty, and with no furnishings of any sort, barely high enough for Hugh to stand upright in, barely large enough for all of them. Hugh got into it, helped Barbara in, the babies were handed to them and Hughie started to squawl and set off his brother.

Ponse looked annoyed. "My sluts have been spoiling those brats. Hugh, I've decided not to watch it, I'm weary. Good-bye to both of you—and good riddance; neither of you would ever have made a loyal servant. But I'll miss our bridge games. Barba, you must bring those brats back into line. But don't break their spunk doing it; they're fine

301

boys." He turned and left abruptly.

The hatch was closed down on them and fastened; they were alone. Hugh at once took advantage of it to kiss his wife, somewhat hampered by each of them holding a baby.

"I don't care what happens now," Barbara said as soon as her mouth was free. "That's what I've been longing for. Oh, dear, Joey is wet again. How about Hughie?"

"It's unanimous, Hughie also. But I thought you just said you didn't care what happens now?"

"Well, I don't, really. But try explaining that to a baby. I would gladly swap one of those rolls of dollars for ten new diapers."

"My dear, do you realize that the human race lasted at least a million years with no diapers at all? Whereas we may not last another hour. So let's not spend it talking about diapers."

"I simply meant— Wups! They're moving us."

"Sit flat on the floor and brace your feet against the wall. Before we have scrambled babies. You were saying?"

"I simply meant, my darling, that I do not care about diapers, I don't care about anything—now that I have you with me again. But if we aren't going to die—if this thing works—I'm going to have to be practical. And do you know of anything more practical than diapers?"

"Yes. Kissing. Making love."

"Well, yes. But they lead to diapers. Darling, could you hold Hughie in your other arm and put this one around me? Uh, they're moving us again. Hugh, is this thing going to work? Or are we going to be very suddenly dead? Somehow I can imagine time travel frontwards—and anyhow we did it. But I can't imagine it *backwards*. I mean, the past has already happened. That's it. Isn't it?"

"Well, yes. But you haven't stated it correctly. The way I see it, there are no paradoxes in time travel, there can't be. If we are going to make this time jump, then we already did; that's what happened. And if it doesn't work, then it's because it didn't happen."

"But it hasn't happened yet. Therefore, you are saying

that it didn't happen, so it can't happen. That's what I said."

"No, no! We don't know whether it has already happened or not. If it did, it will. If it didn't, it won't."

"Darling, you're confusing me."

"Don't worry about it. 'The moving finger writes, and having writ, moves on'—and only then do you find out if it goosed you in passing. I think we've straightened out on a course; we're steady now, just the faintest vibration. If they are taking us where I think they are, James County I mean, then we've got at least an hour before we need worry about anything." He tightened his arm around her. "So let's be happy that hour."

She snuggled in. "That's what I was saying. Beloved, we've come through so many narrow squeaks together that I'm not ever going to worry again. If it's an hour, I'll be happy every second of it. If it's forty years, I'll be happy every second of that, too. If it's together. And if it's not together, I don't want it. But either way, we go on. To the end of our day."

"Yes. 'To the end of our day.'"

She sighed happily, rearranged a wet and sleeping infant, snuggled into his shoulder and murmured, "This feels like our very first day. In the tank room of the shelter, I mean. We were just as crowded and even warmer—and I was never so happy. And we didn't know whether we were going to live through that day, either. That night."

"We didn't expect to. Else we wouldn't have twin boys now."

"So I'm glad we thought we were going to die. Hugh? It isn't any more crowded than it was that night in the tank room."

"Woman, you are an insatiable lecher. You'll shock the boys."

"I don't think once in more than a year is being insatiable. And the boys are too young to be shocked. Aw, come on! You said yourself we might be dead in an hour."

"Yes, we might and you have a point and I'm theoretically in favor of the idea. But the boys do inhibit me and there actually isn't quite as much room even if we weren't cluttered up with eight or nine wet babies and I don't see how it's mechanically possible. The act would be a tesseract, at least."

"Well— I guess you're right. I don't see any way either; we would probably squash them. But it does seem a shame, if we're going to die."

"I refuse to assume that we're going to die. I won't ever make that assumption again. All my figuring is based on the assumption that we are going to live. We go on. No matter what happens—we go on."

"All right. Seven no trump."

"That's better."

"Doubled and redoubled. Hugh? Just as soon as the boys are big enough to hold thirteen cards in their pudgy little hands, we're going to start teaching them contract. Then we'll have a family four of our own."

"Suits. And if they can't learn to play, we'll temper them and try again."

"I don't want ever to hear that word again!"

"Sorry."

"And I don't want to hear that language again, either, dear. The boys should grow up hearing English."

"Sorry again. You're right. But I may slip; I've gotten in the habit of thinking in it—all that translating. So allow me a few slips."

"I'll always allow you a few slips. Speaking of slips— Did you? With Kitten?"

"No."

"Why not? I wouldn't have minded. Well, not much anyhow. She was sweet. She would baby-sit for me any time I would let her. She loved our boys."

"Barbara, I don't want to think about Kitten. It makes me sad. I just hope whoever has her now is good to her. She didn't have any defenses at all—like a kitten before it has its eyes open. Helpless. Kitten means to me everything that is utterly damnable about slavery."

She squeezed his hand "I hope they're good to her, too. But, dear, don't hurt yourself inside about it; there is nothing we can do for her."

"I know it and that's why I don't want to talk about

her. But I do miss her. As a daughter. She was a daughter to me. 'Bedwarmer' never entered into it."

"I didn't doubt it, dear. But— Well, look here, my good man, maybe this place is too cramped. All right, we're going to live through it; we go on. Then don't let me catch you treating *me* like a daughter! I intend to keep your bed very warm indeed!"

"Mmm— You want to remember that I'm an old man."

"'Old man' my calloused feet! We'll be the same age for all practical purposes—namely something over four thousand years, counting once each way. And my purposes are very practical, understand me?"

"I understand you. I suppose 'four thousand years' is one way to look at it. Though perhaps not for 'practical purposes.' "

"You won't get out of it that easily," she said darkly. "I won't stand for it."

"Woman, you've got a one-track mind. All right, I'll do my best. I'll rest all the time and let you do all the work. Hey, I think we're there."

The box was moved several times, then remained stationary a few minutes, then surged straight up with sickening suddenness, stopped with another stomach twister, seemed to hunt a little, and then was perfectly steady.

"You in the experimental chamber," a voice said out of nowhere. "You are warned to expect a short fall. You are advised to stand up, each of you hold one brat, and be ready to fall. Do you understand?"

"Yes," Hugh answered while helping Barbara to her feet. "How much of a fall?"

There was no answer. Hugh said, "Hon, I don't know what they mean. A 'short fall' could be one foot, or fifty. Protect Joey with your arms and better bend your knees a little. If it's quite a fall, then go ahead and go down; don't try to take it stiff-legged. These jokers don't give a hoot what happens to us."

"Bent knees. Protect Joey. All right."

They fell.

22

Hugh never did know how far they fell but he decided later that it could not have been more than four feet. One instant they were standing in a well-lighted, cramped box; the next instant they were outdoors, in the dark of night, and falling.

His boots hit, he went down, landing on the right side of his rump and on two very hard rolls of silver dollars in his hip pocket—rolled with the fall and protected the baby in his arms.

Then he rolled to a sitting position. Barbara was near him, on her side. She was not moving. "Barbara! Are you hurt?"

"No," she said breathlessly. "I don't think so. Just knocked the breath out of me."

"Is Joey all right? Hughie is, but I think he's more than wet now."

"Joey is all right." Joey confirmed this by starting to yell; his brother joined him. "He had the breath knocked out of him, too, I think. Shut up, Joey; Mother is busy. Hugh, where are we?"

He looked around. "We are," he announced, "in a parking lot in a shopping center about four blocks from where I live. And apparently somewhere close to our own proper time. At least that's a 'sixty-one Ford we almost landed on." The lot was empty save for this one car. It occurred to him that their arrival might have been something else than a bump—an explosion, perhaps?—if they had been six feet to the right. But he dropped the thought; enough narrow squeaks and one more didn't matter.

He stood up and helped Barbara up. She winced and in the dim light that came from inside the bank he noticed it. "Trouble?"

"I turned my ankle when I hit."

"Can you walk?"

"I can walk."

"I'll carry both kids. It's not far."

"Hugh, where are we going?"

"Why, home, of course." He looked in the window of the bank, tried to spot a calendar. He saw one but the standing light was not shining on it; he couldn't read it. "I wish I knew the date. Honey, I hate to admit it but it does look as if time travel has some paradoxes—and I think we are about to give somebody a terrible shock."

"Who?"

"Me, maybe. In my earlier incarnation. Maybe I ought to phone him first, not shock him. No, he—I, I mean—wouldn't believe it. Sure you can walk?"

"Certainly."

"All right. Hold our monsters for a moment and let me set my watch." He glanced back into the bank where a clock was visible even though the calendar was shadowed. "Okay. Gimme. And holler if you need to stop."

They set off, Barbara limping but keeping up. He discouraged talk, because he did not have his thoughts in order. To see a town that he had thought of as destroyed so quiet and peaceful on a warm summery night shook him more than he dared admit. He carefully avoided any speculation as to what he might find at his home—except one fleeting thought that if it turned out that his shelter was not yet built, then it never would be and he would try his hand at changing history.

He adjourned that thought, too, and concentrated on being glad that Barbara was a woman who never chattered when her man wanted her to be quiet.

Presently they turned into his driveway, Barbara limping and Hugh beginning to develop cramps in both arms

307

from being unable to shift his double load. There were two cars parked tandem and facing out in the drive; he stopped at the first one, opened the door and said, "Slide in, sit down, and take the load off the ankle. I'll leave the boys with you and reconnoiter." The house was brightly lighted.

"Hugh! Don't do it!"

"Why not?"

"This is my car. *This is the night!*"

He stared at her for a long moment. Then he said quietly, "I'm still going to reconnoiter. You sit here."

He was back in less than two minutes, jerked open the car door, collapsed onto the seat, let out a gasping sob.

Barbara said, "Darling! Darling!"

"Oh, my God!" He choked and caught his breath. *"She's* in there! Grace. And so am *I.*" He dropped his face to the steering wheel and sobbed.

"Hugh."

"What? *Oh, my God!*"

"Stop it, Hugh. I started the engine while you were gone. The keys were in the ignition, I had left them there so that Duke could move it and get out. So let's go. Can you drive?"

He sobered down. "I can drive." He took ten seconds to check the instrument board, adjusted the seat backwards, put it in gear, turned right out of his drive. Four minutes later he turned west on the highway into the mountains, being careful to observe the stop sign; it had occurred to him that this was no night to get stopped and pulled off the road for driving without a license.

As he made the turn a clock in the distance bonged the half hour; he glanced at his wrist watch, noted a one-minute difference. "Switch on the radio, hon."

"Hugh, I'm sorry. The durn thing quit and I couldn't afford to have it repaired."

"Oh. No matter. The news doesn't matter, I mean; time is all that matters. I'm trying to estimate how far we can go in an hour. An hour and some minutes. Do you recall what time the first missile hit us?"

"I think you told me it was eleven-forty-seven."

"That's my recollection, too. I'm certain of it, I just wanted it confirmed. But it all checks. You made crêpes Suzettes, you and Karen fetched them in just in time to catch the end of the ten o'clock news. I ate pretty quickly—they were wonderful—this looney old character rang the doorbell. Me, I mean. And I answered it. Call it ten-twenty or a little after. So we just heard half-past chime and my watch agrees. We've got about seventy-five minutes to get as far from ground zero as possible."

Barbara made no comment. Moments later they passed the city limits; Hugh put the speed up from a careful forty-five to an exact sixty-five.

About ten minutes later she said, "Dear? I'm sorry. About Karen, I mean. Not about anything else."

"I'm not sorry about anything. No, not about Karen. Hearing her merry laugh again shook me up, yes. But now I treasure it. Barbara, for the first time in my life I have a conviction of immortality. Karen is alive right now, back there behind us—and yet we saw her die. So somehow, in some timeless sense, Karen is alive forever, somewhere. Don't ask me to explain it, but that's how it is."

"I've always known it, Hugh. But I didn't dare say so."

"Dare say anything, damn it! I told you that long ago. So I no longer feel sorrow over Karen. I can't feel any honest sorrow over Grace. Some people make a career of trying to get their own way; she's one of them. As for Duke, I hate to think about him. I had great hopes for my son. My first son. But I never had control over his rearing and I certainly had no control over what became of him. And, as Joe pointed out to me, Duke's not too badly off —if welfare and security and happiness are sufficient criteria." Hugh shrugged without taking his hands from the wheel. "So I shall forget him. As of this instant I shall endeavor never to think about Duke again."

Presently he spoke again. "Hon, can you, in spite of being smothered in babies, get at that clock thing on my shoulder and get it off?"

"I'm sure I can."

"Then do it and chuck it into the ditch. I'd rather throw it away inside the circle of total destruction—if we're still in it." He scowled. "I don't want those people *ever* to have time travel. Especially Ponse."

She worked silently for some moments, awkwardly with one hand. She got the radiation clock loose and threw it out into the darkness before she spoke. "Hugh, I don't think Ponse intended us to accept that offer. I think he made the terms such that he knew that I would refuse, even if you were inclined to sacrifice yourself."

"Of course! He picked us as guinea pigs—his white mice—and chivvied us into 'volunteering.' Barbara, I can stand—and somewhat understand but not forgive—a straight-out son of a bitch. But Ponse was, for my money, much worse. He had good intentions. He could always prove why the hotfoot he was giving you was for your own good. I despise him."

Barbara said stubbornly, "Hugh, how many white men of today could be trusted with the power Ponse had and use it with as much gentleness as he did use it?"

"Huh? None. Not even yours truly. And that was a low blow about 'white men.' Color doesn't enter into it."

"I withdraw the word 'white.' And I'm sure that you are one who could be trusted with it. But I don't know any others."

"Not even me. *Nobody* can be trusted with it. The one time I had it I handled it as badly as Ponse. I mean that time I caused a gun to be raised at Duke. I should simply have used karate and knocked him out or even killed him. But not humiliated him. *Nobody,* Barbara. But Ponse was especially bad. Take Memtok. I'm really sorry that I happened to kill Memtok. He was a man who behaved better than his nature, not worse. Memtok had a streak of meanness, sadism, wide as his back. But he held it closely in check so that he could do his job better. But Ponse—Barbie hon, this is probably a subject on which you and I will never agree. You feel a bit soft toward him because he was sweet to you most of the time and always sweet to our boys. But I despised him *because* of that—because he

310

was always showing 'king's mercy'—being less cruel than he could have been, but always reminding his victim of how cruel he could be if he were not such a sweet old guy and such a prince of a fellow. I despised him for it. I despised him long before I found out about his having young girls butchered and served for his dinner."

"What?"

"Didn't you know? Oh, surely you must have known. Ponse and I discussed it in our very last talk. Weren't you listening?"

"I thought that was just heavy sarcasm, on the part of each of you."

"Nope, Ponse is a cannibal. Maybe not a cannibal, since he doesn't consider us human. But he does eat us—they all do. Ponse always ate girls. About one a day for his family table, I gathered. Girls about the age and plumpness of Kitten."

"But— But— Hugh, I ate the same thing he did, lots of times. I must have— I must have—"

"Sure you did. So did I. But not after I knew. Nor did you."

"Honey . . . you better stop the car. I'm going to be sick."

"Throw up on the twins if you must. This car doesn't stop for anything."

She managed to get the window open, got it mostly outside. Presently he said gently, "Feeling better?"

"Some."

"Sweetheart, don't hold what he ate too much against Ponse. He honestly did not know it was wrong—and no doubt cows would feel the same way about us, if they knew. But these other things he *knew* were wrong. Because he tried to justify them. He rationalized slavery, he rationalized tyranny, he rationalized cruelty, and always wanted the victim to agree and thank him. The headsman expected to be tipped."

"I don't want to talk about him, dear. I feel all mixed up inside."

"Sorry. I'm half drunk without a drop and babbling. I'll

311

shut up. Watch the traffic behind, I'm going to make a left turn shortly."

She did so and after they had turned off on a state road, narrower and not as well graded, he said, "I've figured out where we're going. At first I was just putting distance behind us. Now we've got a destination. Maybe a safe one."

"Where, Hugh?"

"A shutdown mine. I had a piece of it, lost some money in it. Now maybe it pays off. The Havely Lode. Nice big tunnels and we can reach the access road from this road. If I can find it in the dark. If we can get there before the trouble starts." He concentrated on herding the car, changing down on the grades both climbing and on the occasional downhill piece, braking hard before going into a curve, then cornering hard with plenty of throttle in the curves.

After a particularly vicious turn with Barbara on the hair-raising outside, she said, "Look, dear, I know you're doing it to save us. But we can be just as dead from a car crash as from an H-bomb."

He grinned without slowing. "I used to drive jeeps in the dark with no headlights. Barbie, I won't kill us. Few people realize how much a car will do and I'm delighted that this had a manual gear shift. You need it in the mountains. I would not dare drive this way with an automatic shift."

She shut up and prayed, silently.

The road dropped into a high alp where it met another road; at the intersection there was a light. When he saw it Hugh said, "Read my watch."

"Eleven-twenty-five."

"Good. We are slightly over fifty miles from ground zero. From my house, I mean. And the Havely Lode is only five minutes beyond here, I know how to find it now. I see Schmidt's Corner is open and we are low on gas. We'll grab some and groceries, too—yes, I recall you told me you had both in this car; we'll get more—and *still* make it before the curtain."

He braked and scattered gravel, stopped by a pump,

jumped out. "Run inside and start grabbing stuff. Put the twins on the floor of the car and close the door. Won't hurt 'em." He stuck the hose into the car's tank, started cranking the old-fashioned pump.

She was out in a moment. "There's nobody here."

"Honk the horn. The Dutchman is probaby back at his house."

Barbara honked and honked and the babies cried. Hugh hung up the hose. "Fourteen gallons we owe him for. Let's go in. Should roll in just ten minutes, to be safe."

Schmidt's Corner was a gasoline station, a small lunch counter, a one-end grocery store, all of the sort that caters to local people, fishermen, hunters, and the tourist who likes to get off the pavement. Hugh wasted no time trying to rouse out the owner; the place told its own story: All lights were on, the screen door stood open, coffee was simmering on a hot plate, a chair had been knocked over, and the radio was tuned to the emergency frequency. It suddenly spoke as he came in:

"Bomb warning. Third bomb warning. This is not a drill. Take shelter at once. Any shelter, God damn it, you're going to be atom-bombed in the next few minutes. I'm damn well going to leave this goddamn microphone and dive for the basement myself when impact is five minutes away! So get the lead out, you stupid fools, and quit listening to this chatter! TAKE SHELTER!"

"Grab those empty cartons and start filling them. Don't pack, just dump stuff in. I'll trot them out. We'll fill the back seat and floor." Hugh started following his own orders, had one carton filled before Barbara did. He rushed it out, rushed back; Barbara had another waiting, and a third almost filled. "Hugh. Stop one second. Look."

The end carton was not empty. Mama cat, quite used to strangers, stared solemnly out at him while four assorted fuzzy ones nursed. Hugh returned her stare.

He suddenly closed the top of the carton over her. "All right," he said. "Load something light into another carton so it weighs this one down while I drive. Hurry." He rushed out to the car with the little family while the mother

313

cat set up agonized complaint.

Barbara followed quickly with a half-loaded carton, put it on top of the cat box. They both rushed back inside. "Take all the canned milk he's got." Hugh stopped long enough to put a roll of dollars on top of the cash register. "And grab all the toilet paper or Kleenex you see, too. Three minutes till we leave."

They left in five minutes but with more cartons; the back seat of the car was well leveled off. "I got a dozen tea towels," Barbara said gleefully, "and six big packs of Chux."

"Huh?"

"Diapers, dear, diapers. Might last us past the fallout. I hope. And I grabbed two packs of playing cards, too. Maybe I shouldn't have."

"Don't be hypocritical, my love. Hang onto the kids and be sure that door is locked." He drove for several hundred yards, with his head hanging out. "Here!"

The going got very rough. Hugh drove in low gear and very carefully.

A black hole in the side of the mountain loomed up suddenly as he turned. "Good, we've made it! And we drive straight inside." He started in and tromped on the brake. "Good Lord! A cow."

"And a calf," Barbara added, leaning out her side.

"I'll have to back out."

"Hugh. A cow. With a calf."

"Uh . . . how the hell would we feed her?"

"Hugh, it may not burn here at all. And that's a real live cow."

"Uh . . . all right, all right. We'll eat them if we have to." There was a wooden wall and a stout door about thirty feet inside the mouth of the mine tunnel. Hugh eased the car forward, forcing the reluctant cow ahead of him, and at last crunched his side of the car against the rock wall to allow the other door to open.

The cow immediately made a break for freedom; Barbara opened her door and thereby stopped her. The calf bawled, the twins echoed him.

Hugh squeezed out past Barbara and the babies, got past the cow and unfastened the door, which was secured by a padlock passed through a hasp but not closed. He shoved the cow's rump aside and braced the door open. "Kick on the 'up' lights. Let it shine in."

Barbara did, then insisted that cow and calf be taken inside. Hugh muttered something about, "Noah's bloody ark!" but agreed, largely because the cow was so very much in the way. The door, though wide, was about one inch narrower than bossie; she did *not* want to go through it. But Hugh got her headed that way, then kicked her emphatically. She went through. The calf followed his mother.

At which point Hugh discovered why the cow was in the tunnel. Someone—presumably someone nearby—had converted the mine to use as a cow barn; there were a dozen or so bales of hay inside. The cow showed no wish to leave once she was at this treasure.

Cartons were carried in, two cartons were dumped and a twin placed in each, with a carton of cat and kittens just beyond and all three weighted down to insure temporary captivity.

While they were unloading Barbara's survival gear from the trunk, everything suddenly became noonday bright. Barbara said, "Oh, heavens! We aren't through."

"We go on unloading. Maybe ten minutes till the sound wave. I don't know about the shock wave. Here, take the rifle."

They had the car empty with jeep cans of water and gasoline out but not yet inside when the ground began to tremble and noise of giant subways started. Hugh put the cans inside, yelled, "Move these!"

"Hugh! Come in!"

"Soon." There was loose hay he had driven over just back of the car. He gathered it up, stuffed it through the door, went back and scavenged, not to save the hay but to reduce fire hazard to gasoline in the car's tank. He considered backing the car out and letting it plunge down the hill. He decided not to risk it. If it got hot enough to set fire to the car's gas tank—well, there were side tunnels, deep inside. "Barbara! Do you have a light yet?"

"Yes! Please come inside. *Please!*"

He went in, barred the door. "Now we remove these bales of hay, far back. You carry the light, I carry the hay. And mind your feet. It is wet a bit farther back. That's why we shut down. Too much pumping."

They moved groceries, livestock (human, bovine, and feline) and gear into a side tunnel a hundred yards inside the mountain. They had to wade through several inches of water on the way but the side tunnel was slightly higher and dry. Once Barbara lost a moccasin. "Sorry," said Hugh. "This mountain is a sponge. Almost every bore struck water."

"I," said Barbara, "am a woman who appreciates water. I have had reason to."

Hugh did not answer as the flash of the second bomb suddenly brightened everything even that deep inside—just through cracks of a wooden wall. He looked at his watch. "Right on time. We're sitting through a second show of the same movie, Barb. This time I hope it will be cooler."

"I wonder."

"If it will be cooler? Sure, it will. Even if it burns outside. I think I know a place where we can go down, and save us, and maybe the cats but not the cow and calf, even if smoke gets pulled in."

"Hugh, I didn't mean that."

"What did you mean?"

"Hugh, I didn't tell you this at the time. I was too upset by it and didn't want you to get upset. I don't own a manual gear shift car."

"Huh? Then whose car is that outside?"

"Mine. I mean my keys were in it—and it certainly had my stuff in the trunk. But mine had automatic shift."

"Honey," he said slowly, "I think you've flipped your lid a little."

"I thought you would think so and that's why I didn't say anything until we were safe. But Hugh—listen to me, dear!—I have *never* owned a manual shift car. I didn't

316

learn to drive that far back. I don't know *how* to drive a manual shift."

He stared thoughtfully. "I don't understand it."

"Neither do I. Darling, when you came away from your house, you said, *'She's* in there. Grace.' Did you mean you saw her?"

"Why, yes. She was nodding over the television, half passed out."

"But, dearest, Grace *had* been nodding over the television. But you put her to bed while I was making crêpes Suzettes. Don't you remember? When the alert came, you went and got her and carried her down—in her nightgown."

Hugh Farnham stood quite still for several moments. "So I did," he agreed. "So I had. Well, let's get the rest of this gear moved. The big one will be along in about an hour and a half."

"But will it be?"

"What do you mean?"

"Hugh, I don't know what has happened. Maybe this is a different world. Or maybe it's the same one but just a tiny bit changed by—well, by us coming back, perhaps."

"I don't know. But right now we go on, moving this stuff."

The big one came on time. It shook them up, did not hurt them. When the air wave hit, it shook them up again. But without casualties other than to the nerves of some very nervous animals—the twins by now seemed to enjoy rough stuff.

Hugh noted the time, then said thoughtfully, "If it is a different world, it is not so very different. And yet—"

"Yet what, dear?"

"Well, it is *some* different. You wouldn't forget that about your own car. And I do remember putting Grace to bed early; Duke and I had a talk afterwards. So, it's different." Suddenly he grinned. "It could be importantly different. If the future can change the past, or whatever, maybe the past can change the future, too. Maybe the United States won't be wholly destroyed. Maybe neither

side will be so suicidal as to use plague bombs. Maybe—
Hell, maybe Ponse will never get a chance to have teen-age
girls for dinner!" He added, "I'm damn' well going to make
a try! To see that he doesn't."

"We'll try! And our boys will try."

"Yes. But that's tomorrow. I think the fireworks are
over for tonight. Madame, do you think you can sleep on
a pile of hay?"

"Just sleep?"

"You're too eager. I've had a long hard day."

"You had had a long hard day the other time, too."

"We'll see."

23

They lived through the missiles, they lived through the bombs, they lived through the fires, they lived through the epidemics—which were not extreme and may not have been weapons; both sides disclaimed them—and they lived through the long period of disorders while civil government writhed like a snake with a broken back. They lived. They went on.

Their sign reads:

FARNHAM'S FREEHOLD
TRADING POST & RESTAURANT
BAR

American Vodka
Corn Liquor
Applejack
Pure Spring Water
Grade "A" Milk
Corned Beef & Potatoes
Steak & Fried Potatoes
Butter & some days Bread
Smoked Bear Meat
Jerked Quisling
    (*by the neck*)
Crêpes Suzettes to order.
  !!!!Any BOOK Accepted as Cash!!!!

DAY NURSERY
!!FREE KITTENS!!
Blacksmithing, Machine Shop, Sheet Metal Work—
You Supply the Metal

FARNHAM SCHOOL OF CONTRACT BRIDGE
Lessons by Arrangement
Social Evening Every Wednesday
WARNING!!!

Ring Bell. Wait. Advance with your Hands *Up*. Stay on path, avoid mines. We lost three customers last week. We can't afford to lose YOU. No sales tax.

> Hugh & Barbara Farnham & Family
> Freeholders

High above their sign their homemade starry flag is flying—and they are *still* going on.